PRAISE FOR
BLACK SUNDAY

"FAST-PACED, ALL TOO REALISTIC . . . WITH A
SHATTERING CLIMAX." —*KIRKUS REVIEWS*

"A FRIGHTENING, SUSPENSEFUL, CLEVERLY PLOTTED CAT-
AND-MOUSE BATTLE PLAYED OUT AGAINST THE CLOCK."
—*PUBLISHERS WEEKLY*

"COULD IT REALLY HAPPEN? THIS IS THE QUESTION YOU
CONTINUALLY ASK YOURSELF AS YOU TIPTOE THROUGH THIS
THRILLER." —*CHICAGO DAILY NEWS*

"A SPELLBINDER . . . THE RACE TO SAVE THE SUPER BOWL
IS HAIR-RAISING, ONE THAT WILL KEEP YOU ROOTED TO
YOUR CHAIR." —*THE HARTFORD COURANT*

"ACTION-PACKED, CRISP, FAST-PACED, TIMELY . . .
A FIRST-CLASS PLOT TOLD IN A FIRST-CLASS FASHION."
—ASSOCIATED PRESS

BY THOMAS HARRIS

BLACK
SUNDAY

———

THOMAS HARRIS

A DELL BOOK

Published by
Dell Publishing
a division of
Random House, Inc.
1540 Broadway
New York, New York 10036

ISBN: 0-440-20614-6

Reprinted by arrangement with G. P. Putnam's Sons
Printed in the United States of America
Published simultaneously in Canada

June 1990

20   19   18   17   16   15   14

OPM

CHAPTER
1

NIGHT FELL AS the airport taxi rattled along the six miles of coastal road into Beirut. From the back seat, Dahlia Iyad watched the Mediterranean surf fade from white to gray in the last light. She was thinking about the American. She would have to answer many questions about him.

The taxi turned onto the Rue Verdun and threaded its way into the heart of the city, the Sabra district, filled with many of the refugees from Palestine. The driver needed no instructions. He scanned his rear-view mirror closely, then turned off his lights and pulled into a small courtyard near the Rue Jeb el-Nakhel. The courtyard was pitch dark. Dahlia could hear distant traffic sounds and the ticking of the motor as it cooled. A minute passed.

The taxi rocked as the four doors were snatched open and a powerful flashlight blinded the driver. Dahlia could smell the oil on the pistol held an inch from her eye.

The man with the flashlight came to the rear door of the taxi, and the pistol was withdrawn.

"Djinniy," she said softly.

"Get out and follow me." He ran the Arabic words together in the accent of the Jabal.

A hard tribunal waited for Dahlia Iyad in the quiet room in Beirut. Hafez Najeer, head of Al Fatah's elite Jihaz al-Rasd (RASD) field intelligence unit, sat at a desk leaning his head back against the wall. He was a tall man with a small head. His subordinates secretly called him "The Praying Mantis." To hold his full attention was to feel sick and frightened.

Najeer was the commander of Black September. He did not believe in the concept of a "Middle East situation." The restoration of Palestine to the Arabs would not have elated him. He believed in holocaust, the fire that purifies. So did Dahlia Iyad.

And so did the other two men in the room: Abu Ali, who controlled the Black September assassination squads in Italy and France, and Muhammad Fasil, ordnance expert and architect of the attack on the Olympic Village at Munich. Both were members of RASD, the brains of Black September. Their position was not acknowledged by the larger Palestinian guerrilla movement, for Black September lives within Al Fatah as desire lives in the body.

It was these three men who decided that Black September would strike within the United States. More than fifty plans had been conceived and discarded. Meanwhile, U.S. munitions continued to pour onto the Israeli docks at Haifa.

Suddenly a solution had come, and now, if Najeer

gave his final approval, the mission would be in the hands of this young woman.

She tossed her djellaba on a chair and faced them. "Good evening, Comrades."

"Welcome, Comrade Dahlia," Najeer said. He had not risen when she entered the room. Nor had the other two. Her appearance had changed during her year in the United States. She was chic in her pants suit and a little disarming.

"The American is ready," she said. "I am satisfied that he will go through with it. He lives for it."

"How stable is he?" Najeer seemed to be staring into her skull.

"Stable enough. I support him. He depends on me."

"I understand that from your reports, but code is clumsy. There are questions. Ali?"

Abu Ali looked at Dahlia carefully. She remembered him from his psychology lectures at the American University of Beirut.

"The American always appears rational?" he asked.

"Yes."

"But you believe him to be insane?"

"Sanity and apparent rationality are not the same, Comrade."

"Is his dependency on you increasing? Does he have periods of hostility toward you?"

"Sometimes he is hostile, but not as often now."

"Is he impotent?"

"He says he was impotent from the time of his release in North Vietnam until two months ago." Dahlia watched Ali. With his small, neat gestures and his moist eyes, he reminded her of a civet cat.

"Do you take credit for overcoming his impotence?"

"It is not a matter of credit, Comrade. It is a matter of control. My body is useful in maintaining that control. If a gun worked better, I would use a gun."

Najeer nodded approval. He knew she was telling the truth. Dahlia had helped train the three Japanese terrorists who struck at Lod Airport in Tel Aviv, slaying at random. Originally there had been four Japanese terrorists. One lost his nerve in training, and, with the other three watching, Dahlia blew his head off with a Schmeisser machine pistol.

"How can you be sure he will not have an attack of conscience and turn you in to the Americans?" Ali persisted.

"What would they get if he did?" Dahlia said. "I am a small catch. They would get the explosives, but the Americans have plenty of *plastique* already, as we have good reason to know." This was intended for Najeer, and she saw him look up at her sharply.

Israeli terrorists almost invariably used American C-4 plastic explosive. Najeer remembered carrying his brother's body out of a shattered apartment in Bhandoum, then going back inside to look for the legs.

"The American turned to us because he needed explosives. You know that, Comrade," Dahlia said. "He will continue to need me for other things. We do not offend his politics, because he has none. Neither does the term 'conscience' apply to him in the usual sense. He will not turn me in."

"Let's look at him again," Najeer said. "Comrade Dahlia, you have studied this man in one setting. Let me show him to you in quite different circumstances. Ali?"

Abu Ali set a 16-millimeter movie projector on the desk and switched out the lights. "We got this quite recently from a source in North Vietnam, Comrade Dahlia. It was shown once on American television, but that was before you were stationed in the House of War. I doubt that you have seen it."

The numbered film leader blurred on the wall and distorted sound came from the speaker. As the film picked up speed, the sound tightened into the anthem of the Democratic Republic of Vietnam, and the square of light on the wall became a whitewashed room. Seated on the floor were two dozen American prisoners of war. A cut to a lectern with a microphone clamped to it. A tall, gaunt man approached the lectern, walking slowly. He wore the baggy uniform of a POW, socks and thong sandals. One of his hands remained in the folds of his jacket, the other was placed flat on his thigh as he bowed to the officials at the front of the room. He turned to the microphone and spoke slowly.

"I am Michael J. Lander, Lieutenant Commander, U.S. Navy, captured February 10, 1967, while firebombing a civilian hospital near Ninh Binh . . . near Ninh Binh. Though the evidence of my war crimes is unmistakable, the Democratic Republic of Vietnam has not done to me punishment, but showed me the suffering which resulted from American war crimes like those of my own and others . . . and others. I am sorry for what I have done. I am sorry we killed children. I call upon the American people to stop this war. The Democratic Republic of Vietnam holds no . . .

holds no animosity toward the American people. It is the warmongers in power. I remain ashamed of what I have done."

The camera panned over the other prisoners, sitting like an attentive class, their faces carefully blank. The film ended with the anthem.

"Clumsy enough," said Ali, whose English was almost flawless. "The hand must have been tied to his side." He had watched Dahlia closely during the film. Her eyes had widened for a second at the close-up of the gaunt face. Otherwise she remained impassive.

"Firebombing a hospital," Ali mused. "He has experience in this sort of thing, then."

"He was captured flying a rescue helicopter. He was trying to retrieve the crew of a downed Phantom," Dahlia said. "You have seen my report."

"I have seen what he told you," Najeer said.

"He tells me the truth. He is beyond lying," she said. "I have lived with him for two months. I know."

"It's a small point, anyway," Ali said. "There are other things about him of much more interest."

During the next half-hour, Ali questioned her about the most intimate details of the American's behavior. When he had finished, it seemed to Dahlia that there was a smell in the room. Real or imagined, it took her back to the Palestinian refugee camp at Tyre when she was eight years old, folding the wet bedroll where her mother and the man who brought food had groaned together in the dark.

Fasil took over the questioning. He had the blunt, capable hands of a technician, and there were calluses on the tips of his fingers. He sat forward in his chair, his small satchel on the floor beside him.

"Has the American handled explosives?"

"Only packaged military ordnance. But he has planned carefully and in minute detail. His plan appears reasonable," Dahlia answered.

"It appears reasonable to *you,* Comrade. Perhaps because you are so intimately involved with it. We will see how reasonable it is."

She wished for the American then, wished these men could hear his slow voice as, step by step, he reduced his terrible project into a series of clearly defined problems, each with a solution.

She took a deep breath and began to talk about the technical problems involved in killing 80,000 people all at once, including the new President of the United States, with an entire nation watching.

"The limitation is weight," Dahlia said. "We are restricted to 600 kilos of *plastique*. Give me a cigarette please, and a pen and paper."

Bending over the desk, she drew a curve that resembled a cross section of a bowl. Inside it and slightly above, she drew another, smaller curve of the same parameter.

"This is the target," she said, indicating the larger curve. Her pen moved to the smaller curve. "The principle of the shaped charge, it—"

"Yes, yes," Fasil snapped. "Like a great Claymore mine. Simple. The density of the crowd?"

"Seated shoulder to shoulder, entirely exposed at this angle from the pelvis up. I need to know if the *plastique*—"

"Comrade Najeer will tell you what you need to know," Fasil said loftily.

Dahlia continued unfazed. "I need to know if the explosive Comrade Najeer may choose to give me is prepackaged antipersonnel *plastique* with steel balls, such as a Claymore contains. The weight requested is of *plastique* only. The containers and this type of shrapnel would not be of use."

"Why?"

"Weight, of course." She was tired of Fasil.

"And if you have no shrapnel? What then, Comrade? If you are counting on concussion, allow me to inform you—"

"Allow me to inform *you*, Comrade. I need your help and I will have it. I do not pretend to your expertise. We are not contending, you and I. Jealousy has no place in the Revolution."

"Tell her what she wants to know." Najeer's voice was hard.

Instantly Fasil said, "The *plastique* is not packaged with shrapnel. What will you use?"

"The outside of the shaped charge will be covered with layers of .177 caliber rifle darts. The American believes they will disperse over 150 degrees vertically through a horizontal arc of 260 degrees. It works out to an average of 3.5 projectiles per person in the kill zone."

Fasil's eyes widened. He had seen an American Claymore mine, no bigger than a schoolbook, blast a bloody path through a column of advancing troops and mow down the grass in a swath around them. What she proposed would be like a thousand Claymores going off at once.

"Detonation?"

"Electric blasting cap fired by a 12-volt system already in the craft. There is an identical backup system with separate battery. Also a fuse."

"That's all," the technician said. "I am finished."

Dahlia looked at him. He was smiling—whether from satisfaction or fear of Hafez Najeer, she could not tell. She wondered if Fasil knew the larger curve represented Tulane Stadium, where on January 12 the first 21 minutes of the Super Bowl game would be played.

Dahlia waited for an hour in a room down the hall. When she was summoned back to Najeer's office, she found the Black September commander alone. Now she would know.

The room was dark except for the area lit by a reading lamp. Najeer, leaning back against the wall, wore a hood of shadow. His hands were in the light and they toyed with a black commando knife. When he spoke, his voice was very soft.

"Do it, Dahlia. Kill as many as you can."

Abruptly he leaned into the light and smiled as though relieved, his teeth bright in his dark face. He seemed almost jovial as he opened the technician's case and withdrew a small statue. It was a figure of the Madonna, like the ones in the windows of religious articles stores, the painting bright and hurriedly executed. "Examine it," he said.

She turned the figure in her hands. It weighed about a half-kilo and did not feel like plaster. A faint ridge ran around the sides of the figure as though it had been pressed in a mold rather than cast. Across the bottom were the words "Made in Taiwan."

"*Plastique*," Najeer said. "Similar to the American C-4 but made farther east. It has some advantages over C-4. It's more powerful for one thing, at some small cost to its stability, and it is very malleable when heated above 50 degrees centigrade.

"Twelve hundred of these will arrive in New York two weeks from tomorrow aboard the freighter *Leticia*. The manifest will show they were transshipped from Taiwan. The importer, Muzi, will claim them on the dock. Afterward you will make sure of his silence."

Najeer rose and stretched. "You have done well, Comrade Dahlia, and you have come a long way. You will rest now with me."

Najeer had a sparsely furnished apartment on an upper floor of 18 Rue Verdun, similar to the quarters Fasil and Ali had on other floors of the building.

Dahlia sat on the side of Najeer's bed with a small tape recorder in her lap. He had ordered her to make a tape for use on Radio Beirut after the strike was made. She was naked, and Najeer, watching her from the couch, saw her become visibly aroused as she talked into the microphone.

"Citizens of America," she said, "today the Palestinian freedom fighters have struck a great blow in the heart of your country. This horror was visited upon you by the merchants of death in your own land, who supply the butchers of Israel. Your leaders have been deaf to the cries of the homeless. Your leaders have ignored the ravages by the Jews in Palestine and have committed their own crimes in Southeast Asia. Guns, warplanes, and hundreds of millions of dollars have flowed from your country to the hands of warmongers while millions of your own people starve. The people will not be denied.

"Hear this, people of America. We want to be your brothers. It is you who must overthrow the filth that rules you. Henceforth, for every Arab that dies by an Israeli hand, an American will die by Arab hands. Every Moslem holy place, every Christian holy place destroyed by Jewish gangsters will be avenged with the destruction of a property in America."

Dahlia's face was flushed and her nipples were erect as she continued. "We hope this cruelty will go no further. The choice is yours. We hope never to begin another year with bloodshed and suffering. Salaam aleikum."

Najeer was standing before her, and she reached for him as his bathrobe fell to the floor.

Two miles from the room where Dahlia and Najeer were locked together in the tangled sheets, a small Israeli missile launch sliced quietly up the Mediterranean.

The launch hove to 1,000 meters south of the Grotte aux Pigeons, and a raft was slipped over the side. Twelve armed men climbed down into it. They wore business suits and neckties tailored by Russians, Arabs, and Frenchmen. All wore crepe-soled shoes and none carried any identification. Their faces were hard. It was not their first visit to Lebanon.

The water was smoky gray under the quarter moon,

and the sea was riffled by a warm off-shore breeze.
Eight of the men paddled, stretching to make the longest strokes possible as they covered the 400 meters to
the sandy beach of the Rue Verdun. It was 4:11 A.M.,
23 minutes before sunrise and 17 minutes before the
first blue glaze of day would spread over the city. Silently they pulled the raft up on the sand, covered it
with a sand-colored canvas, and walked quickly up the
beach to the Rue Ramlet el-Baida, where four men and
four cars awaited them, silhouetted against the glow
from the tourist hotels to the north.

They were only a few yards from the cars when a
brown-and-white Land Rover braked loudly 30 yards
up the Rue Ramlet, its headlights on the little convoy.
Two men in tan uniforms leaped from the truck, their
guns leveled.

"Stand still. Identify yourselves."

There was a sound like popping corn, and dust flew
from the Lebanese officers' uniforms as they collapsed
in the road, riddled by 9-mm bullets from the raiders'
silenced Parabellums.

A third officer, at the wheel of the truck, tried to
drive away. A bullet shattered the windshield and his
forehead. The truck careened into a palm tree at the
roadside, and the policeman was thrown forward onto
the horn. Two men ran to the truck and pulled the dead
man off the horn, but lights were going on in some of
the beachfront apartments.

A window opened, and there was an angry shout in
Arabic. "What is that hellish racket? Someone call the
police."

The leader of the raid, standing by the truck,

shouted back in hoarse and drunken Arabic, "Where is Fatima? We'll leave if she doesn't get down here soon."

"You drunken bastards get away from here or I'll call the police myself."

"Aleikum salaam, neighbor. I'm going," the drunken voice from the street replied. The light in the apartment went out.

In less than two minutes the sea closed over the truck and the bodies it contained.

Two of the cars went south on the Rue Ramlet, while the other two turned onto the Corniche Ras Beyrouth for two blocks, then turned north again on the Rue Verdun . . .

Number 18 Rue Verdun was guarded round the clock. One sentry was stationed in the foyer, and another armed with a machine gun watched from the roof of the building across the street. Now the rooftop sentry lay in a curious attitude behind his gun, his throat smiling wetly in the moonlight. The sentry from the foyer lay outside the door where he had gone to investigate a drunken lullaby.

Najeer had fallen asleep when Dahlia gently pulled free from him and walked into the bathroom. She stood under the shower for a long time, enjoying the stinging spray. Najeer was not an exceptional lover. She smiled as she soaped herself. She was thinking about the American, and she did not hear the footsteps in the hall.

Najeer half-started from the bed as the door to his apartment smashed open and a flashlight blinded him.

"Comrade Najeer!" the man said urgently.

"Aiwa."

The machine gun flickered, and blood exploded from Najeer as the bullets slammed him back into the wall. The killer swept everything from the top of Najeer's desk into a bag as an explosion in another part of the building shook the room.

The naked girl in the bathroom doorway seemed frozen in horror. The killer pointed his machine gun at her wet breast. His finger tightened on the trigger. It was a beautiful breast. The muzzle of the machine gun wavered.

"Put on some clothes, you Arab slut," he said, and backed out of the room.

The explosion two floors below, which tore out the wall of Abu Ali's apartment, killed Ali and his wife instantly. The raiders, coughing in the dust, had started for the stairs, when a thin man in pajamas came out of the apartment at the end of the hall, trying to cock a submachine gun. He was still trying when a hail of bullets tore through him, blowing shreds of his pajamas into his flesh and across the hall.

The raiders scrambled to the street and their cars were roaring southward toward the sea as the first police sirens sounded.

Dahlia, wearing Najeer's bathrobe and clutching her purse, was on the street in seconds, mingling with the crowd that had poured out of the buildings on the block. She was trying desperately to think, when she felt a hard hand grip her arm. It was Muhammad Fasil. A bullet had cut a bloody stripe across his cheek. He wrapped his tie around his hand and held it to the wound.

"Najeer?" he asked.

"Dead."

"Ali, too, I think. His window blew out just as I turned the corner. I shot at them from the car, but—listen to me carefully. Najeer has given the order. Your mission must be completed. The explosives are not affected, they will arrive on schedule. Automatic weapons also—your Schmeisser and an AK-47, packed separately with bicycle parts."

Dahlia looked at him with smoke-reddened eyes. "They will pay," she said. "They will pay 10,000 to one."

Fasil took her to a safe house in the Sabra to wait through the day. After dark he took her to the airport in his rattletrap Citroën. Her borrowed dress was two sizes too large, but she was too tired to care.

At 10:30 P.M., the Pan Am 707 roared out over the Mediterranean, and, before the Arabian lights faded off the starboard wing, Dahlia fell into an exhausted sleep.

CHAPTER
2

AT THAT MOMENT, Michael Lander was doing the only thing he loved. He was flying the Aldrich blimp, hovering 800 feet above the Orange Bowl in Miami, providing a steady platform for the television crew in the gondola behind him. Below, in the packed stadium, the world-champion Miami Dolphins were pounding the Pittsburgh Steelers.

The roar of the crowd nearly drowned out the crackling radio above Lander's head. On hot days above a stadium, he felt that he could smell the crowd, and the blimp seemed suspended on a powerful rising current of mindless screaming and body heat. That current felt dirty to Lander. He preferred the trips between the towns. The blimp was clean and quiet then.

Only occasionally did Lander glance down at the field. He watched the rim of the stadium and the line-of-sight he had established between the top of a flag-pole and the horizon to maintain exactly 800 feet of altitude.

Lander was an exceptional pilot in a difficult field. A dirigible is not easy to fly. Its almost neutral buoyancy and vast surface leave it at the mercy of the wind unless it is skillfully handled. Lander had a sailor's instinct for the wind, and he had the gift the best dirigible pilots have—anticipation. A dirigible's movements are cyclical, and Lander stayed two moves ahead, holding the great gray whale into the breeze as a fish points upstream, burrowing the nose slightly into the gusts and raising it in lulls, shading half the end zone with its shadow. During intervals in the action on the field, many of the spectators looked up at it and some of them waved. Such bulk, such great length suspended in the clear air fascinated them.

Lander had an autopilot in his head. While it dictated the constant, minute adjustments that held the blimp steady, he thought about Dahlia. The patch of down in the small of her back and how it felt beneath his hand. The sharpness of her teeth. The taste of honey and salt.

He looked at his watch. Dahlia should be an hour out of Beirut now, coming back.

Lander could think comfortably about two things: Dahlia and flying.

His scarred left hand gently pushed forward the throttle and propeller pitch controls, and he rolled back the big elevator wheel beside his seat. The great airship rose quickly as Lander spoke into the microphone.

"Nora One Zero, clearing stadium for a 1,200-foot go-around."

"Roger, Nora One Zero," the Miami tower replied cheerily.

Air controllers and tower radio operators always liked to talk to the blimp, and many had a joke ready when they knew it was coming. People felt friendly toward it as they do toward a panda. For millions of Americans who saw it at sporting events and fairs, the blimp was an enormous, amiable, and slow-moving friend in the sky. Blimp metaphors are almost invariably "elephant" or "whale." No one ever says "bomb."

At last the game was over and the blimp's 225-foot shadow flicked over the miles of cars streaming away from the stadium. The television cameraman and his assistant had secured their equipment and were eating sandwiches. Lander had worked with them often.

The lowering sun laid a streak of red-gold fire across Biscayne Bay as the blimp hung over the water. Then Lander turned northward and cruised 50 yards off Miami Beach, while the TV crew and the flight engineer fixed their binoculars on the girls in their bikinis. Some of the bathers waved.

"Hey, Mike, does Aldrich make rubbers?" Pearson the cameraman was yelling around a mouthful of sandwich.

"Yeah," Lander said over his shoulder. "Rubbers, tires, de-icers, windshield wiper blades, bathtub toys, children's balloons, and body bags."

"You get free rubbers with this job?"

"You bet. I've got one on now."

"What's a body bag?"

"It's a big rubber bag. One size fits all," Lander said.

"They're dark inside. Uncle Sam uses them for rubbers. You see some of them, you know he's been fooling around." It would not be hard to push the button on Pearson; it would not be hard to push the button on any of them.

The blimp did not fly often in the winter. Its winter quarters were near Miami, the great hangar dwarfing the rest of the buildings beside the airfield. Each spring it worked northward at 35 to 60 knots, depending on the wind, dropping in at state fairs and baseball games. The Aldrich company provided Lander with an apartment near the Miami airfield in winter, but on this day, as soon as the great airship was secured, he caught the National flight to Newark and went to his home near the blimp's northern base at Lakehurst, New Jersey.

When Lander's wife deserted him, she left him the house. Tonight the lights burned late in the garage-workshop, as Lander worked and waited for Dahlia. He was stirring a can of epoxy resin on his workbench, its strong odor filling the garage. On the floor behind him was a curious object 18 feet long. It was a plug mold that Lander had made from the hull of a small sailboat. He had inverted the hull and split it along the keel. The halves were 18 inches apart and were joined by a broad common bow. Viewed from above, the mold looked like a great streamlined horseshoe. Building the mold had taken weeks of off-duty time. Now it was slick with grease and ready.

Lander, whistling quietly, applied layers of fiberglass cloth and resin to the mold, feathering the edges precisely. When the fiberglass shell cured and he popped it off the mold, he would have a light, sleek nacelle that would fit neatly under the gondola of the Aldrich blimp. The opening in the center would accommodate the blimp's single landing wheel and its transponder antenna. The load-bearing frame that would be enclosed by the nacelle was hanging from a nail on the garage wall. It was very light and very strong, with twin keels of Reynolds 5130 chromemoly tubing and ribs of the same material.

Lander had converted the double garage into a workshop while he was married, and he had built much of his furniture there in the years before he went to Vietnam. The things his wife had not wanted to take were still stored above the rafters—a highchair, a folding camp table, wicker yard furniture. The fluorescent light was harsh, and Lander wore a baseball cap as he worked around the mold, whistling softly.

He paused once, thinking, thinking. Then he went on smoothing the surface, raising his feet carefully as he walked to avoid tearing the newspapers spread on the floor.

Shortly after 4 A.M. the telephone rang. Lander picked up the garage extension.

"Michael?" The British clip in her speech always surprised him, and he imagined the telephone buried in her dark hair.

"Who else?"

"Grandma is fine. I'm at the airport and I'll be along later. Don't wait up."

"What—"

"Michael, I can't wait to see you." The line went dead.

It was almost sunrise when Dahlia turned into the

driveway at Lander's house. The windows were dark. She was apprehensive, but not so much as before their first meeting—then she had felt that she was in the room with a snake she could not see. After she came to live with him, she separated the deadly part of Michael Lander from the rest of him. When she was with him now, she felt that they were both in a room with the snake, and she could tell where it was, and whether it was sleeping.

She made more noise than necessary coming into the house and sang his name softly against the stillness as she came up the stairs. She did not want to startle him. The bedroom was pitch dark.

From the doorway she could see the glow of his cigarette, like a tiny red eye.

"Hello," she said.

"Come here."

She walked through the darkness toward the glow. Her foot touched the shotgun, safely on the floor beside the bed. It was all right. The snake was asleep.

Lander was dreaming about the whales, and he was reluctant to come out of sleep. In his dream the great shadow of the Navy dirigible moved over the ice below him as he flew through the endless day. It was 1956 and he was going over the Pole.

The whales were basking in the Arctic sun, and they did not see the dirigible until it was almost over them. Then they sounded, their flukes rising under a chandelier of spray as they slid beneath a blue ice ledge under the Arctic Sea. Looking down from the gondola, Lander still could see the whales suspended there beneath the ledge. In a cool blue place where there was no noise.

Then he was over the Pole and the magnetic compass was going wild. Solar activity interfered with the omni, and, with Fletcher at the elevator wheel, he steered by the sun as the flag on its weighted spear fluttered down to the ice.

"The compass," he said, walking in his house. "The compass."

"The omni beam from Spitsbergen, Michael," Dahlia said, her hand on his cheek. "I have your breakfast."

She knew the dream. She hoped he would dream often of the whales. He was easier then.

Lander was facing a hard day, and she could not be with him. She opened the curtains and sunlight brightened the room.

"I wish you didn't have to go."

"I'll tell you again," Lander said. "If you have a pilot's ticket they watch you really close. If I don't check in, they'll send some VA caseworker out here with a questionnaire. He's got a form. It goes like this—'A. Note the condition of the grounds. B. Does the subject seem dejected?' Like that. It goes on forever."

"You can manage that."

"One call to the FAA, one little half-assed hint that I might be shaky and that's it. They'll ground me. What if a caseworker looks in the garage?" He drank his orange juice. "Besides, I want to see the clerks one more time."

Dahlia was standing by the window, the sun warm on her cheek and neck. "How do you feel?"

"You mean am I crazy today? No, as a matter of fact I'm not."

"I didn't mean that."

"Shit you didn't. I'll just go into a little office with one of them and we'll close the door and he'll tell me the new things the government is going to do for me." Something lunged behind Lander's eyes.

"All right, are you crazy today? Are you going to spoil it? Are you going to grab a VA clerk and kill him and let the others hold you down? Then you can sit in a cell and sing and masturbate. 'God Bless America and Nixon.'"

She had used two triggers at once. She had tried them separately before, and now she watched to see how they worked together.

Lander's memory was intense. Recollections while awake could make him wince. Asleep, they sometimes made him scream.

Masturbation: The North Vietnamese guard catching him at it in his cell and making him do it in front of the others.

"God Bless America and Nixon": The hand-lettered sign the Air Force officer held up to the window of the C-141 at Clark Air Force Base in the Philippines when the prisoners were coming home. Lander, sitting across the aisle, had read it backwards with the sun shining through the paper.

Now his eyes were hooded as he looked at Dahlia. His mouth opened slightly and his face was slack. This was the dangerous time. It hung in slow seconds while the motes swarmed in the sunlight, swarmed around Dahlia and the short, ugly shotgun by the bed.

"You don't have to get them one at a time, Michael," she said softly. "And you don't have to do the other for yourself. I want to do it for you. I love to do it."

She was telling the truth. Lander could always tell. His eyes opened wide again, and in a moment he could no longer hear his heart.

Windowless corridors. Michael Lander walking through the dead air of the government office building, down the long floors where the buffer had swung from side to side in shining arcs. Guards in the blue uniform of the General Services Administration checking packages. Lander had no packages.

The receptionist was reading a novel entitled *A Nurse to Marry*.

"My name is Michael Lander."

"Did you take a number?"

"No."

"Take a number," the receptionist said.

He picked up a numbered disc from a tray at the side of the desk.

"What is your number?"

"Thirty-six."

"What is your name?"

"Michael Lander."

"Disability?"

"No. I'm supposed to check in today." He handed her the letter from the Veterans Administration.

"Take a seat, please." She turned to the microphone beside her. "Seventeen."

Seventeen, a seedy young man in a vinyl jacket,

brushed past Lander and disappeared into the warren
behind the secretary.

About half the fifty seats in the waiting room were
filled. Most of the men were young, former Spec 4's,
who looked as slovenly in civilian clothes as they had
in uniform. Lander could imagine them playing the
pinball machine in a bus terminal in their wrinkled
Class A's.

In front of Lander sat a man with a shiny scar above
his temple. He had tried to comb his hair over it. At
two-minute intervals he took a handkerchief from his
pocket and blew his nose. He had a handkerchief in every pocket.

The man beside Lander sat very still, his hands gripping his thighs. Only his eyes moved. They never
rested, tracking each person who walked through the
room. Often he had to strain to turn his eyes far
enough, because he would not turn his head.

In a small office in the maze behind the receptionist,
Harold Pugh was waiting for Lander. Pugh was a GS-
12 and rising. He thought of his assignment to the special POW section as "a feather in my cap."

A considerable amount of literature came with
Pugh's new job. Among the reams of advisories was
one from the Air Force surgeon general's national
consultant on psychiatry. The advisory said, "It is not
possible for a man exposed to severe degrees of abuse,
isolation, and deprivation not to develop depression
born out of extreme rage repressed over a long period
of time. It is simply a question of when and how the de-
pressive reaction will surface and manifest itself."

Pugh meant to read the advisories as soon as he

could find the time. The military record on Pugh's desk was impressive. Waiting for Lander, he glanced through it again.

Lander, Michael J. 0214278603. Korea 1951, Naval OCS. Very high marks. Lighter-than-air training at Lakehurst, N.J., 1954. Exceptional rating. Commendation for research in aircraft icing. Navy polar expedition 1956. Shifted to Administration when the Navy phased out its blimp program in 1964. Volunteered for helicopters 1964. Vietnam. Two tours. Shot down near Dong Hoi February 10, 1967. Six years a prisoner of war.

Pugh thought it peculiar that an officer with Lander's record should resign his commission. Something was not quite right there. Pugh remembered the closed hearings after the POW's came home. Perhaps it would be better not to ask Lander why he resigned.

He looked at his watch. Three-forty. Fellow was late. He pushed a button on his desk telephone and the receptionist answered.

"Is Mr. Lander here yet?"

"Who, Mr. Pugh?"

Pugh wondered if she was making a deliberate rhyme with name. "Lander. Lander. He's one of the specials. Your instructions are to send him right in when he comes."

"Yes, Mr. Pugh. I will."

The receptionist returned to her novel. At 3:50, needing a bookmark, she picked up Lander's letter. The name caught her eye.

"Thirty-six. Thirty-six." She rang Pugh's office. "Mr. Lander is here now."

Pugh was mildly surprised at Lander's appearance. Lander was sharp in his civilian flight captain's uniform. He moved briskly and his gaze was direct. Pugh had pictured himself dealing with hollow-eyed men.

Pugh's appearance did not surprise Lander. He had hated clerks all his life.

"You're looking well, Captain. You've bounced back nicely, I'd say."

"Nicely."

"Good to be back with the family, I'm sure."

Lander smiled. His eyes were not involved in the smile. "The family is fine, I understand."

"They're not with you? I believe you're married, it says here, let's see, yes. Two children?"

"Yes, I have two children. I'm divorced."

"I'm sorry. My predecessor on your case, Gorman, left very few notes, I'm afraid." Gorman had been promoted for incompetence.

Lander was watching Pugh steadily, a faint smile on his lips.

"When were you divorced, Captain Lander? I have to bring this up-to-date." Pugh was like a domestic cow grazing placidly near the edge of the swamp, not sensing what was downwind in the black shade watching him.

Suddenly Lander was talking about the things he could never think about. Never think about.

"The first time she filed was two months before my release. While the Paris talks were stalled on the point of elections, I believe. But she didn't go through with it then. She moved out a year after I got back. Please don't feel badly, Pugh, the government did everything it could."

"I'm sure, but it must—"

"A naval officer came around several times after I was captured and had tea with Margaret and counseled her. There is a standard procedure for preparing POW wives, as I'm sure you know."

"I suppose that sometimes—"

"He explained to her that there is an increased incidence of homosexuality and impotence among released POW's. So she would know what to expect, you understand." Lander wanted to stop. He must stop.

"It's better to let—"

"He told her that the life expectancy of a released POW is about half the average." Lander was wearing a wide smile now.

"Surely, Captain, there must have been some other factors."

"Oh sure, she was already getting some dick on the side, if that's what you mean." Lander laughed, the old spike through him, the pressure building behind his eyes. *You don't have to get them one at a time, Michael. Sit in a cell and sing and masturbate.*

Lander closed his eyes so that he could not see the pulse in Pugh's throat.

Pugh's reflex was to laugh with Lander, to ingratiate himself. But he was offended in a Baptist sort of way by glib, cheap references to sex. He stopped the laugh in time. That action saved his life.

Pugh picked up the file again. "Did you receive counseling about it?"

Lander was easier now. "Oh yes. A psychiatrist at

St. Alban's Naval Hospital discussed it with me. He was drinking a Yoo-Hoo."

"If you feel the need of further counseling I can arrange it."

Lander winked. "Look, Mr. Pugh. You're a man of the world and so am I. These things happen. What I want to see you about is some compensation for the old flipper here." He held up his disfigured hand.

Now Pugh was on familiar ground. He pulled Lander's Form 214 from the file. "Since you obviously are not disabled, we'll have to find a way, but"—he winked at Lander—"we'll take care of you."

It was 4:30 P.M. and the evening rush had begun when Lander came out of the Veterans Administration building into the soiled Manhattan afternoon. The sweat was cold on his back as he stood on the steps and watched the garment district crowds funnel toward the 23rd Street subway station. He could not go in there with them and be jammed in the train.

Many of the VA personnel were taking an early slide from their jobs. A stream of them fanned the doors of the building and jostled him back against the wall. He wanted to fight. Margaret came over him in a rush, and he could smell her and feel her. Talking about it over a plywood desk. He had to think about something. The teapot whistle. Not that, for God's sake. Now he had a cold ache in his colon and he reached for a Lomotil tablet. Too late for Lomotil. He would have to find a restroom. Quick. Now he walked back to the waiting room, the dead air like cobwebs on his face. He was pale and sweat stood out on his forehead as he entered the small restroom. The single stall was occupied and

another man was waiting outside it. Lander turned and
walked back through the waiting room. Spastic colon,
his medical profile said. No medication prescribed. He
had found Lomotil for himself.

Why didn't I take some before?

The man with the moving eyes tracked Lander as far
as he could without turning his head. The pain in Lander's bowels was coming in waves now, making goose-
bumps on his arms, and he was gagging.

The fat janitor fumbled through his keys and let
Lander into the employee's washroom. Waiting outside, the janitor could not hear the unpleasant sounds.
At last, Lander turned his face up to the Celotex ceiling. Retching had made his eyes water and the tears ran
down his face.

*For a second he was squatting beside the path with
the guards watching on the forced march to Hanoi.*

It was the same, the same. The teapot whistle came.

"Cocksuckers," Lander croaked. "Cocksuckers."
He wiped his face with his ugly hand.

Dahlia, who had had a busy day with Lander's
credit cards, was on the platform when he got off the
commuter train. She saw him ease down off the step
and knew he was trying not to joggle his insides.

She filled a paper cup with water from the fountain
and took a small bottle from her purse. The water
turned milky as she poured in the paregoric.

He did not see her until she was beside him, offering
the cup.

It tasted like bitter licorice and left a faint numbness
in his lips and tongue. Before they reached the car, the

opium was soothing the ache and in five minutes it was gone. When they reached the house, he fell into bed and slept for three hours.

Lander woke confused and unnaturally alert. His defenses were working, and his mind recoiled from painful images with the speed of a pinball. His thoughts rolled over the safe, painted images between the buzzers and the bells. He had not blown it today, he could rest on that.

The teapot—his neck tightened. He seemed to itch somewhere between his shoulders and his cortex in a place he could not reach. His feet would not keep still.

The house was completely dark, its ghosts just beyond the firelight of his will. Then, from the bed, he saw a flickering light coming up the stairs. Dahlia was carrying a candle, her shadow huge on the wall. She wore a dark floor-length robe that covered her completely and her bare feet made no sound. Now she was standing by him, the candlelight a pinpoint in her great, dark eyes. She held out her hand.

"Come, Michael. Come with me."

Slowly backing down the dark hall, she led him, looking into his face. Her black hair down over her shoulders. Backing, feet peeping white from under the hem. Back to what had been the playroom, empty these seven months. Now in the candlelight Lander could see that a huge bed waited at the end of the room and heavy drapes covered the walls. Incense touched his face and the small blue flame of a spirit lamp flickered on a table near the bed. It was no longer the room where Margaret had—no, no, no.

Dahlia put her candle beside the lamp and with a feather touch removed Lander's pajama top. She undid the drawstring and knelt to slip the trousers off his feet, her hair brushing against his thigh. "You were so strong today." She gently pressed him back upon the bed. The silk beneath him was cool and the air was a cool ache upon his genitals.

He lay watching her as she lit two tapers in holders on the walls. She passed him the slender hash pipe and stood at the foot of the bed, the candle shadows moving behind her.

Lander felt that he was falling into those bottom-less eyes. He remembered as a child lying in the grass on clear summer nights, looking into heavens suddenly dimensional and deep. Looking up until there was no up and he was falling out into the stars.

Dahlia dropped her robe and stood before him.

The sight of her pierced him as it had the first time, and his breath caught in his throat. Dahlia's breasts were large, and their curves were not the curves of a vessel but of a dome, and she had a cleavage even when they were unconfined. Her nipples darkened as they came erect. She was opulent, but not forbidden, her curves and hollows lapped by candlelight.

Lander felt a sweet shock as she turned to take the vessel of sweet oil from above the spirit lamp and the light played over her. Kneeling astride him, she rubbed the warm oil on his chest and belly, her breasts swaying slightly as she worked.

As she leaned forward, her belly rounded slightly and receded again into the dark triangle.

It grew thick and soft and springy up her belly, a

black explosion radiating tufts as though it tried to climb. He felt it touch his navel and, looking down, he saw suspended in the whorls like pearls in the candle-light, the first drops of her essence.

It would bathe him he knew, and be warm on his scrotum and it would taste like bananas and salt.

Dahlia took a mouthful of the warm, sweet oil and held him in it, nodding gently, deeply to the rhythm of his blood, her hair spilling warm over him.

And all the while her eyes, wide-set as a puma's and full of the moon, never left his face.

CHAPTER
3

A SOUND LIKE a slow roll of thunder shivered the air in the bedroom and the candle flames quivered, but Dahlia and Lander, fixed in each other, did not notice it. It was a common sound—that late jet shuttle from New York to Washington. The Boeing 727 was 6,000 feet above Lakehurst and climbing.

Tonight it carried the hunter. He was a broad-shouldered man in a tan suit, and he was seated on the aisle just behind the wing. The stewardess was collecting fares. He handed her a new $50 bill. She frowned at it. "Don't you have anything smaller?"

"For two fares," he said, indicating the big man asleep beside him. "For his and mine." He had an accent the stewardess could not place. She decided he was German or Dutch. She was wrong.

He was Major David Kabakov of the Mossad Aliyah Beth, the Israeli Secret Service, and he was hoping the three men seated across the aisle behind him had smaller bills with which to pay their fare. Otherwise the stewardess might remember them. He should have tended to it in Tel Aviv, he thought. The connection at Kennedy Airport had been too close to permit getting change. It was a small error, but it annoyed him. Major Kabakov had lived to be thirty-seven because he did not make many errors.

Beside him, Sgt. Robert Moshevsky was snoring softly, his head back. On the long flight from Tel Aviv, neither Kabakov nor Moshevsky had given any sign of recognition to the three men behind them, though they had known them for years. The three were burly men with weathered faces, and they wore quiet, baggy suits. They were what the Mossad called a "tactical incursion team." In America they would be called a hit squad.

In the three days since he had killed Hafez Najeer in Beirut, Kabakov had had very little sleep, and he knew that he must give a detailed briefing as soon as he reached the American capital. The Mossad, analyzing the material he brought back from the raid on the Black September leadership, acted instantly when the tape recording was played. There was a hurried conference at the American embassy and Kabakov was dispatched.

It had been clearly understood at the Tel Aviv meeting between American and Israeli intelligence that Kabakov was being sent to the United States to help the Americans determine if a real threat existed and to help identify the terrorists if they could be located. His official orders were clear.

But the high command of the Mossad had given him an additional directive that was flat and unequivocal.

He was to stop the Arabs by whatever means necessary.

Negotiations for the sale of additional Phantom and Skyhawk jets to Israel were at a critical stage, and Arab pressure against the sale was intensified by the Western shortage of oil. Israel must have the airplanes. On the first day that no Phantoms flashed over the desert, the Arab tanks would roll.

A major atrocity within the United States would tip the balance of power in favor of the American isolationists. For the Americans, helping Israel must not have too high a price.

Neither the Israeli nor the American state departments knew about the three men sitting behind Kabakov. They would settle into an apartment near National Airport and wait for him to call. Kabakov hoped the call would not be necessary. He would prefer to handle it himself, quietly.

Kabakov hoped the diplomats would not meddle with him. He distrusted both diplomats and politicians. His attitude and approach were reflected in his Slavic features—blunt but intelligent.

Kabakov believed that careless Jews die young and weak ones wind up behind barbed wire. He had been a child of war, fleeing Latvia with his family just ahead of the German invasion and later fleeing the Russians. His father died in Treblinka. His mother took Kabakov and his sister to Italy in a journey that killed her. As she struggled toward Trieste, there was a fire inside her that gave her strength while it consumed her flesh.

When Kabakov remembered, across thirty years, the road to Trieste, he saw it with his mother's arm swing

ing diagonally across his vision as she walked ahead, holding his hand, her elbow, knobby in the thin arm, showing through her rags. And he remembered her face, almost incandescent as she woke the children before the first light reached the ditch where they were sleeping.

In Trieste she turned the children over to the Zionist underground and died in a doorway across the street.

David Kabakov and his sister reached Palestine in 1946 and they stopped running. By the age of ten he was a courier for the Palmach and fought in the defense of the Tel Aviv–Jerusalem road.

After twenty-seven years of war, Kabakov knew better than most men the value of peace. He did not hate the Arab people, but he believed that trying to negotiate with Al Fatah was a lot of shit. That was the term he used when he was consulted about it by his superiors, which was not often.

The Mossad regarded Kabakov as a good intelligence officer, but his combat record was remarkable and he was too successful in the field to be put behind a desk. In the field, he risked capture and so he was necessarily excluded from the inner councils of the Mossad. He remained in the intelligence service's executive arm, striking again and again at the Al Fatah strongholds in Lebanon and Jordan. The innermost circle of the Mossad called him "The final solution."

No one had ever said that to his face.

The lights of Washington wheeled beneath the wing as the plane turned into the National Airport traffic pattern. Kabakov picked out the Capitol, stark white in its floodlights. He wondered if the Capitol was the target.

The two men waiting in the small conference room at the Israeli embassy looked carefully at Kabakov as he entered with Ambassador Yoachim Tell. Watching the Israeli major, Sam Corley of the Federal Bureau of Investigation was reminded of a Ranger captain of twenty years ago, his commander at Fort Benning.

Fowler of the Central Intelligence Agency had never been in the military service. Kabakov made him think of a pit bulldog. Both men had studied hastily assembled dossiers on the Israeli, but the dossiers were mostly concerned with the Six-Day War and the October War, old Xeroxes from the CIA's Middle East section. Clippings. "Kabakov, the Tiger of Mitla Pass"—journalism.

Ambassador Tell, still wearing his dinner clothes from an embassy function, made brief introductions.

The room fell silent and Kabakov pressed the switch on his small tape recorder. The voice of Dahlia Iyad filled the silence. "Citizens of America . . ."

When the tape had ended, Kabakov spoke slowly and carefully, weighing his words. "We believe that the Ailul al Aswad—Black September—is preparing to strike here. They are not interested in hostages or negotiations or revolutionary theatrics this time. They want maximum casualties—they want to make you sick. We believe the plan is well advanced and that this woman is a principal." He paused. "We believe it likely that she is in this country now."

"Then you must have information to supplement the tape," Fowler said.

"It is supplemented by the fact that we know they want to strike here, and the circumstances in which the tape was found. They have tried before," Kabakov said.

"You took the tape from Najeer's apartment after you killed him?"

"Yes."

"You didn't question him first?"

"Questioning Najeer would have been useless."

Sam Corley saw anger in Fowler's face. Corley glanced at the file before him. "Why do you think it was the woman you saw in the room who made the tape?"

"Because Najeer had not had time to put it in a safe place," Kabakov said. "He was not a careless man."

"He was not careful enough to keep you from killing him," Fowler said.

"Najeer lasted a long time," Kabakov said. "Long enough for Munich to happen, Lod Airport, too long. If you are not careful now, American arms and legs will fly."

"Why do you think the plan would go on now that Najeer is dead?"

Corley looked up from the paper clip he was examining and answered Fowler himself. "Because the tape was dangerous. Making it would have been very nearly the final step. The orders would have been given. Am I right, Major?"

Kabakov recognized an expert interrogator when he saw one. Corley was being the advocate. "Exactly," he said.

"An operation might be mounted in another country

and moved here at the last minute," Corley said. "Why do you think the woman is based here?"

"Najeer's apartment had been under surveillance for some time," Kabakov explained. "She was not seen in Beirut before or after the night of the raid. Two linguists in the Mossad analyzed the tape independently and came to the same conclusion: She learned English as a child from a Briton, but has been exposed to American English for the last year or two. American-made clothing was found in the room."

"Maybe she was just a courier, taking final instructions from Najeer," Fowler said. "Instructions could be passed on anywhere."

"If she were only a courier, she would never have seen Najeer's face," Kabakov said. "Black September is compartmented like a wasp's nest. Most of their agents know only one or two others in the apparatus."

"Why didn't you kill the woman, too, Major?" Fowler was not looking at Kabakov when he said this. If he had been looking, he would not have looked long.

The ambassador spoke for the first time. "Because there was no reason to kill her at the time, Mr. Fowler. I hope you do not come to wish he had."

Kabakov blinked once. These men did not understand the danger. They would not be warned. Behind his eyes, Kabakov saw the Arab armor thundering across the Sinai and into the cities, herding Jewish civilians. Because there were no planes. Because the Americans had been sickened. Because he had spared the woman. His hundred victories were ashes in his mouth. The fact that he could not possibly have known that the woman was important did not excuse him in the slightest in his own eyes. The mission to Beirut had not been perfect.

Kabakov stared into Fowler's jowly face. "Do you have a dossier on Hafez Najeer?"

"He appears in our files on a list of Al Fatah officers."

"A complete dossier on him is included with my report. Look at the pictures, Mr. Fowler. They were taken after some of Najeer's earlier projects."

"I've seen atrocities."

"Not like these you haven't." The Israeli's voice was rising.

"Hafez Najeer is dead, Major Kabakov."

"And the good was interred with his bones, Fowler. If this woman is not found, Black September will rub your nose in guts."

Fowler glanced at the ambassador as though he expected him to intervene, but Yoachim Tell's small, wise eyes were hard. He stood with Kabakov.

When the major spoke again, his voice was almost too quiet. "You must believe it, Mr. Fowler."

"Would you recognize her again, Major?" Corley asked.

"Yes."

"If she were based here, why would she go to Beirut?"

"She needed something she could not get here. She needed something that only Najeer could get for her, and she had to confirm something personally for him in order to get it." Kabakov knew this sounded vague and he was not happy about it. He was also displeased with himself for using the word "something" three times in a row.

Fowler opened his mouth, but Corley interrupted him. "That wouldn't be guns."

"Coals to Newcastle, bringing guns here," Fowler said gloomily.

"It would have to be either equipment or access to another cell or to a highly placed agent," Corley continued. "I doubt that she needed access to an agent. As far as I can tell, U.A.R. intelligence here is a sorry lot."

"Yes," the ambassador said. "The embassy handyman sells them the contents of my wastebasket. He also buys from their handyman the contents of theirs. We load ours with junk mail and fictitious correspondence. Theirs runs heavily to duns from creditors and advertisements for unusual rubber products."

The meeting continued for another thirty minutes before the Americans rose to go.

"I'll try to get this on the agenda at Langley in the morning," Corley said.

"If you wish, I could—"

Fowler interrupted Kabakov. "Your report and the tape will be sufficient, Major."

It was after 3 A.M. when the Americans left the Embassy.

"Oy, the Arabs are coming," Fowler said to Corley as they walked to the cars.

"What do you think?"

"I think I don't envy you having to take up Blue Eyes Bennett's time with that stuff tomorrow," Fowler said. "If there are some crackpots here, the Agency is

out of it, old buddy. No fooling around in the U.S.A."
The CIA was still smarting from Watergate. "If the
Middle East section turns up anything, we'll let you
know."

"Why were you so pissed off in there?"

"I'm tired of it," Fowler said. "We've worked with
the Israelis in Rome, in London, Paris, once even in To-
kyo. You finger an Arab, cut them in on it, and what
happens? Do they try to turn him? No. Do they watch
him? Yes. Just long enough to find out who his friends
are. Then there is a big bang. The Arabs are wiped out,
and you are left holding your schwantz."

"They didn't have to send Kabakov," Corley said.

"Oh yes they did. You'll notice the military attaché
Weisman wasn't there. We both know he has an intelligence function. But he's coordinating the Phantom
sale. They don't want to connect the two things officially at all."

"You'll be at Langley tomorrow?"

"I'll be there all right. Don't let Kabakov get your
ass in a crack."

Each Thursday morning the American intelligence
community meets in a windowless, lead-shielded room
in Central Intelligence Agency headquarters at Langley,
Va. Represented are the CIA, FBI, National Security
Agency, the Secret Service, the National Reconnais-
sance Office, and the military intelligence advisors to
the Joint Chiefs of Staff. Specialists are called in when
necessary. The agenda has a subscription list of fourteen. There are many subjects to be discussed and time
is strictly limited.

Corley spoke for ten minutes, Fowler for five, and the representative from the Immigration and Naturalization subversive section had less time than that.

Kabakov was waiting in Corley's small office at FBI headquarters when he returned from the meeting.

"I'm supposed to thank you for coming," Corley said. "State is going to thank the ambassador. Our ambassador in Tel Aviv is going to thank Yigal Allon."

"You're welcome, now what are you going to do?"

"Damn little," Corley said, lighting his pipe. "Fowler brought a stack of tapes recorded off Radio Cairo and Radio Beirut. He said they were all threats of various kinds that came to nothing. The Agency is voiceprinting your tape against them."

"This tape is not a threat. It was made to be used afterward."

"The Agency is checking its sources in Lebanon."

"In Lebanon the CIA buys the same shit we do, from a lot of the same people," Kabakov said. "The kind of stuff that's two hours ahead of the newspapers."

"Sometimes not even two hours," Corley said. "In the meantime, you can look at pictures. We've got about a hundred known Al Fatah sympathizers on file, people we think are in the July 5th movement here. Immigration and Naturalization doesn't advertise it, but they have a file on suspicious Arab aliens. You'll have to go to New York for that."

"Can you put out a general customs alert on your own authority?"

"I've done that. It's our best bet. For a major job they probably would have to bring in the bomb from outside, that is *if* it's a bomb," Corley said. "We've had three small explosions linked to the July 5th movement in the past two years, all at Israeli offices in New York. From that—"

"One time they used plastic, the other two were dynamite," Kabakov said.

"Exactly. You do keep up, don't you? Apparently there's not much plastic available here or they wouldn't be lugging dynamite around and wouldn't blow themselves up trying to extract nitroglycerine."

"The July 5th movement is full of amateurs," Kabakov said. "Najeer would not have trusted them with this. The ordnance would be separate. If it's not already here, they'll bring it in." The Israeli rose and walked to the window. "So your government is making its files available to me and telling customs to watch out for fellows with bombs and that's all?"

"I'm sorry, Major, but I don't know what else we can do with the information we have."

"The U.S. could ask its new allies in Egypt to pressure Khadafy in Libya. He bankrolls Black September. The bastard gave them $5 million from the Libyan treasury as a reward for the Munich killings. He might be able to call it off if Egypt pushed him hard enough."

Colonel Muammar Khadafy, head of Libya's Revolutionary Command Council, was wooing Egypt again in his drive to build a solid power base. He might respond to pressure from the Egyptians now.

"The State Department is staying out of it," Corley said.

"U.S. intelligence doesn't think they're going to strike here at all, do they, Corley?"

"No," Sam Corley said wearily. "They think the Arabs wouldn't dare."

CHAPTER

4

AT THAT MOMENT the freighter *Leticia* was crossing the 21st meridian en route to the Azores and New York City. In her deepest forward hold in a locked compartment were 1,200 pounds of *plastique* packed in gray crates.

Beside the crates in the total darkness of the hold, Ali Hassan lay semiconscious. A large rat was on his stomach and it was walking toward his face. Hassan had lain there for three days, shot in the stomach by Captain Kemal Larmoso.

The rat was hungry, but not ravenous. At first Hassan's groans had frightened him, but now he heard only shallow, glottal breathing. He stood in the crust on the distended stomach and sniffed the wound, then moved forward onto the chest.

Hassan could feel the claws through his shirt. He must wait. In Hassan's left hand was the short crowbar Captain Larmoso had dropped when Hassan surprised him at the crates. In his right hand was the Walther

PPK automatic he had drawn too late. He would not
fire the gun now. Someone might hear. The traitor
Larmoso must think him dead when he came into the
hold again.

The rat's nose was almost touching Hassan's chin.
The man's labored breathing stirred the rat's whiskers.

With all his strength, Hassan jabbed the crowbar
sideways across his chest and felt it gouge into the rat's
side. The claws dug in as the rat leaped off him, and he
heard the claws rasp on the metal deck as it ran.

Minutes passed. Then Hassan was aware of a faint
rustling. He believed it came from inside his trouser
leg. He could feel nothing below his waist and he was
grateful for that.

The temptation to kill himself was with him all the
time now. He had the strength to bring the Walther to
his head. He would do it too, he told himself, as soon
as Muhammad Fasil came. Until then he would guard
the boxes.

Hassan did not know how long he had lain in the
darkness. He knew his mind would be clear for only a
few minutes this time, and he tried to think. The
Leticia was a little more than three days from the
Azores when he caught Larmoso snooping at the
boxes. When Muhammad Fasil did not receive Hassan's scheduled cable from the Azores on November 2,
he would have two days to act before the *Leticia* sailed
again—and the Azores were the last stop before New
York.

Fasil will act, Hassan thought. *I will not fail him.*

Every stroke of the *Leticia's* aged diesel vibrated the
deck plates beneath his head. The red waves were

spreading behind his eyes. He strained to hear the diesel and thought it was the pulse of God.

Sixty feet above the hold where Hassan lay, Captain Kemal Larmoso was relaxing in his cabin, drinking a bottle of Sapporo beer while he listened to the news. The Lebanese army and the guerrillas were fighting again. *Good,* he thought. *Turds to them both.*

The Lebanese threatened his papers and the guerrillas threatened his life. When he put into Beirut or Tyre or Tobruk, both had to be paid. The guerrillas not so much as the camel-fucking Lebanese customs.

He was in for it with the guerrillas now. He knew he was committed from the moment Hassan caught him at the boxes. Fasil and the others would be after him when he returned to Beirut. Maybe the Lebanese had learned from King Hussein and would drive the guerrillas out. Then there would be only one faction to pay. He was sick of it. "Take him there." "Bring the guns." "Speak nothing." *I know about speak nothing,* Larmoso thought. *My ear did not get this way from a hasty shave.* Once he had found a limpet mine attached to the *Leticia*'s scaly hull, fuse ready to be set if he should refuse the guerrillas' demands.

Larmoso was a large, hairy man, whose body odor made even his crew's eyes water, and his weight sagged his bunk halfway to the floor. He opened another bottle of Sapporo with his teeth and brooded while he drank it, his small eyes fixed on an Italian magazine foldout depicting heterosexual buggery, which was taped to the bulkhead.

Then he lifted the small Madonna from the floor beside his bunk and stood it on his chest. It was scarred where he had probed it with his knife before realizing what it was.

Larmoso knew of three places where he might turn explosives into money. There was a Cuban exile in Miami with more money than sense. In the Dominican Republic there was a man who paid Brazilian cruzeios for anything that would shoot or explode. The third possible customer was the U.S. government.

There would be a reward, of course, but Larmoso knew that there would also be other advantages in a deal with the Americans. Certain prejudices held against him by U.S. Customs might be forgotten.

Larmoso had opened the crates because he wanted to put the bite on the importer, Benjamin Muzi, for an unusually large payoff, and he needed to know the value of the contraband in order to figure out how much he could demand. Larmoso had never trifled with Muzi's shipments before, but persistent rumors had reached him that Muzi was going out of business in the Middle East, and if that happened Larmoso's illicit income would drop sharply. This could very well be Muzi's final shipment, and Larmoso wanted to make all he could.

He had expected to find a whopping shipment of hashish, a commodity Muzi often bought from Al Fatah sources. Instead he found *plastique,* and then Hassan was there, going for his pistol like a fool. *Plastique* was heavy business, not like a normal drug deal where friends could put the squeeze on one another.

Larmoso hoped that Muzi could solve the problem with the guerrillas and still turn a profit on the *plas-*

tique. But Muzi would be furious at him for fooling with the crates.

If Muzi did not want to cooperate, if he refused to pay off Larmoso and make amends to the guerrillas for him, then Larmoso intended to keep the *plastique* and sell it elsewhere. Better to be a wealthy fugitive than a poor one.

But first he must take an inventory of what he had to sell, and he must get rid of certain garbage in the hold.

Larmoso knew that he had hit Hassan squarely. And he had given him plenty of time to die. He decided he would sack up Hassan, weight him in the harbor at Ponta Delgada while there was only an anchor watch aboard, and dump him in deep water when he cleared the Azores.

Muhammad Fasil checked the cable office in Beirut hourly all day. At first he hoped Hassan's cable from the Azores had only been delayed. Always before, the cables had come by noon. There had been three of them—from Benghazi, Tunis, and Lisbon—as the old freighter plowed westward. The wording varied in each, but they all meant the same thing—the explosives had not been disturbed. The next one should be "Mother much improved today" and it should be signed Jose. At 6 P.M., when the cable had still not arrived, Fasil drove to the airport. He was carrying the credentials of an Algerian photographer and a gutted speed graphic camera containing a .357 Magnum revolver. Fasil had made the reservations as a precaution two weeks before. He knew he could be in Ponta Delgada by 4 P.M. the next day.

Captain Larmoso relieved his first mate at the helm when the *Leticia* raised the peaks of Santa Maria early on the morning of November 2. He skirted the small island on the southwest side, then turned north for San Miguel and the port of Ponta Delgada.

The Portuguese city was lovely in the winter sun, white buildings with red-tiled roofs, and evergreens between them rising nearly as high as the bell tower. Behind the city were gentle mountain slopes, patched with fields.

The *Leticia* looked scalier than ever tied at the quay, her faded Plimsoll line creeping up out of the water as the crew off-loaded a consignment of reconditioned light agricultural equipment and creeping down again as crates of bottled mineral water were loaded aboard.

Larmoso was not worried. The cargo handling involved only the aft hold. The small, locked compartment in the forward hold would not be disturbed.

Most of the work was completed by the afternoon of the second day, and he gave the crew shore leave, the purser doling out only enough cash to each man for one evening in the brothels and bars.

The crew trooped off down the quay, walking quickly in anticipation of the evening, the foremost sailor with a blob of shaving cream beneath his ear. They did not notice the thin man beneath the colonnade of the Banco Nacional Ultramarino, who counted them as they passed.

The ship was silent now except for Captain Larmoso's footsteps as he descended to the engine room workshop, a small compartment dimly lit by a bulb in a wire cage. Rummaging through a pile of cast-off parts he selected a piston rod, complete with wrist-pin assembly, which had been ruined when the *Leticia*'s engine seized off Tobruk in the spring. The rod looked like a great metal bone as he hefted it in his hands. Confident that it was heavy enough to take Hassan's body down the long slide to the bottom of the Atlantic, Larmoso carried the rod aft and stowed it in a locker near the stern along with a length of line.

Next he took from the galley one of the cook's big burlap garbage bags and carried it forward through the empty wardroom toward the forward companionway. He draped the bag over his shoulder like a serape and whistled between his teeth, his footfalls loud in the passageway. Then he heard a slight sound behind him. Larmoso paused, listening. Probably the noise was only the old man on anchor watch walking on the deck above his head. Larmoso stepped through the ward-room hatch into the companionway and went down the metal steps to the level of the forward hold. But instead of entering the hold, he slammed its hatch loudly and stood against the bulkhead at the foot of the com-panionway, looking up the metal shaft to the hatch at the top of the dark steps. The five-shot Smith & Wes-son Airweight looked like a child's licorice pistol in his big fist.

As he watched, the wardroom hatch swung open and, as slowly as a questing snake, the small, neat head of Muhammad Fasil appeared.

Larmoso fired, the blast incredible inside the metal walls, the bullet screaming off the handrail. He ducked into the hold and slammed the hatch behind him. He was sweating now, and the rank smell of him mixed with the smells of rust and cold grease as he waited in the darkness.

The footsteps descending the companionway were slow and evenly spaced. Larmoso knew Fasil was holding the railing with one hand and keeping his gun trained on the closed hatch with the other. Larmoso scrambled behind a crate twelve feet from the hatch Fasil had to enter. Time was on his side. Eventually the crew would straggle back. He thought of the deals and excuses he might offer Fasil. Nothing would work. He had four shots left. He would kill Fasil when he came through the hatch. It was settled.

The companionway was quiet for a second. Then Fasil's Magnum roared, the bullet blasting through the hatch and sending metal fragments flying through the hold. Larmoso fired back at the closed hatch, the .38 special bullet only dimpling the metal, and fired again and again as the hatch flew open and the dark shape tumbled through.

Even as he fired the last round, Larmoso saw by the muzzle flash that he had shot a sofa pillow from the wardroom. Now he was running, tripping and cursing, through the dark hold toward the forward compartment.

He would get Hassan's pistol. He would kill Fasil with it.

Larmoso moved well for a big man, and he knew the layout of the hold. In less than 30 seconds he was at the compartment hatch, fumbling with the key. The stench that puffed over him when he opened the hatch gagged him as he plunged inside. He did not want to show a light, and he crawled across the deck in the black compartment, feeling for Hassan and muttering softly to himself. He butted into the crates and crawled around them. His hand touched a shoe. Larmoso felt his way up the trouser leg and over the belly. The gun was not in the waistband. He felt on either side of the body. He found the arm, he felt it move, but he did not find the gun until it exploded in his face.

Fasil's ears were ringing and several minutes passed before he could hear the hoarse whisper from the forward compartment.

"Fasil. Fasil."

The guerrilla shone his small flashlight into the compartment, tiny feet scurrying from the beam. Fasil played the light over the red mask of Larmoso, lying dead on his back, then stepped inside.

Kneeling, he took the rat-ravaged face of Ali Hassan in his hands. The lips moved.

"Fasil."

"You have done well, Hassan. I'll get a doctor." Fasil could see that it was hopeless. Hassan, swollen with peritonitis, was beyond help. But Fasil could kidnap a doctor a half-hour before the *Leticia* sailed and make him come along. He could kill the physician at sea before the ship reached New York. Hassan deserved no less. It was the humane thing to do.

"Hassan, I will be back in five minutes with the medical kit. I will leave the light with you."

A faint whisper. "Is my duty done?"

"It is done. Hold on, old friend, I will bring morphine now and then a doctor."

Fasil was feeling his way aft through the dark hold

when Hassan's pistol went off behind him. He paused and leaned his head against the ship's cold iron. "You will pay for this," he whispered. He was talking to a people that he had never seen.

The old man on anchor watch was still unconscious, with a swollen lump on the back of his head where Fasil had slugged him. Fasil dragged him to the first mate's cabin and laid him on the bunk, then sat down to think.

Originally the plan was to have the crates picked up at the Brooklyn dock by the importer, Benjamin Muzi. There was no way of knowing if Larmoso had contacted Muzi and enlisted his aid in this treachery. Muzi would have to be dealt with anyway because he knew far too much. Customs would be curious at the absence of Larmoso. Questions would be asked. It seemed unlikely that the others on the ship knew what was in the crates. Larmoso's keys were still dangling from the lock on the forward compartment when the captain was killed. Now they were in Fasil's pocket. The *plastique* must not go into New York Harbor, that was clear.

First Mate Mustapha Fawzi was a reasonable man and not a brave one. At midnight when he returned to the ship, Fasil had a brief conversation with him. In one hand Fasil held a large black revolver. In the other he held $2,000. He inquired about the health of Fawzi's mother and sister in Beirut, then suggested that their continued health depended largely on Fawzi's cooperation. The thing was quickly done.

It was 7 P.M. Eastern Standard Time when the telephone rang in Michael Lander's house. He was working in his garage and picked up the extension. Dahlia was mixing a can of paint.

From the amount of line noise, Lander guessed the caller was very far away. He had a pleasant voice with a British clip, similar to Dahlia's. He asked for the "lady of the house."

Dahlia was at the phone in an instant and began a rather tedious conversation in English about relatives and real estate. Then the conversation was punctuated with 20 seconds of rapid-fire slangy Arabic.

Dahlia turned from the phone, covering the mouthpiece with her hand.

"Michael, we have to pick up the *plastique* at sea. Can you get a boat?"

Lander's mind worked furiously. "Yes. Make sure of the rendezvous point. Forty miles due east of the Barnegat Light a half-hour before sunset. We'll make visual contact with the last light and close after dark. If the winds are over force five, postpone it for exactly 24 hours. Tell him to pack it in units one man can lift."

Dahlia spoke quickly into the telephone, then hung up.

"Tuesday the twelfth," she said. She was looking at him curiously. "Michael, you worked that out rather quickly."

"No, I didn't," Lander said.

Dahlia had learned very early never to lie to Lander. That would be as stupid as programming a computer with half-truths and expecting accurate answers. Besides, he could always tell when she had even the temptation to lie. Now she was glad that she had confided in him from the beginning on the arrangements for bringing in the *plastique*.

He listened calmly as she told him what had happened on the ship.

"Do you think Muzi put Larmoso up to it?" he asked.

"Fasil doesn't know. He never had a chance to question Larmoso. We have to assume Muzi put him up to it. We can't afford to do otherwise, can we, Michael? If Muzi dared to interfere with the shipment, if he planned to keep our advance payment and sell the *plastique* elsewhere, then he has sold us out to the authorities here. He would have to do that for his own protection. Even if he has not betrayed us, he would have to be dealt with. He knows far too much, and he has seen you. He could identify you."

"You intended to kill him all along?"

"Yes. He is not one of us, and he is in a dangerous business. If the authorities threatened him on some other matter, who knows what he might tell them?" Dahlia realized she was being too assertive. "I couldn't stand the thought of him always being a threat to you, Michael," she added in a softer voice. "You didn't trust him either, did you, Michael? You had a pickup at sea all worked out in advance, just in case, didn't you? That's amazing."

"Yeah, amazing," Lander said. "One thing. Nothing happens to Muzi until after we have the plastic. If he has gone to the authorities, to get immunity for himself in some other matter or whatever, the trap will be set at the dock. As long as they think we are coming to the dock, they are less likely to fly a stakeout team out to the ship. If Muzi is hit before the ship comes in, they'll know we're not coming to the dock. They'll be waiting for us when we go out to the ship." Suddenly Lander was furious and white around the mouth. "So Muzi was the best your camel-shit mastermind could come up with."

Dahlia did not flinch. She did not point out that it was Lander who went to Muzi first. She knew that this anger would be suppressed and added to Lander's general fund of rage as, irresistibly, his mind was drawn back to the problem.

He closed his eyes for a moment. "You'll have to go shopping," he said. "Give me a pencil."

CHAPTER
5

NOW THAT HAFEZ NAJEER and Abu Ali were dead, only Dahlia and Muhammad Fasil knew Lander's identity, but Benjamin Muzi had seen him several times, for Muzi had been Lander's first link to Black September and the plastic.

From the beginning, the great problem had been obtaining the explosives. In the first white heat of his epiphany, when he knew what he would do, it had not occurred to Lander that he would need help. It was part of the aesthetic of the act that he do it alone. But as the plan flowered in his mind, and as he looked down on the crowds again and again, he decided they deserved more than the few cases of dynamite that he could buy or steal. They should have more attention than the random shrapnel from a shattered gondola and a few pounds of nails and chain.

Sometimes, as he lay awake, the upturned faces of the crowd filled his midnight ceiling, mouths open, shifting like a field of flowers in the wind. Many of the faces became Margaret's. Then the great fireball lifted off the heat of his face and rose to them, swirling like the Crab nebula, searing them to charcoal, soothing him to sleep.

He must have plastic.

Lander traveled across the country twice looking for plastic. He went to three military arsenals to case the possibilities for theft and saw that it was hopeless. He went to the plant of a great corporation that manufactures baby oil and napalm, industrial adhesives and plastic explosives, and he found that plant security was as tight as that of the military and considerably more imaginative. The instability of nitroglycerine ruled out extracting it from dynamite.

Lander checked newspapers avidly for stories about terrorism, explosions, bombs. The pile of clippings in his bedroom grew. It would have offended him to know that this was patterned behavior, to know in how many bedrooms sick men keep clippings, waiting for their day. Many of Lander's clippings carried foreign datelines—Rome, Helsinki, Damascus, The Hague, Beirut.

In a Cincinnati motel in mid-July the idea came to him. He had flown over a fair that day and was getting mildly drunk in the motel lounge. It was late. A television set was suspended from the ceiling over the end of the bar. Lander sat almost directly beneath it, staring into his drink. Most of the customers were facing him, turned on their stools, the bloodless light of the TV playing over their uplifted faces.

Lander stirred and came alert. Something in the expression on the faces of the customers watching television. Apprehension. Anger. Not fear exactly, for they were safe enough, but they wore the look of a man watching wolves from his cabin window. Lander picked up his drink and walked down the bar until he could see the screen. Film of a Boeing 747 sitting in the desert with heat shimmer around it. The forward end of the fuselage exploded, then the center section, and the plane was gone in a belch of flame and smoke. The program was a rerun of a news special on Arab terrorism.

Cut to Munich. The horror at the Olympic Village. The helicopter at the airport. Muffled gunfire inside it as the Israeli athletes were shot. The embassy at Khartoum where the American and Belgian diplomats were slain. Al Fatah leader Yasir Arafat denying responsibility.

Yasir Arafat again at a news conference in Beirut, bitterly accusing England and the United States of aiding the Israelis in terrorist raids against the guerrillas. "When our revenge comes, it will be big," Arafat said, his eyes reflecting double moons from the television lights.

A statement of support from Col. Khadafy, student of Napoleon and Al Fatah's constant ally and banker: "The United States deserves a strong slap in the face." A further comment from Khadafy—"God damn America."

"Scumbag," said a man in a bowling jacket who stood next to Lander. "Bunch of scumbags."

Lander laughed loudly. Several of the drinkers turned to him.

"That funny to you, Jack?"

"No. I assure you, sir, that is not funny at all. You scumbag." Lander put money on the bar and walked out with the man shouting after him.

Lander knew no Arabs. He began to read accounts of the Arab-American groups sympathetic to the cause of the Palestinian Arabs, but the one meeting he attended in Brooklyn convinced him that Arab-American citizens' committees were far too straight for him. They discussed subjects such as "justice" and "individual rights" and encouraged writing to Congressmen. If he put out feelers there for militants, he rightly suspected, he would soon be approached by an undercover cop with a Kel transmitter strapped to his leg.

Demonstrations in Manhattan on the Palestinian question were no better. At United Nations Plaza and Union Square he found less than 20 Arab youngsters surrounded by a sea of Jews.

No, he needed a competent and greedy crook with good contacts in the Middle East. And he found one. Lander obtained the name of Benjamin Muzi from an airline pilot he knew who brought back interesting packages from the Middle East in his shaving kit and delivered them to the importer.

Muzi's office was gloomy enough, set in the back of a shabby warehouse on Sedgwick Street in Brooklyn. Lander was shown to the office by a very large and odorous Greek, whose bald head reflected the dim overhead light as they wound through a maze of crates.

Only the office door was expensive. It was of steel with two deadbolts and a Fox lock. The mail slot was belly-high, with a hinged metal plate in the inside that could be bolted shut.

Muzi was very fat, and he grunted as he lifted a pile of invoices off a chair and motioned for Lander to sit down.

"May I offer you something? A refreshment?"

"No."

Muzi drained his bottle of Perrier water and fished a fresh bottle out of his ice chest. He dropped in two aspirin tablets and took a long swallow. "You said on the telephone that you wished to speak to me on a matter of the utmost confidence. Since you haven't offered your name, do you have any objection to being called Hopkins?"

"None whatever."

"Excellent. Mr. Hopkins, when people say 'in confidence' they generally mean contravention of the law. If that is the case here, then I will have nothing whatever to do with you, do you understand me?"

Lander removed a packet of bills from his pocket and placed it on Muzi's desk. Muzi did not touch the money or look at it. Lander picked up the packet and started for the door.

"A moment, Mr. Hopkins." Muzi gestured to the Greek who stepped forward and searched Lander thoroughly. The Greek looked at Muzi and shook his head.

"Sit down, please. Thank you, Salop. Wait outside." The big man closed the door behind him.

"That's a filthy name," Lander said.

"Yes, but he doesn't know it," Muzi said, mopping his face with a handkerchief. He steepled his fingers under his chin and waited.

"I understand you are a man of wide influence," Lander began.

"I am certainly a wide man of influence."

"Certain advice—"

"Contrary to what you may believe, Mr. Hopkins, it is not necessary to indulge in endless Arabic circumlocutions in dealing with an Arab, especially since, for the most part, Americans lack the subtlety to make it interesting. This office is not bugged. You are not bugged. Tell me what you want."

"I want a letter delivered to the head of the intelligence section of Al Fatah."

"And who might that be?"

"I don't know. You can find out. I am told you can do nearly anything in Beirut. The letter will be sealed in several tricky ways and it must get there unopened."

"Yes, I expect it must." Muzi's eyes were hooded like a turtle's.

"You're thinking letter bomb," Lander said. "It's not. You can watch me put the contents in the envelope from ten feet away. You can lick the flap, then I'll put on the other seals."

"I deal with men who are interested in money. People with politics often don't pay their bills, or they kill you out of ineptitude. I don't think—"

"$2,000 now, $2,000 if the message gets there satisfactorily." Lander put the money back on the desk. "Another thing, I would advise you to open a numbered bank account in The Hague."

"To what purpose?"

"To put a lot of Libyan currency in if you should decide to retire."

There was a prolonged silence. Finally Lander broke it.

"You have to understand that this must go to the right man the first time. It must not be handed around."

"Since I don't know what you want, I am working blind. Certain inquiries could be made, but even inquiry is dangerous. You are aware that Al Fatah is fragmented, contentious within itself."

"Get it to Black September," Lander said.

"Not for $4,000."

"How much?"

"Inquiries will be difficult and expensive and even then you can never be sure—"

"How much?"

"For $8,000, payable immediately, I would do my best."

"$4,000 now and $4,000 afterward."

"$8,000 now, Mr. Hopkins. Afterward I will not know you and you will never come here again."

"Agreed."

"I am going to Beirut in a week's time. I do not want your letter until immediately before my departure. You can bring it here on the night of the seventh. It will be sealed in my presence. Believe me, I do not want to read what is in it."

The letter contained Lander's real name and address and said that he could do a great service for the Palestinian cause. He asked to meet with a representative of Black September anywhere in the Western Hemisphere. He enclosed a money order for $1,500 to cover any expenses.

Muzi accepted the letter and the $8,000 with a gravity just short of ceremony. It was one of his peculiarities that, when his price was met, he kept his word.

A week later, Lander received a picture postcard from Beirut. There was no message on it. He wondered if Muzi had opened the letter himself and gotten the name and address from it.

A third week passed. He had to fly four times out of Lakehurst. Twice in that week he thought he was being followed as he drove to the airfield, but he could not be sure. On Thursday, August 15, he flew a night-sign run over Atlantic City, flashing billboard messages from the computer-controlled panels of lights on the blimp's great sides.

When he returned to Lakehurst and got into his car, he noticed a card stuck under the windshield wiper. Annoyed, he got out and pulled it loose, expecting an advertisement. He examined the card under the dome light. It was a chit good for a swim at Maxie's Swim Club, near Lakehurst. On the back was written "tomorrow 3 P.M. flash once now for yes."

Lander looked around him at the darkened airfield parking lot. He saw no one. He flashed his headlights once and drove home.

There are many private swimming clubs in New Jersey, well maintained and fairly expensive, and they offer a variety of exclusionary policies. Maxie's had a predominantly Jewish clientele, but unlike some of the club owners Maxie admitted a few blacks and Puerto Ricans if he knew them. Lander arrived at the pool at 2:45 P.M. and changed into his swimsuit in a cinder-block dressing room with puddles on the floor. The sun and the sharp smell of chlorine and the noisy children reminded him of other times, swimming at the officers' club with Margaret and his daughters. Afterward a drink at poolside, Margaret holding the stem of her glass with fingers puckered from the water, laughing and tossing her wet hair back, knowing the young lieutenants were watching.

Lander felt very much alone now, and he was conscious of his white body and his ugly hand as he walked out on the hot concrete. He put his valuables in a wire basket and checked them with the attendant, tucking the plastic check tag in his swimsuit pocket. The pool was an unnatural blue and the light danced on it, hurting his eyes.

There are a lot of advantages in a swimming pool, he reflected. Nobody can carry a gun or a tape recorder, nobody can be fingerprinted on the sly.

He swam back and forth lazily for half an hour. There were at least fifteen children in the pool with a variety of inflated seahorses and inner tubes. Several young couples were playing keepaway with a striped beach ball, and one muscle-bound young man was anointing himself with suntan oil on the side of the pool.

Lander rolled over and began a slow backstroke across the deep end, just out of range of the divers. He was watching a small, drifting cloud when he collided with a swimmer in a tangle of arms and legs, a girl in a snorkel mask who had been kicking along, apparently watching the bottom instead of looking where she was going.

"Sorry," she said, treading water. Lander blew water out of his nose and swam on, saying nothing. He stayed in the pool another half-hour, then decided to leave. He was about to climb out when the girl in the snorkel mask surfaced in front of him. She took off the mask and smiled.

"Did you drop this? I found it on the bottom of the pool." She was holding his plastic check tag.

Lander looked down to see that the pocket of his swimsuit was wrong side out.

"You'd better check your wallet and make sure everything is there," she said and submerged again.

Tucked inside the wallet was the money order he had sent to Beirut. He gave his basket back to the attendant and rejoined the girl in the pool. She was in a water fight with two small boys. They complained loudly when she left them. She was splendid to see in the water, and Lander, feeling cold and shriveled inside his swimming trunks, was angered at the sight.

"Let's talk in the pool, Mr. Lander," she said, wading to a depth where the water lapped just below her breasts.

"What am I supposed to do, shoot off in my pants and spill the whole business right here?"

She watched him steadily, multicolored pinpoints of light dancing in her eyes. Suddenly he placed his mangled hand on her arm, staring into her face, watching for the flinch. A gentle smile was the only reaction he saw. The reaction he did not see was beneath the surface of the water. Her left hand slowly turned over, fingers hooked, ready to strike if necessary.

"May I call you Michael? I am Dahlia Iyad. This is a good place to talk."

"Was everything in my wallet satisfactory to you?"

"You should be pleased that I searched it. I don't think you would deal with a fool."

"How much do you know about me?"

"I know what you do for a living. I know you were a prisoner of war. You live alone, you read very late at night, and you smoke a rather inferior grade of marijuana. I know that your telephone is not tapped, at least not from the telephone terminal in your basement or the one on the pole outside your home. I don't know for certain what you want."

Sooner or later he would have to say it. Aside from his distrust of this woman, it was difficult to say the thing, as hard as opening up for a shrink. All right.

"I want to detonate 1,200 pounds of plastic explosive in the Super Bowl."

She looked at him as though he had painfully admitted a sexual aberration that she particularly enjoyed. Calm and kindly compassion, suppressed excitement. Welcome home.

"You have no plastic, do you, Michael?"

"No." He looked away as he asked the question. "Can you get it?"

"That's a lot. It depends."

Water flew off his head as he snapped back to face her. "I don't want to hear that. That is not what I want to hear. Talk straight."

"If I am convinced you can do it, if I can satisfy my commander that you can do it and will do it, then yes, I can get the plastic. I'll get it."

"That's all right. That's fair."

"I want to see everything. I want to go home with you."

"Why not?"

They did not go directly to Lander's house. He was scheduled for a night-sign flight and he took Dahlia with him. It was not common practice to take passengers on night-sign flights, since most of the seats were removed from the gondola to make room for the onboard computer that controlled the 8,000 lights along the sides of the blimp. But with crowding there was room. Farley, the copilot, had inconvenienced everyone on two previous occasions by bringing his Florida girlfriend and was in no position to grumble at giving up his seat to this young woman. He and the computer operator licked their lips over Dahlia and entertained themselves with lewd pantomimes at the rear of the gondola when she and Lander were not looking.

Manhattan blazed in the night like a great diamond ship as they passed over at 2,500 feet. They dropped toward the brilliant wreath of Shea Stadium where the Mets were playing a night game, and the sides of the dirigible became huge flashing billboards, letters moving down its sides. "Don't forget, hire the Vet," was the first message. "Winston tastes God—" this message was interrupted while the technician cursed and fumbled with the perforated tape.

Afterward, Dahlia and Lander watched while the ground crew at Lakehurst secured the floodlit blimp for the night. They paid special attention to the gondola, as the men in coveralls removed the computer and reinstalled the seats.

Lander pointed out the sturdy handrail that runs around the base of the cabin. He led her to the rear of the gondola to watch while the turbojet generator that powers the lights was detached. The generator is a sleek, heavy unit shaped like a largemouth bass, and it has a strong, three-point attachment that would be very useful.

Farley approached them with his clipboard. "Hey, you people aren't going to stay *here* all night."

Dahlia smiled at him vacuously. "It's all so exciting."

"Yeah." Farley chuckled and left them with a wink.

Dahlia's face was flushed and her eyes were bright as they drove home from the airfield.

She made it clear from the first that, inside his house, she expected no performance of any kind from Lander. And she was careful not to show any distaste for him either. Her body was there, she had brought it because it was convenient to do so, her attitude seemed to say. She was physically deferential to Lander in a way so subtle that it does not have a name in English. And she was very, very gentle.

In matters of business it was quite different. Lander quickly found that he could not browbeat her with his superior technical knowledge. He had to explain his plan in minute detail, defining terms as he went along. When she disagreed with him it was usually on methods for handling people, and he found her to be a shrewd judge of people and greatly experienced in the behavior of frightened men under pressure. Even when she was adamant in disagreement she never emphasized a point with a body movement or a facial expression that reflected anything other than concentration.

As the technical problems were resolved, at least in theory, Dahlia could see that the greatest danger to the project was Lander's instability. He was a splendid machine with a homicidal child at the controls. Her role became increasingly supportive. In this area, she could not always calculate and she was forced to feel.

As the days passed, he began to tell her things about himself—safe things that did not pain him. Sometimes in the evenings, a little drunk, he carped endlessly about the injustices of the Navy until she finally went to her room after midnight, leaving him cursing at the television. And then one night, as she sat on the side of his bed, he brought her a story like a gift. He told her about the first time he ever saw a dirigible.

He was a child of eight with impetigo on his knees, and he was standing on the bare clay playground of a country school when he looked up and saw the airship. Silver, wearing for a reach across the wind, it floated over the schoolyard, scattering in the air behind it tiny objects that floated down—Baby Ruth candy bars on small parachutes. Running after the airship, Michael could stay in its shadow the length of the schoolyard, the other children running with him, scrambling for the candy bars. Then they reached the plowed field at the edge of the schoolyard and the shadow moved away, rippling over the rows. Lander in his short pants fell in the field and tore the scabs off his knees. He got to his feet again and watched the dirigible out of sight, rivulets of blood on his shins, a candy bar and parachute clutched in his hand.

While he was lost in the story, Dahlia stretched out beside him on the bed, listening. And he came to her from the playground, with wonder and the light of that old day still in his face.

After that he became shameless. She had heard his terrible wish and had accepted it as her own. She had received him with her body. Not with withering expectations, but with abundant grace. She saw no ugliness in him. Now he felt that he could tell her *anything,* and he poured it out—the things that he could never tell before, even to Margaret. Especially to Margaret.

Dahlia listened with compassion and concerned interest. She never showed a trace of distaste or apprehension, though she learned to be wary of him when he was talking about certain things, for he could become angry at her suddenly for injuries that others had done to him. Dahlia needed to know Lander, and she learned him very well, better than anyone else would ever know him—including the blue-ribbon commission that investigated his final act. The investigators had to rely on their piles of documents and photographs, their witnesses stiff upon the chair. Dahlia had it from the monster's mouth.

It is true that she learned Lander in order to use him, but who will ever listen for free? She might have done a great deal for him if her object had not been murder.

His utter frankness and her own inferences provided her with many windows on his past. Through them, she watched her weapon forged . . .

Willett-Lorance Consolidated School, a rural school between Willett and Lorance, South Carolina, February 2, 1941:

"Michael, Michael Lander, come up here and read your paper. I want you to pay strict attention, Buddy Ives. And you too, Junior Atkins. You two have been fiddling while Rome burns. At six-weeks tests, this class will be divided into the sheep and the goats."

Michael has to be called twice more. He is surprisingly small walking up the aisle. Willett-Lorance has no accelerated program for exceptional children. Instead, Michael has been "skipped" ahead. He is eight years old and in the fourth grade.

Buddy Ives and Junior Atkins, both 12, have spent the previous recess dipping a second-grader's head in the toilet. Now they pay strict attention. To Michael. Not to his paper.

Michael knows he must pay. Standing before the class in his baggy short pants, the only pair in the room, reading in a voice barely audible, he knows he will have to pay. He hopes it will happen on the playground. He would rather be beaten than dipped.

Michael's father is a minister and his mother is a power in the PTA. He is not a cute, appealing child. He thinks there is something terribly wrong with him. For as long as he can remember he has been filled with horrible feelings that he does not understand. He cannot yet identify rage and self-loathing. He has a constant picture of himself as a prissy little boy in short pants, and he hates it. Sometimes he watches the other eight-year-olds playing cowboys in the shrubbery. On a few occasions he has tried to play, yelling "bang bang" and pointing his finger. He feels silly doing it. The others can tell he is not really a cowboy, does not believe in the game.

He wanders over to his classmates, the 11- and 12-year-olds. They are choosing sides to play football. He stands in the group and waits. It is not too bad to be chosen last, as long as you are chosen. He is alone between the two sides. He is not chosen. He notes which team chose last and walks over to the other team. He can see himself coming toward them. He can see his knobby knees beneath the short pants, knows they are talking about him in the huddle. They turn their backs to him. He cannot beg to play. He walks away, his face burning. There is no place on the red clay playground where he can get out of sight.

As a Southerner, Michael is deeply imprinted with the Code. A man fights when called on. A man is tough, straightforward, honorable, and strong. He can play football, he loves to hunt, and he allows no nasty talk around the ladies, although he discusses them in lewd terms among his fellows.

When you are a child, the Code without the equipment will kill you.

Michael has learned not to fight 12-year-olds if he can help it. He is told that he is a coward. He believes it. He is articulate and has not yet learned to conceal it. He is told that he is a sissy. He believes that this must be true.

He has finished reading his paper before the class now. He knows how Junior Atkins' breath will smell in his face. The teacher tells Michael he is a "good classroom citizen." She does not understand why he turns his face away from her.

September 10, 1947, the football field behind Willett-Lorance Consolidated:

Michael Lander is going out for football. He is in the tenth grade and he is going out without his parents' knowledge. He feels that he has to do it. He wants the good feeling his classmates have about the sport. He is curious about himself. The uniform makes him wonderfully anonymous. He cannot see himself when he has it on. The tenth grade is late for a boy to begin playing football, and he has much to learn. To his surprise the others are tolerant of him. After a few days of forearms and cleats, they have discovered that, though he is naive about the game, he will hit and he wants to learn from them. It is a good time for him. It lasts a week. His parents learn that he is going out for football. They hate the coach, a godless man who, it is rumored, keeps alcohol in his home. The Reverend Lander is on the school board now. The Landers drive up to the practice field in their Kaiser. Michael does not see them until he hears his name being called. His mother is approaching the sideline, walking stiff-ankled through the grass. The Reverend Lander waits in the car.

"Take off that monkey suit."

Michael pretends not to hear. He is playing linebacker with the scrubs in scrimmage. He assumes his stance. Each blade of grass is distinct in his eyes. The tackle in front of him has a red scratch on his calf.

His mother is walking the sideline now. Now she is crossing it. She is coming. Two hundred pounds of pondered rage. "I said take off that monkey suit and get in that car."

Michael might have saved himself in that moment. He might have yelled into his mother's face. The coach might have saved him, had he been quicker, less afraid for his job. Michael cannot let the others see any more.

He cannot be with them after this. They are looking at each other now with expressions he cannot stand. He trots toward the prefabricated building they use for a dressing room. There are snickers behind him.

The coach has to speak to the boys twice to resume the practice. "We don't need no mama's boys no way," he says.

Michael moves very deliberately in the dressing room, leaving his equipment in a neat pile on the bench with his locker key on top. He feels only a dull heaviness inside, no surface anger.

Riding home in the Kaiser, he listens to a torrent of abuse. He replies that, yes, he understands how he has embarrassed his parents, that he should have thought of others. He nods solemnly when reminded that he must save his hands for the piano.

July 18, 1948: Michael Lander is sitting on the back porch of his home, a mean parsonage beside the Baptist church in Willett. He is fixing a lawn mower. He makes a little money fixing lawn mowers and small appliances. Looking through the screen, he can see his father lying on a bed, his hands behind his head, listening to the radio. When he thinks of his father, Michael sees his father's white, inept hands, the ring from Cumberland-Macon Divinity School loose behind the knuckle of his ring finger. In the South, as in many other places, the church is an institution of, by, and for women. The men tolerate it for the sake of family peace. The men of the community have no respect for the Reverend Lander because he could never make a crop, could never do anything practical. His sermons are dull and rambling, composed while the choir is singing the offertory hymn. The Reverend Lander spends much of his time writing letters to a girl he knew in high school. He never mails the letters, but locks them in a tin box in his office. The combination padlock is childishly simple. Michael has read the letters for years. For laughs.

Puberty has done a great deal for Michael Lander. At fifteen he is tall and lean. He has, by considerable effort, learned to do convincingly mediocre school-work. Against all odds, he has developed what appears to be an affable personality. He knows the joke about the bald-headed parrot, and he tells it well.

A freckle-faced girl two years older has helped Michael discover that he is a man. This is a tremendous relief to him after years of being told that he is a queer, with no evidence to judge himself either way.

But in the blossoming of Michael Lander, part of him has stood off to the side, cold and watchful. It is the part of him that recognized the ignorance of the classroom, that constantly replays little vignettes of grade school making the new face wince, that flashes the picture of the unlovely little scholar in front of him in moments of stress, and can open under him a dread void when his new image is threatened.

The little scholar stands at the head of a legion of hate and he knows the answer every time, and his creed is *God Damn You All*. At fifteen Lander functions very well. A trained observer might notice a few things about him that hint at his feelings, but these in themselves are not suspicious. He cannot bear personal competition. He has never experienced the gradients of controlled aggression that allow most of us to survive. He cannot even endure board games, he can never gamble. Lander understands limited aggression objectively, but he cannot take part in it. Emotionally, for him there is no middle ground between a pleasant, uncompetitive atmosphere and total war to the death with the corpse defiled and burned. So he has no outlet. And he has swallowed his poison longer than most could have done.

Though he tells himself that he hates the church, Michael prays often during the day. He is convinced that assuming certain positions expedites his prayers. Touching his forehead to his knee is one of the most effective ones. When it is necessary for him to do this in public places, he must think of a ruse to keep it from being noticeable. Dropping something beneath his chair and bending to get it is a useful device. Prayers delivered in thresholds or while touching a door lock are also more effective. He prays often for persons who appear in the quick flashes of memory that sear him many times a day. Without willing it, despite his efforts to stop, he conducts internal dialogues often during his waking hours. He is having one now:

"There's old Miss Phelps working in the teacher-age yard. I wonder when she'll retire. She's been at that schoolhouse for a long time."

"Do you wish she was rotten with cancer?"

"No! Dear Jesus forgive me, I don't wish she was rotten with cancer. I wish I was rotten with cancer first. [He touches wood.] Dear God, let me be rotten with cancer first, oh Father."

"Would you like to take your shotgun and blow her rotten ignorant old guts out?"

"No! No! Jesus Father no I don't. I want her to be

*safe and happy. She can't help what she is. She's a kind
and good lady. She's all right. Forgive me for saying
God Damn."*

*"Would you like to stick her face in the lawn
mower?"*

*"I wouldn't, I wouldn't, Christ help me stop think-
ing that."*

"Fuck the Holy Ghost."

*"No! I mustn't think it, I won't think it, that's the
mortal sin. I can't get forgiven. I won't think fuck the
Holy Ghost. Oh, I thought it again."*

Michael reaches behind him to touch the latch of the
screen door. He touches his forehead to his knee. Then
he concentrates hard on the lawn mower. He is anxious to finish it. He is saving his money for a flying lesson.

From the first, Lander was attracted to machinery
and he had a gift for working with machines. This did
not become a passion until he discovered machines that
enveloped him, that became his body. When he was inside them, he saw his actions as those of the machine,
he never saw the little scholar.

The first was a Piper Cub on a grass airfield. At the
controls he saw nothing of Lander, but he saw the little
plane banking, stalling, diving, and its shape was his
and its grace and strength were his and he could feel
the wind on it and he was free.

Lander joined the Navy when he was sixteen, and he
never went home again. He was not accepted for flight
school the first time he applied, and he served throughout the Korean War handling ordnance on the carrier

Coral Sea. A picture in his album shows him standing before the wing of a Corsair with a ground crew and a rack of fragmentation bombs. The others in the crew are smiling, and they have their arms around one another's shoulders. Lander is not smiling. He is holding a fuse.

On June 1, 1953, Lander awoke in the enlisted men's barracks at Lakehurst, N.J., shortly after dawn. He had arrived at his new assignment in the middle of the night and he needed a cold shower to wake up. Then he dressed carefully. The Navy had been good for Lander. He liked the uniform, liked the way he looked in it and the anonymity it gave him. He was competent and he was accepted. Today he would report for his new job, handling pressure-actuated depth-charge detonators being prepared for experiments in anti-submarine warfare. He was good with ordnance. Like many men with deep-seated insecurities, he loved the nomenclature of weapons.

He walked through the cool morning toward the ordnance complex, looking around curiously at all he had not seen when he arrived in darkness. There were the giant hangars that held the airships. The doors on the nearest one were opening with a rumble. Lander checked the time, then stopped on the sidewalk, watching. The nose came out slowly and then the great length of it. The airship was a ZPG-1 with a capacity of a million cubic feet of helium. Lander had never been so close to one before. Three hundred twenty-four feet of silver airship, the rising sun touching it with fire. Lander trotted across the asphalt apron. The ground crew was swarming under the air-ship. One of the portside engines roared and a puff of blue smoke hung in the air behind it.

Lander did not want to arm airships with depth charges. He did not want to work on them or roll them in and out of hangars. He saw only the controls.

He qualified easily for the next competitive examination for officer candidate school. Two hundred eighty enlisted men took the test on a hot July afternoon in 1953. Lander placed first. His standing in OCS won him a choice of assignments. He went to the airships.

The extension of the kinesthetic sense in controlling moving machines has never been satisfactorily explained. Some people are described as "naturals," but the term is inadequate. Mike Hailwood, the great motorcycle racer, is a natural. So was Betty Skelton, as anyone will testify who has seen her do an outside Cuban Eight in her little biplane. Lander was a natural. At the controls of an airship, freed of himself, he was sure and decisive, pressure-proof. And while he flew, part of his mind was free to race ahead, weighing probabilities, projecting the next problem and the next.

By 1955, Lander was one of the most proficient airship pilots in the world. In December of that year, he was second officer on a series of hazardous flights from South Weymouth Naval Air Station in Massachusetts, testing the effects of ice accumulation in bad weather. The flights won for the crew the Harmon Trophy for that year.

And then there was Margaret. He met her in January at the officers' club at Lakehurst, where he was being lionized after the flights from South Weymouth. It was the beginning of the best year of his life.

She was twenty years old and good-looking and fresh from West Virginia. Lander the lion, in his perfect uniform, knocked her out. Oddly, he was the first man for her and, while teaching her was a great satisfaction to him, the memory of it made things much more difficult for him later when he believed that she had others.

They were married in the chapel at Lakehurst with its plaque made of wreckage from the airship *Akron*.

Lander came to define himself in terms of Margaret and his profession. He flew the biggest, longest, sleekest airship in the world. He thought Margaret was the best-looking woman in the world.

How different Margaret was from his mother! Sometimes when he awakened from dreaming of his mother, he looked at Margaret for a long time, admiring her as he checked off the physical differences.

They had two children, they went to the Jersey shore in the summer with their boat. They had some good times. Margaret was not a very perceptive person, but gradually she came to realize that Lander was not exactly what she had thought. She needed a fairly constant level of reinforcement, but he swung between extremes in his treatment of her. Sometimes he was cloyingly solicitous. When he was thwarted in his work or at home, he became cold and withdrawn. Occasionally he showed flashes of cruelty that terrified her.

They could not discuss their problems. Either he adopted an annoying pedantic attitude or he refused to talk at all. They were denied the catharsis of an occasional fight.

In the early sixties he was away much of the time, flying the giant ZPG-3W. At 403 feet, it was the biggest non-rigid airship ever built. The 40-foot radar antenna revolving inside its vast envelope provided a key link in the country's early warning system. Lander was happy, and his behavior while he was at home was correspondingly good. But the extension of the Distant Early Warning Line, the "DEW Line" of permanent radar installations, was eating into the airships' defense role, and in 1964 the end came for Lander as a Navy airship pilot. His group was disbanded, the airships were dismantled, and he was on the ground. He was transferred to Administration.

His behavior toward Margaret deteriorated. Scalding silences marked their hours together. In the evenings he cross-examined her about her activities during the day. She was innocent enough. He would not believe it. He grew physically indifferent to her. By the end of 1964, her activities in the daytime were no longer innocent. But, more than sex, she sought warmth and friendship.

Lander volunteered for helicopters during the Vietnam expansion, and he was readily accepted. He was distracted now by his training. He was flying again. He gave Margaret expensive presents. She felt uncomfortable and uneasy about them, but this was better than the way he had acted before.

On his final leave before shipping out to Vietnam they went to Bermuda for a good vacation. If Lander's conversation was tiresomely larded with the technicalities of rotary-wing aircraft, he was at least attentive, sometimes loving. Margaret responded. Lander thought he had never loved her so much.

On February 10, 1967, Lander flew his 114th air-sea rescue mission off the carrier *Ticonderoga* in the South China Sea. A half-hour after moonset, he hung over the dark ocean off Dong Hoi. He was in a holding pattern 15 miles at sea, waiting for some F-4s and Skyraiders coming home from a raid. One of the Phantoms was hit. The pilot reported that his starboard engine had conked and he was showing a fire light. He would try to make it to the sea before he and the second officer ejected.

Lander, in the rattling cockpit of his helicopter, was talking to the pilot all the time, Vietnam a dark mass to his left.

"Ding Zero One, when you're well over the water gimme some lights if you gottem." Lander could find the Phantom crew on the water by their homing device, but he wanted to cut down on the time as much as possible. "Mr. Dillon," he said to the door gunner, "we'll go down with you facing landward. Ops confirms no friendly vessels are close by. Any boat that ain't rubber ain't ours."

The voice of the Phantom pilot was loud in his earphones. "Mixmaster, I've got a second fire light and she's filling up with smoke. We're punching out." He yelled the coordinates, and before Lander could repeat them for confirmation he was gone.

Lander knew what was happening—the two-man crew pulling down their face curtains, the canopy blowing off, the fliers rocketing up into the cold air, turning in their ejection seats, the seats falling away, and then the jar and the cool rush down through the darkness to the jungle.

He wheeled the big helicopter landward, blades slapping the heavy sea air. He had a choice now. He could wait for air cover, hang around trying to contact the men by radio, waiting for protection, or he could go in.

"There it is, sir." The copilot was pointing.

Lander could see a shower of fire a mile inland as the Phantom blew up in the air. He was over the beach when the homing signal came through. He called for air cover, but he did not wait for it. The helicopter, showing no lights, skimmed over the double canopy forest.

The light signal blinked from the narrow, rutted road. The two on the ground had the good sense to mark a landing zone for him. There was room for the rotor between the banks of trees flanking the road. Setting it down would be quicker than pulling them up with the hook one by one. Down, sinking between the banks of trees, blowing the weeds flat at the sides of the road, and suddenly the night was full of orange flashes and the cockpit ripped around him. Splattered with the copilot's blood, falling, rocking crazily, the smell of burning rubber.

The bamboo cage was not long enough for Lander to stretch out in it. His hand had been smashed by a bullet, and the pain was constant and terrible. He was delirious part of the time. His captors had nothing to treat him with except a little sulfa powder from an old

French medical kit. They took a thin plank from a crate and bound the hand flat against it. The wound throbbed constantly. After three days in the cage, Lander was marched northward to Hanoi, prodded along by the small, wiry men. They were dressed in muddy black pajamas and carried very clean AK-47 automatic rifles.

During the first month of his confinement in Hanoi, Lander was half crazy with the pain in his hand. He was in a cell with an Air Force navigator, a thoughtful former zoology teacher named Jergens. Jergens put wet compresses on the mangled hand and tried to comfort Lander as best he could, but Jergens had been confined for a long time and he was very shaky himself. Thirty-seven days after Lander arrived, Jergens reached the point where he could not stop yelling in the cell and they took him away. Lander cried when he was gone.

One afternoon in the fifth week, a young Vietnamese doctor came into the cell carrying a small black bag. Lander shrank away from him. He was seized by two guards and held while the doctor injected a powerful local anesthetic into his hand. The relief was like cool water flowing over him. In the next hour, while he could think, Lander was offered a deal.

It was explained to him that the Democratic Republic of Vietnam's medical facilities were terribly inadequate to treat even their own wounded. But a surgeon would be provided to repair his hand and drugs would be administered to ease the pain—if he signed a confession of his war crimes. It was clear to Lander that if the mangled meat at the end of his arm were not repaired, he would lose the hand and possibly the entire arm. He would never fly again. He did not believe that a confession signed under these circumstances would be regarded seriously at home. Even if it was, he preferred the hand to anyone's good opinion. The anesthetic was wearing off. Pain was beginning to shoot up his arm again. He agreed.

He was not prepared for what came next. When he saw the lectern, the room full of prisoners sitting like a class, when he was told that he must read his confession to them, he froze.

He was hustled into an anteroom. A powerful hand smelling of fish was clamped over his mouth while a guard twanged his metacarpals. He was about to faint. He nodded frantically, straining against the hand over his face. He was given another shot while the hand was tied out of sight beneath his jacket.

He read, blinking in the lights, while the movie camera whirred.

Sitting in the front row was a man with the leathery, scarred head of a plucked hawk. He was Colonel Ralph DeJong, senior American officer at the Plantation prison camp. In his four years of imprisonment, Colonel DeJong had done 258 days of solitary confinement. As Lander completed his confession, Colonel DeJong spoke suddenly, his voice carrying through the room. "It's a lie."

Two guards were on DeJong instantly. They dragged him from the room. Lander had to read the conclusion a second time. DeJong served 100 days in solitary confinement on reduced rations.

The North Vietnamese fixed Lander's hand at a hospital on the outskirts of Hanoi, a stark building white-

washed inside, with cane screens over the openings
where the windows had been blown out. They did not
do a pretty job. The red-eyed surgeon who worked on
Lander did not have the training for cosmetic surgery
on the red spider clamped to his table, and he had few
drugs. But he had stainless-steel wire and ligatures and
patience and, eventually, the hand functioned again.
The doctor spoke English and exercised his English on
Lander in maddeningly tedious conversations while he
worked.

Lander, desperate for some distraction, looking anywhere but at his hand while the work went on, saw an
old French-made resuscitator, obviously unused, in the
corner of the operating room. It was driven by a DC
motor with an eccentric flywheel pumping the bellows.
Gasping, he asked about it.

The motor was burned out, the doctor said. No one
knew how to fix it.

Driving his attention into any corner where it might
escape the pain, Lander talked about armatures and
how they are rewound. Beads of sweat stood out on his
face.

"Could you repair it?" The doctor's brow was fur-
rowed. He was tying a tiny knot. The knot was no bigger than the head of a fire ant, no bigger than a tooth
pulp, bigger than the blazing sun.

"Yes." Lander talked about copper wire and reels,
and some of the words were cut off in the middle.

"There," the doctor said. "That finishes you for
now."

The majority of American POW's behaved in a manner admirable in the eyes of the American military.

They endured for years to return to their country with a crisp salute slanting above their sunken eyes. They were determined men with strong, resilient egos. They were men for whom beliefs were possible.

Colonel DeJong was one of these. When he emerged from solitary confinement to resume command of the POW's he weighed 140 pounds. Deep in his skull his eyes glowed redly, as a martyr's eyes reflect the fire. He had not passed judgment on Lander until he saw him in a cell with a spool of copper wire, rewinding the armature on a North Vietnamese motor, a few fishbones beside him on a plate.

Colonel DeJong passed the word and Lander received the Silence in the compound. He became an outcast.

Lander had never been able to bring his usual level of craftsmanship to bear on the jerry-built system of defenses that allowed him to survive. His disgrace before the other prisoners, the isolation that came later, were all the old, bad times come back again. Only Jergens would talk to him and Jergens was often in solitary. He was taken away whenever he could not stop yelling.

Weakened by his wound, raddled with malaria, Lander was stripped down to his two ill-matched parts— the child, hated and hating, and the man he had created in the image of what he wanted to be. The old dialogues in his head resumed, but the voice of the man, the voice of sanity remained the stronger. He endured in this state for six years. It took more than prison for Lander to let go and allow the child to teach the man to kill.

On the last Christmas of his captivity, he was given one letter from Margaret. She had a job, it said. The children were all right. A picture was enclosed, Margaret and the children in front of the house. The children were longer. Margaret had gained a little weight. The shadow of the person who took the picture lay in the foreground. The shadow was wide. It fell on their legs. Lander wondered who had taken the picture. He looked at the shadow more than he looked at his wife and children.

On February 15, 1973, Lander was led aboard an Air Force C-141 at Hanoi. An orderly fastened his seat belt. He did not look out the window.

Colonel DeJong was also on the plane, though he was hard to recognize. His nose had been broken and his teeth kicked out in the past two years as he set an example of noncooperation for his men. Now he set an example by ignoring Lander. If Lander noticed, he did not show it. He was gaunt and sallow and subject any second to a malarial chill. The Air Force doctor aboard the plane kept a close eye on him. A refreshment cart went up and down the aisle constantly.

A number of officers had been sent along on the plane to talk with the POW's, if they wanted to talk. One of these men sat by Lander. Lander did not want to talk. The officer called his attention to the goodie wagon. Lander took a sandwich and bit into it. He chewed several times, then spit the bite into his barf bag. He put the sandwich in his pocket. Then he put another sandwich in his pocket.

The officer beside him started to reassure him that

there would be plenty of sandwiches, then decided against it. He patted Lander's arm. No response.

Clark Air Force Base, the Philippines. A band was there, and the base commander, ready to greet the men. Television cameras were waiting. Colonel DeJong was to be first off the plane. He walked down the aisle toward the door, saw Lander, and stopped. For a second there was hate in DeJong's face. Lander looked up at him and quickly turned away. He was trembling. DeJong opened his mouth, then his expression softened by a millimeter and he walked on, into the cheers, into the sun.

Lander was taken to St. Alban's Naval Hospital in Queens. There he began a journal, a project he would not continue long. He wrote very slowly and carefully. He was afraid that if he went any faster, the pen might get away from him and write something he did not wish to see.

Here are the first four entries:

St. Alban's, March 2.
     I am free. Margaret came to see me every day for the first eight days. She has come three times this week. The other days she had car pool. Margaret looks well, but not like I thought about her back there. She looks like she is satisfied all the time. She brought the girls twice. They were here today. They just sat and looked at me and looked around the room. I kept my hand under the sheet. There is not much for them to do in the hospital. They can go down to the rec room and get a coke. I must remember to get some change. Margaret had to give them

the change. I suppose I look strange to them. Margaret is very good and patient and they obey her. I dreamed about the Weasel again last night and I was absent-minded talking to them today. Margaret keeps up the conversation.

St. Alban's, March 12.

The doctors say I have falciparum malaria and that is why the chill cycle is irregular. They are giving me chloroquine, but it doesn't work immediately. A chill caught me today while Margaret was here. She has her hair cut short now. It does not look like her too much, but it smells good. She held me during the chill. She was warm, but she turned her face away. I hope I don't smell bad. Maybe it's my gums. I'm afraid Margaret will hear something. I hope she never saw the film.

Good news. The medics rate my hand only ten per cent impaired. It should not affect my flying status. Margaret and the kids will have to see it sooner or later.

St. Alban's, March 20.

Jergens is down the hall. He hopes to go back to teaching, but he is in bad shape. We were cellmates exactly two years, I think. He says it was 745 days. He is dreaming too. Sometimes the Weasel. He has to have the door of his room open. It was all the solitary toward the last that brought him down. They would not believe that he wasn't yelling deliberately in the cell at night. The Weasel yelled at him and called General Smegma. Smegma's real name was Capt. Lebron Nhu, I must remember that. Half French, half Vietnamese. They shoved Jergens back against the wall and slapped him and this is what Jergens said:

"Various species of plants and animals carry lethal factors which, when homozygous, stop development at some stage and the individual dies. A conspicuous case is that of the yellow race of the house mouse, *mus musculus,* which never breeds true. This should be of interest to you, Smegma. (That was where they started trying to drag him out of the cell.) If a yellow mouse is mated to some nonyellow, half the young are yellow and half are nonyellow (Jergens was holding onto the bars then and Weasel went outside to kick his fingers), a ratio to be expected from mating a heterozygous animal, yellow, with a homozygous recessive, any non-yellow such as agouti, a small voracious rodent, slender legged, resembling a rabbit but with smaller ears. If two yellows are mated together, the young average two yellow and one non-yellow, whereas the expected ratio among the young would be one pure yellow to two heterozygous yellow to one nonyellow. (His hands were bleeding and they were dragging him down the hall and him still yelling.) *But,* the 'homozygous yellow' dies as an embryo. That's you, Smegma. The 'creeper fowl' with short, crooked legs behaves genetically like the yellow mouse."

Jergens had six months solitary for that and lost his teeth on the diet. He had that about the yellow mouse scratched on the slats in his bunk and I used to read it after he was gone.

I am not going to think about that any more. Yes I am. I can say it to myself during the other things. I must raise this mattress and see if anyone in the hospital has scratched on the slats.

St. Alban's, April 1, 1973.

In four days I can go home. I told Margaret. She will trade days in the car pool to come get me. I have to be careful with my temper, now that I am stronger. I blew up today when Margaret told me she had arranged to trade cars. She told me she ordered the station wagon in December, so it's already done. She should have waited. I could have gotten a better deal. She said the dealer was giving her a very special deal. She looked smug.

If I had a protractor, a level, navigation tables and a string I could figure out the date without a calendar. I get one hour of direct sunlight through my window. The strips of wood between the windowpanes make a cross on the wall. I know the time and I know the latitude and longitude of the hospital. That and the angle of the sun would give me the date. I could measure it on the wall.

Lander's return was difficult for Margaret. She had begun to build a different life with different people in his absence, and she interrupted that life to take him home. It is probable that she would have left him had he come home from his last tour in 1968, but she would not file for a divorce while he was imprisoned.

She tried to be fair, and she could not bear the thought of leaving him while he was sick.

The first month was awful. Lander was very nervous, and his pills did not always help him. He could not stand to have the doors locked, even at night, and he prowled the house after midnight, making sure they were open. He went to the refrigerator twenty times a day to reassure himself that it was full of food. The children were polite to him, but their conversation was about people he did not know.

He gained strength steadily and talked of returning to active duty. The records at St. Alban's Hospital showed a weight gain of 18 pounds in the first two months.

The records of the Judge Advocate General of the Department of the Navy show that Lander was summoned to a closed hearing on May 24 to answer charges of collaboration with the enemy lodged by Colonel Ralph DeJong.

The transcript of the hearing records that Exhibit Seven, a piece of North Vietnamese propaganda film, was shown at the hearing, and that, immediately afterward, the hearing was recessed for fifteen minutes while the defendant excused himself. Subsequently, testimony by the defendant and by Colonel DeJong was heard.

The transcript on two occasions records that the accused addressed the hearing board as "Mam." Much later, these quotations were considered by the blue-ribbon commission to be typographical errors in the transcript.

In view of the accused's exemplary record prior to

capture and his decoration for going after the downed air crew, the action that led to his capture, the officers at the hearing were inclined to be lenient.

A memorandum signed by Colonel DeJong is affixed to the transcript. It states that, in view of the Defense Department's expressed wish to avoid adverse publicity regarding POW misconduct, he is willing to drop the charges "for the larger good of the service" if Lander offers his resignation.

The alternative to resignation was court-martial. Lander did not think he could sit through the film again.

A copy of his resignation from the United States Navy is attached to the transcript.

Lander was numb when he left the hearing room. He felt as if one of his limbs had been struck off. He would have to tell Margaret soon. Although she had never mentioned the film, she would know the reason for his resignation. He walked aimlessly through Washington, a solitary figure on a bright spring day, neat in the uniform he could never wear again. The film kept running in his head. Every detail was there, except that, somehow, his POW uniform was replaced with short pants. He sat down on a bench near the Ellipse. It was not so far to the bridge into Arlington, not so far to the river. He wondered if the undertaker would cross his hands on his chest. He wondered if he could write a note requesting that the good hand be placed on top. He wondered if the note would dissolve in his pocket. He was staring at the Washington Monument without really seeing it. He saw it with the tunnel vision of a suicide, the monument standing up in the bright circle like a post reticule in a telescopic sight. Something moved into his field of vision, crossing the bright circle, above and behind the pointed reticule.

It was the silver airship of his childhood, the Aldrich blimp. Behind the still point of the monument he could see it porpoising gently in a headwind and he gripped the end of his bench as though it were the elevator wheel. The ship was turning, turning faster now as it caught the wind on the starboard side, making a little leeway as it droned over him. Hope drifted down upon Lander through the clear spring air.

The Aldrich Company was glad to have Michael Lander. If the company officials were aware that for 98 seconds his face had appeared on network television denouncing his country, they never mentioned it. They found that he could fly superbly and that was enough.

He trembled half the night before his flight test. Margaret had great misgivings as she drove him to the airfield, only five miles away from their house. She needn't have worried. He changed even as he walked toward the airship. All the old feeling flooded him and invigorated him and left his mind calm and his hands steady.

Flying appeared to be marvelous therapy for him, and for part of him it was. But Lander's mind was jointed like a flail, and as he regained his confidence the half of his mind held steady by that confidence gave strength to the blows from the other half. His humiliation in Hanoi and Washington loomed ever greater in his mind during the fall and winter of 1973. The contrast between his self-image and the way he had been treated grew larger and more obscene.

His confidence did not sustain him through the hours of darkness. He sweated, he dreamed, he remained impotent. It was at night that the child in him, the hater, fed by his suffering, whispered to the man.

"*What else has it cost you? What else? Margaret tosses in her sleep, doesn't she? Do you think she gave away a little while you were gone?*"

"No."

"*Fool. Ask her.*"

"*I don't have to ask her.*"

"*You stupid limpdick.*"

"*Shut up.*"

"*While you were squalling in a cell, she was straddling one.*"

"No. No. No. No. No. No."

"*Ask her.*"

He asked her one cold evening near the end of October. Her eyes filled with tears and she left the room. Guilty or not?

He became obsessed with the thought that she had been unfaithful to him. He asked her druggist if her prescription for birth control pills had been renewed regularly over the past two years and was told that it was none of his business. Lying beside her after yet another of his failures, he was tormented by graphic scenes of her performing acts with other men. Sometimes the men were Buddy Ives and Junior Atkins, one on Margaret, the other awaiting his turn.

He learned to avoid her when he was angry and suspicious, and he spent some of his evenings brooding in his garage workshop. Others he passed trying to make light conversation with her, feigning an interest in the details of her daily routine, in the doings of the children at school.

Margaret was deceived by his physical recovery, and his success at his job. She thought he was practically well. She assured him that his impotence would pass. She said the Navy counselor had talked to her about it before he came home. She used the word impotence.

The blimp's first spring tour in 1974 was confined to the Northeast, so Lander could stay at home. The second was to be a run down the East Coast to Florida. He would be away three weeks. Some of Margaret's friends had a party the night before his departure and the Landers were invited. Lander was in a good humor. He insisted that they attend.

It was a pleasant gathering of eight couples. There was food and dancing. Lander did not dance. Talking rapidly, a film of sweat on his forehead, he told a captive group of husbands about the balonet and damper systems in airships. Margaret interrupted his discourse to show him the patio. When he returned, the talk had turned to professional football. He took the floor to resume his lecture where he had left off.

Margaret danced with the host. Twice. The second time, the host held her hand for a moment after the music had stopped. Lander watched them. They were talking quietly. He knew they were talking about him. He explained all about catenary curtains while his audience stared into their drinks. Margaret was being very careful, he thought. But he could see her soaking up the attention of the men. She drew it in through her skin.

Driving home he was silent, white with rage.

Finally, in the kitchen of their house, she could stand his silence no longer.

"Why don't you just start yelling and get it over with?" she said. "Go ahead and say what you're thinking."

Her kitten came into the kitchen and rubbed itself on Lander's leg. She scooped it up, fearful that he might kick it.

"Tell me what I did, Michael. We were having a good time, weren't we?"

She was so very pretty. She stood convicted by her loveliness. Lander said nothing. He approached her quickly, looking into her face. She did not back away. He had never struck her, could never strike her. He grabbed the kitten and went to the sink. When she realized what he was doing, the kitten was already in the garbage disposal. She ran to the sink and tore at his arms as he switched it on. She could hear the kitten until the disposal's ablative action disposed of its extremities and reached its vitals. All the time, Lander was staring into her face.

Her screams woke the children. She slept in their room. She heard him when he left shortly after daylight.

He sent her flowers from Norfolk. He tried to call her from Atlanta. She did not answer the telephone. He wanted to tell her that he realized his suspicions were groundless, the product of a sick imagination. He wrote her a long letter from Jacksonville, telling her he was sorry, that he knew he had been cruel and unfair and crazy and that he would never behave that way again.

On the tenth day of the scheduled three-week tour, the copilot was bringing the blimp to the landing mast when a freak gust of wind caught it and swung it into the maintenance truck, tearing the fabric of the envelope. The airship would stand down for a day and a night while repairs were made. Lander could not face a motel room for a day and a night with no word from Margaret.

He caught a flight to Newark. At a Newark pet store he bought a fine Persian kitten. He arrived at his house at midday. The house was quiet, the children were at camp. Margaret's car was in the driveway. Her teapot was heating on a low fire. He would give her the kitten and tell her he was sorry and they could hold each other and she would forgive him. He took the kitten out of the carrier and straightened the ribbon around its neck. He climbed the stairs.

The stranger was reclining on the daybed, Margaret astride him pumping, her breasts bouncing. They did not see Lander until he screamed. It was a short fight. Lander did not have all his strength back and the stranger was big, fast and frightened. He slugged Lander hard on the temple twice and he and Margaret fled together.

Lander sat on the playroom floor, his back against the wall. His mouth was open and bleeding and his eyes were vacant. The teapot whistle shrilled for half an hour. He did not move, and when the water boiled away, the house was filled with the smell of scorched metal.

———

When pain and rage reach levels far above the mind's capacity to cope, a curious relief is possible but it requires a partial death.

Lander smiled an awful smile, a bloody rictus smile, when he felt his will die. He believed that it passed out through his mouth and nose in a thin smoke riding on a sigh. The relief came to him then. It was over. Oh, it was over. For half of him.

The remains of the man Lander would feel some pain, would jerk galvanically like frogs' legs in a skillet, would cry out for relief. But he would never again sink his teeth into the pumping heart of rage. Rage would never again cut out his heart and rub it pumping in his face.

What was left could live with rage because it was made in rage and rage was its element and it thrived there as a mammal thrives in air.

He rose and washed his face, and when he left the house, when he returned to Florida, he was steady. His mind was as cool as snake's blood. There were no more dialogues in his head. There was only one voice now. The man functioned perfectly because the child needed him, needed his quick brain and clever fingers. To find its own relief. By killing and killing and killing and killing. And dying.

He did not yet know what he would do, but as he hung over the crowded stadiums week after week, it would come to him. And when he knew what he must do, he sought the means, and before the means came Dahlia. And Dahlia heard some of these things and inferred much of the rest.

He was drunk when he told her about finding Margaret and her lover in the house and afterward he became violent. She caught him behind the ear with the heel of her hand, knocking him unconscious. In the morning, he did not remember that she had hit him.

Two months passed before Dahlia was sure of him, two months of listening, of watching him build and scheme and fly, of lying next to him at night.

When she was sure, she told Hafez Najeer these things and Najeer found it good.

Now, with the explosives at sea, moving toward the United States at a steady 12 knots in the freighter *Leticia,* the entire project was threatened by Captain Larmoso's treachery and perhaps by the treachery of Benjamin Muzi himself. Had Larmoso interfered with the crates at Muzi's orders? Perhaps Muzi had decided to keep the advance payment, sell Lander and Dahlia to the authorities, and peddle the plastic elsewhere. If so, they could not risk picking up the explosives on the New York dock. They must pick up the plastic at sea.

C H A P T E R

6

THE BOAT WAS fairly standard in appearance—a sleek
sportfisherman 38 feet long—a "canyon runner" of the
kind used by men with a lot of money and not much
time. Each weekend in the season many of them blast
eastward through the swells, carrying paunchy men in
Bermuda shorts to the sudden deeps off the New Jersey
coast where the big fish feed.

But in an age of fiberglass and aluminum boats, this
one was made of wood—double planked with Philip-
pine mahogany. It was beautifully and strongly made
and it had cost a great deal. Even the superstructure
was wood, but this was not noticeable because much of
the brightwork had been painted over. Wood is a very
poor radar reflector.

Two big turbocharged diesels were crammed into
the engine room and much of the space used for dining
and relaxing in ordinary craft had been sacrificed to
make room for extra fuel and water. For much of the
summer, the owner used it in the Caribbean, running

hashish and marijuana out of Jamaica into Miami in the dark of the moon. In the winter he came north and the boat was for hire, but not to fishermen. The fee was $2,000 a day, no questions asked, plus a staggering deposit. Lander had mortgaged his house to get the deposit.

It was in a boathouse at the end of a row of deserted piers in Toms River off Barnegat Bay, fully fueled, waiting.

At 10 A.M. on November 12 Lander and Dahlia arrived at the boathouse in a rented van. A cold, drizzling rain was falling and the winter piers were deserted. Lander opened the double doors on the landward side of the boathouse and backed the van in until it was 6 feet from the stern of the big sportfisherman. Dahlia exclaimed at the sight of the boat, but Lander was busy with his checklist and paid no attention. For the next 20 minutes they loaded equipment aboard: extra coils of line, a slender mast, two long-barreled shotguns, a shotgun with the barrel sawed off to 18 inches, a high-powered rifle, a small platform lashed onto four hollow floats, charts to supplement the already well-stocked chart bin, and several neat bundles that included a lunch.

Lander lashed every object down so tightly that even if the boat had been turned upside down and shaken, nothing would have fallen out.

He flicked a switch on the boathouse wall and the big door on the water side creaked upward, admitting the gray winter light. He climbed to the flying bridge. First the port diesel roared and then the starboard, blue smoke rising in the dim boathouse. His eyes darted from gauge to gauge as the engines warmed up.

At Lander's signal, Dahlia cast off the stern lines and joined him on the flying bridge. He eased the throttles forward, the water swelling like a muscle at the stern, the exhaust ports awash and burbling, and the boat nosed slowly out into the rain.

When they had cleared Toms River, Lander and Dahlia moved to the lower control station inside the heated cabin for the run down the bay to Barnegat Inlet and the open sea. The wind was from the north, raising a light chop. They sliced through it easily, the windshield wipers slowly swiping away fine raindrops. No other boats were out that they could see. The long sandspit that protected the bay lay low in the mist off to port and on the other side they could make out a smokestack at the head of Oyster Creek.

In less than an hour they reached Barnegat Inlet. The wind had shifted to the northeast and the ground swells were building in the inlet. Lander laughed as they met the first of the big Atlantic rollers, spray bursting from the bows. They had mounted to the exposed upper control station again to run the inlet, and cold spray stung their faces.

"The waves won't be so big out there, sport," Lander said as Dahlia wiped her face with the back of her hand.

She could see that he was enjoying himself. He loved to feel the boat under him. Buoyancy had a fascination for Lander. Fluid strength, giving, pushing with support reliable as rock. He turned the wheel slowly from side to side, slightly altering the angle at which the boat met the seas, extending his kinesthetic sense to feel the changing forces on the hull. The land was falling astern now on both sides, the Barnegat Light flashing off to starboard.

They ran out of the drizzle into watery winter sunlight as they cleared the shore and, looking back, Dahlia watched the gulls wheeling, very white against the gray clouds banked behind them. Wheeling as they had above the beach at Tyre when she was a child standing in the warm sand, her feet small and brown beneath her ragged hem. She had followed too many strange corridors in Michael Lander's mind for too long. She wondered how the presence of Muhammad Fasil would change the chemistry between them, if Fasil was still alive and waiting with the explosives out there beyond the 90-fathom curve. She would have to speak with Fasil quickly. There were things that Fasil must understand before he made a fatal mistake.

When she turned back to face the sea, Lander was watching her from the helmsman's seat, one hand on the wheel. The sea air had brought color to her cheeks and her eyes were bright. The collar of her sheepskin coat was turned up around her face and her Levis were taut around her thighs as she balanced against the motion of the boat. Lander, with two big diesels beneath his hand, doing something that he did well, threw back his head and laughed and laughed again. It was a real laugh and it surprised her. She had not heard it often.

"You are a dynamite lady, you know that?" he said, wiping his eye with his knuckle.

She looked down at the deck and then raised her

head again, smiling, looking into him. "Let's go get some plastic."

"Yeah," Lander said, bobbing his head. "All the plastic in the world."

He held a course of 110 degrees magnetic, a hair north of east with the compass variation, then altered it north 5 more degrees as the bell and whistle buoys off Barnegat showed him more precisely the effect of the wind. The seas were on the port bow, moderating now, and only a little spray blew back as the boat sliced through them. Somewhere out there beyond the horizon, the freighter was waiting, riding the winter sea.

They paused at mid-afternoon while Lander made a fix of their position with the radio direction finder. He did it early to avoid the distortion that would be present at sundown and he did it very carefully, taking three bearings and plotting them on his chart, noting times and distances in meticulous little figures.

As they roared on eastward toward the "X" on the chart, Dahlia made coffee in the galley to go with the sandwiches she had brought, then cleared away the counter. With small strips of adhesive tape, she fastened to the countertop a pair of surgical scissors, compress bandages, three small disposable syringes of morphine, and a single syringe of Ritalin. She laid a set of splints along the fiddle rail at the counter edge and fastened them in place with a strip of tape.

They reached the approximate rendezvous point, well beyond the northbound Barnegat-to-Ambrose sealane, an hour before sunset. Lander checked his position with the RDF and corrected it slightly northward.

They saw the smoke first, a smudge on the horizon

to the east. Then two dots under the smoke as the freighter's superstructure showed. Soon she was hull up, steaming slowly. The sun was low in the southwest, behind Lander as he ran toward the ship. It was as he had planned. He would come out of the sun to look her over, and any gunman on the ship with a telescopic sight would be dazzled by the light.

Throttled back, the sportsfisherman eased toward the scabby freighter, Lander studying her through his binoculars. As he watched, two signal flags shot up the outboard halyards on the port side. He could make out a white "X" on a blue field and, below it, a red diamond on a white field.

"M.F.," Lander read.

"That's it. Muhammad Fasil."

Forty minutes of sunlight remained. Lander decided to take advantage of it. With no other vessels in sight, it was better to risk the transfer in daylight than to take a chance on mischief from the freighter in the dark. While there was light, he and Dahlia could keep the rail of the freighter covered.

Dahlia broke out the Delta pennant. Closer and closer the boat crept, its exhaust burbling. Dahlia and Lander pulled on stocking masks.

"Big shotgun," Lander said.

She put it in his hand. He opened the windshield in front of him and laid the shotgun on the instrument panel, muzzle out on the foredeck. It was a Remington 12-gauge automatic with a long barrel and full choke, and it was loaded with 00 buckshot. Lander knew it would be impossible to fire a rifle accurately from the moving boat. He and Dahlia had gone over it many times. If Fasil had lost control of the ship and they were fired on, Lander would shoot back, blast the stern around, and run into the sun while Dahlia emptied the other long shotgun at the freighter. She would switch to the rifle when the range increased.

"Don't worry about trying to hit somebody with the boat pitching," he had told her. "Rattle enough lead around their ears and you'll suppress their fire." Then he remembered that she had more experience with small arms than he.

The freighter turned slowly and hove to with the seas nearly abeam. From 300 yards, Lander could see only three men on her deck and a single lookout high on the bridge. One of the men ran to the signal halyard and dipped the flags once, acknowledging the Delta Lander was flying. It would have been easier to use radio, but Fasil could not be on deck and in the radio shack at the same time.

"That's him, that's Fasil in the blue cap," Dahlia said, lowering her binoculars.

When Lander was within 100 yards, Fasil spoke to the two men beside him. They swung a lifeboat davit out over the side, then stood with their hands in sight on the rail.

Lander idled his engines and scrambled aft to rig a fender board on the starboard side, then mounted to the flying bridge carrying the short shotgun.

Fasil appeared to be in control of the ship. Lander could see a revolver in his belt. He must have ordered the deck cleared except for the mate and one crewman. The rust streaks on the freighter's side glowed orange in the lowering sun as Lander brought the boat under her lee and Dahlia threw a line to the crewman. The sailor started to make it fast to a deck cleat, but Dahlia shook her head and beckoned. Then he understood and passed the line around the cleat and threw the end back.

She and Lander had rehearsed this carefully, and she quickly rigged a doubled after bowspring—a connection that could be cast off instantly from the smaller craft. With the rudder hard over, the engines held the boat's stern against the ship.

Fasil had repacked the plastic explosive in 25-pound bags. Forty-eight of them were piled on the deck beside him. The fender board scraped against the side of the freighter as the boat rose and fell on the muted seas in the lee of the ship. A ladder was flung over the *Leticia*'s side.

Fasil called down to Lander, "The mate is coming down. He is not armed. He can help stow the bags."

Lander nodded and the man scrambled down the side. He obviously was trying not to look at Dahlia or Lander, sinister in their masks. Using the lifeboat davit as a miniature cargo crane, Fasil and the sailor lowered a cargo net containing the first six bags and the automatic weapons in a canvas-wrapped bundle. It was a tricky business in the lively boat to time exactly the moment to release the load from the hook, and once Lander and the mate went sprawling.

With twelve bags in the cockpit, the loading operation paused while the three in the boat passed the bags forward, stowing them in the cabin in the bow. It was all Lander could do to keep himself from ripping open a bag and looking at the stuff. It felt electric in his hands. Then came the next twelve bags and the next. The three working in the boat were wet with sweat despite the cold.

The hail from the lookout on the bridge was nearly carried away by the wind. Fasil spun around and cupped his hands behind his ears. The man was waving his arms and pointing. Fasil leaned over the rail and yelled down, "Something's coming, from that way— east. I'm going to look."

In less than 15 seconds he was on the bridge, snatching the binoculars from the frightened lookout. He was back on the deck in an instant, wrestling with the cargo net, yelling over the side.

"It's white with a stripe near the bow."

"Coast Guard," Lander said. "What's the range— how far away?"

"About 8 kilometers, he's coming fast."

"Swing it down, God dammit."

Fasil slapped the face of the crewman beside him and put the man's hands on the lifting tackle. The cargo net bulging with the last twelve bags of plastic swayed over the sea and dropped quickly, ropes squealing in the blocks. It dropped into the cockpit with a heavy thump and was quickly lashed down.

On the freighter deck, Muhammad Fasil turned to the sweating crewman. "Stand at the rail with your hands in sight." The man fixed his eyes on the horizon and appeared to be holding his breath as Fasil went over the side.

The mate standing in the cockpit could not take his eyes off Fasil. The Arab handed the man a roll of bills and pulled out his revolver, touching the muzzle to the man's upper lip. "You have done well. Silence and health are one. Do you understand me?"

The man wanted to nod, but was prevented by the pistol under his nose.

"Go in peace."

The man went up the ladder as rapidly as an ape. Dahlia was casting off the bowsprit.

While this was going on, Lander looked almost pensive. He had demanded from his mind a projection of possibilities based on all he knew.

The patrol boat, approaching from the other side of the ship, could not see him yet. Probably the sight of the freighter hove to had aroused the Coast Guard's curiosity, unless they had been tipped off. Patrol boat. Six in these waters, all 82 feet, twin diesels, 1,600 shaft horsepower, good for 20 knots. Sperry-Rand SPB-5 radar, crew of eight. One .50 caliber machine gun and an 81 mm mortar. In a flash Lander considered setting fire to the freighter, forcing the cutter to stop and render aid. No, the first mate would scream piracy and the hue and cry would go up. Search planes would come, some of them with infrared equipment that would pick up the heat of his engines. Darkness coming. No moon for five hours. Better a chase.

Lander snapped back to the present. His deliberations had taken five seconds.

"Dahlia, rig the reflector." He slammed the throttles open and heeled the big boat over in a foaming curve away from the freighter. He headed toward the land, forty miles away, the engines roaring at full throttle and spray flying back as they smashed through moderate seas. Even heavily laden, the powerful boat was doing close to 19 knots. The cutter had a slight edge in speed. He would keep the freighter between them as long as he could. He yelled down to Fasil in the cockpit. "Monitor 2182 kilocycles." This was the International Radio-Telephone Distress frequency and a "calling frequency" used in initial contacts between vessels.

The freighter was well astern now, but as they watched, the cutter appeared, still beyond the freighter but coming hard, throwing a big bow wave. As Lander looked back over his shoulder he saw the cutter's bow swing slightly until it pointed dead at him.

Fasil scrambled up the ladder until his head was above the level of the flying bridge. "He's ordering us to halt."

"Fuck him. Switch to the Coast Guard frequency. It's marked on the dial. We'll see if he calls for help."

With the running lights off, the boat raced toward the last glow in the west. Behind them, graceful white bow and bow wave gleaming in the last light, the Coast Guard cutter charged like a terrier.

Dahlia had finished clamping the passive radar reflector to the handrail on the bridge. It was a kiteshaped assembly of metal rods which she had bought in a marine supply store for $12, and it trembled as the boat plunged through the seas.

Lander sent her below to check the lashings. He wanted nothing to come adrift in the pounding the boat would have to take.

She checked the cockpit first and then worked forward to the cabin where Fasil frowned at the radio.

"Nothing yet," he said in Arabic. "Why the radar reflector?"

"The Coast Guard would have seen us anyway," Dahlia said. She had to yell in his ear to be heard in the plunging boat. "When the Coast Guard captain sees that the chase will continue into darkness, he will have his radar operator get a fix on us and track us while he can still follow visually—then there will be no problem identifying the blip we make on his screen after the light is gone." Lander had explained all this at tiresome length. "With that reflector, it is a big, fat blip, distinct from interference from the waves. Like the image of a metal boat."

"Is—"

"Listen to me," she said urgently, glancing upward toward the bridge above their heads. "You must not act familiar with me in any way, or touch me, do you understand? You must speak only English in his presence. Never come upstairs in his house. Never surprise him. For the sake of the mission."

Fasil's face was lit from beneath by the radio dials, his eyes glowing in their shadowed sockets. "For the mission, then, Comrade Dahlia. As long as he functions, I will humor him."

Dahlia nodded. "If you don't humor him, you may find out how well he functions," she said, but the words were lost in the wind as she climbed aft.

It was dark now. There was only the faint light of the binnacle on the bridge, visible to Lander alone. He could see the red and green running lights of the cutter clearly and its big searchlight boring into the dark. He estimated that the government vessel had about a half-knot advantage and his lead was about four-and-a-half miles. Fasil climbed up beside him. "He's radioed customs about the *Leticia*. He says he's going to take us himself."

"Tell Dahlia it's almost time."

They were pounding toward the sealanes now. Lander knew that the men in the cutter could not see him, yet the vessel matched every slight course alteration he made. He could almost feel the fingers of the radar on his back. It would be better if there were some ships . . . yes! Off the port bow were the white range lights of a ship, and as the minutes passed he raised her running lights. A freighter northbound and plowing along at a good rate. He altered course slightly to pass under her bows as closely as possible. Lander saw in his mind the patrol boat's radar screen, its green light glowing on the face of the operator watching the big image of the freighter and the smaller one of the speedboat converge, the blips glowing bright each time the sweep went around.

"Get ready," he yelled to Dahlia.

"Let's go," she said to Fasil. He did not ask questions. Together they pulled the little platform with the floats clear of the lashed-down explosives. Each float was made of a five-gallon drum and each had a pinhole in the top and an ordinary faucet in its underside. Dahlia brought the mast from the cabin and the radar reflector from the bridge. They clamped the reflector to the top of the mast and set the mast in a socket on the platform. With Fasil's help she attached a 6-foot line to the underside of the platform and secured the other end to a heavy lead weight. They looked up from their work to see the lights of the freighter hanging almost over them, its bow like a cliff. In a flash they were past it.

Lander, angling north, looked back over the stern to keep the freighter between him and the patrol boat. Now the radar blips had merged, the greater height of the freighter shielding Lander's boat from the radar impulses.

He estimated the distance back to the cutter. "Half turn on the faucets." A moment later, he cut the engines. "Overboard."

Dahlia and Fasil dropped the floating platform over the side, the mast wagging wildly until the weight hanging down beneath the platform steadied it like a keel, holding the radar reflector high above the water. The device rocked again as Lander rammed the throttles home and headed straight south in the blacked-out boat.

"The radar operator can't be sure if the image of the reflector is us or something new, or if we're running along on the other side of the freighter," Fasil said. "How long will it float?"

"Fifteen minutes with the faucets half open," Dahlia said. "It will be gone when the cutter gets there."

"Then he will follow the ship north to see if we're alongside?"

"Perhaps."

"How much can he see of us now?"

"A wooden boat at this range, not much if anything. Even the paint is not lead-based. There will be some wake interference from the ship. The engine noise from the ship will help too, if he stops to listen. We don't know yet if he's taken the bait."

From the bridge, Lander watched the lights of the patrol boat. He could see the two high white range lights and the red portside running light. If she turned toward him, he would see the green starboard light come around.

Dahlia was beside him now and together they watched the cutter's lights. They saw only red, and then as the distance increased they could make out only the white range lights, then nothing but an occasional beam of the searchlight, raised by a wave, probing the empty dark.

Lander was aware of a third presence on the bridge.

"A nice piece of work," Muhammad Fasil said. Lander did not answer him.

CHAPTER
7

MAJOR KABAKOV'S EYES were red and he was irritable. The clerks in the New York office of the Immigration and Naturalization Service had learned to walk softly around him as he sat, day after day, studying mug shots of Arab aliens living in the United States.

The ledger-sized books piled on either side of him at the long table contained, in all, 137,000 photos and descriptions. He was determined to look at every one. If the woman was on a mission in this country, she would have established a cover first, he was convinced of it. The "suspicious Arab" file maintained sub rosa by Immigration had contained few women, and none of them resembled the woman in Hafez Najeer's bedroom. Immigration and Naturalization estimated there were some 85,000 Arabs on the Eastern Seaboard who had entered the country illegally over the years and appeared in nobody's file. Most of them worked quietly at inconspicuous jobs, bothered no one and rarely came to the attention of the authorities. The possibility plagued him that the woman might be one of these.

Wearily, he turned another page. Here's a woman. Katherine Ghalib. Working with retarded children in Phoenix. Fifty years old and looks it.

A clerk was at his elbow. "Major, there's a call for you in the office."

"Very well. Don't move these damned books. I'll lose my place."

The caller was Sam Corley in Washington.

"How's it going?"

"Nothing yet. I've got about 80,000 Arabs to go."

"I got a report from the Coast Guard. It may not be anything, but one of their cutters spotted a power boat next to a Libyan freighter off the Jersey coast yesterday afternoon. The boat ran from them when they went to take a look."

"Yesterday?"

"Yeah, they had been busy with a ship fire way out and they were coming back. The freighter was out of Beirut."

"Where's the ship now?"

"Impounded in Brooklyn. Captain's missing. I don't know the details yet."

"What about the boat?"

"Gave them the slip in the dark."

Kabakov swore viciously. "Why did it take them so long to tell us?"

"Damned if I know, but there it is. I'll call Customs up there. They'll give you a rundown."

———

The *Leticia*'s first mate and acting captain, Mustapha Fawzi, talked with customs officers for an hour in his little cabin, waving his arms in air thick with the acrid smoke of his Turkish cigarettes.

Yes, the boat approached his ship, Fawzi told them. The boat was low on petrol and requested assistance. Following the law of the sea, he helped them. His description of the boat and its occupants was vague. This event took place in international waters, he stressed. No, he would not voluntarily permit a search of his vessel. The ship, under international law, was Libyan territory and was his responsibility after the most unfortunate falling overboard of Captain Larmoso.

Customs did not want an incident with the Libyan government, particularly now with the Middle East inflamed. What the Coast Guard saw would not constitute sufficient probable cause for a search warrant to be issued. Fawzi promised a deposition on Larmoso's accident, and the customs officers left the ship to confer with the departments of Justice and State.

Fawzi drank a bottle of the late Captain's beer and fell soundly asleep for the first time in days.

A voice seemed to be calling Fawzi from far away. His name was repeated in a deep voice and something was hurting his eyes. Fawzi awoke and raised his hand to shield his eyes from the blinding flashlight beam.

"Good evening, Mustapha Fawzi," Kabakov said. "Please keep your hands above the sheet."

Sergeant Moshevsky, looming huge behind Kabakov, flicked on the lights. Fawzi sat up in bed and called upon God.

"Freeze," Moshevsky said, holding a knife beneath Fawzi's ear.

Kabakov pulled up a chair and sat down at the bedside. He lit a cigarette. "I would appreciate a quiet conversation now. Will it be quiet?"

Fawzi nodded and Kabakov motioned Moshevsky away. "Now Mustapha Fawzi, I am going to explain to you how you will help me at no risk to yourself. You see, I will not hesitate to kill you if you do not cooperate, but I have no reason to kill you if you are helpful. It's very important that you understand that."

Moshevsky stirred impatiently and delivered his line. "First let me cut—"

"No, no," Kabakov said, raising his hand. "You see, Fawzi, with men less intelligent than yourself it is often necessary to establish, first, that you will suffer terrible pain and mutilation if you displease me and, second, that you will get some marvelous reward if you are useful. We both know what the reward usually is." Kabakov flicked the ash from his cigarette with the tip of his little finger. "Ordinarily, I would let my friend break your arms before we talked. But you see, Fawzi, you have nothing to lose by telling me what has happened here. Your noncooperation with customs is a matter of record. Your cooperation with me will remain our secret." He flipped his Israeli identification onto the bed. "Will you help me?"

Fawzi looked at the card and swallowed hard. He said nothing.

Kabakov rose and sighed. "Sergeant, I am going out for a breath of air. Perhaps Mustapha Fawzi would like some refreshments. Call me when he has finished eating his testicles." He turned toward the cabin door.

"I have relatives in Beirut." Fawzi was having trouble controlling his voice. Kabakov could see the heart pounding in his thin body as he sat half-naked in the bunk.

"Of course you do," Kabakov said. "And they have been threatened, I am sure. Lie to Customs all you like. But don't lie to me, Fawzi. There is no place where you will be safe from me. Not here, not at home, not in any port on earth. I have respect for your relatives. I understand these things and I'll cover for you."

"The Lebanese killed Larmoso in the Azores," Fawzi began.

Moshevsky had no taste for torture. He knew Kabakov hated it as well. It took a conscious effort for Moshevsky to keep from smiling as he searched the cabin. Each time Fawzi's recitation faltered, Moshevsky paused in his work to scowl at him, trying to look disappointed at not getting to carve him up.

"Describe the Lebanese."

"Slender, medium height. He had a cut on his face, scabbed over."

"What was in the bags?"

"I don't know. As Allah is my witness. The Lebanese packed them from the crates in the forward hold. He allowed no one near them."

"How many were in the boat?"

"Two."

"Describe them."

"One tall and thin, the other smaller. They wore masks. I was frightened, I did not look."

"What did they speak?"

"The bigger spoke English with the Lebanese."

"The smaller?"

"The smaller said nothing."

"Could the smaller have been a woman?"

The Arab flushed. He did not want to admit being frightened by a woman. It was unthinkable.

"With the Lebanese holding a gun, with your relatives threatened—it was these thoughts that made you cooperate, Fawzi," Kabakov said gently.

"The smaller could have been a woman," Fawzi said finally.

"You saw her hands on the bags?"

"She wore gloves. But there was a lump at the back of her mask that might have been her hair. And there is the thing of her bottom."

"The thing of her bottom?"

"Rounded, you know. Wider than a man's. Perhaps a shapely boy?"

Moshevsky, rummaging through the refrigerator, helped himself to a bottle of beer. Something was behind the bottle. He pulled it out and handed it to Kabakov.

"Did Captain Larmoso's religion require him to keep religious articles in his refrigerator?" Kabakov asked, holding the knife-scarred figure of the Madonna close to Fawzi's face.

Fawzi looked at it with genuine incomprehension and the distaste a Moslem feels toward religious statuary. Kabakov, deep in thought, smelled the statue and dug into it with his fingernail. Plastic. Larmoso had known what it was, but had not known much about its properties, he reasoned. The captain had thought it safest to keep the thing cold, as cold as the rest of the explosive down in the hold. He needn't have bothered, Kabakov thought. He turned the statue in his hands. If they went to this trouble to disguise the plastic, then they originally had planned to bring it through Customs.

"Get me the ship's books," Kabakov snapped.

Fawzi found the manifest with the bill of lading after a short delay. Mineral water, unrestricted hides, flatware—there it was. Three crates of religious statues. Made in Taiwan. Shipped to Benjamin Muzi.

Muzi watched from Brooklyn Heights as the *Leticia* labored into New York harbor escorted by the Coast Guard cutter. He swore in several languages. What had Larmoso done? Muzi walked to a telephone booth at top speed, approximately two-and-a-half miles per hour. He moved with the dignity of an elephant, and like an elephant he had surprising grace in his extremities and loved orderly progressions. This business was most disorderly.

His size prevented him from entering the booth, but he could reach inside and dial. He called Coast Guard Search and Rescue, identifying himself as a reporter for El Diario-La Prensa. The helpful young man at the Coast Guard communications center told him the details that could be gleaned from radio traffic concerning the *Leticia* and her missing captain and the pursuit of the speedboat.

Muzi drove along the Brooklyn-Queens Expressway overlooking the Brooklyn docks. On the pier beside the

Leticia he could see both Customs and Port Authority police. He was relieved that neither the freighter nor the cutter flew the red swallow-tailed Bravo that means dangerous cargo aboard. Either the authorities had not yet found the explosives or the speedboat had taken the plastic off the ship. If the speedboat had taken the plastic, which was very likely, then he had a little time as far as the law was concerned. It would take days for the authorities to inventory the *Leticia*'s cargo and pinpoint the missing shipment. Probably he was not yet hot with the law. But he was hot all right, and he could feel it.

Something was terribly wrong. It did not matter whose fault it was, he would be blamed. He had a quarter of a million dollars of Arab money in a bank in the Netherlands and his employers would accept no excuse. If they took the plastic at sea, then they believed he was ready to betray them, had betrayed them. What had that fool Larmoso done? Whatever it was, Muzi knew he would never get a chance to explain that he was innocent. Black September would kill him at the first opportunity. Clearly he would have to take early retirement.

From his safe deposit box in a lower Manhattan bank, Muzi took a thick wad of banknotes and a number of bankbooks. One of the bankbooks bore the name of the Netherlands' oldest and most prestigious financial house. It showed a balance of $250,000, all deposited at once and available only to him.

Muzi sighed. It would have been so nice to collect the second $250,000 when the plastic was delivered. Now the guerrillas would stake out the bank in Holland for a while, he was sure. Let them. He would transfer the account and pick up the money elsewhere.

The items that worried him most were not in the lockbox. His passports. For years he had kept them in the lockbox, but after his last trip to the Middle East, inexcusably he had left them in his home. He would have to get them. Then he would fly from Newark to Chicago to Seattle and over the Pole to London. Where was it that Farouk had dined in London? Muzi, who greatly admired Farouk's taste and style, determined to find out.

Muzi had no intention of returning to his office. Let them interrogate the Greek. His ignorance would astound them. The odds were very good that the guerrillas were watching his home as well. But they would not watch long. With the explosives in hand, they would have other things to do. It would be stupid to rush home immediately. Let them think that he had already fled.

He checked into a motel on the West Side, signing the register "Chesterfield Pardue." He iced down 12 bottles of Perrier in the bathroom sink. For a moment he felt a nervous chill. He had a sudden urge to sit in the dry bathtub with the shower curtain closed, but he feared that his wide behind would get stuck in the tub as it had in Atlantic City once.

The chill passed and he lay on the bed, hands folded on his great mound of a stomach, frowning at the ceiling. Fool that he was to get mixed up with those scabby guerrillas. Skinny, oafish fellows, all of them, enjoying nothing but politics. Beirut had been bad news for him before, in the failure of the Intra Bank in

1967. The bank failure had put a dent in his retirement fund. If it had not occurred he would have retired already.

He had been close to recouping when the Arab offer came along. The whopping fee for bringing in the plastic would put him over the top. For that reason, he had decided to take the risk. Well, half the guerrilla money would still do it.

Retirement. To his exquisite little villa near Naples with no difficult steps to climb. It had been a long time coming.

He had started as a cabin boy on the freighter *Ali Bey*. At 16, his bulk already made climbing the companionways a chore. When the *Ali Bey* came to New York in 1938, Muzi took one look at the city and immediately jumped ship. Fluent in four languages and quick with figures, he soon found employment on the Brooklyn waterfront as a warehouse checker for a Turk named Jahal Bezir, a man of almost Satanic cunning who cleaned up in the black market during World War II.

Bezir was greatly impressed with Muzi, for he could never catch him stealing. By 1947 Muzi was keeping books for Bezir, and as time passed the old man relied on him more and more.

The old Turk's mind remained clear and active, but increasingly he lapsed into the Turkish of his childhood, dictating his correspondence in that language and leaving the translation to Muzi. Bezir made a great show of reading the translations, but if there were several letters, he sometimes was unaware of which one was in his hand. This puzzled Muzi. The old man's eye-

sight was good. He was far from senile. He was fluent
in English. With a few judicious tests, Muzi confirmed
that Bezir could no longer read. A visit to the public library told Muzi a great deal about aphasia. The old
man had it all right. Muzi thought about this development for a long time. Then he began to make modest
currency speculations on the foreign exchanges, taking
advantage of the Turk's credit without his knowledge
or consent.

The postwar currency fluctuations were good for
Muzi. Almost the only exception was one awful three-
day period, when a cartel of speculators red-dogged
Muscat military scrip with Muzi holding 10,000 certifi-
cates at 27 to the pound sterling and the Turk snoring
peacefully upstairs. That cost him $3,000 U.S. out of
his own pocket, but by then he could afford it.

Meanwhile he had delighted Bezir by devising a hollow docking hawser for the importation of hashish.
When the Turk died, distant relatives appeared to seize
his business and ruin it. Muzi was left with $65,000 he
had made in currency speculation and some excellent
smuggling connections. That was all he needed to become a dealer in anything and everything that would
turn a dollar, with the exception of hard narcotics. The
astronomical profit potential of heroin tempted him,
but Muzi saw past the fast buck. He did not want to be
branded for the rest of his life. He did not want to have
to sleep in a safe at night. He did not want the risks,
and he did not like the people who dealt in heroin.
Hashish was another matter entirely.

By 1972, the Jihaz al-Rasd section of Al Fatah was
heavily engaged in the hashish trade. Many of the half-

kilo sacks Muzi bought in Lebanon were decorated with their trademark—a feda'i holding a submachine gun. It was through his hashish connections that Muzi had delivered the letter for the American, and it was through them that he had been approached about smuggling in the plastic.

In recent months, Muzi had been extricating himself from the hash trade and systematically closing out his other interests in the Middle East. He wanted to do it gradually and leave no one on the hook. He wanted to make no enemies who might interfere with a peaceful retirement and an endless succession of dinners *al fresco* on his terrace overlooking the Bay of Naples. Now this business of the *Leticia* threatened everything. Perhaps the guerrillas were unsure of him because he was pulling out of the Middle East. Larmoso, too, must have gotten wind of his liquidations and been uneasy, ready for a chance to go into business for himself. Whatever Larmoso had done, he had spooked the Arabs badly.

Muzi knew he could manage all right in Italy. He had to take one sizable chance here in New York, and then he was home free. Lying on his motel bed, waiting to make his move, his stomach rumbling, Muzi pretended he was dining at Lutèce.

Kabakov sat on a coil of garden hose, shivering. A cold draft whistled through the tool shed atop the warehouse and there was frost on the walls, but the shed offered concealment and a good view of Muzi's house across the street. The sleepy man watching out the side window of the shack unwrapped a chocolate bar and began to gnaw it, the cold chocolate breaking off with little popping sounds. He and the other two members of the tactical incursion team had driven up from Washington in a rented van after they received Kabakov's call.

The hard five-hour drive on the turnpike had been necessary because the team's luggage would have aroused a great deal of interest under an airport fluoroscope—submachine guns, snipers' rifles, grenades. Another member of the team was on a roof down the block on the opposite side of the street. The third was with Moshevsky at Muzi's office.

The sleepy Israeli offered Kabakov some of the chocolate. Kabakov shook his head and continued to watch the house through his binoculars, peering through the crack in the partially opened shed door. Kabakov wondered if he had been right in not telling Corley and the other American authorities about Muzi and the Madonna. He snorted through his nose. Of course he was right. At best, the Americans might have let him talk to Muzi in some precinct anteroom with a lawyer present. This way he would speak to Muzi under more favorable circumstances—if the Arabs hadn't killed him already.

Muzi lived on a pleasant, tree-lined street in the Cobble Hill section of Brooklyn. His building, a brownstone, contained four apartments. His was the largest apartment on the ground floor. The only entrance was in the front and Kabakov felt sure that he would use it, if he came. Muzi was far too fat to go in a window, judging from the enormous clothes in his closet.

Kabakov hoped to complete his business very quickly, if Muzi gave him a good lead on the explosives. He would tell Corley when it was over. He looked at his watch through red-rimmed eyes: 7:30 A.M. If Muzi did not come during the day, he would have to set up alternating watches so that his men could sleep. Kabakov told himself again and again that Muzi would come. The importer's passports—three of them in various names—were in Kabakov's breast pocket. He had found them in a quick search of Muzi's bedroom. He would have preferred to wait in the apartment, but he knew that Muzi's time of greatest danger would be on the street and he wanted to be in a position to cover him.

Once again he scanned the windows across the street. In one apartment building to the left a window shade went up. Kabakov tensed. A woman stood at the window in her slip. As she turned away, he could see a child behind her, sitting at a kitchen table.

A few early commuters were on the sidewalk now, still pale with sleep and hurrying to the bus stop on Pacific Street, a block away. Kabakov flicked open the passports and studied Muzi's fat face for the fiftieth time. His legs were cramping and he rose to stretch them. The walkie-talkie beside him crackled.

"Jerry Dimples, front door your position a man with keys."

"Roger Dimples," Kabakov said into the microphone. With any luck it was the relief for the watchman who had snored the night away on the ground floor of the warehouse. A moment later the radio spat again, and the Israeli on the rooftop down the street confirmed that the night watchman was leaving the building. The watchman crossed the street into Kabakov's field of vision and walked to the bus stop.

Kabakov turned back to watch the windows, and when he looked at the bus stop again, the big green city bus was there, discharging a clutch of cleaning ladies. They began to waddle along the block, sturdy, middle-aged women with shopping bags. Many of them had Slavic features similar to Kabakov's own. They looked much like the neighbors he had had as a small child. He followed them with his field glasses. The group grew smaller as the women, one by one, dropped out at the buildings where they worked. They were passing Muzi's house now, and a fat one from the center of the group turned up the walk toward the entrance, umbrella under one arm and a shopping bag in each hand. Kabakov focused his glasses on her. Something peculiar—the shoes. They were large Cordovans and one of the bulging calves above them bore a fresh razor cut.

"Dimples Jerry," Kabakov said into his walkie-talkie. "I think the fat woman is Muzi. I'm going in. Cover the street."

Kabakov put his rifle aside and picked up a sledge-hammer from the corner of the shed. "Cover the street," he repeated to the man beside him. Then he was pounding down the stairwell, not caring if the day watchman heard him. A quick look outside, a dash across the street, carrying the hammer at port arms.

The building entrance was unlocked. He stood outside Muzi's door, straining to hear. Then he swung the hammer sideways with all his strength, dead center on the lock.

The door smashed open, carrying part of the door facing with it, and Kabakov was inside before the splinters hit the floor, leveling a large pistol at the fat man in the dress.

Muzi stood in the doorway to his bedroom, his hands full of papers. His jowls quivered, and he had a sick, dull look in his eyes as he watched Kabakov. "I swear I didn't—"

"Turn around, hands on the wall." Kabakov searched Muzi carefully, removing a small automatic pistol from his purse. Then he closed the scarred door and leaned a chair against it.

Muzi had composed himself with the speed of thought. "Do you mind if I remove this wig? It itches, you know."

"No. Sit down." Kabakov spoke into the radio. "Dimples Jerry. Get Moshevsky. Tell him to bring the truck." He took the passports from his pocket. "Muzi, do you want to live?"

"A rhetorical question, no doubt. May I ask who you are? You have neither displayed a warrant nor killed me. Those are the only two credentials I would recognize immediately."

Kabakov passed Muzi his identification. The fat man's expression did not change, but inside his head the wet implements of scheming were pumping hard, for he saw a chance that he might live. Muzi folded his hands across his apron and waited.

"They've already paid you, haven't they?"

Muzi hesitated. Kabakov's pistol bucked, silencer hissing, and a bullet slammed through the chair back beside Muzi's neck.

"Muzi, if you do not help me, you are a dead man. They will not let you live. If you stay here, you will go to prison. It should be obvious to you that I am your only hope. I will make this proposal once. Tell me everything and I will put you on an airplane at Kennedy Airport. I and my men are the only ones who can get you on a plane alive."

"I recognize your name, Major Kabakov. I know what you do and I think it rather unlikely that you would leave me alive."

"Do you keep your word in business?"

"Frequently."

"So do I. You have their money already, or a lot of it, I expect. Tell me and go spend it."

"In Iceland?"

"That's your problem."

"All right," Muzi said heavily. "I'll tell you. But I want to fly out tonight."

"If the information checks out, agreed."

"I don't know where the plastic is, that's the truth. I was approached twice, once here and once from Beirut." Muzi mopped his face with his apron, relief spreading through his body like brandy. "Do you mind if I get a Perrier? This talking is thirsty work."

"You know the house is surrounded."

"Believe me, Major, I do not want to run."

Only a serving counter separated the kitchen area from the living room. Kabakov could watch him all the time. He nodded.

"First there was the American," Muzi said at the refrigerator.

"The *American*?"

Muzi opened the refrigerator door and he saw the device for an instant before the explosion blew him piecemeal through the kitchen wall. The room heaved, Kabakov turning in the air, blood flying from his nose, falling, shattered furniture rattling around him. Blackness. A ringing silence and then the crackle of flames.

The first alarm went in at 8:05. The fire dispatcher called it "a four-brick, 75 by 125, fully involved, Engine 224, Ladder 118 and Emergency Service responding."

Police teleprinters rattled in the stationhouses, printing this message:

SLIP 12 0820 HRS 76 PRECINCT REPORTS SUSPICIOUS EXPLOSION AND FIRE 382 VINCENT ST. TWO DOAS TO KINGS COUNTY HOSP OPR 24 ZZZZZZZZZZZZZZZZZZZZZZZZZZ

The paper feed clanked twice, the carriage returned, then this message:

SLIP 13 0820 HRS CQN SLIP 12 ONE DOA ONE INJURED AUTH LONG ISLAND COLLEGE HOSP OPR 24 ZZZZZZZZZZZZZZZZZZZZZZZZZZZZ

Reporters from the *Daily News*, *The New York Times*, and AP were waiting in the corridor of Long Island College Hospital when the fire marshal came out of the room red-faced and angry. Beside him were Sam Corley and a deputy chief. The fire marshal cleared his throat.

"I think it was a gas explosion in the kitchen," the fire marshal said, looking away from the cameras. "We're checking it out."

"ID's?"

"Only on the dead guy." He consulted the slip of paper in his hand. "Benjamin Muzi, or maybe you say it 'Muzzy.' Community relations will give it to you." He brushed past the reporters and stalked out. The back of his neck was very red.

CHAPTER
8

THE BOMB THAT killed Benjamin Muzi on Thursday morning had been placed in the refrigerator 28 hours before by Muhammad Fasil, and it had almost cost Fasil his hand before a detonator was ever stuck into the plastic. For Fasil had made an error, not with the explosive, but with Lander.

It had been nearly midnight Tuesday when Lander, Fasil, and Dahlia secured the boat and it was almost 2 A.M. when they arrived at Lander's house with the plastic.

Dahlia could still feel the boat moving under her as she walked into the house. She fixed a quick hot meal and Fasil wolfed it down at the kitchen table, his face gray with fatigue. She had to take Lander's food into the garage. He would not leave the plastic. He had opened a bag and lined up six Madonnas on his work-bench. Like a raccoon with a clam, he turned one in his hand and sniffed and tasted it. It must be Hexogen of Chinese or Russian manufacture mixed with TNT or kamnikite and some kind of synthetic rubber binder, he decided. The bluish-white substance had a faint smell that touched the back of the nasal passages, like the smell of a garden hose left in the sun, the smell of a body bag. Lander knew he must pace himself to get everything done in the remaining six weeks before the Super Bowl. He put down the statuette and forced himself to sip his soup until his hands were steady. He hardly glanced at Dahlia and Fasil as they came into the garage, Fasil popping an amphetamine tablet into his mouth. The guerrilla started for the workbench and the row of Madonnas, but Dahlia stopped him with a touch on the arm.

"Michael, I need a half-kilo of plastic, please," she said. "For what we were discussing." She spoke as a woman speaks to her lover, leaving things half-said in the presence of a third person.

"Why don't you shoot Muzi?"

Fasil had been under a strain for a week guarding that plastic on the ship, and his bloodshot eyes narrowed at Lander's indifferent tone. " 'Why don't you shoot Muzi?'" he mimicked. "You don't have to do anything, just give me the plastic." The Arab moved to the workbench. Lander's arm blurred with speed as he brought the electric saw off the bottom shelf and pulled the trigger, the shrieking blade a half-inch from Fasil's reaching hand.

Fasil stood very still. "I'm sorry, Mr. Lander. I meant no disrespect." Carefully, carefully. "We may not get a shot. I want to cover every eventuality. Your project must not be interrupted."

"All right," Lander said. He spoke so quietly Dahlia

could not hear him over the sound of the saw. He released the trigger and the blade whirred to a stop, each black tooth distinct. Lander cut a Madonna in two with a knife. "You have a detonator and wire?"

"Yes, thank you."

"Will you need a battery? I have several."

"No, thank you."

Lander turned back to his work and did not look up as Dahlia and Fasil drove away in his car, heading north toward Brooklyn to arrange the death of Muzi.

WCBS "Newsradio 88" broadcast the first bulletin on the explosion at 8:30 A.M. Thursday and confirmed Muzi's identity by 9:45. Now the deed was done. The last possible connection between him and the plastic was cut. Thursday was beginning auspiciously. Lander heard Dahlia come into the workshop. She brought him a cup of coffee. "Good news," he said.

She listened carefully as the newscast recycled. She was eating a peach. "I wish they would identify the injured one. There's a fair chance it's the Greek."

"I'm not worried about the Greek," Lander said. "He only saw me once and he didn't hear what we said. Muzi showed no respect for him. I doubt if he trusted him at all."

Lander paused in his work to watch her as she leaned against the wall eating the peach. Dahlia relished fruit. He liked to see her absorbed in a simple pleasure. Displaying appetite. It made him feel that she was uncomplicated, unthreatening, that he moved around her unseen. He was the benign bear watching the camper unload the goodies in the firelight. When she first came to him, he had often turned suddenly to

look at her, expecting to see malice or cunning or distaste. But she was always the same—insolence in her
posture and welcome in her face.

Dahlia was aware of all this. She appeared to be
watching with interest as he turned back to the wiring
harness he was making. Actually she was worrying.

Fasil had slept most of yesterday and most of this
morning. But soon he would awaken. He would be
elated at the success of his device, and he must be restrained from showing it. Dahlia was sorry that Fasil
had completed his training before 1969, when the Chinese instructors came to Lebanon. They could have
taught him much about self-effacement, something he
never learned in training in North Vietnam and certainly not in East Germany. She watched Lander's long
fingers deftly moving the soldering iron. Fasil had made
a near-fatal mistake with Lander, and she must make
sure it did not happen again. She must make Fasil understand that if he were not very careful, the project
might come to a bloody end here in Lander's house.
The project needed Fasil's quick, savage mind, and his
muscle and firepower would be essential at the penulti-
mate moment, when the explosive was being attached
to the blimp. But she had to keep him in line.

Fasil nominally was her superior in the terrorist organization, but this mission had been acknowledged as
hers by no less than Hafez Najeer himself. Further, she
was the key to Lander and Lander was irreplaceable.
On the other hand, Hafez Najeer was dead and Fasil
no longer feared his wrath. And Fasil was not very pro-
gressive in his view of women. It would be so much

easier if they all spoke French. That simple difference would have been invaluable, she thought.

Like many educated Arabs, Fasil practiced two sets of social behavior. In Western-style social situations, speaking French, his treatment of women was as gracious and egalitarian as anyone could wish. Back among traditional Arabs, his ingrained sexual chauvinism reasserted itself strongly. A woman was a vessel, a servant, a draft animal with no control over her sexual urges, a sow perpetually in heat.

Fasil might be cosmopolitan in his manners and radical in his politics, but Dahlia could tell that in the send and ebb of his emotions he was not greatly removed from the time of his grandfather, the time of female circumcision, clitoridectomy and infibulation, the bloody rites which ensured that female children would not bring dishonor on their houses. She always detected a faint sneer in his voice when he called her comrade.

"Dahlia." Lander's voice shifted her attention back to him. The change did not register in her face at all. It was a trick she had. "Hand me the needle-nosed pliers." His voice was calm, his hands steady. Good omens for what might be a difficult day. She was determined there would be no wasteful squabbling. Dahlia had confidence in Fasil's basic intelligence and dedication, if not in his attitude. She had confidence in the strength of her own will. She believed in the genuine understanding and affection she shared with Lander, and she believed in the 50 milligrams of chlorpromazine she had dissolved in his coffee.

CHAPTER

9

KABAKOV STRUGGLED BACK to consciousness like a desperate diver thrashing upward to the air. He felt the fire in his chest and tried to raise his hands to his burning throat, but his wrists were held with a grip like padded iron. He realized that he was in a hospital. He felt the rough-dried hospital sheet under him and felt the loom of someone standing beside the bed. He did not want to open his smarting eyes. His body was seized by his will. *He would relax. He would not struggle and bleed.* It was not the first time he had regained consciousness in a hospital.

Moshevsky, towering over the bed, relaxed his grip on Kabakov's wrists and turned to an orderly at the door of the room. He used his softest growl. "He's coming around. Tell the doctor to get in here. Move!"

Kabakov opened and shut one hand, then the other. He moved his right leg, then his left. Moshevsky nearly smiled with relief. He knew what Kabakov was doing.

He was taking inventory. Moshevsky had done it himself on several occasions.

Minutes passed as Kabakov drifted back and forth between the darkness and the hospital room. Moshevsky, swearing softly, had started for the door when the doctor came in with a nurse following him. The doctor was a slight young man with sideburns.

He glanced at the chart while the nurse opened the oxygen tent and peeled back the top sheet, suspended tentlike on a metal frame to keep it from touching the patient. The doctor shined a penlight into each of Kabakov's eyes. The eyes were red and tears welled out when he opened them. The nurse administered eyedrops and shook down a thermometer while the doctor listened to Kabakov's breathing.

The skin quivered under the cold stethoscope and the doctor was inconvenienced by the tape covering the left side of the rib cage. The emergency room had done a neat job. The doctor looked with some professional curiosity at the old scars that dotted and seamed Kabakov's body. "Do you mind standing out of the light?" he said to Moshevsky.

Moshevsky shifted from one foot to the other. Finally, in a position that resembled parade rest, he stared fixedly out the window until the examination was completed. He followed the doctor outside.

Sam Corley was waiting in the hall. "Well?"

The young doctor raised his eyebrows and looked annoyed. "Oh, yes. You're the FBI." He might have been identifying a plant. "He has a mild concussion. The X-rays look good. Three fractured ribs. Second-degree burns on the left thigh. Smoke inhalation has him very raw in the throat and lungs. He's got a ruptured sinus that may require a drain. An ENT man will be in this afternoon. His eyes and ears appear to be okay, but I expect his ears are ringing. It's not unusual."

"The hospital administrator spoke to you about listing him as very critical?"

"The administrator can list him any way he pleases. I would call his condition fair or even good. He has a remarkably tough body, but he's battered it around a lot."

"But you'll—"

"Mr. Corley, the administrator can tell the public he's pregnant for all I care. I won't contradict him. How did this happen, or may I ask?"

"I think a stove exploded."

"Yes, I'm sure it did." The doctor snorted through his nose and walked off down the hall.

"What's an ENT man?" Moshevsky asked Corley.

"An ear, nose, and throat specialist. By the way, I thought you didn't speak English."

"Poorly, if at all," Moshevsky said, hurriedly reentering the room with Corley staring balefully at his back.

Kabakov slept through most of the afternoon. As his sedative wore off, his eyes began to twitch beneath the lids and he dreamed, the colors in his dreams drug-bright. He was in his apartment in Tel Aviv and the red telephone was ringing. He could not reach it. He was entangled in a pile of clothing on the floor, and the clothing stank of cordite.

Kabakov's hands clutched the hospital sheet. Moshevsky heard the cloth rip and came out of his chair with the speed of a Cape buffalo. He unclenched Kabakov's fists and put them back at his sides, relieved to see that only the sheet was torn and not the bandage.

Kabakov woke remembering. The events at Muzi's house did not come back to him in order, and it was maddening to have to rearrange the pieces as he recalled them. By nightfall the oxygen tent had been removed and the ringing in his ears had subsided enough for him to listen while Moshevsky filled him in on the aftermath of the explosion—the ambulance, the cameramen, the press temporarily deceived but suspicious.

And Kabakov had no trouble hearing Corley when he was admitted to the room.

"What about Muzi?" Corley was pale with anger.

Kabakov did not want to talk. Talking made him cough and coughing aggravated the fire in his chest. He nodded to Moshevsky. "Tell him," he croaked.

Moshevsky's accent showed marked improvement. "Muzi was an importer—"

"Jesus Christ, I know all that. I've got the paper on him. Tell me what you saw and heard."

Moshevsky cut his eyes toward Kabakov and received a slight nod. He began with the questioning of Fawzi, the discovery of the Madonna, and the examination of the ship's papers. Kabakov filled in the scene in Muzi's apartment. When they had finished, Corley picked up Kabakov's bedside telephone and issued a rapid series of orders—warrants for the *Leticia* and crew, a lab team for the ship. Kabakov interrupted him once.

"Tell them to abuse Fawzi in front of the crew."

"What?" Corley's hand was over the mouthpiece.

"Say he's being arrested for not cooperating. Shove him around a little. I owe him a favor. He has relatives in Beirut."

"It's our ass if he complains."

"He won't."

Corley turned back to the telephone and continued his instructions for several minutes. ". . . yeah, Pearson, and call Fawzi a—"

"Pig-eating crotch cannibal," prompted Moshevsky.

". . . yeah, that's what I said call him," Corley said finally. "When you advise him of his rights, yeah. Don't ask questions, Pearson, just do it." He hung up the receiver.

"Okay, Kabakov. You were dragged out of that house by two guys with golf bags who just *happened* to be passing by, the fire department's report says. Some *golfers*." Corley stood in the middle of the room in his rumpled suit, flipping his keys. "These fellows just *happened* to leave the scene in a panel truck as soon as the ambulance arrived. What was the truck—a shuttle to some golf club where everybody talks funny? I quote to you from the police 'aided card': 'They both talked funny.' Like you talk funny. What are you running here, Kabakov? Are you gonna shit me or what?"

"I would have called you when I knew something." Kabakov's faint croak carried no apology.

"You would have sent me a postcard from fucking Tel Aviv. 'Sorry about the crater and the tidal wave.'" Corley looked out the window for a full minute. When he turned back to the bed, the anger had gone out of him. He had beaten the anger and he was ready to go again. It was a capacity Kabakov appreciated. "An American," Corley muttered. "Muzi said an American. Muzi was very clean, by the way. The police yellow sheet listed only one arrest. Assault and battery and disorderly conduct in a French restaurant. Charges dropped.

"We didn't get much from the house. The bomb was plastic, a little over a pound. We think it was wired into the light bulb socket inside the refrigerator. Someone unplugged the box, wired it up, closed the refrigerator door and plugged it back again. Unusual."

"I have heard of it once before," Kabakov said quietly, too quietly.

"I'm having you transferred to Bethesda Naval Hospital first thing tomorrow. We can set up adequate security there."

"I'm not staying—"

"Oh, yes you are." Corley took the late edition of the New York *Post* from his jacket pocket and held it up. Kabakov's picture was on page 3. It had been shot over the shoulder of an ambulance attendant as Kabakov was carried into the emergency room. The face was smoke-stained but the features were distinct. "They have your name as 'Kabov,' no address or occupation. We put the lid on the police community news unit before your identity was cleared up. Washington is climbing my ass. The director thinks the Arabs might recognize this picture and hit you."

"Splendid. We can take one alive and discuss it with him."

"Oh, no. Not in this hospital we can't. The whole wing would have to be evacuated first. Besides, they might succeed. You're no good to me dead. We don't want you to be another Yosef Alon."

Colonel Alon, the Israeli air attaché in Washington, was shot down in his driveway in Chevy Chase, Md., by guerrilla assassins in 1973. Kabakov had known and liked Alon, had stood beside Moshe Dayan at Lod Airport when his body was carried off the plane, wind rippling the flag that draped his casket.

"Possibly they would send the same people who killed Colonel Alon," Moshevsky said with the smile of a crocodile.

Corley shook his head wearily. "They'd send goons and you know it. No. We're not going to have a hospital shot up. Later, if you want to, you can make a speech on the steps of the UAR mission in a red jumpsuit for all I care. My orders are to keep you alive. The doctor says you must be flat on your back for a week, minimum. In the morning, pack your bedpan. You're moving to Bethesda. The press will be told you're transferred to the Brooke Army burn unit in San Antonio."

Kabakov closed his eyes for several seconds. If he were in Bethesda, he would be in the hands of the bureaucrats. They would have him looking at pictures of suspicious Arab pita bakers for the next six months.

But he had no intention of going to Bethesda. He needed a little medical attention, absolute privacy, and a place to rest for a day or two, with nobody giving orders about his convalescence. And he knew where he might get these things. "Corley, I can make better arrangements for myself. Did they tell you specifically Bethesda?"

"They said it was my responsibility to see that you were safe. You *will* be safe." The unspoken threat was there. If Kabakov did not cooperate, the State Department would see to it that he was ordered back to Israel.

"All right, look. By morning I'll have things set up. You can check it out until you're satisfied."

"I'll promise nothing."

"But you'll keep an open mind?" Kabakov hated to wheedle.

"We'll see. Meanwhile, I'm keeping five men on this floor. It really burns you to lose a round, doesn't it?"

Kabakov looked at him, and suddenly Corley was reminded of a badger he had trapped in Michigan as a boy. The badger had come at him dragging the trap, the broken end of his femur furrowing the dirt. His eyes had looked like Kabakov's.

As soon as the FBI agent had left the room, Kabakov tried to sit up, then fell back dizzy with the effort.

"Moshevsky, call Rachel Bauman," he said.

Bauman, Rachel, M.D., was in the medical listings of the Manhattan Telephone Directory. Moshevsky dialed the number with his little finger, the only finger that would go in the holes, and got an answering service. Dr. Bauman was away for three days.

He found "Bauman, R." in the Manhattan residence listing. The same answering service operator replied. Yes, she said, Dr. Bauman might check in, but she wasn't sure. Did she have a number where Dr. Bauman might be reached? Sorry, but she couldn't give out that information.

Moshevsky got one of the federal marshals on guard in the corridor to speak to the answering service. They waited while the operator checked his identification and called back.

"Dr. Bauman's at Mt. Murray Lodge in the Pocono Mountains," the marshal said at last. "She told the answering service she'd call with the room number later. That was yesterday. She hasn't called yet. If she planned to call back with the room number, she knew she wouldn't be registering in her own name."

"Yes, yes," Kabakov croaked.

"Shacked up, probably." The man would not be quiet.

Well, Kabakov was thinking, what can you expect when you don't call somebody for seven years? "How far away is this place?"

"About three hours."

"Moshevsky, go get her."

Seventy miles from the hospital, in Lakehurst, N.J., Michael Lander fiddled with the controls on his television set. It had an excellent picture—all of his appliances worked flawlessly—but he was never satisfied. Dahlia and Fasil gave no sign of their impatience. The 6 P.M. newscast was well underway before Lander finally left the set alone.

"An explosion in Brooklyn early today took the life of importer Benjamin Muzi. A second man was critically injured," the newscaster was saying. "Here's Frank Frizzell with an on-the-scene report.

The newscaster stared into the camera for an awkward moment before the film rolled. There was Frank Frizzell standing in a tangle of fire hoses on the sidewalk in front of Muzi's house.

". . . blew out the kitchen wall and caused minor damage to the house next door. Thirty-five firemen with six pieces of equipment battled the fire for more than half an hour before bringing it under control. Six firemen were treated for smoke inhalation."

The scene switched to the side of the house, with its gaping hole. Lander leaned forward eagerly, trying to gauge the force of the blast. Fasil watched as though hypnotized.

The firemen were taking up their hoses. Clearly the TV crew had arrived when the operation was almost completed. Now film from the ramp outside the hospital. Some intelligent television deskman, knowing Long Island College Hospital was the designated receiver for disaster victims in the 76th Precinct, must have sent a camera crew directly to the hospital immediately after the alarm. The news team had arrived just before the ambulance. Here was the ambulance crew bringing out the stretcher, two men rolling it and a third holding up a bottle of intravenous fluid. The picture jerked as the cameraman was jostled by the crowd. Picture bouncing now as the cameraman trotted along with the stretcher. A pause as they reached the emergency room ramp. A closeup of the smoke-stained face. "David Kabov, no address, remained in Long Island College Hospital, his condition described as very critical."

"Kabakov!" Fasil shouted. His lip was drawn back from his teeth and he lapsed into Arabic in a string of filthy oaths. Now Dahlia was speaking Arabic too. She was pale, remembering the room in Beirut, the black muzzle of the machine gun swinging toward her, Najeer slack against the splattered wall.

"Speak English." Lander repeated it twice before they heard him. "Who is that?"

"I can't be positive," Dahlia said, breathing deeply.

"I can." Fasil held the bridge of his nose between thumb and forefinger. "It's a filthy Israeli coward who comes in the night to kill and kill and kill, women, children . . . he doesn't care. The bastard Jew killed our leader, killed many others, nearly killed Dahlia." Unconsciously, Fasil's hand had moved to the bullet stripe on his cheek, suffered in the Beirut raid.

Lander's mainspring was hate, but his hate came from injury and madness. Here was conditioned hatred, and though Lander could not have defined the difference, was not consciously aware of the difference, it made him uneasy. "Maybe he'll die," he said.

"Oh, yes," Fasil said. "He will."

CHAPTER
10

KABAKOV LAY AWAKE for hours in the middle of the night, after the noise of the hospital had diminished to the rustle of nylon uniforms, the squeak of soft-soled shoes on waxed floors, the toothless cry of an elderly patient down the hall calling for Jesus. He was holding onto himself as he had before, lying awake listening to the traffic in a hospital hall. Hospitals threaten us all with the old disasters of childhood, the uncontrolled bowel, the need to weep.

Kabakov did not think in terms of bravery and cowardice. When he thought about it at all, he was a behaviorist. His citations credited him with various virtues, some of which he believed to be nonexistent. The fact that his men were somewhat in awe of him was useful in leading them, but it was not a source of pride to him. Too many had died beside him.

He had seen courage. He would define it as doing what was necessary, regardless. But the operative word was *necessary*. Not *regardless*. He had known two or three men who had been utterly without fear. They were all psychotic. Fear could be controlled and channeled. It was the secret of a successful soldier.

Kabakov would laugh at the suggestion that he was an idealist, but there was inside him a dichotomy that is close to the center of what is called Jewishness. He could be utterly pragmatic in his view of human behavior and still feel on the very heart of his heart the white hot fingerprint of God.

Kabakov was not a religious man as the world sees religious men. He was not learned in the rites of Judaism. But he had known that he was a Jew every day that he lived. He believed in Israel. He would do his best and leave the rest to the rabbis.

He was itching under the tape on his ribs. He found that by twisting slightly, he could make the tape pull on the itching place. It was not as satisfactory as scratching, but it helped. The doctor, young what's-his-name, had kept asking questions about his old scars. Kabakov laughed to himself, remembering how the doctor's curiosity had offended Moshevsky. Moshevsky told the man Kabakov was a professional motor-cycle racer. He did not tell the doctor about the fight for Mitla Pass in 1956, or the Syrian bunkers at Rafid in 1967, or the other, less conventional battlefields that had marked Kabakov—a hotel roof in Tripoli, the docks on Crete with the bullets splintering the planks—all the places where the Arab terrorists had nested.

It was the doctor's question about old wounds that had started Kabakov thinking about Rachel. Now, lying in the dark, he thought about how it began with her.

June 9, 1967: He and Moshevsky lying on stretchers outside a field hospital in Galilee, the wind blowing sand against the canvas sides with a hissing sound and the generator roaring over the moans of the wounded. A doctor, stepping high like an ibis over the litters, carrying on the awful business of triage. Kabakov and Moshevsky, both hit with small arms fire storming the Syrian Heights in darkness, were carried inside the field hospital, into the light, emergency lanterns swinging beside the operating room lamps. Numbness spreading from the needle, the masked doctor bending over him. Kabakov, watching like a stranger, not looking down at himself, mildly surprised to see that the doctor's hands, extended for fresh sterile gloves, were the hands of a woman. Dr. Rachel Bauman, psychiatric resident at Mt. Sinai Hospital in New York turned volunteer battlefield surgeon, removed the slug that had notched Kabakov's collarbone.

He was recuperating in a Tel Aviv hospital when she came into his ward on a round of postoperative examinations. She was an attractive woman of about 26 with dark red hair gathered into a bun. Kabakov's eyes never left her after she began her rounds with an older staff doctor and a nurse.

The nurse pulled down the sheet. Dr. Bauman did not speak to Kabakov. She was engrossed by the wound, pressing the skin around it with her fingers. The staff doctor examined it in turn.

"A very nice job, Dr. Bauman," he said.

"Thank you, Doctor. They gave me the easier ones."

"You did this?" Kabakov said.

She looked at him as though she had just realized he was there. "Yes."

"You have an American accent."

"Yes, I'm an American."

"Thank you for coming."

A pause, a blink, she reddened. "Thank you for breathing," she said and walked away down the ward. Kabakov's face showed his surprise.

"Dummy," the older doctor said. "How would you like it if a Jew said to you 'Thank you for acting like a Jew all day today'?" He patted Kabakov's arm as he left the bedside.

A week later, leaving the hospital in uniform, he saw her on the front steps.

"Dr. Bauman."

"Major Kabakov. I'm glad to see you out." She did not smile. The wind pressed a strand of hair across her cheek.

"Have dinner with me."

"There isn't time, thank you. I have to go." She disappeared into the hospital.

Kabakov was away from Tel Aviv for the next two weeks, reestablishing contact with intelligence sources along the Syrian front. He conducted one probe across the ceasefire line, moving through a moonless night to a Syrian rocket launcher position that persisted in violation of the ceasefire despite United Nations surveillance. The Russian-made rockets all detonated simultaneously in their storage racks, leaving a crater in the hillside.

When his orders brought him back to the city, he sought out some of the women he knew and found them to be as satisfactory as ever. And he persisted in his invitations to Rachel Bauman. She was helping in the operating room and working with head injury cases as much as 16 hours a day now. Finally, wearily, smelling of disinfectant, she began to meet Kabakov near the hospital for hurried meals. She was a reserved woman and she protected herself, protected the direction of her life. Sometimes, after the last surgery of the evening, they sat on a park bench and sipped brandy from a flask. She was too tired for much conversation, but she drew comfort from sitting beside the large, dark form of Kabakov. She would not come to his apartment.

This arrangement ended suddenly. They were in the park and, though Kabakov could not tell it in the darkness, she was close to tears. A desperate four-hour operation had failed, a case of brain damage. Knowledgeable in head trauma, she had been called in to aid in the diagnosis, had confirmed the signs of subdural hematoma in a seventeen-year-old Arab soldier. The increased cerebrospinal fluid pressure and the presence of blood in the fluid left no doubt. She helped the neurosurgeon. There was an unavoidable intracerebral hemorrhage and the young man was dead. Wasted even as she watched his face.

Kabakov, laughing and unaware, told her a story about a tank driver with a scorpion in his underwear, who flattened a Quonset hut. She did not respond.

"Thinking?" he said.

A column of armored personnel carriers rumbled along the street behind them, and she had to speak loudly to be heard. "I'm thinking that in some Cairo hospital they're working just as hard to clean up the messes *you* make. Even in peacetime you do it, don't you? You and the fedayeen."

"There is no peacetime."

"They gossip at the hospital. You're some sort of super commando, aren't you?" She could not stop now and her voice was shrill. "Do you know what? I was passing through the lounge at the hotel, going to my room, and I heard your name. A little fat man, a second secretary from one of the foreign missions, was drinking with some Israeli officers. He was saying that if real peace ever comes they'll have to gas you like a war dog."

Nothing. Kabakov still, his profile indistinct against the dark trees.

The anger went out of her suddenly, leaving her slack, sick that she had struck at him. It was an effort for her to speak, but she owed him the rest of the story. "The officers stood up. One of them slapped the fat man's face and they walked away with their drinks still on the table," she finished miserably.

Kabakov stood in front of her. "Get some sleep, Dr. Bauman," he said, and then he was gone.

Kabakov's duties chafed him in the next month—office work. He had been transferred back to the Mossad, which was working furiously to determine the full damage wrought on Israel's ring of enemies in the Six-Day War and to estimate their potential for a second strike. There were exhaustive debriefings of pilots, unit commanders, and individual soldiers. Kabakov conducted many of the debriefings, collating the material with information provided by sources within the Arab countries and reducing the results to terse memoranda carefully studied by his chiefs. It was tiresome, tedious work and Rachel Bauman intruded only occasionally into his thoughts. He neither saw nor called her. Instead, he confined his attentions to a ripe Sabra sergeant with a bulging blouse, who could have ridden a Brahma bull without holding onto the rope. His Sabra was soon transferred and he was alone again, remaining alone by choice, numbed by the routine of his work, until a party brought him out.

The party was his first real celebration since the war ended. It was organized by two dozen of the men who served in Kabakov's paratroop section and was attended by a wild and friendly group of fifty—men and women, soldiers all. They were bright-eyed and sunburned and most of them were younger than Kabakov. The Six-Day War had scorched the youth off their faces, and now, indomitable as a hardy crop, it was coming back again. The women were glad to be in skirts and sandals and bright blouses instead of uniform, and it was good to look at them. There was little discussion of the war, no mention of the men they had lost. *Kaddish* had been said and would be said again.

The group took over a café on the outskirts of Tel Aviv beside the road to Haifa, an isolated building blue-white under the moon. Kabakov heard the party from 300 yards away as he approached in his jeep. It sounded like a riot with musical accompaniment. Couples were dancing inside the café and under an arbor on the terrace. A ripple of attention swept over the room as Kabakov entered, weaving his way through the dancers, acknowledging a dozen greetings yelled above the crashing music. Some of the younger soldiers

pointed him out to their companions with a glance and
a nod of the head. Kabakov was pleasantly aware of all
this, though he made an elaborate effort not to show it.
He knew that it was wrong to make anything special of
him. Every man took his own chances. These people
were just young enough to want to indulge themselves
in this bullshit, he thought. He wished Rachel were
here, wished she had come in with him, and he believed
innocently that the wish had nothing to do with his
welcome. Damn Rachel!

He made his way to a long table at the end of the
terrace, where Moshevsky was seated with some lively
girls. Moshevsky had an assortment of bottles before
him, and he was telling lewd knock-knock jokes as fast
as he could think of them. Kabakov felt good and the
wine made him feel better. The men at the party held a
variety of ranks, commissioned and noncommissioned,
and no one thought it strange that a major and a sergeant should carouse side-by-side. The discipline that
had carried the Israelis across the Sinai was born of
mutual respect and sustained by *esprit,* and it was like
a coat-of-mail that could be hung by the door on these
occasions. This was a good party: the people understood each other, the wine was Israeli, and the dances
were the dances of the kibbutz.

Just before midnight, through the whirling dancers,
Kabakov spotted Rachel hesitating at the edge of the
light. She walked toward the arbor where the couples
danced, clapping their hands and singing.

The air was soft on her arms and brushed her legs
beneath the short denim dress, air scented with wine
and strong tobacco and warm flowers. She saw

Kabakov, lounging back like Nero at his long table. Someone had put a flower behind his ear and a cigar was in his teeth. A girl leaned toward him talking.

Shyly, Rachel approached his table, through the dancers and the music. A very young lieutenant grabbed her and spun her in the dance and, when the room stopped whirling, Kabakov was standing before her, his eyes wine-bright. She had forgotten how big he was. "David," she said, looking up into his face, "I want to tell you—"

"That you need a drink," Kabakov said, holding out a glass.

"I go home tomorrow—they said you were here and I couldn't leave without—"

"Without dancing with me? Of course not."

Rachel had danced during her kibbutz summer years before, and the steps came back to her now. Kabakov had a remarkable facility for dancing with a glass in his hand, obtaining refills in full flight, and they drank from it by turns. With his other hand he reached behind her and plucked the pins from her hair. It tumbled in a dark red mass down her back and around her cheeks, more hair than Kabakov would have believed possible. The wine warmed Rachel, and she found herself laughing as she danced. The other, the pain and mutilation she had been steeped in, seemed distant.

Quite suddenly it was late. The noise had dropped and many of the revelers had left without Kabakov or Rachel noticing. Only a few couples still danced beneath the arbor. The musicians were asleep, their heads down on a table by the bandstand. The dancers were very close together, moving to an old Edith Piaf song played on the jukebox near the bar. The terrace was strewn with crushed flowers and cigar ends and puddled with wine. A very young soldier, his foot in a cast propped up on a chair, was singing along with the record, holding a bottle at his side. It was late, late, the hour when the moon fades and objects harden in the half-light to take the weight of day. Kabakov and Rachel barely moved to the music. They stopped entirely, warm against each other. Kabakov kissed away a trickle of sweat on the side of her neck, tasted the sweat, a drop of the moving sea. The air that she had warmed and scented rose to touch his eyes and throat. She swayed, a short sidestep to keep her balance, thigh sliding over his, around his, holding, remembering absurdly the first time she had laid her check on the warm hard side of a horse's neck.

They parted slowly in a deepening V that let the light between them, and walked outside in the still dawn, Kabakov hooking a bottle of brandy off a table as he passed. The beaded grass wet Rachel's ankles as they climbed the hillside path, and they saw details of the rocks and brush with the unnatural clarity of vision that follows a sleepless night.

Sitting with their backs against a rock, they watched the sun come up. In the light of that clear day, Kabakov could see the tiny flaws in her complexion, the freckles, the lines of fatigue beneath her eyes, the good cheekbones. He wanted her very much and time had run out.

He kissed her for minutes, his hand warm beneath her hair.

A couple came down the path from the thickets

above, bashful in the light, brushing leaves from their clothing. They stumbled over the feet of Kabakov and Rachel sitting beside the path, and passed on, unnoticed.

"David, I am shook," Rachel said at last, shredding a blade of grass. "I didn't mean for this to get started, you know?"

"Shook?"

"Disturbed, upset Slang."

"Well, I—" Kabakov tried to think of a nice phrase, then snorted at himself. He liked her. Talk was nothing. Damn talking. He talked. "Wet drawers and vague regrets are fifth-form nonsense. Come with me to Haifa. I can get a week's leave. I want you to come with me. We'll talk about your responsibilities next week."

"Next week. Next week I might not have any sense at all. I have obligations in New York. What would be different about it next week?"

"Knocking the slats out of a bed and lying in the sun and looking at each other would make it different."

She turned away quickly.

"Don't get pissed off, either."

"I'm not pissed off," she said.

"Stop saying words like pissed off, then. It sounds like you are." He was smiling. She smiled too. An awkward silence.

"Will you come back?" Kabakov said.

"Not soon. I have my residency to finish. Not unless the war breaks out again. But it hasn't stopped for you, not even for a little while, has it, David? It's never over for you."

He said nothing.

"It's funny, David. Women are supposed to have busy little flexible lives, men have Their Duty. What I do is real and valuable and important. And if I say it's *my* duty, because I want it to be my duty, then that is just as real as your uniform. We won't 'talk about it next week.'"

"Fine," Kabakov said. "Go do your duty."

"Don't get pissed off, either."

"I'm not pissed off."

"Hey, David, thank you for asking me. If I could, I would ask you. To go to Haifa. Or somewhere. And knock the slats out of a bed." A pause, then quickly, "Goodbye, Major David Kabakov. I'll remember you."

And then she was running down the trail. She did not realize she was crying until her jeep picked up speed and the wind spread the tears in cold patches on her cheeks. Tears the wind dried, seven years ago, in Israel.

A nurse came into Kabakov's room, interrupting his thoughts, and the hospital walls closed in on him again. She carried a pill in a paper cup. "I'm going off now, Mr. Kabov," the nurse said. "I'll see you tomorrow afternoon." Kabakov looked at his watch. Moshevsky should have called from the lodge by now, it was nearly midnight.

From a car parked across the street, Dahlia Iyad watched a group of late-shift nurses filing through the front entrance of the hospital. She, too, made a note of the time. Then she drove away.

CHAPTER
11

As Kabakov took his pill, Moshevsky was standing just inside the doorway of the Boom-Boom Room, the nightclub at Mt. Murray Lodge. He was glowering at the crowd. It had been a tiresome three-hour drive through the runty Pocono Mountains in a light snow, and he was disgruntled. As he had expected, the registration desk did not list a Rachel Bauman. He had not spotted her in the dinner crowd downstairs, though his surveillance had on three occasions attracted the head-waiter, who uneasily offered him a table. The band in the Boom-Boom Room was loud, but not bad, and the "activities director" was master of ceremonies. A moving spotlight slid over the tables, pausing on each. Often the patrons waved when the light touched them.

Rachel Bauman, sitting with her current fiancé and a couple they had met at the lodge, did not wave in the spotlight. She thought this was an ugly lodge with no view. She thought the Poconos were stupid little mountains. She thought the crowd was frumpy. Numerous new art-carved engagement and wedding rings made the room flash like a muddy constellation. This depressed her because she was reminded that she had agreed, sort of, to marry the personable, dull young lawyer at her side. He was not the type to interfere with her life.

Furthermore, their room was vulgar, cost $60 a day, and had hairs in the bathtub. The furniture was Brooklyn oriental, the bathtub hairs unmistakably pubic. Her fiancé, sort of, sported an ascot with his dressing gown and wore his watch to bed. Holy God, look at me, Rachel was thinking. I have little enameled rings on my fingers.

Moshevsky appeared beside the table like a whale peering down into a rowboat. He had gone over what he would say. He would open with humor.

"Dr. Bauman, I always see you making a party. You remember me, Moshevsky, Israel 1967, now could we have some words?"

"I beg your pardon?"

That was all Moshevsky had been prepared to say for openers. He hesitated, then rallied, bending over as though showing his face to a short dermatologist. "Robert Moshevsky, Israel 1967. With Major Kabakov? At the hospital and the party?"

"Of course! Sergeant Moshevsky. I didn't recognize you in your civvies."

Moshevsky was nonplussed. He thought she had said "skivvies," a term he understood. He looked down at himself quickly. No problem there. Rachel's boyfriend and the other couple were staring at him now.

"Marc Taubman, this is Robert Moshevsky, a good

friend of mine," Rachel was saying to her escort. "Please sit down, Sergeant."

"Yes, do," Taubman said dubiously.

"What in the world—" Rachel's face changed suddenly. "Is David all right?"

"Almost." Enough of this social stuff. His instructions did not include sitting around and talking. What would Kabakov say? He bent close to her ear. "I have to speak with you privately, please," he rumbled. "Most urgent."

"Would you excuse us?" She put her hand on Taubman's shoulder as he started to rise. "I'll only be a moment, Marc. It's all right."

In five minutes Rachel returned to the table to summon Marc Taubman outside. Ten minutes later he was sitting alone in the bar with his chin in his hand. Rachel and Moshevsky were speeding back to New York, snow streaking level into the windshield like tracer fire.

To the south, the snow had changed to sleet that rattled off the roof and windshield of Lander's station-wagon as Dahlia Iyad drove down the Garden State Parkway. The parkway had been sanded, but Route 70 was slick as she turned west toward Lakehurst. It was 3 A.M. when she reached Lander's house and ran inside. Lander was pouring a cup of coffee. She put the two-star edition of the *Daily News* on the kitchen counter and opened it to the centerfold picture section. The face of the man on the stretcher was clear. It was Kabakov all right. Cold drops of water trickled onto her scalp as the sleet melted in her hair.

"So it's Kabakov, so what?" Lander said.

"So what indeed," Fasil said, coming out of his room. "He had a chance to talk to Muzi, he may have your description. He must have found Muzi through the ship, and at the ship he would have gotten my description also. He may not have fixed on my identity yet, but he knows of me. It will occur to him. He has seen Dahlia. He has to go."

Lander set his cup down with a clatter. "Don't shit me, Fasil. If the authorities knew anything they'd have been here by now. You just want to kill him for revenge. He shot your leader, didn't he? Strolled right in and blew off his ass."

"In his sleep, he sneaked—"

"You people really get me. This is why the Israelis beat you with such regularity, you're always thinking about revenge, trying to get them back for what happened last week. And you're willing to risk this whole thing, just for revenge."

"Kabakov must die," Fasil said, his voice rising.

"It's not just revenge, either. You're afraid that if you don't get him while he's injured, sooner or later he'll come to see *you* in the middle of the night."

The word "afraid" hung in the air between them. Fasil was exerting a tremendous effort to hold his temper. An Arab could swallow a toad more easily than an insult. Dahlia moved quietly to the coffeepot, breaking their eye contact. She poured a cup and stood leaning against the counter, her behind firmly against the drawer containing the butcher knives.

When Fasil spoke, his throat seemed very dry. "Kabakov is the best they have. If he dies, he will be replaced, true, but it will not be the same. Let me point out, Mr. Lander, that Muzi was destroyed because he had seen you. He had seen your face and your—" Fasil's Arab tongue could be artful when he wished. He hesitated just long enough for Lander to anticipate the word "hand," then diverted the sentence with what appeared to be tact—"your accent was known to him. Besides, are we not all marked with our wounds?" He tapped the scar on his cheek. Lander said nothing, so Fasil continued. "Now we have a man who knows Dahlia on sight. There are places where he might find her picture."

"Where?"

"My picture is in the alien registry. I was well disguised in that one," she said. "But in the annuals of the American University at Beirut—"

"School annuals? Come on, he'd never—"

"They have done it before, Michael. They know we are often recruited there and at the university in Cairo. Many times the pictures are taken and the annual published before a person becomes involved in the movement. He will be looking."

"If Dahlia is identified, her picture will be circulated," Fasil added. "When the time comes for you to strike, there will be Secret Service all around—if the President attends."

"He'll attend, he'll attend. He's said he would attend."

"Then Secret Service likely will come to the airfield. They might have seen Dahlia's picture, perhaps a picture of me, probably a description of you," Fasil said. "All because of Kabakov—if he is allowed to live."

"I will not risk you or Dahlia being captured," Lander snapped. "It would be stupid to go myself."

"That is not necessary," Dahlia said. "We can do it by remote control." She was lying.

At Long Island College Hospital, Rachel had to show her identification at two federal checkpoints before she could accompany Moshevsky to Kabakov's floor.

Kabakov awakened at the slight sound of the opening door. She crossed the dark room and put her hand on his cheek, felt his eyelashes brush her hand, knew he was awake.

"David, I'm here," she said.

Six hours later Corley returned to the hospital. Visiting hours had begun and patients' relatives were carrying flowers down the halls and conferring in worried groups outside the doors where the signs said "No visitors. No smoking, oxygen in use."

Corley found Moshevsky seated on a bench outside Kabakov's room eating a Big Mac hamburger. Beside him in a wheelchair was a girl of about eight. She also was eating a Big Mac.

"Kabakov asleep?"

"Bathing," Moshevsky said, his mouth full.

"Good morning," the child said.

"Good morning. When will he be finished, Moshevsky?"

"When the nurse finishes scrubbing him," the child said. "It tickles. Did a nurse ever bathe you?"

"No. Moshevsky, tell her to hurry up. I've got to—"

"Would you like a bite of this hamburger?" the child

said. "Mr. Moshevsky and I send out for them. The food here is terrible. Mr. Moshevsky won't let Mr. Kabakov have a hamburger. Mr. Kabakov said some very bad words about it."

"I see," Corley said, biting his thumbnail.

"I have a burn just like Mr. Kabakov."

"I'm sorry to hear it."

She gingerly leaned sideways in her wheelchair to take some french-fried potatoes from a sack in Moshevsky's lap. Corley opened the door, stuck his head in, spoke briefly to the nurse and withdrew again. "One leg to go," he muttered. "One leg to go."

"I was cooking and I spilled a pan of hot water on myself," the child said.

"I beg your pardon?"

"I said I was cooking and I burned myself with some hot water."

"Oh, I'm sorry."

"I was telling Mr. Kabakov, the same thing happened to him you know, I was telling him that most home accidents happen in the kitchen."

"*You've* been talking to Mr. Kabakov?"

"Sure. We watched the softball game on the playground across the street from his window. They play before school every morning. I can just see a brick wall from the window in my room. He knows some pretty good jokes. Want to hear one?"

"Thank you, no. He's told me a few already."

"I have one of those tent beds too, and—"

The nurse came out into the hall carrying a basin of water. "You can go in now."

"Good," the child said.

"Wait, Dotty," Moshevsky rumbled. "Stay with me. We haven't finished these chips."

"French fries," she said.

Corley found Kabakov propped up in bed. "Now that you're clean, here's what we have. We got warrants for the *Leticia*. Three crew members saw the boat. Nobody remembers the numbers, but they would be fake anyway. We got a little paint where they scraped the side of the ship. It's being analyzed."

Kabakov made a small gesture of impatience. Corley ignored it and went on. "The electronics people talked to the radar operator on the Coast Guard cutter. They think the boat was wood. We know it's fast. We're guessing it has turbo-charged diesels from the description of the sound. It adds up to a smuggler's boat. Sooner or later we'll find it. It had to be built somewhere, at a very good yard."

"What about the American?"

"Nothing. This country is lousy with them. We've got the *Leticia* crewmen working with an Identikit trying to make up a composite of the man who came over on the ship. We're having to work through an interpreter, though. It's slow going. 'Eyes like a pig's ass,' they tell us. Descriptions like that. I'll get you an Identikit and you can do one on the woman. Lab's working on the Madonna."

Kabakov nodded.

"Now, I've got a medevac laid on for 11:30. We'll leave here at 11, drive to the Marine Air Terminal at La Guardia—"

"May I talk to you, Mr. Corley?" Rachel spoke

from the doorway. She carried Kabakov's X-rays and charts and wore her stiffest white coat.

"I could have gone to the Israeli mission already," Kabakov said. "You couldn't touch me there. Talk to her, Corley."

Half an hour later, Corley spoke to the hospital administrator, who spoke to the hospital's public information officer, who was trying to leave early on this Friday. The information officer stuck a memo for the press under the telephone and did not bother to post the patient condition book.

The television stations, putting together their six o'clock news, called at mid-afternoon to check on the victims of various disasters. Referring to the memo, the clerk told them "Mr. Kabov" had been medevaced to Brooke Army Hospital. It was a crowded news day. None of them used the story.

The *New York Times*, thorough as always, prepared a brief item on Mr. Kabov being moved. The *Times'* call was the last and the memo was thrown away. The first edition of the *Times* does not appear on the street until 10:30 P.M. By then it was too late. Dahlia was on the road.

THE IRT EXPRESS train rumbled under the East River and stopped in the Boro Hall station near Long Island College Hospital. Eleven nurses, due to report at 11:30 P.M. for the overnight shift, got off the train. By the time they had climbed the stairs to the street, they numbered an even dozen. The women moved in a tight group along the dark Brooklyn sidewalk, turning their heads only slightly to scan the shadows with the keen survival instincts of city women. A wino was the only other person visible. He swayed toward them. The nurses had sized him up from 25 yards away and, pocketbooks shifted to their inboard arms, they skirted him and passed on, leaving in the air a pleasant scent of toothpaste and hairspray that he could not appreciate because his nose was stopped up. Most of the hospital windows were dark. An ambulance siren wailed and wailed again, louder this time.

"They're playing our song," a resigned voice said.

A yawning security guard opened the glass doors. "ID cards, ladies, let's see 'um."

Grumbling, the women rummaged their purses and held up their identification—building passes for the staff nurses, lime-green State University of New York ID cards for the private nurses. This was the only special security measure they would encounter.

The guard swept the upheld cards with a glance as though he were polling a class. He waved the nurses on and they scattered toward their duty stations in the big building. One of them entered the women's restroom opposite the elevator bank on the ground floor. The room was dark, as she had expected.

She switched on the light and looked in the mirror. The blonde wig was a flawless fit and the effect of bleaching her eyebrows had been well worth the effort. With cotton pads filling out her cheeks and the glasses with fancy frames altering the proportions of her face, it was difficult to recognize Dahlia Iyad.

She hung her coat inside the toilet stall and took from its inside pocket a small tray. She placed two bottles, a thermometer, a plastic tongue depressor, and a paper pill cup on the tray and covered them with a cloth. The tray was a prop. The important piece of equipment was in her uniform pocket. It was a hypodermic syringe filled with potassium chloride, enough to cause cardiac arrest in a robust ox.

She put the crisp nurse's cap on her head and secured it carefully with hairpins. She gave her appearance a final check in the mirror. The loose-fitting nurse's uniform did her figure no justice, but it concealed the flat Beretta automatic stuffed into the top of her pantyhose. She was satisfied.

The ground-floor hall containing the administrative offices was dim and deserted, lighting cut to a minimum in the energy shortage. She ticked off the signs as she passed along the hall. Accounting, Records, there it was—Patient Information. The inquiry window with its round conversation hole was dark.

A simple snap lock secured the door. Thirty seconds' work with the tongue depressor forced back the beveled bolt and the door swung open. She had given considerable thought to her next move, and though it went against her instinctive wish to be hidden, she turned on the office lights instead of using the flashlight. One by one the banks of fluorescent lights buzzed and lit up.

She went to the large ledger on the inquiry desk and flipped it open. K. No Kabakov. Now she would have to go from door to door checking the nurses' stations, watching out for guards, risking exposure. Wait. The television news had pronounced it Kabov. The papers had spelled it Kabov. Bottom of the page, here it was. Kabov, D. No address. All inquiries to be directed to the hospital administrator. Inquiries in person reported to administrator, hospital security, and the Federal Bureau of Investigation, LE 5-7700. He was in Room 327.

Dahlia took a deep breath and closed the book.

"How did you get in there?"

Dahlia in a double reflex nearly jumped, did not jump, looked up calmly at the security guard peering at her through the inquiry window. "Hey, you want to make yourself useful," she said, "you could take this book up to the night administrator and I won't have to go all the way back upstairs. It weighs ten pounds."

"How did you get in there?"

"The night administrator's key." If he asked to see the key, she would kill him.

"Nobody is supposed to be in here at night."

"Look, you want to call upstairs and tell them they have to have your permission, that's fine with me. I was just told to come bring it, that's all." If he tried to call, she would kill him. "What, should I check in with you if they send me down here? I would have done that, but I didn't know."

"I'm responsible for this, see. I have to know who is here. I see this light, I don't know who's here. I have to leave the door to find out. What if somebody is waiting at the front to come in? Then they're mad at me, see, because I'm not at the door. You check with me when you come down here, all right?"

"All right, sure. I'm sorry."

"Be sure you lock this up and turn out the light, all right?"

"Sure."

He nodded and walked slowly down the hall.

Room 327 was quiet and dark. Only the streetlights below shone through the venetian blinds, casting faint bars of light on the ceiling. Eyes accustomed to the dark could make out the bed, fitted with its aluminum frame to hold the covers up off the patient. In the bed, Dotty Hirschburg slept the deep sleep of childhood, the tip of her thumb just touching the roof of her mouth, fingers spread on the pillow. She had watched the play-ground from the window of her new room all afternoon, and she had tired herself out. She was accustomed by now to the comings and goings of the night nurses and she did not stir when the door slowly opened. A column of light widened on the opposite wall, was blotted by a shadow, and then narrowed again as the door quietly closed.

Dahlia Iyad stood with her back against the door, waiting for her pupils to dilate. The light from the hall had shown her that the room was empty except for the patient, the cushions of the chair still deeply dented from Moshevsky's vigil. Dahlia opened her mouth and throat to silence her breathing. She could hear other breathing in the darkness. Nurse's footsteps in the hall behind her, pausing, entering the room across the hall.

Dahlia moved silently to the foot of the tentlike bed. She set her tray down on the rolling bed table and took the hypodermic from her pocket. She removed the cap from the long needle and depressed the plunger until she could feel a tiny bead of the fluid at the tip of the needle.

Anywhere would do. The carotid then. Very quick. She moved up beside the bed in the dark and felt gently for the neck, touched hair and then the skin. It felt soft. Where was the pulse? There. Too soft. She felt with thumb and fingers around the neck. Too small. The hair too soft, the skin too soft, the neck too small. She put the hypo in her pocket and switched on her penlight.

"Hello," said Dotty Hirschburg, blinking against the light. Dahlia's fingers rested cool on her throat.

"Hello," Dahlia said.

"The light hurts my eyes. Do I have to have a shot?"

She looked up anxiously at Dahlia's face, lighted from beneath. The hand moved to her cheek.

"No. No, you don't have to have a shot. Are you all right? Do you want anything?"

"Do you go around and see if everybody is asleep?"

"Yes."

"Why do you wake them up then?"

"To make sure they're all right. You go back to sleep now."

"It seems pretty silly to me. Waking people up to see if they're asleep."

"When did you move in here?"

"Today. Mr. Kabakov had this room. My mother asked for it so I can see the playground."

"Where is Mr. Kabakov?"

"He went away."

"Was he very sick, did they take him away covered up?"

"You mean dead? Heck no, but they shaved a place on his head. We watched the ballgame together yesterday. The lady doctor took him away. Maybe he went home."

Dahlia hesitated in the hall. She knew she should not push it now. She should leave the hospital. She should fail. She pushed it. At the icemaker behind the nurses' station, she spent several minutes packing a pitcher with cubes. The head nurse, all starch and spectacles and iron gray hair, was talking with a nurse's aide in one of those listless conversations that drift on through the night with no beginning or end. At last the head nurse rose and marched down the hall in response to a call from a floor nurse.

Dahlia was at her desk in a second, flipping through
the alphabetical index. No Kabakov. No Kabov. The
nurse's aide watched her. Dahlia turned to the woman.

"What happened to the patient in 327?"

"Who?"

"The man in 327."

"I can't keep up with them. I haven't seen you before, have I?"

"No, I've been at St. Vincent's." This was true—she
had stolen her credentials at St. Vincent's Hospital in
Manhattan during the afternoon shift change. Dahlia
had to hurry this up, even if she aroused the woman's
suspicions. "If he was moved, there would be a record,
right?"

"It would be downstairs locked up. If he's not in the
file, he's not on this floor, and if he's not on this floor
he's most likely not in this hospital."

"The girls were saying there was such a flap when he
came in."

"There's a flap all the time, honey. Woman doctor
come in here yesterday morning about 3 A.M. wanting
to see his X-rays. Had to go upstairs and open up radiology. They must have moved him in the daytime after
I left."

"Who was the doctor?"

"I don't know. Nothing would do but she was going
to have those X-rays."

"Did she sign for them?"

"Up in radiology she had to sign them out, just like
everybody signs them out."

The head nurse was coming. Quickly now. "Is radiology on four?"

"Five."

The head nurse and the aide were talking as Dahlia entered the elevator. The doors closed. She did not see the aide nod toward the elevator, did not see the head nurse's expression change as she remembered instructions from the night before, did not see her reach for the telephone fast.

In the emergency room Policeman John Sullivan's belt beeper sounded. "Now shut your mouth!" he said to the cursing, bloody drunk his partner was holding. Sullivan unclipped his walkie-talkie and responded to the call.

"Complainant third-floor head nurse Emma Ryan reports a suspicious person, white female, blonde, about five-seven, late twenties, nurse's uniform, possibly in radiology on the fifth floor," the precinct dispatcher told Sullivan. "Security guard will meet you at the elevators. Unit seven-one is on the way."

"Ten-four," Sullivan said, switching off. "Jack, cuff this bastard to the bench and cover the stairs until seven-one gets here. I'm going up."

The security guard was waiting with a bunch of keys.

"Freeze all the elevators except the first one," Sullivan said. "Let's go."

Dahlia had no trouble with the lock on the radiology lab. She closed the door behind her. In a moment she made out the bulk of the X-ray table, the vertical slab of the fluoroscope. She rolled one of the heavy leaded screens in front of the frosted glass door and turned on her penlight. The small beam played over the coiled barium hose, the goggles and gloves hanging beside the fluoroscope. Faintly a siren. An ambulance? Police? Looking around quickly. This door—a darkroom. An alcove lined with big filing cabinets. Drawer opening on loud rollers—X-rays in envelopes. Here a small office, a desk, and a book. Footsteps in the hall. A circle of light on the pages. Flip, flip. Yesterday's date. A page of signatures and case numbers. It had to be a woman's name. Go by the time in the left column—4 A.M., case number, no patient's name, X-ray signed out to Dr. Rachel Bauman. Not signed back in.

The footsteps stopping at the door. A tinkle of keys. The first one didn't work. Throw the wig behind the cabinet, glasses with it. Door bumping against the leaded screen. A bulky policeman and a security guard coming in.

Dahlia Iyad was standing before an illuminated X-ray viewer. A chest X-ray was clamped over the lighted screen of the viewer, ribs projecting bars of light and shadow on her uniform. The shadows of the bones moved over her face as she turned her head toward the men. The policeman's gun was out.

"Yes, officer?" Pretending to notice the gun for the first time. "My goodness, is something wrong?"

"Stand right there, ma'am." With his free hand, Sullivan fumbled for the light switch and found it. The room lit up, Dahlia seeing details of the office she had not noticed in the darkness. The policeman looked over the room with quick snaps of his head.

"What are you doing in here?"

"Examining an X-ray, obviously."

"Is anyone else in here?"

"Not now. There was a nurse a few minutes ago."

"Blonde, about your height?"

"Yes, I think so."

"Where did she go?"

"I have no idea. What's happening?"

"We're finding out."

The security guard looked in the other rooms adjoining the X-ray lab and returned, shaking his head. The policeman stared at Dahlia. Something about her did not seem quite right to him but he couldn't identify it. He should search her and take her downstairs to the complainant. He should secure the floor. He should radio his partner. Nurses make the air white around them. He did not want to put his hands on the white uniform. He did not want to offend a nurse. He did not want to appear a fool, handcuffing a nurse.

"You'll have to come with me for a few minutes, ma'am. We'll have to ask you some questions."

She nodded. Sullivan put away his gun, but did not fasten the retaining strap. He told the security guard to check the other doors along the hall and unclipped his radio from his belt.

"Six-five, six-five."

"Yeah, John," came the reply.

"One woman in the lab. She says the perpetrator was here and left."

"Back and front are covered. Want I should come up? I'm at the third-floor landing now."

"I'll bring her down to three. Ask the complainant to stand by."

"John, the complainant advises no one should be in the lab at this time."

"I'll bring her down. Stand by."

"Who said that?" Dahlia asked hotly. "She—honestly."

"Let's go." He walked behind her to the elevator, watching her, his thumb hooked in his holster. She stood by the panel of buttons in the elevator. The doors closed.

"Three?" she said.

"I'll do it." He reached for the button with his gun hand.

Dahlia's hand snaked to the light switch. Black in the elevator. The sound of scuffling feet, rasp of a holster, a grunt of pain, a curse, thrashing, a wheezing effort to breathe, the indicator lights blinking in succession in the dark elevator.

On the third floor, Officer Sullivan's partner watched the blinking lights over the door to the elevator shaft. Three. He waited. It did not stop. Two. It stopped.

Puzzled, he pushed the "up" button, and waited while the elevator rose again. He stood before the doors. They opened.

"John? My God, John!"

Officer John Sullivan sat against the back wall of the elevator, his mouth open, his eyes wide, the hypodermic needle hanging from his neck like a banderilla.

Dahlia was running now, the long second-floor hall rocking in her vision, lights whipping overhead, past a startled orderly and around the corner into a linen room. Slipping into a light green surgical smock. Tucking her hair into a cap. Hanging the cloth mask around her neck. Down the stairs to the emergency room at the rear of the ground floor. Walking slowly now, seeing the policemen, three of them, looking around like bird dogs. Worried relatives sitting in chairs. The howls of a stabbed drunk. Victims of minor fights waiting for treatment.

A small Puerto Rican woman was sitting on a bench, sobbing into her hands. Dahlia went to her, sat down beside her, and put her arm around the plump little woman. "No tenga miedo," Dahlia said.

The woman looked up at her, tooth gold in her nut-brown face. "Julio?"

"He's going to be all right. Come, come with me. We'll walk around and get some air, you'll feel better."

"But—"

"Shush now, do as I say."

She had the woman up now, standing childlike under the comforting arm with her ruined, blown-out belly and her split shoes.

"I tole him. Ten times I tole him—"

"Don't worry now."

Walking toward the side exit of the emergency room. A cop in front of the door. A very big man, sweating in his blue coat.

"Why he don't come home to me? Why is this always to fight?"

"It's all right. Would you like to say a rosary?"

The woman's lips moved. The policeman did not move. Dahlia looked up at him.

"Officer, this lady needs some air. Could you walk her around outside for a few minutes?"

The woman's head was bowed and her lips were moving. Belt radios were crackling across the room. The alarm would be up any second now. Dead cop.

"I can't leave the door, lady. This way out is closed right now."

"Could I walk her around for a few minutes? I'm afraid she'll faint in here."

The woman was murmuring, beads between the thick brown fingers. The policeman rubbed the back of his neck. He had a big, scarred face. The woman swayed against Dahlia.

"Uh, what's your name?"

"Dr. Vizzini."

"All right, doctor." Leaning his weight on the door. Cold air in their faces. The sidewalk and the street lit in red flashes by the squadcar lights. No running, police around.

"Take deep breaths," Dahlia said. The woman bobbed her head. A yellow cab stopped. An intern got out. Dahlia caught the cabbie's attention, stopped the intern.

"You're going in, right?"

"Yeah."

"Would you walk this lady back inside? Thanks."

Blocks away now, on the Gowanus Parkway. Leaning back in the taxi, arching her neck back against the seat, eyes closed, she spoke to herself. "I really do care about her, you know."

Officer John Sullivan was not a dead cop, not yet, but he was close to death. Kneeling in the elevator, ear against Sullivan's chest, his partner could hear a confused murmuring beneath the rib cage. He pulled Sullivan around and laid him flat on the floor of the elevator. The door was trying to close and the policeman blocked it with his boot. Emma Ryan was not a head nurse for nothing. Her liver-spotted hand slammed down the stop switch on the elevator, and she bellowed once for the trauma team. Then she was kneeling over Sullivan, gray eyes flicking up and down him and her round back rising and falling as she gave him external heart massage. The officer at Sullivan's head gave mouth-to-mouth artificial respiration. The aide took over from the officer so that he could radio the alarm, but precious seconds had been lost.

A nurse arrived with a rolling stretcher. They lifted the heavy body onto it, Emma Ryan hoisting with surprising strength. She plucked the hypodermic from Sullivan's neck and handed it to a nurse. The needle had stitched through the skin, leaving two red holes, like a snake bite. Part of the dose had squirted against the elevator wall after the tip of the needle exited. It had trickled down to form a tiny pool on the floor. "Get Dr. Field, give him the hypo," Ryan snapped to the nurse. Then to another, "Get the blood sample while we're rolling, let's go."

In less than a minute, Sullivan was in a heart-lung machine in the intensive care unit, Dr. Field at his side. Armed with the results of blood test and urinalysis and with a tray of countermeasures at his elbow, Field sweated over Sullivan. He would live. They would make him live.

CHAPTER
13

ATTEMPTING TO KILL a New York City policeman is like touching a lit cigarette to an anaconda. New York's finest have a sudden and terrible wrath. They never stop hunting a cop killer, never forget, never forgive. A successful attempt on Kabakov—with the resultant diplomatic flap and heat from the Justice Department—might have resulted in news conferences by the mayor and the police commissioner, harangues and exhortations by Brooklyn borough command, and the full-time efforts of twenty to thirty detectives. Because a needle had been stuck in Officer John Sullivan's neck, more than 30,000 policemen in the five boroughs were ready to take care of business.

Kabakov, despite Rachel's objections, left the hospital bed she had set up in her spare bedroom and went to Sullivan's bedside at noon the following day. He was beyond rage and had throttled despair. Sullivan was strong enough to use an Identikit, and he had seen the woman, both full face and profile, in good light. Together, with the Identikit and a police artist, Kabakov, Sullivan, and the hospital security guard put together a composite picture that strongly resembled Dahlia Iyad. When the 3 P.M. police shift turned out, every patrolman and every detective had a copy of the composite. The early edition of the *Daily News* carried it on page two.

Six policemen from the Identification Division and four clerks from Immigration and Naturalization, each with a copy of the picture, pored over the Arab alien file.

The connection between the hospital incident and Kabakov was known only to head nurse Emma Ryan, the FBI agents working on the case, and the highest echelon of the New York Police Department. Emma Ryan could keep her mouth shut.

Washington did not want a terrorist scare and neither did the enforcement agencies. They did not want the media breathing down their necks in a case that could end as badly as this one. Police pointed out publicly that the hospital contained both narcotics and valuable radioactive elements, that the intruder might have been after these. This was not entirely satisfactory to the press, but in the crushing work-load of New York City news coverage, newsmen can easily forget yesterday's stories. Authorities hoped that in a few days the media's interest would flag.

And Dahlia hoped that in a few days Lander's anger would subside. He was enraged when he saw her likeness in the paper and knew what she had done. For a moment, she thought he would kill her. She nodded

meekly when he forbade any further attempt on
Kabakov. Fasil stayed in his room for two days.

David Kabakov's convalescence in Dr. Rachel Bauman's apartment was a strange, almost surreal time for
her. Her home was bright and oppressively orderly and
he came into it like a grizzled tomcat home from a fight
in the rain. The sizes and proportions of her rooms and
furnishings seemed all changed to Rachel with
Kabakov and Moshevsky in the place. For large men,
they did not make much noise. This was a relief to Rachel at first, and then it bothered her a little. Size and
silence are a sinister combination in nature. They are
the tools of doom.

Moshevsky was doing his best to be accommodat-
ing. After he had spooked her several times, appearing
suddenly in the kitchen with a tray, he began clearing
his throat to announce his movements. Rachel's friends
across the hall were in the Bahamas and had left their
keys with her. She installed Moshevsky in that apartment after his snoring on her couch became unbear-
able. Kabakov listened respectfully to her instructions
regarding his treatment and followed them, with the
one angry exception of the trip to Sullivan's bedside.
She and Kabakov did not talk much at first. They did
not chat at all. He seemed distracted, and Rachel did
not disturb his thoughts.

Rachel had changed since the Six-Day War, but the
change was one of degree. She had become more intensely what she was before. She had a busy practice,
an ordered life. One man, two men over the years. Two
engagements. Dinners in smart and hollow places,

where the chefs put coy signatures of garnishment on uninspired dishes—places chosen by her escorts. None of her experiences roared in her ears. Men who could have struck fire from her, she rebuffed. Her only high was the best one—working well—and that sustained her. She did much volunteer work, therapy sessions with ex-addicts, parolees, disturbed children. During the October War of 1973, she worked a double shift at Mt. Sinai Hospital in New York so that a staff doctor with more recent surgical experience could go to Israel.

Externally she was molding fast. Bloomingdale's and Bonwit Teller, Lord & Taylor and Saks were the touchstones in her Saturday rounds. She would have looked like a trim Jewish matron, expensively turned out and just a little behind the trends, if she had not spoiled the effect with defiant touches, a hint of the street. For a time she had resembled a woman fighting her thirties with her daughter's accessories. Then she didn't give a damn what she wore anymore and lapsed into quiet business dress because she didn't have to think about it. Her working hours grew longer, her apartment grew tidier and more sterile. She paid an exorbitant price for a cleaning woman who could remember to put everything back precisely as it had been before.

Now, here was Kabakov, poking through her bookshelves and gnawing on a piece of salami. He seemed to delight in examining things and not putting them back where he found them. He had not put on his slippers and he had not buttoned up his pajama jacket. She would not look at him.

Rachel was no longer so concerned about the concussion. He did not seem to worry about it at all. As his periods of dizziness grew less frequent, then abated altogether, their relationship changed. The impersonal doctor-patient attitude she had tried to maintain began to soften.

Kabakov found Rachel's company stimulating. He felt a pleasant necessity to think when talking with her. He found himself saying things that he had not realized he felt or knew. He liked to look at her. She was longlegged and given to angular positions, and she had durable good looks. Kabakov had decided to tell her about his mission, and because he liked her he found it difficult to do. For years he had guarded his tongue. He knew that he was susceptible to women, that the loneliness of his profession tempted him to talk about his problems. Rachel had given him help when he needed it, immediately and with no unnecessary questions. She was involved now and could be in danger—the reason for the assassin's visit to the radiology lab was not lost on Kabakov.

Still, it was not his sense of justice that led him to tell her, no feeling that she had a right to know. His considerations were more practical. She had a first-rate mind and he needed it. Probably one of the plotters was Abu Ali—a psychologist. Rachel was a psychiatrist. One of the terrorists was a woman. Rachel was a woman. Her knowledge of the nuances of human behavior, and the fact that, with this knowledge, she was a product of the American culture, might give her some useful insights. Kabakov believed that he could think like an Arab, but could he think like an American? *Was* there any way to think like an American? He had found them inconsistent. He thought that perhaps when the Americans had been here longer, they might have a way of thinking.

Sitting by a sunny window, he explained the situation to her as she dressed the burn on his leg. He started with the fact that a Black September cell was hidden in the Northeast, ready to strike somewhere with a large quantity of plastic explosive, probably half a ton or more. He explained from Israel's point of view the absolute necessity of his stopping them, and he hastily added the humanitarian considerations. She finished the bandaging and sat cross-legged on the rug listening. Occasionally she looked up at him to ask a question. The rest of the time he could only see the top of her bent head, the part in her hair. He wondered how she was taking it. He could not tell what she was thinking, now that the deadly struggle she had witnessed in the Middle East had come home to this safe place.

Actually, she was feeling relieved about Kabakov himself. Always she wanted to know specifics. Exactly what had been done and said—especially just before the blast at Muzi's house. She was glad to see that his answers were immediate and consistent. When questioned at the hospital about his most recent memories he had given the doctor vague replies, and Rachel could not be sure whether this was deliberate evasion or the result of head trauma. She had been handicapped in evaluating Kabakov's injury by her reluctance to ask him specifics. Now, her minute questioning served two purposes. She needed the information if she was to help him, and she wanted to test his emotional response. She was watching for the irritability under questioning that marks the Korsakoff, or amnesic-confabulatory syndrome, which frequently follows concussion.

Satisfied with his patience, pleased with his clarity, she concentrated on the information. He was more than a patient, she was more like a partner as the story was completed. Kabakov concluded with the questions that were eating at him: Who was the American? Where would the terrorists strike? When he had finished talking he felt vaguely ashamed, as though she had seen him crying.

"How old was Muzi?" she asked quietly.

"Fifty-six."

"And his last words were 'First there was the American'?"

"That's what he said." Kabakov did not see where this was leading. They had talked enough for now.

"Want an opinion?"

He nodded.

"I think there's a fair probability that your American is a non-Semitic Caucasian male, probably past his middle twenties."

"How do you know?"

"I don't know, I'm guessing. But Muzi was a middle-aged man. The person I described is what many men his age call an 'American.' Very likely, if the American he saw was black, he would have mentioned it. He would have used a racial designation. You spoke English the entire time?"

"Yes."

"If the American was a woman, very likely he would

have said 'the woman' or 'the American woman.' A man of Muzi's age and ethnic background would not think of an Arab-American or an American Jew as 'the American.' In all cases, black, female, Semitic or Latin, the word 'American' is an adjective. It's a noun only for non-minority Caucasian males. I'm sounding pedantic probably, but it's true."

Kabakov, conferring with Corley by telephone, told the FBI agent what Rachel had said.

"That narrows it down to about forty million people," Corley said. "No, listen, anything helps, for Christ's sake."

Corley's report on the search for the boat was not encouraging. Customs agents and New York City police had checked every boatyard on City Island. Nassau and Suffolk police had checked every marina on Long Island. The New Jersey state police had questioned boatyard owners along their coast. FBI agents had gone to the best boatyards—to legendary craftsmen like Rybovich, Trumpy, and Huckins—and to the lesser-known yards where craftsmen still built fine wooden boats. None of the yards could identify the fugitive craft.

"Boats, boats, boats," Rachel said to herself.

Kabakov stared out the window at the snow while Rachel fixed dinner. He was trying to remember something, going at it indirectly, the way he would use peripheral vision to see in the dark. The technique employed in blowing up Muzi teased Kabakov ceaselessly. Where had it happened before? One of the thousands of reports that had crossed his desk in the past five or six years had mentioned a bomb in a refrigerator. He remembered that the report had an old-style jacket, the manila kind, bound along the spine. That meant he had seen it before 1972, when the Mossad changed the bindings to facilitate micro-filming. One other flash came to him. A memo on booby-trap techniques issued to commando units on his orders years ago. The memo had explained mercury switches, then in fashion among the fedayeen, with an addendum on electrical appliances.

He was composing a cable to Mossad headquarters with the scraps of information he recalled when quite suddenly he remembered. Syria 1971. A Mossad agent was lost in an explosion at a house in Damascus. The charge had not been heavy, but the refrigerator was shattered. A coincidence? Kabakov called the Israeli consulate and dictated the cable. The cable clerk pointed out that it was 4 A.M. in Tel Aviv.

"It's 0200 Zulu all over the world, my friend," Kabakov said. "We never close. Get that cable out."

A cold December drizzle stung Moshevsky's face and neck as he waited on the corner to flag a cab. He let three Dodges pass and finally spotted what he was looking for, a big Checker barging through the morning rush. He wanted the extra room so Kabakov would not have to bend his sore leg. Moshevsky told the driver to stop in front of Rachel's apartment building in the middle of the block. Kabakov hobbled out and climbed in beside him. He gave the address of the Israeli consulate.

Kabakov had rested as Rachel prescribed. Now he would roll. He could have called Ambassador Tell from the apartment, but his business required the safest of telephones—one equipped with a scrambler. He had decided to ask Tel Aviv to suggest that the U.S. State Department approach the Russians for help. Kabakov's request must be cleared through Tell. Going to the Russians was not a pleasant thought from the standpoint of his professional pride. At the moment, Kabakov could not afford professional pride. He knew that and accepted it, but he did not like it.

Since the spring of 1971, the Soviet Komitet Gosudarstvennoy Bezopastveny, the infamous KGB, has had a special section providing technical assistance to Black September through Al Fatah field intelligence. This was the source Kabakov wanted to tap.

He knew the Russians would never help Israel, but in light of the new East-West detente, he thought they might cooperate with the United States. The request to Moscow must come from the Americans, but Kabakov could not suggest the move without the approval of Tel Aviv. Precisely because he hated so much to ask, he would sign the message to Tel Aviv himself, instead of putting the primary responsibility on Tell.

Kabakov decided to swear that the plastic was Russian, whether it was or not. Maybe the Americans would swear to it too. That ought to put the onus on the Russians.

Why such a large quantity of explosives? Did the amount signify some special opportunity the Arabs had in this country? On that point the KGB might be of help.

The Black September cell in America would be sealed off now, even from the guerrilla leadership in

Beirut. It would be hell to find. The heat from the woman's picture would drive the terrorists far down in their burrow. They had to be close by—they had reacted too fast after the explosion. Damn Corley for not staking out the hospital. Damn that pipe-smoking son of a bitch.

What had been planned in the Black September headquarters in Beirut, and who had taken part? Najeer. Najeer was dead. The woman. She was hiding. Abu Ali? Ali was dead. There was no way to be positive that Ali was in on the plot, but it was very likely, for he was one of the few men in the world Najeer trusted. Ali was a psychologist. But then Ali was many things. Why might they need a psychologist? Ali would never be able to tell anyone.

Who was the American? Who was the Lebanese who brought in the explosives? Who blew up Muzi? Was it the woman he saw in Beirut—the woman who came to the hospital to kill him?

The taxi driver pushed the big car to the limit the wet pavement would allow, slamming over the potholes and nosediving to a halt at the first red light. Moshevsky, with a resigned expression, climbed out and got into the front seat beside the driver. "Take it slowly. Neither bang nor jar," he said.

"Why?" the driver said. "Time is money, buddy."

Moshevsky leaned toward him confidentially. "Why is to keep me from breaking your fucking neck, that's why."

Kabakov looked absently at the crowds hurrying along the sidewalk. Midafternoon and already the light was failing. What a place. A place with more Jews than

Tel Aviv. He wondered how the Jewish immigrants had felt, crowded on the ships, herded through Ellis Island, some of them even losing their names as semiliterate immigration officials scrawled "Smith" and "Jones" on the entry papers. Spilled from Ellis Island into a bleak afternoon on this cold rock where nothing was free except what they could give each other. Broken families, men alone.

What happened here then to a man alone who died before he could make a place and send for his family? A man alone? Who sat *shivah*—the neighbors?

The plastic madonna on the dashboard of the taxi caught Kabakov's attention, and his thoughts shifted guiltily back to the problem that plagued him. Closing his eyes against the cold afternoon, he started over from the beginning, with the mission to Beirut that had ultimately brought him here.

Kabakov had been briefed minutely before the raid. The Israelis knew Najeer and Abu Ali would be in the apartment house and that other Black September officers might be present. Kabakov had studied the dossiers on guerrilla leaders known to be in Lebanon until he knew what was in them by heart. He could see the folders now, stacked alphabetically on his desk.

First, Abu Ali. Abu Ali, killed in the Beirut raid, had no relatives, no family except his wife, and she, too, was dead. He—*a man alone!* Before the thought was completed, Kabakov was rapping on the plastic shield that separated him from the driver. Moshevsky slid open the partition.

"Tell him to step on it."

"So now you want me to step on it," the driver said over his shoulder.

Moshevsky showed the man his teeth.

"So I'm stepping," the driver said.

The Israeli consulate and mission to the United Nations share a white brick building at 800 Second Avenue in Manhattan. The security system is well thought-out and thorough. Kabakov fumed in the confines of the holding room, then went quickly to the communications center.

His coded cable to Tel Aviv regarding Abu Ali was acknowledged in less than a minute. It set delicate machinery in motion. Within fifteen minutes, a stocky young man left Mossad headquarters for Lod Airport. He would fly to Nicosia, Cyprus, switch passports and catch the next flight into Beirut. His first business in the Lebanese capital would be to enjoy a cup of coffee in a small café with an excellent view of the central Beirut police station, where, hopefully, waiting for the statutory period in the police property room was a numbered carton containing the effects of Abu Ali. Now there was someone to claim them.

Kabakov was on the scrambler with Tell for half an hour. The ambassador expressed no surprise at Kabakov's request for roundabout Russian aid. Kabakov had the feeling that Yoachim Tell had never been surprised in his life. He thought he had detected a bit of extra warmth in the ambassador's voice as he said goodbye. Was it sympathy? Kabakov reddened and stalked toward the door of the communications center. The telex in the corner rattled and the clerk's voice stopped him in the doorway. An answer was coming to his query about the Syrian bombing in 1971.

The bombing took place August 15, the telex said. It occurred during Al Fatah's major recruiting effort in Damascus that year. Three organizers were known to have been in Damascus at that time:

—Fakhri el-Amari, who led the team that assassinated Jordanian prime minister Wasfi el-Tel and drank his blood. Amari was believed to be in Algeria at the present time. Inquiries were under way.

—Abdel Kadir, who once bazookaed an Israeli school bus; killed when his bomb factory near Cheikh Saad blew up in 1973. The telex added that doubtless Kabakov would not need his memory refreshed on Kadir's demise, as he had been present at the time.

—Muhammad Fasil, alias Yusuf Halef, alias Sammar Tufiq. Believed to be the architect of the Munich atrocity and one of the men most wanted by the Mossad. Fasil was last reported operating in Syria. The Mossad believed him to be in Damascus at the time of Kabakov's Beirut raid, but recent reports, not yet confirmed, placed him in Beirut within the past three weeks. Israeli intelligence was pressing sources in Beirut and elsewhere on Fasil's whereabouts.

Photos of el-Amari and Fasil were being transmitted via satellite to the Israeli embassy in Washington to be forwarded to Kabakov. The negatives would follow. Kabakov winced at that. If they were sending negatives, the pictures must be poor—too poor to be very useful when transmitted electronically. Still, it was something. He wished that he had waited to ask about the Russians. "Muhammad Fasil," Kabakov muttered. "Yes. This is your kind of show. I hope you came personally this time."

He went back into the rain for the trip to Brooklyn. Moshevsky and the trio of Israelis under his direction combed the Cobble Hill bars and short-order restaurants and klabash games looking for traces of Muzi's Greek assistant. Perhaps the Greek had seen the American. Kabakov knew the FBI had covered this ground, but his own men did not look like police, they fit better into the ethnic mix of the neighborhood and they could eavesdrop in several languages. Kabakov stationed himself in Muzi's office, examining the incredible rat's nest of papers the importer had left, in the hope that he could find some scrap of information about the American or about Muzi's contacts in the Middle East. A name, a place, anything. If there was one person between Istanbul and the Gulf of Aden who knew the nature of the Black September mission in the United States, and Kabakov could find out his name, he would kidnap that person or die trying. By mid-evening he had discovered that Muzi kept at least three sets of books, but he had learned little else. Wearily, he returned to Rachel's apartment.

Rachel was waiting up for him. She seemed somehow different and, looking at her, he was no longer weary. Their separation during the day had made something clear to both of them.

Very gently they became lovers. And their encounters thereafter began and ended with great gentleness, as though they feared they might tear the fragile tent their feelings built in air around their bed.

"I'm silly," she said once, resting. "I don't care if I'm silly."

"I certainly don't care if you're silly," Kabakov said. "Want a cigar?"

Ambassador Tell's call came at seven A.M., while Kabakov was in the shower. Rachel opened the bathroom door and called his name into the steam. Kabakov came out quickly, while Rachel was still in the doorway. He wrapped a towel around himself and padded to the telephone. Rachel began to work very hard on her fingernails.

Kabakov was uneasy. If the ambassador had an answer on the Russians, he would not have used this telephone. Tell's voice was calm and very businesslike.

"Major, we've gotten an inquiry about you from *The New York Times.* Also some uncomfortable questions about the incident on the *Leticia.* I'd like for you to come down here. I'll be free a little after three, if that's convenient."

"I'll be there."

Kabakov found the *Times* on Rachel's doormat. *Page one:* ISRAELI FOREIGN MINISTER IN WASHINGTON FOR MIDEAST TALKS. *Read that later.* COST OF LIVING. GM RECALLS TRUCKS. *Page two. Oh, hell. Here it is:* ARAB TORTURED HERE BY ISRAELI AGENTS, CONSUL ALLEGES
By Margaret Leeds Finch

A Lebanese seaman was questioned under torture by Israeli agents aboard a Libyan merchant vessel in

New York harbor last week prior to his arrest by U.S. customs officials on smuggling charges, the Lebanese consul said Tuesday night.

In a strongly worded protest to the U.S. State Department, Consul Yusuf el-Amedi said first mate Mustapha Fawzi of the freighter *Leticia* was beaten and subjected to electric shock by two men who identified themselves as Israelis. He said he did not know what the agents were after and refused to comment on smuggling conspiracy charges pending against Fawzi.

An Israeli spokesman emphatically denied the allegations, saying the charge was "a clumsy attempt to arouse anti-Israeli feeling."

Department of Corrections physician Carl Gillette said he examined Fawzi at the Federal House of Detention on West Street and found no evidence of a beating.

Consul Amedi said Fawzi was attacked by Major David Kabakov of the Israeli Defense Force and another unidentified man. Kabakov is attached to the Israeli embassy in Washington.

The *Leticia* was impounded . . .

Kabakov skimmed the rest of the article. The customs authorities had kept their mouths shut on the investigation of the *Leticia* and the newspaper did not have the Muzi connection yet, thank God.

"You are being ordered home, officially," Ambassador Tell said.

The corner of Kabakov's mouth twitched. He felt as though he had been kicked in the stomach.

Tell moved the papers on his desk with the tip of his pen. "The arrest of Mustapha Fawzi was reported routinely to the Lebanese consul, as Fawzi is a Lebanese citizen. A lawyer was provided by the consulate. The lawyer apparently is acting on orders from Beirut and he's playing Fawzi like a calliope. The Libyans were informed, since the vessel is of Libyan registry. Once your name came into it, I have no doubt Al Fatah was alerted and so was Colonel Khadafy, the enlightened Libyan statesman. I haven't seen the deposition supposedly authored by Fawzi, but I understand it's very colorful. Very graphic anatomically. Did you hurt him?"

"I didn't have to."

"The Lebanese and the Libyans will continue to protest until you are withdrawn. Probably the Syrians will join it too. Khadafy owns more than one Arab diplomat. And I doubt that any of them know why you are really here, with the possible exception of Khadafy."

"What does the U.S. State Department say?" Kabakov felt sick inside.

"They don't want a diplomatic uproar over this. They want to quash it. Officially, you are no longer welcome here as an arm of Israel."

"The fat-faced idiots! They deserve—" Kabakov shut his mouth with a snap.

"As you know, Major, the United Nations entertains the U.A.R. motion for a censure of Israel this week over the action against the fedayeen camps in

Syria last month. This matter should not be exacerbated by another disturbance now."

"What if I resign my commission and get an ordinary passport? Then Tel Aviv could disown me if it became necessary."

Ambassador Tell was not listening. "It's tempting to think that if the Arabs succeed in this project, God forbid, the Americans would be enraged and would redouble their support for Israel," he said. "You and I both know that won't happen. The salient fact will be that the atrocity happened *because* the United States has helped Israel. Because they got involved in another dirty little war. Indochina has made them sick of involvement, just as it did the French, and understandably so. I wouldn't be surprised to see Al Fatah strike in Paris if the French sell us Mirages.

"Anyway, if it happens here, the Arab governments will denounce Al Fatah for the four hundredth time and Khadafy will give Al Fatah some millions of dollars. The United States can't afford to be angry at the Arabs too long. It sounds horrible, but the U.S. will find it convenient to blame only Al Fatah. This country consumes too much oil for it to be otherwise.

"If the Arabs succeed, and we have tried to stop them, then it won't be quite so bad for us. If we stop helping, even at State Department request, and the Arabs are successful, then we are still at fault.

"The Americans won't ask the Russians for any intelligence from the Middle East, by the way. The State Department gave us the news that the Middle East is a 'sphere of continuing East-West tension' and no such request is possible. They don't want to admit to the

Russians that the CIA can't get the information themselves. You were right to try it anyway, David.

"And now there is this." Tell passed Kabakov a
cable from Mossad headquarters. "The information
has also been relayed to you in New York."

The cable reported that Muhammad Fasil was seen
in Beirut the day after Kabakov's raid. He had a wound
on his cheek similar to the one described by Mustapha
Fawzi, the first mate of the *Leticia*.

"Muhammad Fasil," Tell said quietly, "the worst
one of all."

"I'm not going—"

"Wait, wait, David. This is a time for utter frankness. Is there anyone you know, in the Mossad or elsewhere, who might be better equipped to deal with this
matter than you?"

"No sir." Kabakov wanted to say that if he had not
taken the tape in Beirut, had not questioned Fawzi, if
he had not searched the cabin on the ship, checked the
ship's books, caught Muzi at a disadvantage, they
would know nothing at all. All he said was "No sir."

"That's our consensus also." Tell's telephone rang.
"Yes? Five minutes, very well." He turned back to
Kabakov. "Major, would you please report to the conference room on the second floor? And you might
straighten your tie."

Kabakov's collar was cutting into his neck. He felt
as though he were strangling, and he paused outside
the conference room to get hold of himself. Maybe the
military attaché was about to read him his orders to go
home. Nothing would be accomplished by screaming
in the man's face. What was Tell talking about anyway,

what consensus? If he had to go back to Israel he would by God go, and the guerrillas in Syria and Lebanon would wish to hell he was back in the United States.

Kabakov opened the door. The thin man at the window turned.

"Come in, Major Kabakov," said the foreign minister of Israel.

In 15 minutes Kabakov was back in the hall, trying to suppress a smile. An embassy car took him to National Airport. He arrived at the El Al terminal at Kennedy International 20 minutes before the scheduled departure of Flight 601 to Tel Aviv. Margaret Leeds Finch of the *Times* was lurking near the counter. She asked him questions while he checked his bag and while he went through the metal detector. He answered in polite monosyllables. She followed him into the gate, waving her press pass at the airline officials, and dogged him down the very boarding ramp to the door of the plane where she was politely but firmly stopped by El Al security men.

Kabakov passed through first class, through the tourist section, back to the galley where hot dinners were being loaded aboard. With a smile at the stewardess, he stepped out the open door into the elevated bed of the catering truck. The bed whirred downward, and the truck returned to its garage. Kabakov climbed out and entered the car where Corley and Moshevsky were waiting.

Kabakov had been officially withdrawn from the United States. Unofficially, he had returned.

He must be very careful now. If he fouled up, his country would lose a great deal of face. Kabakov wondered what had been said at the foreign minister's luncheon with the Secretary of State. He would never know the details, but clearly the situation had been discussed at some length. His instructions were the same as before: stop the Arabs. His team was being withdrawn, with the exception of Moshevsky. Kabakov was to be an ex officio advisor to the Americans. He felt sure the last part of his instructions had not been discussed over lunch; if it was necessary to do more than advise, he was to leave no unfriendly witnesses.

There was a strained silence in the car on the way back into Manhattan. Finally Corley broke it. "I'm sorry this happened, old buddy."

"I am not your old buddy, old buddy," Kabakov said calmly.

"Customs saw that piece of plastic and they were screaming to bust those guys. We had to bust them."

"Never mind, Corley. I'm here to help you, old buddy. Here, look at this." Kabakov handed him one of the pictures given him as he left the embassy. It was still wet from the darkroom.

"Who is it?"

"Muhammad Fasil. Here, read the file."

Corley whistled. "Munich! How can you be sure he's the one? The *Leticia* crew won't identify him. On advice of counsel, you can bet on that."

"They won't have to identify him. Read on. Fasil was in Beirut the day after our raid. We should have gotten him with the others, but we didn't expect him to be there. He got a bullet stripe on the cheek. The Lebanese on the freighter had a scab across his cheek. Fawzi said so."

The picture had been taken in a Damascus café in poor light and it was fuzzy.

"If you've got the negative, we can improve it with the NASA computer," Corley said. "The way they enhance the pictures from the Mariner project." Corley paused. "Has anybody from State talked to you?"

"No."

"But your own people have talked to you."

"Corley, 'my own people' always talk to me."

"About working through us. They made it clear you're going to help with the thinking and we're stuck with the work, right?"

"Right. You bet, old buddy."

The car dropped Kabakov and Moshevsky at the Israeli mission. They waited until it was out of sight and took a cab to Rachel's building.

"Corley knows where we are anyway, doesn't he?" Moshevsky said.

"Yes, but I don't want the son of a bitch to think he can drop by whenever he feels like it," Kabakov said. As he spoke, he was not thinking about Corley or Rachel's apartment at all. He was thinking about Fasil, Fasil, Fasil.

Muhammad Fasil was also deep in thought as he lay on his bed in Lander's ground-floor guestroom. Fasil had a passion for Swiss chocolates, and he was eating some now. In the field he ate the rough fare of the fedayeen, but in private he liked to rub Swiss chocolates between his fingers until the chocolate melted.

Then he licked the chocolate off his fingers. Fasil had a number of little private pleasures of this kind.

He had a certain amount of surface passion and a range of visible emotion that was wide and not deep. But he was deep, all right, and cold, and those cold depths held sightless, savage things that brushed and bit one another in the dark. He had learned about himself very early. At the same time he had taught his schoolmates about himself and then he was left alone. Fasil had splendid reflexes and wiry strength. He had no fear and no mercy, but he did have malice. Fasil was living proof that physiognomy is a false science. He was slim and fairly good-looking. He was a monster.

It was curious how only the most primitive and the keenest found him out. The fedayeen admired him from a distance and praised his behavior under fire, not recognizing that his coolness was something other than courage. But he could not afford to mix with the most illiterate and ignorant among them, the ones gnawing mutton and gobbling chickpeas around a fire. These superstitious men had no calluses on their instincts. They soon became uneasy with him, and as quickly as manners permitted they moved away. If he was to lead them all someday, then he must solve that problem.

Abu Ali, too. That clever little man, a psychologist who made a long, circuitous trip through his own mind, had recognized Fasil. Once, over coffee, Ali had described one of his own earliest memories—a lamb walking around in the house. Then he asked Fasil his earliest memory. Fasil had replied that he remembered his mother killing a chicken by holding its head in the fire. After Fasil had spoken, he realized that this was not an idle conversation at all. Fortunately, Abu Ali had not been able to hurt Fasil in the eyes of Hafez Najeer, for Najeer was strange enough himself.

The deaths of Najeer and Ali had left a gap in the leadership of Black September that Fasil intended to fill. For this reason, he was anxious to get back to Lebanon. In the internecine slaughterhouse of fedayeen politics, a rival might grow too strong in Fasil's absence. He had enjoyed considerable prestige in the movement after the Munich massacre. Had not President Khadafy himself embraced Fasil when the surviving guerrillas arrived in Tripoli to a hero's welcome? Fasil thought the ruler of Libya had embraced the men who had actually been at Munich with somewhat greater fervor than he embraced Fasil, who planned the mission, but Khadafy had definitely been impressed. And had not Khadafy given $5 million to Al Fatah as a reward for Munich? That was another result of his efforts. If the Super Bowl strike was successful, if Fasil claimed credit for it, he would be the most prestigious guerrilla in the world, even better known than that idealist Guevara. Fasil believed that he could then count on support from Khadafy—and the Libyan treasury— in taking over Black September, and eventually he might replace Yasir Arafat as maximum leader of Al Fatah. Fasil was well aware that all those who had tried to replace Arafat were dead. He needed lead time to set up a secure base, for when he made his move to take over, Arafat's assassins would come.

None of his ends would be served by getting himself killed in New Orleans. Originally, he had not intended to take part in the action, anymore than he had at Munich. He was not afraid to do it, but he was fixed on the thought of what he might become if he lived. If the trouble on the *Leticia* had not occurred, he would still be in Lebanon.

Fasil could see that the odds of his getting away clean from New Orleans were not good under the current plan. His job was to provide muscle and covering fire at New Orleans Lakefront Airport while the bomb was being attached to the blimp. It was not possible to clamp the nacelle to the blimp at some other location— the ground crew and the mooring mast were necessary because the airship must be held rock-steady while the work was going on.

Lander might be able to fool the ground crew for a few vital seconds by claiming the nacelle contained some esoteric piece of television equipment, but the ruse would not last long. There would be violence, and after the takeoff Fasil would be left in the open on the airfield, possibly in a converging ring of police. Fasil did not think his role worthy of his abilities. Ali Hassan would have performed this function if he had not been killed on the freighter. It was certainly not a job that would justify the loss of Muhammad Fasil.

If he was not trapped at the takeoff site, the best chance of escape was an air hijack to a friendly country. But at Lakefront Airport, a private facility on the shore of Lake Pontchartrain, there were no long-range passenger flights. He might take over a private aircraft with range enough to reach Cuba, but that would not do. Cuba could not be depended upon to shield him. Fidel Castro was tough on hijackers, and in the face of an enraged America he might hand Fasil over. Besides, he would not have the advantage of a planeload of hostages, and no private plane would be fast enough to escape the American fighters screaming into the sky from a half-dozen coastal bases.

No, he had no desire to fall into the Gulf of Mexico in some smoke-filled cockpit, knowing it was all over as the water rushed up to smash him. That would be stupid. Fasil was fanatic enough to die gladly if it were necessary to his satisfactions, but he was not willing to die stupidly.

Even if he could slip across the city to New Orleans International, there were no commercial flights with range enough to reach Libya without refueling, and the probabilities of making a successful refueling stop were low.

The House of War would be enraged as it had not been since Pearl Harbor. Fasil recalled the words of the Japanese admiral after the strike at Pearl: "I fear we have awakened a sleeping giant and filled him with a terrible resolve."

They would take him when he stopped to refuel—if he ever got off the ground. Very likely air traffic would be frozen within minutes of the blast.

It was clear to Fasil that his place was in Beirut, leading the new army of front-fighters who would flock to him after this triumph. It would be a disservice to the cause for him to die in New Orleans.

Now. Lander clearly had the qualifications to carry out the technical end. Having seen him, Fasil was confident that he was willing to do it. Dahlia appeared to have control of him. There simply remained the problem of last-minute muscle at the airport. If Fasil could arrange for that, then there was no need for his actual presence. He could be waiting in Beirut with a microphone in his hand. A satellite link to New York would have his picture and his statement on worldwide television in minutes. He could hold a news conference. He would be in a stroke the most formidable Arab in the world.

All that would be required at the New Orleans airport was a couple of skilled gunmen, imported at the last minute, under Dahlia's command and ignorant of their mission until just before they went into action. That could be accomplished. Fasil had made up his mind. He would see the nacelle through the final stages of its construction, would see that it got to New Orleans. Then he would leave.

To Fasil, Lander's progress with the huge bomb was maddeningly slow. Lander had asked for the maximum amount of explosives the blimp could carry, with shrapnel, under ideal conditions. He had not really expected to get as much as he asked for. Now that it was here he intended to take full advantage of it. The problem was weight and weather—the weather on January 12 in New Orleans. The blimp could fly in any conditions in which football could be played, but rain meant extra weight and New Orleans had received 77 inches of rain in the past year, far more than the national average. Even a dew covering the blimp's great skin weighed 700 pounds, detracting that much from its lifting power. Lander had calculated the lift very carefully, and he would be straining the blimp to the utmost when it rose into the sky carrying its deadly egg. On a clear day, with sunshine, he could count on some help from the "superheat" effect, added lift gained when the helium inside the bag was hotter than the outside air. But unless he was prepared, rain could ruin everything. By the time he was ready to take off, some of the ground crew would almost certainly have been shot and there could be no delay in getting airborne. The blimp must fly, and fly immediately. To allow for the possibility of rain, he had split the nacelle, so that part of it could be left behind in bad weather. It was a pity that Aldrich did not use a surplus Navy dirigible instead of the smaller blimp, Lander reflected. He had flown Navy airships when they carried six tons of ice, great sheets of it, that slid down the sides and fell away in a glittering, crashing cascade when the dirigible reached warmer air. But those long-extinct ships had been eight times the size of the Aldrich blimp.

Balance must be close to perfect with either the entire nacelle or three-quarters of it. That meant having optional mounting points on the frame. These changes had taken time, but not so much time as Lander had feared. He had a little over a month before the Super Bowl. Of that month he would lose most of the last two weeks flying football games. That left him about 17 working days. There was time for one more refinement.

He set up on his workbench a thick sheet of fiberglass five inches by seven and one-half inches in size. The sheet was reinforced with metal mesh and curved in two planes, like a section of watermelon rind. He warmed a piece of plastic explosive and rolled it into a slab of the same size, carefully increasing the thickness of the plastic from the center toward the ends.

Lander attached the slab of plastic to the convex side of the fiberglass sheet. The device now looked like a warped book with a cover on only one side. Smoothed over the plastic explosive were three layers of rubber sheeting cut from a sickroom mattress cover. On top of these went a piece of light canvas bristling with .177 caliber rifle darts. The darts sat on their flat bottoms, glued to the canvas closer together than the nails in a fakir's bed. As the dart-studded canvas was pulled tight around the convex surface of the device, the sharp tips of the darts diverged slightly. This divergence was the purpose of curving the device. It was necessary if the darts were to spread out in flight in a predetermined pattern. Lander had marked out the ballistics with great care. The shape of the darts should stabilize them in flight just like the steel flechettes used in Vietnam.

Now he attached three more layers of dart-covered canvas. In all, the four layers contained 944 darts. At a range of 60 yards, Lander calculated, they would riddle an area of 1,000 square feet, one dart striking in each 1.07 square feet with the velocity of a high-powered rifle bullet. Nothing could live in that strike zone. And this was only the small test model. The real one, the one that would hang beneath the blimp, was 317 times bigger in surface area and weight and carried an average of 3.5 darts for every one of the 80,985 persons Tulane Stadium could seat.

Fasil came into the workshop as Lander was attaching the outside cover, a sheet of fiberglass the same thickness as the skin of the nacelle.

Lander did not speak to him.

Fasil appeared to pay little attention to the object on the workbench, but he recognized what it was, and he was appalled. The Arab looked around the workshop for several minutes, careful not to touch anything. A technician himself, trained in Germany and North Vietnam, Fasil could not help admiring the neatness and economy with which the big nacelle was constructed.

"This material is hard to weld," he said, tapping the Reynolds alloy tubing. "I see no heliarc equipment, did you farm out the work?"

"I borrowed some equipment from the company over the weekend."

"The frame is stress-relieved as well. Now that, Mr. Lander, is a conceit." Fasil intended this as a joking compliment to Lander's craftsmanship. He had decided his duty lay in getting along with the American.

"If the frame warped and cracked the fiberglass shell, someone might see the darts as we rolled it out of the truck," Lander said in a monotone.

"I thought you would be packing in the plastic by now, with only a month remaining."

"Not ready yet. I have to test something first."

"Perhaps I can be of assistance."

"Do you know the explosive index of this material?"

Fasil shook his head ruefully. "It's very new."

"Have you ever seen any of it detonated?"

"No. I was instructed that it is more potent than C-4. You saw what it did to Muzi's apartment."

"I saw a hole in the wall and I can't tell enough from that. The most common mistake in making an antipersonnel device is putting the shrapnel too close to the charge, so the shrapnel loses its integrity in the explosion. Think about that, Fasil. If you don't know it you should know it. Read this field manual and you will find out all about it. I'll translate the big words for you. I don't want these darts fragmented in the blast. I am not interested in merely filling 75 institutes for the deaf. I don't know how much buffer is necessary between the darts and the plastic to protect them."

"But look at how much is in a claymore-type device—"

"That's no indication. I'm dealing with longer ranges and infinitely more explosive. Nobody has ever built one this big before. A claymore is the size of a schoolbook. This is the size of a lifeboat."

"How will the nacelle be positioned when it is detonated?"

"Over the 50-yard line at precisely 100 feet altitude, lined up lengthwise with the field. You can see how the curve of the nacelle conforms to the curve of the stadium."

"So—"

"So, Fasil, I have to also be sure that the darts will disperse in the correct arc, rather than blowing out in big lumps. I've got some leeway inside the skin. I can exaggerate the curves if I have to. I'll find out about the buffer and about the dispersal when we detonate this," Lander said, patting the device on his workbench.

"It's got at least a half-kilo of plastic in it."

"Yes."

"You can't set it off without drawing the authorities."

"Yes, I can."

"You would have no time to examine the results before the authorities came."

"Yes, I will."

"This is—" He nearly said "madness," but stopped himself in time. "This is very rash."

"Don't worry about it, A-rab."

"May I check your calculations?" Fasil hoped he could devise a way to stop the experiment.

"Help yourself. Remember, this is not a scale model of the side of the nacelle. It just contains the two compound curves used in dispersing the shrapnel."

"I'll remember, Mr. Lander."

Fasil spoke privately with Dahlia as she was carrying out the trash. "Talk to him," he said in Arabic. "We know the thing will work as it is. This business of the test is not an acceptable risk. He will lose everything."

"It might not work perfectly," she replied in English. "It must be without flaw."

"It does not have to be *that* perfect."

"For him, it does. For me too."

"For the purpose of the mission, for what we set out to do, it will work adequately the way it is."

"Comrade Fasil, pushing the button in that gondola on January 12 will be the last act of Michael Lander's life. He won't see what comes after. Neither will I, if he needs me to fly with him. We have to *know* what's coming after, do you understand that?"

"I understand that you are beginning to sound more like him than like a front-fighter."

"Then you are of limited intelligence."

"In Lebanon I would kill you for that."

"We're a long way from Lebanon, Comrade Fasil. If either of us ever sees Lebanon again, you may try at your convenience."

CHAPTER

14

RACHEL BAUMAN, M.D., sat behind a desk at Halfway House in the South Bronx, waiting. The addict rehabilitation center held many memories for her. She looked around the bright little room with its amateurish paint job and pickup furniture and thought about some of the ravaged, desperate minds she had tried to reach, the things that she had listened to, in her volunteer work here. It was because of the memories the room evoked that she had chosen this place to meet with Eddie Stiles.

There was a light rap on the door and Stiles came in, a slight, balding man looking around with quick glances. He had shaved for the occasion. A patch of tissue was stuck to a nick on his jaw. Stiles smiled awkwardly and fiddled with his cap.

"Sit down, Eddie. You're looking well."

"Never better, Dr. Bauman."

"How's the tugboat business?"

"To tell you the truth, dull. But I like it, I like it, understand," he added quickly. "You done me a good turn getting me that job."

"I didn't get you that job, Eddie. I just asked the man to look you over."

"Yeah, well, I'd never have got it otherwise. How's with you? You look kind of different, I mean like you feel good. What am I talking, you're the doctor." He laughed self-consciously.

Rachel could see that he had gained weight. When she met him three years ago, he had just been arrested for smuggling cigarettes up from Norfolk in a 40-foot trawler, trying to feed a $75 a day heroin habit. Eddie had spent many months at Halfway House, many hours talking to Rachel. She had worked with him when he was screaming.

"What did you want to see me about, Dr. Bauman? I mean, I'm glad to see you and all and if you was wondering if I'm clean—"

"I know you're clean, Eddie. I want to ask you for some advice." She had never before presumed on a professional relationship, and it disturbed her to do so now. Stiles noted this instantly. His native wariness warred with the respect and warmth he felt for her.

"It's got nothing to do with you," she said. "Let me lay it out for you and see what you think."

Stiles relaxed a little. He was not being asked to commit himself about anything immediately.

"I need to find a boat, Eddie. A certain boat. A funny-business boat."

His face revealed nothing. "I told you I would tugboat and that's all I do is tugboat, you know that."

"I know that. But you know a lot of people, Eddie. I

don't know any people who carry on funny business in boats. I need your help."

"We level with each other, always have, right?"

"Yes."

"You never blabbed none of the stuff I told you when I was on the couch, right?"

"Nope."

"Okay, you tell me the question and who wants to know."

Rachel hesitated. The truth was the truth. Nothing else would do. She told him.

"The feds already asked me," Stiles said when she had finished. "This guy comes right on board in front of everybody to ask me, which I don't appreciate too much. I know they asked some other—guys of my acquaintance."

"And you told them zip."

Stiles smiled and reddened. "I didn't know anything to tell them, you know? To tell you the truth I didn't concentrate too hard. I guess nobody else did either, they're still asking around, I hear."

Rachel waited, she did not push him. The little man tugged at his collar, stroked his chin, deliberately put his hands back in his lap.

"You want to talk to the guy who owns this boat? I don't mean you yourself, that wouldn't be—I mean, your friends want to."

"Right."

"Just talk?"

"Just talk."

"For money? I mean, not for me, Dr. Bauman. Don't think that, for God's sake, I owe you enough already. But I mean, if I was to know some guy, very few things are free. I got a couple hundred, you're welcome, but it might—"

"Don't worry about the money," she said.

"Tell me again from where the Coast Guard first spotted the boat and who did what."

Stiles listened, nodding and asking an occasional question. "Frankly, maybe I can't help you at all, Dr. Bauman," he said finally. "But some things occur to me. I'll listen around."

"Very carefully."

"You know it."

CHAPTER
15

HARRY LOGAN DROVE his battered pickup along the perimeter of United Coal Company's heavy equipment compound on his hourly watchman's round, looking down the rows of bulldozers and dirt buggies. He was supposed to watch for thieves and conservation-minded saboteurs, but none ever came. Nobody was within miles of the place. All was well, he could slip away.

He turned onto a dirt track that followed the giant scar the strip mine had gouged in the Pennsylvania hills, red dust rising behind the pickup. The scar was eight miles long and two miles wide, and it was growing longer as the great earthmoving machines chewed down the hills. Twenty-four hours a day, six days a week, two of the largest earthmovers in the world slammed their maws against the hillsides like hyenas opening a belly. They stopped for nothing except the Sabbath, the president of United Coal being a very religious man.

This was Sunday, when nothing but dustdevils moved on the raw wasteland. It was the day when Harry Logan made a little extra money. He was a scavenger and he worked in the condemned area that would shortly be uprooted by the mining. Each Sunday Logan left his post at the equipment compound and drove to the small abandoned village on a hill in the path of the earthmovers.

The peeling houses stood empty, smelling of urine left by the vandals who smashed the windows. The householders had taken everything they thought was valuable when they moved out, but their eye for salable scrap was not so keen as Logan's. He was a natural scavenger. There was good lead to be found in the old-fashioned gutters and plumbing. Electrical switches could be pried from the walls and there were showerheads and copper wire. He sold these things to his son-in-law's junkyard. Logan was anxious to make a good haul on this Sunday because only an eighth of a mile of woods remained between the village and the strip mine. In two weeks the village would be devoured.

He backed his truck into the garage beside a house. It was very quiet when he turned off the motor. There was only the wind, whistling through the scattered, windowless houses. Logan was loading a stack of wallboard into his truck when he heard the airplane.

The red four-seater Cessna made two low passes over the village. Looking downhill through the trees, Logan saw it settle toward the dirt road in the strip mine. If Logan had appreciated such things, he would have enjoyed watching a superb cross-wind landing; a sideslip, a flare-out, and the little plane rolling smoothly with dust blowing off to one side.

He scratched his head and his behind. Now what could they want? Company inspectors maybe. He could say he was checking the village. The plane had rolled out of sight behind a thick grove. Logan worked his way cautiously down through the trees. When he could see the airplane again it was empty, and the wheels were chocked. He heard voices through the trees to his left and walked quietly in that direction. A big empty barn was over there with a three-acre feedlot beside it. Logan knew very well that it contained nothing worth stealing. Watching from the edge of the woods, he could see two men and a woman in the feedlot, ankle deep in bright green winter wheat.

One of the men was tall and wore sunglasses and a ski jacket. The other was darker and had a mark on his face. The men unrolled a long piece of cord and measured a distance from the side of the barn out into the feedlot. The woman set up a surveyor's transit and the tall man sighted through it while the dark one made marks on the barn wall with paint. The three gathered around a clipboard, gesturing with their arms.

Logan stepped out of the woods. The swarthy one saw him first and said something Logan couldn't hear.

"What are you folks doing out here?"

"Hello," the woman said, smiling.

"Have you got any company identification?"

"We're not with the company," the taller man said.

"This is private property. You're not allowed out here. That's what I'm out here for, to keep people off."

"We just wanted to take a few pictures," the tall man said.

"There ain't nothing to take pictures of out here," Logan said suspiciously.

"Oh yes there is," the woman said. "Me." She licked her lips.

"We're shooting a cover for what you might call a private kind of magazine, you know, a daring sort of magazine?"

"You talking about a nudie book?"

"We prefer to call it a naturist publication," the tall man said. "You can't do this sort of thing just anywhere."

"I might get arrested," the woman said, laughing. She was a looker all right.

"It's too cold for that stuff," Logan said.

"We're going to call the picture 'Goose Bumps.'"

Meanwhile, the swarthy one was unrolling a spool of wire from the tripod to the trees.

"Don't you fool with me now, I don't know anything about this. The office never said anything to me about letting anybody in here. You'd better go on back where you came from."

"Do you want to make $50 helping us? It will only take a half hour and we'll be gone," the tall man said.

Logan considered a moment. "Well, I won't take off my clothes."

"You won't have to. Is there anyone else around here?"

"No. Nobody for miles."

"We'll manage just fine then." The man was holding out $50. "Does my hand offend you?"

"No, no."

"Why are you staring at it then?" The woman shifted uncomfortably beside the tall man.

"I didn't mean to," Logan said. He could see his reflection in the man's sunglasses.

"You two get the big camera from the plane, and this gentleman and I will get things ready." The swarthy man and the woman disappeared into the woods.

"What's your name?"

"Logan."

"All right, Mr. Logan, if you'll get a couple of boards and put them down in the grass right here at the center of the barn wall for the lady to stand on."

"Do what?"

"Put some boards there, right in the middle. The ground is cold and we want her feet up out of the grass where they will show. Some people like feet."

While Logan found the boards, the tall man removed the transit and fastened a peculiar-looking curved object to the tripod. He turned and called to Logan. "No, no. One board on top of the other." He made a frame with his hands and squinted through it. "Now stand on it and let me see if it's right. Hold it right there, don't move, here they come with the viewfinder." The tall man disappeared into the trees.

Logan reached up to scratch his head. For an instant his brain registered the blinding flash, but he never heard the roar. Twenty darts shredded him and the blast slammed him back against the barn wall.

Lander, Fasil, and Dahlia came running through the smoke.

"Ground meat," Fasil said. They turned the slack body over and examined the back. Rapidly, they took pictures of the barn wall. It was bowed in and looked like a giant colander. Lander went inside the barn. Hundreds of small holes in the wall admitted points of light that freckled him as his camera clicked and clicked again.

"Very successful," Fasil said.

They dragged the body into the barn, sloshed gasoline over it and over the dry wood around it, and poured a trail of gasoline out the door for 20 yards. The fire flashed inside and lit the pools of gas with a "Whump" they felt on their faces.

Black smoke rose from the barn as the Cessna climbed out of sight.

"How did you find that place?" Fasil asked, leaning forward from the rear seat to be heard over the engine noise.

"I was hunting dynamite last summer," Lander said.

"Do you think the authorities will come soon?"

"I doubt it, they blast there all the time."

CHAPTER
16

EDDIE STILES SAT by the window in the New York
City Aquarium snack bar worrying. From his table he
could see Rachel Bauman below him and 40 yards
away at the rail of the penguin pen. It was not Rachel
Bauman that disturbed him, it was the two men standing with her. Stiles did not like their looks at all. The
one on her left looked like Man Mountain Dean. The
other one was a little smaller, but worse. He had the
easy, economical movements and the balance that Eddie had learned to fear. The predators in Eddie's world
had moved that way. The expensive ones. Very different from the muscle the shylocks employed, the blocky
hard guys with their weight on their heels.

Eddie did not like the way this man's eyes swept
over the high places, the roof of the shark house, the
fences on the dunes between the Aquarium and the Co-
ney Island boardwalk. One slow sweep and then the
man quartered the ground, going over it minutely, in-

fantry style, from close to far, and all the time wagging his finger over an interested penguin's head.

Eddie was sorry he had chosen this place to meet. On a weekday the crowd was not big enough to give him that comfortable, anonymous feeling.

He had Dr. Bauman's word that he would not be involved. She had never lied to him. His life, the life he was trying to build, was based on what he had learned about himself with Dr. Bauman's help. If that was not true, then nothing was true. He drained his coffee cup and walked quickly down the stairs and around to the whale tank. He could hear the whale blowing before he reached the tank. It was a 40-foot female killer whale, elegant with her gleaming black and white markings. A show was underway. A young man stood on a platform over the water holding up a fish in the pale winter sunshine. The surface of the water bulged in a line across the pool as beneath the surface the whale came like a black locomotive. She cannoned vertically out of the water and her great length seemed to hang in the air as she took the fish in her triangular teeth.

Eddie heard the applause behind him as he went down the steps to the underground gallery with its big plate-glass windows. The room was dim and damp, lit by the sun shining down through the blue-green water of the whale tank. Eddie looked into the tank. The whale was moving over the light-dappled bottom, rolling over and over, chewing. Three families came down the stairs and joined him. They all had loud children.

"Daddy, I can't see."

The father hoisted the boy to his shoulders, bumping his head on the ceiling, then took him outside squalling.

"Hi, Eddie," Rachel said.

Her two companions stood on the far side of her, away from Eddie. That was good manners, Eddie thought. Goons would have come up on either side. Cops would have, too. "Hello, Dr. Bauman." His eyes flicked over her shoulder.

"Eddie, this is David and this is Robert."

"Pleased to make your acquaintance." Eddie shook their hands. The big one had a piece under his left arm, no doubt about it. Maybe the other guy had one too, but the coat fit better. This David. Enlarged knuckles on the first two fingers and the edge of his hand like a wood rasp. He didn't get that learning to yo-yo. Dr. Bauman was a very wise and understanding woman, but there were some things she did not know about, Eddie thought. "Dr. Bauman, I'd like to talk to you a second, uh, personal, if you don't mind."

At the other end of the chamber, he spoke close to her ear. Yelling children covered his voice. "Doc. I want to know, do you really know these guys? I know you think you do, but I mean *know* them? Dr. Bauman, these are some very hard guys. There are, you know, hard guys and hard guys. This is a thing I happen to know about. These are the harder type of hard guy, rather than mugs, if you follow me. These don't look like no fuzz to me. I can't see you around these type of fellows. You know, unless they were kin to you or something like that you can't do anything about."

Rachel put her hand on his arm. "Thanks, Eddie. I

know what you're saying. But I've known these two for a long time. They're my friends."

A porpoise had been put in the tank with the whale to provide her company. It was busy hiding pieces of fish in the drain while the whale was distracted by the trainer. The whale slid by the underwater window, taking a full ten seconds to pass by, its small eye looking through the glass at the people talking on the other side.

"This guy I hear about, Jerry Sapp, did a job in Cuba a couple of years ago," Stiles told Kabakov. "Cuba! He ran in under the coastal radar close to Puerta Cabanas with some Cubans from Miami." Stiles looked from Kabakov to Rachel and back again. "They had some business on shore, you know, they ran in through the surf in one of these inflatables, like an Avon or a Zodiac, and they came off with this box. I don't know what the hell it was, but this guy didn't come back to Florida. He got into it with a Cuban patrol boat out of Bahia Honda and ran straight across to Yucatan. Had a big bladder tank on the foredeck."

Kabakov listened, tapping his fingers on the rail. The whale was quiet now, resting on the surface. Her great tail arched down, dropping her flukes ten feet below the surface.

"These kids are driving me nuts," Eddie said. "Let's move."

They stood in the dark corridor of the shark house, watching the long gray shapes endlessly circling, small bright fish darting between them.

"Anyway, I had always wondered how this guy ran in close to Cuba. Since the Bay of Pigs they got radar you wouldn't believe. You said your guy slipped away from the Coast Guard radar. Same thing. So I asked around a little, you know, about this Sapp. He was in Sweeney's in Asbury Park there, about two weeks ago. But nobody's seen him since. His boat's a 38-foot sportfisherman, a Shing Lu job. They're built in Hong Kong, and I mean *built*. This one's all wood."

"Where did he keep his boat?" Kabakov asked.

"I don't know. Nobody seemed to know. I mean, you can't ask too close, you know? But look, the bartender at Sweeney's takes messages for this guy, I think he could get in touch. If it was business."

"What kind of business would he go for?"

"Depends. He has to know he's hot. If he went himself on this job you're interested in, of course he knows he's hot. If it was a contract job, if he let out the boat, then he was listening to the Coast Guard frequency the whole time. Wouldn't you?"

"Where would you run, if you were this man?"

"I would have watched the boat for a day after it was back, to make sure it wasn't staked out. Then if I had a place to work I'd paint it, put the legit registration back on and change it up—I'd put a tuna tower on it. I'd catch a string of Gold Platers running south to Florida along the ditch and I'd get right in with 'em—a string of yachts going down the Intracoastal Waterway," Eddie explained. "Those rich guys like to go in a pack."

"Give me a high-profit item away from here that would make him surface," Kabakov said. "Something that would require the boat."

"Smack," Eddie said, with a guilty glance toward

Rachel. "Heroin. Out of Mexico into, say, Corpus
Christi or Aransas Pass on the Texas coast. He might
go for that. There would have to be some front money,
though. And he would have to be approached very
careful. He would spook easy."

"Think about the contact, Eddie. And thank you,"
Kabakov said.

"I did it for the Doc." The sharks moved silently in
the lighted tank. "Look, I'm gonna split now, I don't
want to look at these things anymore."

"I'll meet you back in town, David," Rachel said.

Kabakov was surprised to see a kind of distaste in
her eyes when she looked at him. She and Eddie walked
away together, their heads bent, talking. Her arm was
around the little man's shoulders.

Kabakov would have preferred to keep Corley out
of it. So far, the FBI agent knew nothing of this business of Jerry Sapp and his boat. Kabakov wanted to
pursue it alone. He needed to talk to Sapp before the
man wrapped himself in the Constitution.

Kabakov did not mind violating a man's rights, his
dignity, or his person if the violation provided immediate benefits. The fact of doing it did not bother him,
but the seed within him that was nourished by the success of these tactics made him uneasy.

He felt himself developing contemptuous attitudes
toward the web of safeguards between the citizen and
the expediency of investigation. He did not try to ratio-
nalize his acts with catchphrases like "the greater
good," for he was not a reflective man. While Kabakov
believed his measures to be necessary—knew that they

worked—he feared that the mentality a man could develop in their practice was an ugly and dangerous thing, and for him it wore a face. The face of Hitler.

Kabakov recognized that the things he did marked his mind as surely as they marked his body. He wanted to think that his increasing impatience with the restraints of the law were entirely the result of his experience, that he felt anger against these obstacles just as he felt stiffness in old wounds on winter mornings.

But this was not entirely true. The seed of his attitudes was in his nature, a fact he had discovered years ago near Tiberias, in Galilee.

He was en route to inspect some positions on the Syrian border when he stopped his jeep at a well on a mountainside. A windmill, an old American Aermotor, pumped the cold water out of the rock. The windmill creaked at regular intervals as the blades slowly revolved, a lonely sound on a bright and quiet day. Leaning against his jeep, the water still cool on his face, Kabakov watched a flock of sheep grazing above him on the mountainside. A sense of aloneness pressed around him and made him aware of the shape and position of his body in these great tilted spaces. And then he saw an eagle, high, riding a thermal, wingtip feathers splayed like fingers, slipping sideways over the mountain's face, his shadow slipping fast over the rocks. The eagle was not hunting sheep, for it was winter and there were no lambs among them, but it was above the sheep and they saw it and baaed among themselves. Kabakov became dizzy watching the bird, his horizontal reference distorted by the mountain

slope. He found himself holding onto the jeep for balance.

And then he realized that he loved the eagle better
than the sheep and that he always would and that, because he did, because it was in him to do it, he could
never be perfect in the sight of God.

Kabakov was glad that he would never have any real
power.

Now, in an apartment in a cliff face in Manhattan,
Kabakov considered how the bait could be presented to
Jerry Sapp. If he pursued Sapp alone, then Eddie Stiles
had to make the contact. He was the only person
Kabakov knew who had access to crime circles along
the waterfront. Without him, Kabakov would have to
use Corley's resources. Stiles would do it for Rachel.

"No," Rachel said at breakfast.

"He would do it if you asked him. We could cover
him all the time—"

"He's not going to do it, so forget it."

It was hard to believe that twenty minutes before,
she had been so warm and morning-rosy over him, her
hair a gentle pendulum that brushed his face and chest.

"I know you don't like to use him, but God dammit—"

"I don't like me using him, I don't like you using me.
I'm using you too, in a different way that I haven't figured out yet. It's okay, our using each other. We have
something besides that and it's good. But no more Eddie."

She was really splendid, Kabakov thought, with the
flush creeping out of the lace and up her neck.

"I can't do it. I won't do it," she said. "Would you like some orange juice?"

"Please."

Reluctantly, Kabakov went to Corley. He gave him the information on Jerry Sapp. He did not give the source.

Corley worked on the bait for two days with the Bureau of Narcotics and Dangerous Drugs. He spent an hour on the telephone to Mexico City. Then he met with Kabakov in the FBI's Manhattan office.

"Anything on the Greek?"

"Not yet," Kabakov said. "Moshevsky is still working the bars. Go on with Sapp."

"The Bureau has no record on a Jerry Sapp," Corley said. "Whoever he is, he's clean under that name. Coast Guard registration does not have him. Their files are not cross-indexed on boat type down to the detail we need. The paint we have will do for positive comparison, but tracing origin is another matter. It's not marine paint. It's a commercial brand of semi-gloss over a heavy sealer, available anywhere."

"Tell me about the dope."

"I'm getting to that. Here's the package. Did you follow the Krapf-Mendoza case in Chihuahua by any chance? Well, I didn't know the details either. From 1970 through 1973 they got 115 pounds of heroin into this country. It went to Boston. Clever method. For each shipment they used a pretext to hire an American citizen to go down to Mexico. Sometimes it was a man, sometimes a woman, but always a loner who had no close relatives. The stooge flew down on a tourist visa and after a few days unfortunately died. The body was shipped home with a belly full of heroin. They had a funeral home on this end. Your hair is growing out nicely by the way."

"Go on, go on."

"Two things we got out of it. The money man in Boston still has a good name with the mob. He helps us out because he's trying to stave off forty years mandatory in the joint. The Mexican authorities left a guy in Cozumel on the street. Better not to ask what he's trying to stave off."

"So if our man sends word down the pipeline that he is looking for a good man with a boat to run the stuff out of Cozumel into Texas, it would look reasonable because the old method was stopped," Kabakov said. "And if Sapp calls our man, he can give references in Mexico and in Boston."

"Yeah. This Sapp would check it out before he showed himself. Even getting the word to him will probably involve a couple of cutouts. This is what bothers me, if we find him we've got almost nothing on him. We might get him on some bullshit conspiracy charge involving the use of his boat, but that would take time to develop. We've got nothing to threaten him with."

Oh, yes we do, Kabakov thought to himself.

By mid-afternoon Corley had asked the U.S. District Court in Newark for permission to tap the two telephones in Sweeney's Bar & Grill in Asbury Park. By 4 P.M. the request had been denied. Corley had no evidence whatsoever of any wrongdoing at Sweeney's, and he was acting on anonymous allegations of little substance, the magistrate explained. The magistrate said that he was sorry.

At 10 A.M. on the following day a blue van pulled into the supermarket parking lot adjacent to Sweeney's. An elderly lady was at the wheel. The lot was full and she drove along slowly, apparently looking for a parking place. In a car parked beside the telephone pole 30 feet from the rear of Sweeney's Bar a man was dozing.

"He's asleep, for Christ's sake," the elderly lady said, apparently speaking to her bosom.

The dozing man in the car awoke as the radio beside him crackled angrily. With a sheepish expression, he pulled out of the parking space. The van backed into the place. A few shoppers rolled carts down the traffic aisle. The man who vacated the parking space got out of his car.

"Lady, I think you got a flat."

"Oh, yeah?"

The man walked to the rear wheel of the van, close beside the pole. Two thin wires, brown against the brown pole, led from the telephone line to the ground and terminated in a double jack. The man plugged the jack into a socket in the fender well of the van.

"No, the tire's just low. You can drive on it all right." He drove away.

In the rear of the van, Kabakov leaned back with his hands behind his head. He was wearing earphones and smoking a cigar.

"You don't have to wear them all the time," said the balding young man at the miniature switchboard. "I say you don't have to wear them all the time. When it rings or when it's picked up on this end, you'll see this light and hear the buzzer. You want some coffee? Here." He leaned close to the partition behind the cab. "Hey, mom. You want coffee?"

"No," came the voice from the front. "And you leave the bialys in the bag. You know they give you gas." Bernie Biner's mother had switched from the driver's seat to the passenger side. She was knitting an afghan. As the mother of one of the best freelance wire men in the business, it was her job to drive, look innocent, and watch for the police.

"$11.40 an hour she charges me and she's supervising my diet," Biner told Kabakov.

The buzzer sounded. Bernie's quick fingers started the tape recorder. He and Kabakov put on the earphones. They could hear the telephone ringing in the bar.

"Hello. Sweeney's."

"Freddy?" A woman's voice. "Listen, honey, I can't come in today."

"Shit, Frances, what is this, twice in two weeks?"

"Freddy, I'm sorry, I got the cramps like you wouldn't believe."

"Every week you get the cramps? You better go to the muff doctor, kid. What about Arlene?"

"I called her house already, she's not home."

"Well, you get somebody over here, I'm not waiting tables and working the bar too."

"I'll try, Freddy."

They heard the bartender hang up and a woman's laughter before the phone was replaced on the other end. Kabakov blew a smoke ring and told himself to be

patient. Corley's stooge had planted an urgent message
for Sapp when Sweeney's opened a half-hour ago. The
stooge had given the bartender $50 to hurry it up. It
was a simple message saying business was available
and asking Sapp to call a number in Manhattan to talk
business or to get references. The number was to be
given to Sapp alone. If Sapp called, Corley would try to
fool him into a meeting. Kabakov was not satisfied.
That was why he had hired Biner, who already received
a weekly retainer to check the Israeli mission phones
for bugs. Kabakov had not consulted Corley about the
matter.

A light on Biner's switchboard indicated the second
telephone in the bar had been picked up. Through the
earphones, they heard ten digits dialed. Then a telephone ringing. It was not answered.

Bernie Biner ran back his tape recording of the dial-
ing, then played it at a slower speed, counting the
clicks. "Three-oh-five area code. That's Florida. Here's
the number. Eight-four-four-six-oh-six-nine. Just a second." He consulted a thick table of prefixes. "It's
somewhere in the West Palm Beach area."

Half an hour passed before the switchboard in the
van signaled that another call was being placed from
the bar. Ten digits again.

"Glamareef Lounge."

"Yeah, I'm calling for Mr. Sapp. He said I could
leave him a message at this number if I needed to."

"Who is this?"

"Freddy Hodges at Sweeney's. Mr. Sapp will
know."

"All right. What is it?"

"I want him to call me."

"I don't know if I can get him on the phone. You say Freddy Hodges?"

"Yeah. He knows the number. It's important, tell him. It's business."

"Uh, look, he may come in around five or six. Sometimes he comes in. I see him, I'll tell him."

"Tell him it's important. That Freddy Hodges called."

"Yeah, yeah, I'll tell him." A click.

Bernie Biner called West Palm Beach information and confirmed that the number was that of the Glamareef Lounge.

The fire on Kabakov's cigar was two inches long. He was elated. He had expected Sapp to use a telephone cutout, a person who did not know his identity, but whom he called under a code name to receive messages. Instead it was a simple message drop in a bar. Now it would not be necessary to go through the intricate process of setting up a meeting with Sapp. He could find him at the bar.

"Bernie, I want a tap until Sapp calls Sweeney's here. When that happens, let me know the second you're sure it's him."

"Where will you be?"

"In Florida. I'll give you a number when I get there." Kabakov glanced at his watch. He intended to be in the Glamareef at 5 P.M. He had six hours.

The Glamareef in West Palm Beach is a cinderblock building on a sandy lot. Like many Southern drinking places constructed after air conditioning became popular, it has no windows. Originally it was a jukebox-and-pool-table beer joint called Shangala, with a loud air conditioner and a block of ice in the urinal. Now it went after a faster crowd. Its naugahyde booths and dim bar drew people from two worlds—the paycheck playboys and the big-money yachting people who liked to slum. The Glamareef, nee Shangala, was a good place to look for young women with marital problems. It was a good place for an older, affluent woman to find a body-and-fender man who had never had it on a silk sheet.

Kabakov sat at the end of the bar drinking beer. He and Moshevsky had rented a car at the airport and their hurried drive past the four nearby marinas had been discouraging. There was a small city of boats in West Palm Beach, many of them sportfishermen. They would have to find the man first, then the boat.

He had been waiting an hour when a husky man in his middle thirties came into the bar. Kabakov ordered another beer and asked for change. He studied the new arrival in the mirrored front of the cigarette machine. He was of medium height and he had a deep suntan and heavy muscles under his polo shirt. The bartender put a drink in front of him and, with it, a note.

The husky man finished his drink in a few long swallows and went to a phone booth in the corner. Kabakov doodled on his napkin. He could see the man's mouth moving in the telephone booth.

The bar telephone rang twice before the bartender picked it up. He put his hand over the mouthpiece. "Is there a Shirley Tatum here?" he said loudly, looking around. "No, I'm sorry." He hung up.

That was Moshevsky, calling the bar from a pay phone outside, relaying the signal from Bernie Biner in Asbury Park. The man Kabakov was watching in the telephone booth was talking to Sweeney's Bar in Asbury Park with Bernie listening in. He was Jerry Sapp.

Kabakov sorted his change in a roadside telephone booth a half-hour before dark. He dialed Rachel's number.

"Hello."

"Rachel, don't wait dinner on me. I'm in Florida."

"You found the boat."

"Yes. I found Sapp first and followed him to it. I haven't examined it yet. Or talked to Sapp. Listen, tomorrow I want you to call Corley. Tell him Sapp and the boat are at the Clear Springs Marina near West Palm Beach. Have you got that? The boat is green now. Number FL 4040 AL. Call him about 10 A.M., not before."

"You're going aboard it tonight, and in the morning, if you're still alive, you're planning to call me and say you've changed your mind about telling Corley, aren't you?"

"Yes." There was a long silence. Kabakov had to break it. "It's a private marina, very exclusive. Lucky Luciano used to keep a boat here years ago. Also other arch-criminals. The man at the bait store told me. I had to buy a bucket of shrimp to find that out."

"Why don't you go in with Corley and a warrant?"

"They don't admit Jews."

"You'll take Moshevsky with you, won't you?"

"Sure. He'll be close by."

"David?"

"Yes."

"I love you, to a certain extent."

"Thank you, Rachel." He hung up.

He did not tell her that the marina was isolated, that the landward side was surrounded by a twelve-foot hurricane fence, floodlit. Or that two tall men with short shotguns manned the gate and patrolled the piers.

Kabakov drove a half-mile down the winding road through the scrub growth, the rented johnboat bouncing on its trailer behind him. He parked the car in a thicket and climbed a small knoll where Moshevsky lay with two pairs of field glasses.

"He's still aboard," the big man said. "There are fleas in this damned sand."

With his binoculars, Kabakov scanned the three long piers jutting into Lake Worth. A guard was on the farthest pier, walking slowly, his hat set back on his head. The whole marina had a sinister, fast-money look. Kabakov could imagine what would happen if a warrant were served at the gate. The alarm would be given and whatever was illegal in any of the boats would go over the side. There must be some clue aboard Sapp's boat. Or in Sapp's head. Something that would lead him to the Arabs.

"He's coming out," Moshevsky said.

Kabakov zeroed in on the green sportfisherman moored stern-to in the line of boats at the center pier. Sapp climbed up through the foredeck hatch and locked it behind him. He was dressed for dinner. He stepped down from the bow into a dinghy and pulled well away from his boat to a vacant slip, then climbed onto the pier.

"Why didn't he just walk back along the boat and get onto the pier," muttered Moshevsky, lowering his field glasses and rubbing his eyes.

"Because the damned thing is wired," Kabakov replied wearily. "Let's get our boat."

Kabakov swam slowly in the darkness under the pier, feeling ahead for the pilings. Cobwebs hanging from the planks above him brushed his face, and, from the smell, there was a dead fish nearby. He paused, hugging a piling he could not see, feet gripping the rough sea growth crusting the piling beneath the water. A little light came under the edges of the long pier, and he could see the dark, square shapes of the motor yachts moored stern-to against it.

He had counted seven on the right side. He had six to go. A foot and a half above him, the underside of the pier was studded with nail points where the planks had been nailed down. High tide would be hard on his scalp. A spider ran across his neck and he submerged to drown it. The water tasted like diesel fuel.

Kabakov heard a woman's laughter and the tinkle of ice. He shifted his equipment bag farther around on his back and swam on. This should be it. He made his way around a tangle of rusty cable and stopped just under the edge of the pier, the stern of the boat rising black above him.

Here the air was not so close, and he breathed deeply as he peered at the luminous dial of his watch. It had been 15 minutes since Moshevsky steered the outboard past the seaward end of the marina and he had slipped over the side. He hoped Sapp would linger over dessert.

The man had some kind of alarm system. Either a pressure-sensitive mat in the open cockpit at the stern or something fancier. Kabakov swam along the stern until he found the cable that carried 110-volt shore power to the craft. He unplugged the cable from the jack in the stern. If the alarm used shore power it was now inoperative. He heard footsteps and slid back under the pier. The heavy tread passed overhead, sending a trickle of grit down in his face.

No, he decided, if it were his alarm system, it would be independent of shore power. He would not go over the stern. He would go in as Sapp had come out.

Kabakov swam along the hull to the darkness under the flaring bow. Two mooring lines, slack to accommodate the tide, ran from the bow to pilings on either side of the slip. Kabakov pulled himself up, hand over hand, until he could lock his arms around the stanchion supporting the bow rail. He could see into the cabin of the yacht next door. A man and a woman were seated on a couch. The backs of their heads were visible. They were necking. The woman's head disappeared. Kabakov climbed up on the foredeck and lay against the windshield, the cabin shielding him from the dock. The windshield was dogged tightly shut. Here was the hatch.

With a screwdriver, he removed the thick plastic window in the center of it. The hole was just big enough for his arm. Reaching inside, he turned the lock and felt around the edges of the hatch until he found the contacts of the burglar alarm sensor. His mind was picturing the wiring as his fingers felt for the wires in the padded overhead. The switch was on the coaming, and it was held open by a magnet on the hatch. Take loose the magnet, then, and hold it in place on the switch. Don't drop it! Ease open the hatch. Don't ring, don't ring, don't ring.

He dropped into the darkness of the forward cabin and closed the hatch, replacing the window and the magnet.

Kabakov felt good. Some of the sting was gone from the debacle at Muzi's house. With his flashlight he found the alarm circuit box and disconnected it from its clutch of dry-cell batteries. Sapp did neat wiring. A timer permitted him to leave without setting off the alarm, a magnet-sensitive cutout against the skin of the boat permitted him to reenter.

Now Kabakov could move around. A quick search of the forward cabin revealed nothing unusual except a full ounce of high-grade crystal cocaine and a coke spoon from which to sniff it.

He switched off his flashlight and opened the hatch leading up to the main cabin. The dock lights shining through the ports provided a little light. Suddenly Kabakov's Parabellum was out and cocked, the trigger squeezed within an ounce of firing.

Something was moving in the cabin. He saw it again, a small, repetitive movement, and again, a flicker of dark against the port. Kabakov lay down in the companionway to silhouette the movement against the light. He smiled. It was Sapp's little surprise for an intruder coming aboard from the dock, an electronic scanner of a new and expensive type. It swept the cockpit constantly, ready to sound the alarm. Kabakov came up behind it and turned off the switch.

For an hour, he searched the boat. In a concealed compartment near the wheel he found a Belgian FN automatic rifle and a revolver. But there was nothing to prove that Sapp or Sapp's boat had been involved in moving the plastic explosive.

It was in the chart bin that he found what he was looking for. A bump at the bow interrupted him. The dinghy. Sapp was coming back. Kabakov slipped into the forward cabin and squeezed into the narrow point of the bow.

Above him, the hatch opened. Feet and then legs appeared. Sapp's head was still out of the hatch when Kabakov's heel slammed into his diaphragm.

Sapp regained consciousness to find himself tied hand and foot on one of the two berths with a sock stuffed in his mouth. A lantern hanging from the ceiling gave off a yellow light and a strong odor of kerosene. Kabakov sat on the opposite bunk smoking a cigar and cleaning his fingernails with Sapp's ice-pick.

"Good evening, Mr. Sapp. Is your head clear or shall I throw some water on you? All right? On November twelfth, you took a load of plastic explosive from a freighter off the New Jersey Coast. I want to know who was with you and where the plastic is. I have no interest in you otherwise.

"If you tell me, you will not be harmed. If you don't, I will leave you worse than dead. I'll leave you blind, dumb, and crippled. Do I have to hurt you now to demonstrate that I'm serious? I don't think so. I'll remove this sock from your mouth now. If you scream, I'll give you something to scream about, do you understand me?"

Sapp nodded. He spat out lint. "Who the hell are you?"

"That doesn't concern you. Tell me about the plastic."

"I don't know anything about it. You got nothing on me."

"Don't think in legalistic terms, Mr. Sapp. You are not protected from me by the law. The people you worked for are not mob-connected, by the way. You don't have to protect them on that account."

Sapp said nothing.

"The FBI is looking for you on a smuggling charge. Soon they will add mass murder to the list. That's a lot of plastic, Sapp. It will kill a lot of people unless you tell me where it is. Look at me when I'm talking to you."

"Kiss my ass."

Kabakov rose and jammed the sock back in Sapp's mouth. He grabbed Sapp by the hair and forced his head back against the wooden bulkhead. The tip of the icepick rested lightly in the corner of Sapp's rolling eye. A growl rumbled from Kabakov's chest as he drew back the icepick and struck, pinning Sapp's ear to the bulkhead. The color had gone from Sapp's face and there was a foul odor in the cabin.

"You really must look at me when I'm talking to you," Kabakov said. "Are you ready to cooperate? Blink for yes. Die for no."

Sapp blinked and Kabakov removed the sock.

"I didn't go. I didn't know it was plastic."

Kabakov believed this was probably true. Sapp was

shorter than the man described by the *Leticia*'s first mate. "But your boat went."

"Yes. I don't know who took it out. *No!* Honestly, I don't know. Look, it's my business not to know. I didn't want to know."

"How were you contacted?"

"A man called me the last week in October. He wanted the boat ready, standing by, during the week of November eighth. He didn't say who he was and I didn't ask." Sapp grimaced with pain. "He wanted to know a few things about the boat, not much. Hours on the engines, whether it had any new electronics."

"Any *new* electronics?"

"Yeah, I told him the loran was out—for God's sake take this thing out of my ear."

"All right. You'll get it through the other one if I catch you in a lie. This man that called, he already knew the boat?"

"Ouch!" Sapp turned his head from side to side and cut his eyes far over, as though he could see his ear. "I guess he knew the boat, he sounded like it. It was worth a thousand to him for it to be available, like a retainer. I got the thousand in the mail at Sweeney's in Asbury Park two days later."

"Do you have the envelope?"

"No, it was a plain envelope, New York City postmark."

"He called you again."

"Yeah, about November tenth. He wanted the boat for the twelfth, a Tuesday. The money was delivered to Sweeney's that night."

"How much?"

"Two thousand for the boat, sixty-five thousand deposit. All cash."

"How was it delivered?"

"A cab brought it in a picnic basket. Food was on top of it. A few minutes later the phone rang again. It was the guy. I told him where to get the boat."

"You never saw him pick it up or return it?"

"No." Sapp described the boathouse in Toms River.

Kabakov had the photo of Fasil and the composite of the woman sealed in a rubber glove in his bag. He took them out. Sapp shook his head at both pictures.

"If you still think I went out with the boat, I've got an alibi for that day. A dentist in Asbury Park fixed my teeth. I have a receipt."

"I expect you have," Kabakov said. "How long have you owned the boat?"

"A long time. Eight years."

"Any previous owners?"

"I had it built."

"How did you return the deposit?"

"I left it in the same basket in the trunk of my car by a supermarket and put the trunk key under the floor mat. Somebody picked it up."

The New Jersey coastal chart Kabakov had found in Sapp's chart bin had the course to the rendezvous marked with a neat black line, departure time and running time checks jotted beside it. The bearings for two radio direction finder fixes were penciled in. Three bearings for each fix.

Kabakov held the chart by the edges, under the lantern where Sapp could see it. "Did you mark this chart?"

"No. I didn't know it was on the boat or I would have gotten rid of it."

Kabakov took another chart from the bin, a Florida chart. "Did you plot the course on this one?"

"Yes."

He compared the two charts. Sapp's handwriting was different. He had used only two bearings for an RDF fix. Sapp's times were written in Eastern Standard. Time for the rendezvous with the *Leticia,* jotted on the New Jersey chart, was 2115. This puzzled Kabakov. He knew the Coast Guard cutter had spotted the speedboat close to the freighter at 1700 Eastern Standard. The boat must have been there for some minutes, loading the plastic, so the rendezvous was about 1615 or 1630. Yet it was marked on the chart for five hours later. Why? The departure time from Toms River and the running time checks were also marked about five hours later than they must have occurred. It didn't make sense. And then it did make sense—the man Kabakov was seeking had not used Eastern Standard time, he had used Greenwich Mean Time—Zulu time—*Pilot time*!

"What fliers do you know?" Kabakov demanded. "Professional pilots."

"I don't know any professional pilots I can think of," Sapp said.

"Think hard."

"Maybe a guy in Jamaica with a commercial license. But he's been in the jug down there ever since the feds vacuumed his luggage compartment. He's the only professional pilot I know. I'm sure of it."

"You know no pilots, you don't know who hired the boat. You know very little, Mr. Sapp."

"I don't. I can't think of any pilots. Look, you can bust me up, you probably will, but I still won't know."

Kabakov considered torturing Sapp. The idea was sickening to him, but he would do it if he thought the results would be worth it. No. Sapp was not a principal in the plot. Threatened with prosecution, fearful that he might be an accessory to a major atrocity involving the explosives, he would try to cooperate. He would try to recall any small detail that would identify the man who hired his boat. Better not to hurt him badly now.

The next step should be an intensive interrogation of Sapp about his activities and associates and a thorough lab analysis of the chart. The FBI was better equipped to do these things. Kabakov had come a long way for very little.

He called Corley from a telephone booth on the pier.

Sapp had not consciously lied to Kabakov, but he was mistaken in saying that he knew no professional pilots. It was an understandable memory lapse—it had been years since he had last seen Michael Lander or thought about the frightening, infuriating day of their first meeting.

Sapp had been on his seasonal migration northward when a floating timber mangled both his propellers off Manasquan, N.J., forcing him to stop. Sapp was strong and capable, but he could not change a jammed and twisted prop in open water with a sea running. The boat was drifting slowly toward the beach, dragging her anchor before a relentless onshore wind. He could not call the Coast Guard because they would smell the same stench that gagged him as he went below to get his storm anchor—the smell of $5,500 worth of black market alligator hides bought from a Florida poacher and bound for New York. When Sapp returned to the deck, he saw a boat approaching.

Michael Lander, out with his family in a trim little cruiser, threw Sapp a line and towed him to a protected inlet. Sapp, not wanting to be stuck at a marina with a disabled boat loaded with hot hides, asked Lander to help him. Wearing snorkle masks and flippers, they worked beneath the boat, and their combined strength was enough to pry one of the propellers off its shaft and fit the spare. Sapp could limp home.

"Excuse the smell," Sapp said uneasily as they sat on the stern, resting. Since Lander had been below in the course of the work, he could not have helped seeing the hides.

"None of my business," Lander said.

The incident began a casual friendship that ended when Lander returned to Vietnam for his second hitch. Sapp's friendship with Margaret Lander had continued, however, for some months after that. On the rare occasions when he thought about the Landers, it was the woman Sapp recalled most clearly, not the pilot.

CHAPTER
17

ON THE FIRST of December the President informed his chief of staff that he would definitely attend the Super Bowl in New Orleans, whether the Washington Redskins were playing or not.

"God dammit," said Earl Biggs, special agent in charge of the White House Secret Service detail. He said this quietly and alone. He was not surprised—the President had indicated previously that he was likely to go—but Biggs had hoped the trip would be canceled.

I should have known better than to hope, Biggs reflected. The Man's honeymoon with the nation was over and he had begun to slip a little in the polls, but he would be assured of a standing ovation in the Deep South, with the whole world watching.

Biggs dialed the number of the Secret Service's Protective Research section. "January 12. New Orleans," he said. "Get on it."

The Protective Research section has three levels of files. The largest contains every threat that has been made against a President by telephone, mail, or reported utterance in the last forty years. Persons who have made repeated threats or who are considered potentially dangerous are listed in a "live file."

The live files are reviewed every six months. Changes in address, job status, and international travel are noted. At present, there are 840 names in the live file.

Of these, the 325 considered most serious are also listed in a geographically indexed "trip file." Before each presidential trip, the persons listed in the area involved are investigated.

With 43 days of lead time, the clerks in Protective Research and the agents in the field had plenty of time to check out New Orleans.

Lee Harvey Oswald was never listed in the Secret Service trip file. Neither was Michael Lander.

On December 3, three agents from the White House Secret Service detail were dispatched to New Orleans to take charge of security arrangements. Forty days' lead time and a three-man team have been standard procedure since 1963. On December 7, Jack Renfro, leader of the three-man detail, sent a preliminary report to Earl Biggs at the White House.

Renfro did not like Tulane Stadium. Anytime the President appeared in public, Renfro could feel the exposure crawling on his own skin. The stadium, home of Tulane's Green Wave, the Sugar Bowl Classic, and the New Orleans Saints, is the largest steel stadium in the world. It is rusty gray and tan and the area beneath the stands is a forest of girders and beams, a nightmare to search. Renfro and the other two Secret Service agents spent two days climbing through the stadium. When Renfro walked out onto the field, every one of the 80,985 seats threatened him. The glassed-in VIP booth high on the west side of the stadium at the end of the press gallery was useless. He knew the President would never consent to use it, even in the case of inclement weather. No one could see the President there. He would use the VIP box, at the front of the west stands on the 50-yard line. For hours Renfro sat in the box. He placed a member of the New Orleans police department in it for an entire day, while he and the other two agents checked the lines-of-sight from various positions in the stands. He personally inspected the cream of the New Orleans police department's Special Events squad—the officers who would be assigned to the stadium.

He tried routes from New Orleans International Airport to the stadium via U.S. 61, state highway 3046, and U.S. 90 and a combination of Interstate 10 and the Claiborne Avenue section of U.S. 90. All routes seemed endless, especially in light of the notorious traffic problem in the stadium area.

The preliminary evaluation Renfro sent to special agent Biggs at the White House said in part:

Suggest we recommend in the strongest terms that the President be helicoptered from New Orleans International Airport to the stadium following this procedure:

1. A motorcade will be ordered to stand by at the

airport, but will be used by peripheral members of traveling party.

2. No helipad will be marked at the stadium until the President's helicopter is airborne from New Orleans International. At that time a portable fabric landing marker will be deployed at the south end of the infield on the track outside the northwest corner of the stadium. (See attached diagram A-1.) The track has no overhead wires and provides a clear landing area in the infield, but has three tall light standards on each side. These standards do not appear on the New Orleans sectional and VFR terminal area chart. Their presence should be emphasized at the pilot's briefing.

3. From the landing pad to Gate 19 is 100 paces. (Note enclosed photograph A-2.) Have requested removal of the unsightly garbage container indicated beside stadium wall. Suggest agents on the ground at landing point check the bushes at the edge of the stadium at Zero minus one minute.

The landing area can be covered from the rear upper floors of five houses on Audubon Boulevard. They are numbers 49, 55, 65, 71, and 73. Preliminary check indicates they are all occupied by citizens considered zero threat. The roofs and windows should be observed during the arrival, however.

In the event a crowd remains at the ticket windows at Gate 19 when the President arrives, Gate 18 and vendor's gate 18A could be used, but these are considered less desirable, as they would necessitate a short walk under the stands.

From Gate 19, the President would be exposed to

the area under the stands for 75 paces before reaching the sideline at the goal line.

The President will use Box 40, a double-size box
at the 50-yard line. (See attached diagram A-3.)
Note the railings allow access at front and rear. Also
note the rear of the box is elevated 6 inches by a
step. Tall agents seated behind the President in Box
40 would give considerable coverage from behind.
Secret Service boxes will be numbers 14 and 13 in
front of the Presidential Box to the right and left. At
least one agent each should be in Boxes 71, 70, 69,
and 68, to the rear.

The railing of box 40 is constructed of iron pipe.
The ends are capped. These caps should be removed
and the interior of the pipes examined immediately
before the President's arrival.

The box contains one telephone terminal box. I
am advising Signal Corps on details. (Memo to Signals attached.) Diagram A-4, stadium overview and
seating chart, shows individual agent assignments
and areas of responsibility.

Our radio frequency is clear.

Details of egress are subject to modification
pending our observation of crowd flow at the Sugar
Bowl game December 31.

Jack Renfro was a careful and conscientious man,
skilled at his trade. He had learned the stadium by
heart. But as he catalogued its dangers, he never once
looked up at the sky.

CHAPTER

18

LANDER FINISHED THE bomb two days after Christmas. Its sleek skin, midnight blue and bearing the bright insignia of the National Broadcasting System, reflected the harsh garage lights as it lay in its loading cradle. The clamps that would fasten it to the gondola of the blimp hung from the upper rim like open hands, and the electrical connections and backup fuse were taped in neat coils on the top. Inside the skin, the 1,316.7 pounds of plastic explosive rested in two great slabs of precise thickness, curving behind the layers of bristling darts. The detonators were packed separately, ready to be plugged into place.

Lander sat staring at the great bomb. He could see his reflection distorted on its side. He thought that he would like to sit on it now, and plug in the detonators and hold the wires like reins, touch them to the battery and ride the mighty firebloom into the face of God. Sixteen days to go.

The telephone had been ringing for some time when he answered it. Dahlia was calling from New Orleans.

"It's finished," Lander said.

"Michael, you've done a beautiful job. It's a privilege to watch you."

"Did you get the garage?"

"Yes. It's near the Galvez Street wharf. Twenty minutes from New Orleans Lakefront Airport. I've driven the route twice."

"You're sure it's big enough."

"It's big enough. It's a walled-off section of a warehouse. I've bought the padlocks and put them on. Now may I come home to you, Michael?"

"You're satisfied?"

"I'm satisfied."

"With the airport too?"

"Yes. I had no trouble getting in. I can make it in the truck when the time comes."

"Come home."

"I'll see you late tonight."

She did well, Lander thought as he hung up the telephone. Still, he would have preferred to make the arrangements in New Orleans himself. There had been no time. He still had to fly a National Football Conference playoff game and the Sugar Bowl in New Orleans before the Super Bowl. His time was used up.

The problem of moving the nacelle to New Orleans had worried him, and the solution he found was less than ideal. He had leased a two-and-one-half-ton truck, which now stood in his driveway, and he had engaged two bonded professional truck drivers to take it to New Orleans. They would leave tomorrow. The back of the truck would be sealed, and even if the drivers did see the device they would not know what it was.

Putting the bomb in the hands of strangers made Lander uneasy anyway. But there was no help for it. Fasil and Dahlia could not drive the truck. Lander was certain that the authorities had broadcast their descriptions in the Northeast. Fasil's forged international driving license was sure to attract attention if he were stopped by the police. Dahlia would be very conspicuous at the wheel of a big truck. She would be ogled at every step. Besides, Lander wanted Dahlia to be with him.

If he could have trusted Fasil to go to New Orleans, Dahlia would be here now, Lander thought bitterly. He had no confidence in Fasil since the Arab announced that he would not be present at the strike. Lander had enjoyed the contempt for Fasil that flashed in Dahlia's eyes. Supposedly Fasil was off arranging for some muscle to be employed at the airport—Dahlia had seen to it that he and Lander were not left in the house together.

One item remained on Lander's checklist of materials—a tarpaulin to tie down over the nacelle. It was 4:45 P.M. The hardware store was still open. He just had time to make it.

Twenty minutes later, Margaret Feldman, formerly Margaret Lander, parked her Dart stationwagon beside the big truck in Lander's driveway. She sat for a moment, looking at the house.

This was the first time she had seen it since her divorce and remarriage. Margaret felt some reservations about coming, but the bassinet and baby carriage were rightfully hers, she would need them in a few more months, and she intended to have them. She had called first to make sure Michael was not at home. She did not want him crying after her. He had been a strong and proud man before he was broken. For the memory of that man, she still had a great affection, in her fashion. She had tried to forget his sick behavior at the end. She still dreamed about the kitten, though, still heard it in her sleep.

Reflexively Margaret glanced in her compact mirror, patting her blonde hair and checking her teeth for lipstick before getting out of the car. It was as much a part of her routine as turning off the ignition. She hoped she would not get dirty loading the carriage and bassinet into the stationwagon. Really, Roger should have come with her. But he did not feel right about going into Lander's house when Lander was not there.

Roger had not always felt that way, she thought drily. Why had Michael tried to fight? It was over anyway.

Stooping in the thin snow on the driveway, Margaret found that the lock on the garage had been replaced with a new, stronger one. She decided to go through the house and open it from the inside. Her old key still fit the front door. She had intended to go straight through to the garage, but once inside the house her curiosity was aroused.

She looked around. There was the familiar spot on the carpet in front of the TV, residue of the children's countless Kool-Aid drippings. She had never been able to get it clean. But the living room was neat and so was the kitchen. Margaret had expected a litter of beer cans and TV dinner trays. She was a little piqued at the neatness of the house.

There is a guilty thrill in being alone in someone else's house, particularly the home of a familiar person. Much can be felt in the arrangement of a person's belongings, and the more intimate the belongings, the better. Margaret went upstairs.

Their old bedroom told her little. Lander's shoes were in a straight line in the closet, the furniture was dusted. She stood looking at the bed and smiled to herself. Roger would be angry if he knew what she was thinking about, did think about sometimes, even with him.

The bathroom. Two toothbrushes. A tiny wrinkle appeared between Margaret's eyes. A shower cap. Face creams, body lotion, bubble bath. Well, well. Now she was glad she had violated Lander's privacy. She wondered what the woman looked like. She wanted to see the rest of her things.

She tried the other bedroom, then opened the playroom door. Margaret stood wide-eyed, staring at the spirit lamp, the wall hangings, candle holders and the great bed. She walked to the bed and touched the pillow. Silk. *Well, la-de-da!* she said to herself.

"Hello, Margaret," Lander said.

She spun around with a gasp. Lander stood in the doorway, one hand on the knob, the other in his pocket. He was pale.

"I was just—"

"You're looking well." It was true. She looked splendid. He had seen her in this room before, in his mind. Crying out to him like Dahlia, touching him like Dahlia. Lander felt a hollow ache inside. He wished Dahlia were here. Looking at his ex-wife, he was trying to see Dahlia, needed to see Dahlia. He saw Margaret. She brightened the air around her.

"You seem to be all right—I mean you look well, too, Michael. I—I must say I didn't expect *this*." Her hand swept around the room.

"What *did* you expect?" Sweat was on his face. Oh, the things that he had found again in this room did not stand up to Margaret.

"Michael, I need the baby things. The bassinet and the carriage."

"I can see that Roger's knocked you up. I'm giving you the benefit of the doubt, of course."

She smiled, unthinkingly, despite the insult, trying to get past the moment, trying to get away. That smile meant to Lander that she thought infidelity was funny, a joke they could laugh about together. It pierced Lander like a red-hot poker.

"I can get the things from the garage." She moved toward the door.

"Have you looked for them yet?" *Show it to her. Show it to her and kill her.*

"No, I was about to—"

"The bassinet and the carriage aren't there. I put them in storage. The sparrows get in the garage and speckle everything. I'll have them sent over." *No! Take her in the garage and show it to her. And kill her.*

"Thank you, Michael. That would be very nice."

"How are the kids?" His own voice sounded strange to him.

"Fine. They had a good Christmas."

"Do they like Roger?"

"Yes, he's good to them. They'd like to see you sometime. They ask about you. Are you moving? I saw the big truck in the driveway and I thought—"

"Is Roger's bigger than mine?"

"What?"

He could not stop now. "You God damned slut." He moved toward her. *I must stop.*

"Goodbye, Michael." She moved sideways toward the door.

The pistol in his pocket was burning his hand. *I must stop. It will be ruined. Dahlia said it is a privilege to watch you. Dahlia said Michael you were so strong today. Dahlia said Michael I love to do it for you. I was your first time, Margaret. No. The elastic left red marks on your hips. Don't think. Dahlia will be home soon, home soon, home soon. Mustn't—. Click.*

"I'm sorry I said that, Margaret. I shouldn't have said it. It's not true, and I'm sorry."

She was still frightened. She wanted to go.

He could hold on a second longer. "Margaret, there's something I've been meaning to send you. For you and Roger. Wait, wait. I've acted badly. It's important to me that you're not angry. I'll be upset if you're angry."

"I'm not angry, Michael. I have to go. Are you seeing a doctor?"

"Yes, yes. I'm all right, it was just a shock, seeing you." His next words choked him, but he forced them out. "I've missed you and I just got disturbed. That's all. Wait one second." He walked quickly to the desk in his room, and when he came out she was going down the stairs. "Here, I want you to take these. Just take them and have a good time and don't be mad."

"All right, Michael. Goodbye now." She took the envelope.

At the door, she stopped and turned to him again. She felt like telling him. She was not sure why. He ought to know. "Michael, I was sorry to hear about your friend Jergens."

"What about Jergens?"

"He *is* the one who used to wake us up calling you in the middle of the night, isn't he?"

"What about him?"

"He killed himself. Didn't you see the paper? The first POW suicide, it said. He took some pills and pulled a plastic bag over his head," she said. "I was sorry. I remembered how you talked to him on the telephone when he couldn't sleep. Goodbye, Michael." Her eyes were like nailheads, and she felt lighter and didn't know why.

When she was three blocks away, waiting at the light, she opened the envelope Michael had given her. It contained two tickets to the Super Bowl.

As soon as Margaret left, Lander ran to the garage. The bottom was out of him. He began to work very rapidly, trying to stay above the thoughts rising like black water in his head. He eased the rented forklift forward, pushing the fork under the cradle that held the nacelle. He switched off the forklift and climbed out of the seat. He was concentrating on forklifts. He thought about all the forklifts he had seen in warehouses and on docks. He thought about the principles of hydraulic leverage. He walked outside and lowered the tailgate of the truck. He attached the sloping metal ramp to the rear of the truck. He thought about landing craft he had seen and the way their ramps were hinged. He thought desperately about loading ramps. He checked the street. Nobody was watching. It didn't matter anyway. He jumped back on the forklift and raised the nacelle off the floor. Gently now. It was a delicate job. He had to think about it. He had to be very careful. He drove the forklift slowly up the loading ramp and into the back of the truck. The truck springs creaked as they took the weight. He lowered the fork bearing the nacelle, locked the brake, chocked the wheels firmly, and secured the nacelle and forklift in place with heavy rope. He thought about knots. He knew all about knots. He could tie 12 different knots. He must remember to put a sharp knife in the back of the truck. Dahlia could cut the ropes when the time came. She would not have time to fool with knots. *Oh Dahlia. Come home, I am drowning.* He put the loading ramp and the duffle bag of small arms inside the truck and locked the tailgate. It was done.

He threw up in the garage. *Mustn't think.* He walked to the liquor cabinet and took out a bottle of vodka. His stomach heaved up the vodka. The second time it stayed down. He took the pistol from his pocket and threw it behind the kitchen stove where he could not reach it. The bottle again, and again. Half of it was gone and it was running down his shirt front, running down his neck. The bottle again, and again. His head was swimming. *I mustn't throw up. Hold it down.* He was crying. The vodka was hitting him now. He sat down on the kitchen floor. *Two more weeks and I'll be dead. Oh thank God I'll be dead. Everybody else will be too. Where it's quiet. And nothing ever is. Oh God it has been so long. Oh God it has been so long. Jergens, you were right to kill yourself. Jergens!* He was yelling now. He was up and staggering to the back door. He was yelling out the back door. Cold rain was blowing in his face as he yelled out into the yard. *Jergens, you were right!* And the back steps were coming up at him, and he rolled off into the dead grass and snow, and lay face up in the rain. A last thought, consciousness glimmering out. *Water is a good conductor of heat. Witness a million engines and my heart cold upon this ground.*

It was quite late when Dahlia set her suitcase down in the living room and called his name. She looked in the workshop and then climbed the stairs.

"Michael." The lights were on and the house was cold. She was uneasy. "Michael." She went into the kitchen.

The back door was open. She ran to it. When she saw him she thought he was dead. His face was white with a bluish tinge and his hair was plastered flat by the cold rain. She knelt beside him and felt his chest through the soggy shirt. His heart was beating. Kicking off her high-heeled shoes, she dragged him toward the door. She could feel the freezing ground through her stockings. Groaning with the effort, she dragged him up the stairs and into the kitchen. She jerked the blankets off the guest-room bed and spread them on the floor beside him, stripped the soggy clothes off him and rolled him in the blankets. She rubbed him with a rough towel, and she sat beside him in the ambulance on the way to the hospital. At daylight, his temperature was 105. He had viral pneumonia.

CHAPTER
19

THE DELTA JET approached New Orleans over Lake Pontchartrain, maintaining considerable altitude over the water, then swooped down toward New Orleans International Airport. The swoop lifted Muhammad Fasil's stomach unpleasantly, and he cursed under his breath.

Pneumonia! The woman's precious pet got drunk and fell out in the rain! The fool was half-delirious and weak as a kitten, the woman sitting beside him in the hospital, bleating expressions of pity. At least she would see to it that he kept his mouth shut about the mission. The chances of Lander being able to fly the Super Bowl in fifteen days were exactly nil, Fasil thought. When the stubborn-headed woman was finally convinced of that, when she saw that Lander could do nothing but puke in her hand, she would kill him and join Fasil in New Orleans. Fasil had her word for it.

Fasil was desperate. The truck bearing the bomb

was moving toward New Orleans on schedule. Now he had a bomb and no delivery system. He must work out an alternate plan, and the place to do it was here, where the strike would be made. Hafez Najeer had erred very badly in allowing Dahlia Iyad to control this mission, Fasil told himself for the hundredth time. Well, she controlled it no longer. The new plan would be his.

The airport was jammed with the crowd arriving for the Sugar Bowl, the college invitational bowl game that would be played in Tulane Stadium in three days. Fasil called eight hotels. All were full. He had to take a room at the YMCA.

The cramped little room was quite a comedown from the Plaza in New York, where he had spent the previous night—the Plaza, with the national flags of foreign dignitaries hanging in front and a switchboard accustomed to placing international calls. The flags of Saudi Arabia, Iran, and Turkey hung among the others during the present United Nations session and calls to the Middle East were common. Fasil could have had a comfortable conversation with Beirut, arranging for the gunmen to report to New Orleans. He had finished encoding his message and was ready to make the call when he was interrupted by Dahlia on the telephone, telling him of Lander's stupid debacle. Angrily, Fasil had torn up his message to Beirut and flushed it down his elegant Plaza toilet.

Now he was stuffed in this shabby cell in New Orleans with the plan a shambles. It was time to look over the ground. Fasil had never seen Tulane Stadium. He had depended on Lander for all that. Bitterly he walked outside and flagged a taxi.

How could he make the strike? He would have the truck. He would have the bomb. He could still send for a couple of gunmen. He would have the services of Dahlia Iyad, even if her infidel was out of it. Although Fasil was an atheist, he thought of Lander as an infidel, and he spat as he muttered the name.

The taxi mounted the U.S. 90 expressway over downtown New Orleans and headed southwest into the afternoon sun. The driver kept up a steady monologue in a dialect barely intelligible to Fasil.

"These bums now don't want to work. They want something for nothing," the driver was saying. "My sister's kid used to work with me when I was plumbing, before my back went out. I never could find him half the time. You can't do any plumbing by yourself. You have to come out from under the house too many times, you don't have nobody to hand you stuff. That's why my back went out, all the time crawling under and coming back out."

Fasil wished the man would shut up. He did not shut up.

"That there's the Superdome, which I think they're never gonna finish. First they thought it would cost $168 million, now it's $200 million. Everybody says Howard Hughes bought it. What a mess. The sheet metal workers took a walk first, and then . . ."

Fasil looked at the great bulge of the domed stadium. Work was underway on it, even through the holiday. He could see tiny figures moving on it. There had been a scare in the early stages of the mission that the

Superdome would not be completed in time for the Super Bowl, rendering the blimp useless. But there were still big gaps visible in the roof. Not that it mattered now anyway, Fasil thought angrily.

He made a mental note to investigate the possible use of toxic gas in closed stadiums. That might be a useful technique at some future time.

The taxi shifted into the high-speed lane, the driver talking over his shoulder. "You know, they were gonna have the Super Bowl there, they thought for a while. Now they got a terrific cost overrun because the city thinks it looks bad, embarrassing you know, not to be through with it. Double time and a half they're paying to work on it through the holidays, you know. Put on a show of really hustling to finish it by spring. I wouldn't mind some of that overtime myself."

Fasil started to ask the man to be quiet. Then he changed his mind. If he were rude, the driver would remember him.

"You know what happened in Houston with the Astrodome. They got cutesy with the Oilers and now they play in Rice Stadium. These guys don't want that to happen. They got to have the Saints, you know? They want everybody to see they're getting on with it, the NFL and all, so they work over the holidays too. You think I wouldn't work Christmas and New Year's double time and a half? Ha. The old lady could hang up the stockings by herself."

The taxi followed the curve of U.S. 90, turning northwest, and the driver adjusted his sunshade. They were nearing Tulane University now. "That's the Ursu-

line College on the left there. What side of the stadium
you want, Willow Street?"

"Yes."

The sight of the great, shabby tan-and-gray stadium
aroused Fasil. The films of Munich were running in his
head.

It was big. Fasil was reminded of his first close view
of an aircraft carrier. It went up and up. Fasil climbed
out of the taxi, his camera banging against the door.

The southeast gate was open. Maintenance men
were coming in and out in the last rush before the
Sugar Bowl game. Fasil had his press card ready, and
the same credentials he had brought on his flight to the
Azores, but he was not stopped. He glanced at the vast,
shadowy spaces under the stands, tangled with iron,
then walked out into the arena.

It was so big! Its size elated him. The artificial turf
was new, the numbers gleaming white against the
green. He stepped on the turf and almost recoiled. It
felt like flesh underfoot. Fasil walked across the field,
feeling the presence of the endless tiers of seats. It is difficult to walk through the focal area of a stadium, even
an empty stadium, without feeling watched. He hurried
to the west side of the field and climbed the stands
toward the press boxes.

High above the field, looking out at the curve of the
stands, Fasil recalled the matching curves of the shaped
charge and, in spite of himself, he was impressed with
the genius of Michael Lander.

The stadium spread its sides open to the sky, labial,
passive, waiting. The thought of those stands filled
with 80,985 people, moving in their seats, the stands

squirming with life, filled Fasil with an emotion that was very close to lust. This was the soft aperture to the House of War. Soon those spreading sides would be engorged with people, full and waiting.

"Quss ummak," Fasil hissed. It is an ancient Arab insult. It means "your mother's vulva."

He thought of the various possibilities. Any explosion in or close to the stadium would guarantee worldwide headlines. The gates were not really substantial. The truck possibly could plow through one of the four entrances and make it onto the field before the charge was set off. There would certainly be many casualties, but much of the explosion would be wasted in blowing a great crater in the earth. There was also the problem of traffic in the small, choked streets leading to the stadium. What if emergency vehicles were parked in the entrances? If the President was here, surely there would be armed men at the gates. What if the driver were shot before he could detonate the charge? Who would drive the truck? Not himself, certainly. Dahlia, then. She had the guts to do it, there was no question about that. Afterward, he would praise her posthumously at his news conference in Lebanon.

Perhaps an emergency vehicle, an ambulance, might have a better chance. It could be rushed onto the field, siren wailing.

But the nacelle was too big to fit inside an ordinary ambulance, and the truck that now carried it did not look anything like an emergency vehicle. But it did look like a television equipment truck. Still, an emergency vehicle was better. A big panel truck, then. He could paint it white and put a red cross on it. Whatever he did, he would have to hurry. Fourteen days remained.

The empty sky pressed on Fasil as he stood at the top of the stands, wind fluttering the collar of his coat. The open, easy sky gave perfect access, he thought bitterly. Getting the nacelle into an airplane and then hijacking it would be next to impossible. If it could be done through some ruse of carrying the nacelle as freight, he was not sure Dahlia could force a pilot to dive close enough to the stadium, even with a gun at the man's temple.

Fasil looked to the northeast at the New Orleans skyline; the Superdome two miles away, the Marriott Hotel, the International Trade Mart. Beyond that skyline, a scant eight miles away, lay New Orleans Lakefront Airport. The fat and harmless blimp would come over that skyline to the Super Bowl on January 12 while he struggled like an ant on the ground. Damn Lander and his putrid issue to the tenth generation.

Fasil was seized with a vision of what the strike might have been. The blimp shining silver, coming down, unnoticed at first by the crowd intent on the game. Then more and more of the spectators glancing up as it came lower, bigger, impossibly big, hanging over them, the long shadow darkening the field and some of them looking directly at the bright nacelle as it detonated with a flash like the sun exploding, the stands heaving, possibly collapsing, filled with 12 million pounds of ripped meat. And the roar and shock wave rolling out across the flats, deafening, blasting the windows out of homes 20 miles away, ships heeling as to a monsoon. The wind of it screaming around the towers of the House of War, screaming

F a s e e e e e e l!

It would have been incredibly beautiful. He had to sit down. He was shaking. He forced his mind back to the alternatives. He tried to cut his losses. When he was calm again, he felt proud of his strength of character, his forbearance in the face of misfortune. He was Fasil. He would do the best he could.

Fasil's thoughts were concerned with trucks and paint as he rode back toward downtown New Orleans. All was not lost, he told himself. It was perhaps better this way. The use of the American had always sullied the operation. Now the strike was all his. Not so spectacular perhaps, not a maximum-efficiency air burst, but he would still gain enormous prestige—and the guerrilla movement would be enhanced, he added in a quick afterthought.

There was the domed stadium, on his right this time. The sun was gleaming off the metal roof. And what was that rising behind it? A helicopter of the "skycrane" type. It was lifting something, a piece of machinery. Now it was moving over the roof. A party of workmen waited beside one of the openings in the roof. The shadow of the helicopter slid across the dome and covered them. Slowly, delicately, the helicopter lowered the heavy object into the gap on the roof. The hat of one of the workmen blew away and tumbled, a tiny dot bouncing down the dome and out into space, tumbling on the wind. The helicopter rose again, freed of its burden, and sank out of sight behind the unfinished Superdome.

Fasil no longer thought about trucks. He could always get a truck. Sweat stood out on his face. He was wondering if the helicopter worked on Sundays. He tapped the driver and told him to go to the Superdome.

Two hours later, Fasil was in the public library studying an entry in "Jane's All the World's Aircraft." From the library he went to the Monteleone Hotel, where he copied the number from a telephone in a lobby booth. He copied another number from a pay phone in the Union Passenger Terminal, then went to the Western Union office. On a cable blank, he carefully composed a message, referring frequently to a small card of coded numbers glued inside his camera case. In minutes, on the long line beneath the sea, the brief personal message flashed toward Benghazi, Libya.

Fasil was back in the passenger terminal at 9 A.M. the next day. He removed a yellow out-of-order sticker from a pay phone near the entrance and placed it on the telephone he had selected, a booth at the end of the row. He glanced at his watch. A half-hour to go. He sat down with a newspaper on a bench near the telephone.

Fasil had never before presumed on Najeer's Libyan connections. He would not dare to do it now, if Najeer were still alive. Fasil had only picked up the plastic explosive in Benghazi after Najeer's arrangements were made, but the code name "Sofia," coined by Najeer for the mission, had opened the necessary doors for Fasil in Benghazi. He had included it in his cable, and he hoped it would work again.

At 9:35 P.M., the telephone rang. Fasil picked it up on the second ring. "Hello?"

"Yes, I am trying to reach Mrs. Yusuf." Despite the

scratchy connection, Fasil recognized the voice of the Libyan officer in charge of liaison with Al Fatah.

"You are calling for Sofia Yusuf, then."

"Go ahead."

Fasil spoke quickly. He knew the Libyan would not stay on the telephone long. "I need a pilot capable of flying a Sikorsky S-58 cargo helicopter. The priority is absolute. I must have him in New Orleans in six days. He must be expendable." Fasil knew he was asking something of extreme difficulty. He also knew that there were great resources available to Al Fatah in Benghazi and Tripoli. He went on quickly, before the officer could object. "It is similar to the Russian machines used on the Aswan High Dam. Take the request to the very highest level. The *very* highest level. I carry the authority of Eleven." "Eleven" was Hafez Najeer.

The voice on the other end was soft, as though the man were trying to whisper over the telephone. "There may not be such a man. This is very hard. Six days is nothing."

"If I cannot have him in that time, it will be useless. Much will be lost. I *must* have him. Call me in 24 hours at the alternate number. The priority is absolute."

"I understand," said the voice 6,000 miles away. The line went dead.

Fasil walked away from the telephone and out of the terminal at a lively pace. It was terribly dangerous to communicate directly with the Middle East, but the shortage of time demanded taking the chance. The request for a pilot was a very long shot. There were none in the fedayeen ranks. Flying a cargo helicopter with a heavy object suspended beneath it is a fine art. Pilots capable of doing it are not common. But the Libyans had come through for Black September before. Had not Colonel Khadafy helped with the strike at Khartoum? The very weapons used to slay the American diplomats were smuggled into the country in the Libyan diplomatic pouch. Thirty million dollars a year flows to Al Fatah from the Libyan treasury. How much could a pilot be worth? Fasil had every reason to hope. If only they could find one, and soon.

The six-day time limit Fasil had stressed was not strictly true, since two weeks remained before the Super Bowl. But modifications on the bomb would be necessary to fit it to a different aircraft, and he needed lead time and the pilot's skilled help.

Fasil had weighed the odds against finding a pilot, and the risk involved in asking for one, against the splendid result if one could be located. He found the risk worth taking.

What if his cable, innocent as it appeared to be, was examined by the U.S. authorities? What if the number code for the telephones was known to the Jew Kabakov? That was hardly likely, Fasil knew, but still he was uneasy. Certainly the authorities were looking for the plastic, but they could not know the nature of the mission. There was nothing to point to New Orleans.

He wondered if Lander was delirious. Nonsense. People didn't lie around delirious with fever anymore. But crazy people sometimes rave, fever or no. If he were on the point of blabbing, Dahlia would kill him.

In Israel, at that moment, a sequence of events was underway that would have far greater bearing on Fasil's request than any influence of the late Hafez Najeer. At an airstrip near Jaffa, fourteen Israeli airmen were climbing into the cockpits of seven F-4 Phantom fighter-bombers. They taxied onto the runway, the heat distorting the air behind them like rippled glass. By twos they drove down the asphalt and leaped into the sky in a long, climbing turn that took them out over the Mediterranean and westward, toward Tobruk, Libya, at twice the speed of sound.

They were on a retaliatory raid. Still smoking at Rosh Pina was the rubble of an apartment house hit by Russian Katyusha rockets, supplied to the fedayeen by Libya. This time the reply would not be against the fedayeen bases in Lebanon and Syria. This time the supplier would suffer.

Thirty-nine minutes after takeoff, the flight leader spotted the Libyan freighter. She was exactly where the Mossad said she would be, 18 miles out of Tobruk and steaming eastward, heavily laden with armaments for the guerrillas. But they must be sure. Four Phantoms remained at altitude to provide cover from Arab aircraft. The other three went down. The lead plane, throttled back to 200 knots, passed the ship at an altitude of 60 feet. There was no mistake. Then the three of them were howling down upon her in a bomb run, and up again, pulling three and a half G's as they streaked back into the sky. There were no cries of victory in the cockpits as the ship ballooned in fire. On the way home, the Israelis watched the sky hopefully. They would feel better if the MIGs came.

Rage swept Libya's Revolutionary Command Council after the Israeli attack. Who on the Council knew of the Al Fatah strike in the United States will never be determined. But somewhere in the angry halls at Benghazi, a cog turned.

The Israelis had struck with airplanes given to them by the Americans.

The Israelis themselves had said it: "The suppliers will suffer."

So be it.

CHAPTER

20

"I TOLD HIM he could go to bed, but he said his orders are to put the box in your hands," Colonel Weisman, the military attaché, told Kabakov, as they walked toward the conference room in the Israeli embassy.

The young captain was nodding in his chair as Kabakov opened the door. He snapped to his feet.

"Major Kabakov, I'm Captain Reik. The package from Beirut, sir."

Kabakov fought down the urge to grab the box and open it. Reik had come a long way. "I remember you, Captain. You had the howitzer battery at Qanaabe." They shook hands, the younger man obviously pleased.

Kabakov turned to the fiberboard carton on the table. It was about two feet square and a foot deep and was tied with twine. Scrawled in Arabic across the lid was "Personal property of Abu Ali, 18 Rue Verdun, deceased. File 186047. Hold until February 23." There was a hole gouged through the corner of the box. A bullet hole.

"Intelligence went through it in Tel Aviv," Reik said. "There was dust in the knots. They think it hadn't been opened for some time."

Kabakov removed the lid and set the contents out on the table. An alarm clock with the crystal smashed. Two bottles of pills. A bankbook. A clip for a Llama automatic pistol—Kabakov felt sure the pistol had been stolen—a cufflink box without the cufflinks, a pair of bent spectacles, and a few periodicals. Doubtless any items of value had been taken by the police and what was left had been carefully sifted by Al Fatah. Kabakov was bitterly disappointed. He had hoped that for once the obsessive secrecy of Black September would work against the terrorist organization, that the person assigned to "sanitize" Abu Ali's effects would not know what was harmless and what was not, and thus might miss some useful clue. He looked up at Reik. "What did this cost?"

"Yoffee got a flesh wound across the thigh. He sent you a message, sir. He—" the captain stammered.

"Go on."

"He said you owe him a bottle of Remy Martin and—and not that goat piss you passed around at Kuneitra, sir."

"I see." Kabakov grinned in spite of himself. At least the box of junk had not cost any lives.

"Yoffee went in," Reik said. "He had some funny credentials from a Saudi law firm. He had decided he would try to do it in one move, instead of bribing the clerk ahead of time—so they wouldn't have time to fool with the box and the clerk couldn't sell him a box of garbage. He gave the property clerk in the police station three Lebanese pounds and asked to see the box. The clerk brought it out, but set it behind the counter and said he would have to get clearance from the duty officer. That normally would have only meant another bribe, but Yoffee did not have great confidence in the credentials. He slugged the clerk and grabbed the box. He had a Mini-Cooper outside, and he was all right until two radio cars blocked the Mazraa in front of him at the Rue Unesco. Of course he went around them on the sidewalk, but they got a couple of rounds into the car. He had a five-block lead going down the Ramlet el Baida. Jacoby was flying the Huey, coming in to take him off. Yoffee climbed up through the sun roof of the car while it was still moving and we plucked him off. We came back at about a hundred feet in the dark. The chopper has the new terrain-following autopilot system and you just hang on."

"You were in the helicopter?"

"Yes sir. Yoffee owes me money."

Kabakov could imagine the heaving, dipping ride in the dark as the black helicopter snaked over the hills. "I'm surprised you had the range."

"We had to put down at Gesher Haziv."

"Did the Lebanese scramble any planes?"

"Yessir, finally. It took a little time for the word to get around. We were back in Israel in 24 minutes from the time the police saw the chopper."

Kabakov would not display his disappointment at the contents of the box, not after three men had risked their lives to get it. Tel Aviv must think him a fool.

"Thank you, Captain Reik, for a remarkable job. Tell Yoffee and Jacoby the same for me. Now go to bed. That's an order."

Kabakov and Weisman sat at the table with Abu Ali's effects between them. Weisman maintained a tactful silence. There were no personal papers of any kind, not even a copy of "Political and Armed Struggle," the omnipresent Fatah handbook. They had picked over Ali's belongings all right. Kabakov looked at the periodicals. Two copies of Al-Tali'ah, the Egyptian monthly. Here was something underlined in an interview. ". . . the rumor about the strength of the Israeli Intelligence Services is a myth. Israel is not particularly advanced in its Intelligence as such." Kabakov snorted. Abu Ali was mocking him from the grave.

Here were a few back issues of the Beirut newspaper Al-Hawadess. *Paris-Match.* A copy of *Sports Illustrated* dated January 21, 1974. Kabakov frowned at it. He picked it up. It was the only publication in English in the box. The cover bore a dark stain, coffee probably. He flipped through it once, then again. It was mostly concerned with football. Arabs follow soccer, but the principal article was about—Kabakov's mind was racing. Fasil. Munich. Sports. The tape had said, "Begin another year with bloodshed."

Weisman looked up quickly at the sound of Kabakov's voice. "Colonel Weisman, what do you know about this 'Super Bowl'?"

FBI Director John Baker took off his glasses and rubbed the bridge of his nose. "That's a hypothesis of considerable size, gentlemen."

Corley stirred in his chair.

Kabakov was tired of talking into Baker's blank face, tired of the caution with which Corley phrased remarks to his boss. "It's more than a hypothesis. Look at the facts—"

"I know, I know, Major. You've made it very clear. You think the target is the Super Bowl because this man—Fasil, is it?—organized the Black September attack at the Olympic Village; because the tape you captured at Beirut refers to a strike at the beginning of the year, and because the President plans to attend the game." He might have been naming the parts of speech.

"And because it would happen on live television with maximum shock value," Corley said.

"But this entire line of reasoning proceeds from the fact that this man, Ali, had a copy of *Sports Illustrated,* and you are not even positive that Ali was involved in the plot." Baker peered out the window at the gray Washington afternoon, as though he might find the answer in the street.

Baker had Corley's 302 file on his desk—the raw information on the case. Kabakov wondered why he had been called in, and then he realized that Baker, professionally paranoid, wanted to look at him. Wanted to expose the source to his own cop instincts. Kabakov could see a stubborn set in Baker's face. *He knows he will have to do something,* Kabakov thought. *But he needs for me to argue with him. He does not like to be told his business, but he wants to observe the telling. He's got to do something, now. Let him stew about it.*

It's his move. "Thank you for your time, Mr. Baker," Kabakov said, rising.

"Just a moment, Major, if you don't mind. Since you have seen this kind of thing, how do you think they would go about it? Would they conceal the plastic in the stadium and then, when the crowd arrives, threaten to blow it up if certain demands are not met— freedom for Sirhan Sirhan, no more aid to Israel, that kind of thing?"

"They won't demand anything. They'll blow it up and then crow about it."

"Why do you think so?"

"What could you give them? Most of the terrorists arrested in skyjackings are already freed. Those at Munich were freed to save hostages in a subsequent skyjacking. Lelia Khaled was freed in the same way. The guerrillas who shot your own diplomats in Khartoum were turned back to their people by the Sudanese government. They're all free, Mr. Baker.

"Stop aid to Israel? Even if the promise were made, no guarantees are possible. The promise would never be made in the first place and would not be kept anyway, if it were made under duress. Besides, to use hostages you must contain them. In a stadium that could not be done. There would be panic and the crowd would rush the gates, trampling a few thousand on the way. No, they'll blow it up all right."

"How?"

"I don't know. With a half-ton of plastic they could collapse both sides of the stands, but to be sure of doing that they would have to put charges in several locations and detonate them simultaneously. That would not be easy. Fasil is no fool. There are too many radio transmissions at an event like that to use a remote electronic signal to set it off, and multiple locations increase the chance of discovery."

"We can make sure the stadium is clean," Corley said. "It will be a bitch to search, but we can do it."

"Secret Service will want to handle that themselves, I expect, but they'll ask for some manpower," Baker said.

"We can check all the personnel involved with the Super Bowl, check hot dog wagons, cold drink boxes, we can prohibit any packages being carried in," Corley continued. "We can use dogs and the electronic sniffer. There's still time to train the dogs on that piece of plastic from the ship."

"What about the sky?" Kabakov said.

"You're thinking of that pilot business with the chart, of course," the FBI director said. "I think we might shut down private aviation in New Orleans for the duration of the game. We'll check with the FAA. I'm calling in the concerned agencies this afternoon. We'll know more after that."

I doubt it, Kabakov reflected.

C H A P T E R
21

THE SOUND OF Abdel Awad's endless pacing was beginning to annoy the guard in the hall. The guard raised the slide in the cell door and cursed Awad through the grate. Having done that, he felt a little ashamed. The man had a right to pace. He raised the slide again and offered Awad a cigarette, cautioning him to put it out and hide it if he heard approaching footsteps.

Awad had been listening for footsteps, all right. Sometime—tonight, tomorrow, the next day—they would be coming. To cut off his hands.

A former officer in the Libyan Air Force, he had been convicted of theft and narcotics trafficking. His sentence of death had been commuted to double amputation in view of his former service to his country. This type of sentence, prescribed by the Koran, had fallen into disuse until Colonel Khadafy assumed power and reinstated it. It must be said, however, that in line with his policy of modernization, Khadafy has replaced the

axe in the marketplace with a surgeon's knife and anti-
septic conditions at a Benghazi hospital.

Awad had tried to write down his thoughts, had
tried to write to his father apologizing for the shame he
had brought on the family, but the words were difficult
to find. He was afraid he would have the letter only
half-finished when they came for him and he would
have to mail it that way. Or finish it with the pen held
between his teeth.

He wondered if the sentence permitted anesthesia.

He wondered if he could hook one leg of his trousers on the door hinge and tie the other around his
neck and hang himself by sitting down. For a week
since his sentencing he had entertained these considerations. It would be easier if they would tell him *when*.
Perhaps not knowing was part of the sentence.

The slide flew up. "Put it out. Put it out," the guard
hissed. Numbly, Awad stepped on the cigarette and
kicked it under his cot. He heard the bolts sliding back.
He faced the door, his hands behind him, finger-nails
digging into his palms.

I am a man and a good officer, Awad thought. *They
could not deny that even at the trial. I will not shame
myself now.*

A small man in neat civilian dress came into the cell.
The man was saying something, his mouth was moving
under the small mustache. ". . . Did you hear me,
Lieutenant Awad? It is not yet time to—it is not yet
time for your punishment. But it *is* time for a serious
conversation. Speak English, please. Take the chair. I
will sit on the bunk." The little man's voice was soft,

and his eyes were constantly on Awad's face as he spoke.

Awad had very sensitive hands, the hands of a helicopter pilot. When he was offered a chance to keep them, to gain full reinstatement, he was quick to agree to the conditions.

Awad was removed from the Benghazi prison to the garrison at Ajdabujah, where, under tight security, he was checked out in a Russian MIL-6 helicopter, the heavy-duty model that carries the NATO code name "Hook." It is one of three owned by the Libyan armed forces. Awad was familiar with the type, though his experience was mostly in smaller craft. He handled it well. The MIL-6 was not exactly like the Sikorsky S-58, but it was close enough. At night, he pored over a Sikorsky flight manual, procured in Egypt. With a careful hand on the throttle and pitch controls and a vigilant eye on the manifold pressure, he would be all right when the time came.

The reign of President Khadafy is a strongly moralistic one, backed by terrible penalties, and as a result certain crimes have been sharply repressed in Libya. The civilized art of forgery does not flourish there, and it was necessary to contact a forger in Nicosia for the manufacture of Awad's papers.

Awad was to be thoroughly sanitized—no evidence of his origin would remain on his person. All that was necessary, really, was sufficient identification to get him into the United States. He would not be leaving, since he would be vaporized in the explosion. Awad was not aware of this last consideration. In fact, he had only been told to report to Muhammad Fasil and follow orders. He had been assured that he would get out of it all right. To preserve this illusion it was necessary to provide Awad with an escape plan and the papers to go with it.

On December 31, the day after Awad's release from prison, his Libyan passport, several recent photographs, and samples of his handwriting were delivered to a small printshop in Nicosia.

The concept of providing an entire "scene"—a set of mutually supportive papers such as passport, driving license, recent correspondence properly postmarked, and receipts—is a relatively recent development among forgers in the West, coming into wide practice only after the narcotics trade was able to pay for such elaborate service. Forgers in the Middle East have been creating "scenes" for their customers for generations.

The forger used by Al Fatah in Nicosia did marvelous work. He also supplied blank Lebanese passports to the Israelis, who filled in the details themselves. And he sold information to the Mossad.

It was an expensive job the Libyans wanted—two passports, one Italian bearing a U.S. entry stamp and one Portuguese. They did not quibble at the price. What is valuable to one party is often valuable to another, the forger thought as he put on his coat.

Within the hour, Mossad headquarters in Tel Aviv knew who Awad was and whom he would become. Awad's trial had received considerable attention in Benghazi. A Mossad agent there had only to look in the public prints to find out Awad's particular skill.

In Tel Aviv, they put it together. Awad was a helicopter pilot who was going into the United States one way and coming out another. The long line to Washington hummed for 45 minutes.

CHAPTER

22

ON THE AFTERNOON of December 30, a massive
search was begun at Tulane Stadium in New Orleans in
preparation for the Sugar Bowl Classic to be played on
New Year's Eve. Similar searches were scheduled for
December 31 at stadiums in Miami, Dallas, Houston,
Pasadena—every city that would host a major college
bowl game on New Year's Day.

Kabakov was glad that the Americans finally had
marshaled their great resources against the terrorists,
but he was amused by the process that prompted them.
It was typical of bureaucracy. FBI Director John Baker
had called a top-level meeting of FBI, National Security
Agency, and Secret Service personnel the previous afternoon, immediately after his talk with Kabakov and
Corley. Kabakov, sitting in the front row, felt many
pointed stares while the assembled officials emphasized
the flimsiness of the evidence pointing to the target—a
single magazine, unmarked, containing an article about
the Super Bowl.

Each of the heavyweights from the FBI and the National Security Agency seemed determined not to let another out-skepticize him as Corley outlined the theory of an attack on the Super Bowl game in New Orleans.

Only the Secret Service representatives, Earl Biggs and Jack Renfro, remained silent. Kabakov thought the Secret Service agents were the most humorless men he had ever seen. That was understandable, he decided. They had much to be humorless about.

Kabakov knew that the men in this meeting were not stupid. Each of them would have been more receptive to an uncommon idea if the idea were presented to him in privacy. When surrounded by their peers, most men have two sets of reactions—the real ones and those designed for evaluation by their fellows. Skepticism was established as the proper attitude early in the meeting and, once established, prevailed throughout Corley's presentation.

But the herd principle also worked in the other direction. As Kabakov recounted Black September's maneuvers before the strike at Munich and the abortive attempt on the World Cup soccer matches six months ago, the seed of alarm was planted. On the face of it, was an attack on the Super Bowl less plausible than an attack on the Olympic Village? Kabakov asked.

"There's not a Jewish team playing," was an immediate rejoinder. It did not get a laugh. As the officials listened to Kabakov, dread was present in the room, subtly communicated from one listener to the next by small body movements, a certain restiveness. Hands fidgeted, hands rubbed faces. Kabakov could see the

men before him changing. For as long as he could remember, Kabakov had disturbed policemen, even Israeli policemen. He attributed this to his own
impatience with them, but it was more than that. There
was something about him that affected policemen as a
trace of musk carried on the wind sets the dogs on
edge, makes them draw closer to the fire. It says that
out there is something that does not love the fire; it is
watching and it is not afraid.

The evidence of the magazine, supplemented by
Fasil's track record, began to loom large and was ex-
trapolated by the men in the meeting room. Once the
possibility of danger was admitted, one official would
not call for less stringent measures than the next: Why
just the Super Bowl as a possible target? The magazine
showed a packed stadium—why not any packed stadium? My God, the Sugar Bowl is New Year's Eve—
day after tomorrow—and there are bowl games all
over the country on New Year's Day. Search them all.

With apprehension came hostility. Suddenly Kabakov was acutely aware that he was a foreigner, and a
Jew at that. Kabakov was instantly aware that a number of the men in the room were thinking about the
fact that he was a Jew. He had expected that. He was
not surprised when, in the minds of these men with
their crisp haircuts and law school rings, he was identified with the problem rather than with the solution.
The threat was from a bunch of foreigners, of which he
was one. The attitude was unspoken, but it was there.

"Thank you, old buddies," Kabakov said, as he sat
down. You don't know from foreigners, old buddies,
he thought. But you may find out on January 12.

Kabakov did not think it reasonable that, once Black September had the capability to strike at a stadium, they would hit one that did not contain the President in preference to one that did. He stuck with the Super Bowl.

On the afternoon of December 30 he arrived in New Orleans. The search was already underway at Tulane Stadium in preparation for the Sugar Bowl. The task force at Tulane Stadium was composed of 50 men—members of the FBI and police bomb sections, police detectives, two dog handlers from the Federal Aviation Administration with dogs trained to smell explosives, and two U.S. Army technicians with an electronic "sniffer" calibrated on the Madonna recovered from the *Leticia.*

New Orleans was unique in the fact that Secret Service personnel aided in the search and in the necessity for doing the job twice—today for the Sugar Bowl and on January 11, the eve of the Super Bowl. The men went about their work quietly, largely ignored by the crew of maintenance men putting the final touches on the stadium.

The search did not interest Kabakov much. He did not expect the searchers to find anything. What he did was stare into the face of every employee of Tulane Stadium. He remembered how Fasil had sent his guerrillas to find employment in the Olympic Village six weeks ahead of time. He knew the New Orleans police were running background checks on stadium employees, but still he stared into their faces as though hoping for an instinctive, visceral reaction if he saw a terrorist. Looking at the workers, he felt nothing. The background check exposed one bigamist, who was held for extradition to Coahoma County, Mississippi.

On New Year's Eve, the Tigers of Louisiana State University lost to Nebraska 13-7 in the Sugar Bowl Classic. Kabakov attended.

He had never seen a football game before and he did not see much of this one. He and Moshevsky spent most of the time prowling under the stands and around the gates, ignored by the numerous FBI agents and police in the stadium. Kabakov was particularly interested in how the gates were manned and what access was allowed through them after the stadium was full.

He found most public spectacles annoying, and this one, with the pompoms and the pennants and the massed bands, was particularly offensive. He had always considered marching bands ridiculous. The one pleasant moment of the afternoon was the flyover at halftime by the Navy's Blue Angels, a neat diamond of jets catching the sun during a beautiful slow roll high above the droning blimp that floated around the stadium. Kabakov knew there were other jets too—Air Force interceptors poised on runways nearby in the unlikely event that an unknown aircraft approached the New Orleans area while the game was in progress.

The shadows were long across the field as the last of the crowd filtered out. Kabakov felt numbed by the hours of noise. He had difficulty understanding the English of the people he heard in conversation, and he was generally aggravated. Corley found him standing at the edge of the track outside the stadium.

"Well, no bang," Corley said.

Kabakov looked at him quickly, watching for a

smirk. Corley just looked tired. Kabakov imagined that the expression "wild goose chase" was in wide use at the stadiums in other cities, where tired men were searching for explosives in preparation for the games on New Year's Day. He expected plenty was being said here, out of his hearing. He had never claimed that the target was a college bowl game, but who remembered that? It didn't matter anyway. He and Corley walked back through the stadium together, heading for the parking lot. Rachel would be waiting at the Royal Orleans.

"Major Kabakov."

He looked around for an instant before he realized the voice came from the radio in his pocket. "Kabakov, go ahead."

"Call for you in the command post."

"Right."

The FBI command post was set up in the Tulane public relations office under the stands. An agent in shirtsleeves handed Kabakov the telephone.

Weisman was calling from the Israeli embassy. Corley tried to deduce the nature of the conversation from the brief replies Kabakov made.

"Let's walk outside," Kabakov said, as he handed back the telephone. He did not like the way the agents in the office pointedly avoided looking at him after this day of extra effort.

Standing at the sideline, Kabakov looked up at the flags blowing in the wind at the top of the stadium. "They're bringing in a helicopter pilot. We don't know if it's for this job, but we know he's coming. From Libya. And they're in a hell of a hurry."

There was a brief silence as Corley digested this information.

"How much of a make have you got on him?"

"The passports, a picture, everything. The embassy is turning our file over to your office in Washington. They'll have the stuff here in a half hour. You'll probably get a call in a minute."

"Where is he?"

"Still on the other side, we don't know where. But his papers will be picked up in Nicosia tomorrow."

"You won't interfere—"

"Of course not. We are leaving the operation strictly alone on that side. In Nicosia we're watching the place where they get the papers at the airport. That's all."

"An air strike! Here or somewhere. That's what they had in mind all the time."

"Maybe," Kabakov said. "Fasil may be running a diversion. It depends on how much he knows we know. If he is watching this stadium or any stadium, he knows we know plenty."

In the New Orleans office of the FBI, Corley and Kabakov studied the report on the pilot from Libya. Corley tapped the yellow Telex sheet. "He'll be coming in on the Portuguese passport and leaving on the Italian one with the U.S. entry stamp already on it. If he flashes that Portuguese passport at any entry point, anywhere, we'll know it within ten minutes. If he is part of this project, we've got them, David. He'll lead us to the bomb and to Fasil and the woman."

"Perhaps."

"But where were they planning to get a chopper for

him? If the target is the Super Bowl, one of the people here has it set up."

"Yes. And close by. They don't have a lot of range." Kabakov ripped open a large manila envelope. It contained 100 pictures of Fasil in three-quarter profile and 100 prints of the composite drawing of the woman. Every agent in the stadium carried the pictures. "NASA did a good job on these," Kabakov said. The pictures of Fasil were remarkably clear, and a police artist had added the bullet stripe on his cheek.

"We'll get them around to the flying services, the naval station, every place that has helicopters," Corley said. "What's the matter with you?"

"Why should they get the pilot so late? It all fits very nicely except for that. A big bomb, an air strike. But why so late with the pilot? It was the chart from the boat that first suggested a pilot might be involved, but if it was a pilot who marked the chart, he was already here."

"Nautical charts are available all over the world, David. It might have been marked on the other side, in the Middle East. A safety factor. An emergency rendezvous at sea, just in case. The chart could have come over with the woman. And as it turned out, they needed the rendezvous when they thought Muzi was unreliable."

"But the last-minute rush for the papers doesn't fit. If they had known far in advance that they were going to use the Libyan, they would have had the passports ready long ago."

"The later he was brought into it, the less chance of exposure."

"No," Kabakov said, shaking his head. "Rushing around for papers is not Fasil's style. You know how far ahead he made the arrangements for Munich."

"Anyway, it's a break. I'll get the troops out to the airports with these pictures first thing tomorrow," Corley said. "A lot of the flying services will be closed over New Year's. It may take a couple of days to talk to them all."

Kabakov rode up in the elevator at the Royal Orleans Hotel with two couples, both laughing loudly, the women in elaborate beehive hairdos. He practiced understanding their speech and decided the conversation would not have made sense if he had understood it.

He found the number and knocked on the door. Hotel-room doors all look blank. They do not admit that there are people we love behind them. Rachel was there all right, and she hugged Kabakov for several seconds without saying anything.

"I'm glad the flatfeet gave you my message at the stadium. You could have invited me to meet you down here, you know."

"I was going to wait until it was over."

"You feel like a robot," she said, releasing him. "What have you got under your coat?"

"A machine gun."

"Well take it off and have a drink."

"How did you get a place like this on short notice? Corley had to go home with a local FBI agent."

"I know someone at the Plaza in New York, and the same people own this hotel. Do you like it?"

"Yes." It was a small suite, very plush.

"I'm sorry I couldn't fix Moshevsky up."

"He's right outside the door. He can sleep on the couch—no, I'm kidding. He's all right at the consulate."

"I sent for some food."

He was not listening.

"I said some food is on the way. A Chateaubriand."

"I think they're bringing in a pilot." He told her the details.

"If the pilot leads you to the rest of them, then that's it," she said.

"If we get the plastic and we can get all of them, yes."

Rachel started to ask another question and bit it off.

"How long can you stay?" Kabakov asked.

"Four or five days. Longer if I can help you. I thought I'd go back to New York and catch up on my practice and then come back on, say, the tenth or the eleventh—if you'd like me to."

"Of course I'd like you to. When this is over, let's really do New Orleans. It looks like a good town."

"Oh, David, you'll see what a town it is."

"One thing. I don't want you to come to the Super Bowl. Come to New Orleans, fine, but I don't want you around that stadium."

"If it's not safe for me, it's not safe for anybody. In that case people should be warned."

"That's what the President told the FBI and the Secret Service. If there *is* a Super Bowl, he's coming."

"It might be canceled?"

"He called in Baker and Biggs and said that if the Super Bowl crowd cannot be adequately protected, himself included, he will cancel the game and announce the reason. Baker told him the FBI could protect it."

"What did the Secret Service say?"

"Biggs doesn't make foolish promises. He's waiting to see what happens with this pilot. He isn't inviting a damned soul to the Super Bowl and neither am I. Promise me you won't come to the stadium."

"All right, David."

He smiled. "Now tell me about New Orleans."

Dinner was splendid. They ate beside the window and Kabakov relaxed for the first time in days. Outside, New Orleans glittered in the great curve of the river, and inside was Rachel, soft beyond the candles, talking about coming to New Orleans as a child with her father and how she had felt like a great lady when her father took her to Antoine's, where a waiter tactfully slipped a pillow onto her chair when he saw her coming.

She and Kabakov planned a mighty dinner at Antoine's for the night of January 12, or whenever his business was concluded. And full of Beaujolais and plans, they were happy together in the big bed. Rachel went to sleep smiling.

She awoke once after midnight and saw Kabakov propped against the headboard. When she stirred he patted her absently, and she knew he was thinking of something else.

The truck carrying the bomb entered New Orleans at 11 P.M. on December 31. The driver followed U.S. 10 past the Superdome to the intersection with U.S. 90, turned south and came to a stop near the Thalia Street wharf beneath the Mississippi River Bridge, an area deserted at that time of night.

"This is the place he said," the man at the wheel told his companion. "I'm damned if I see anybody. The whole wharf is closed."

A voice at his ear startled the driver. "Yes, this is the place," Fasil said, mounting the running board. "Here are the papers. I've signed the receipt." While the driver examined the documents with his flashlight, Fasil inspected the seals on the tailgate of the truck. They were intact.

"Buddy, could you let us have a ride to the airport? There's a late flight to Newark we're trying to catch."

"Sorry, but I can't," Fasil said. "I'll drop you where you can get a taxi."

"Christ Jesus, it'll be ten bucks to the airport."

Fasil did not want a row. He gave the man $10 and dropped the drivers off a block from a cab stand. He smiled and whistled tunelessly between his teeth as he drove toward the garage. He had been smiling all day, ever since the voice on the pay phone at the Monteleone Hotel told him the pilot was coming. His mind was alive with plans, and he had to force himself to concentrate on his driving.

First he must establish complete dominance over this man Awad. Awad must fear and respect him. That Fasil could manage. Then he must give Awad a thorough briefing and include a convincing story on how they would escape after the strike.

Fasil's plan for the strike itself was based largely on what he had learned at the Superdome. The Sikorsky S-58 helicopter that had attracted his attention was a venerable machine, sold as surplus by the West German Army. With its lift capacity of 5,000 pounds, it could not compare with the new Skycranes, but it was more than adequate for Fasil's purpose.

To make a lift requires three persons—the pilot, the "belly-man," and the loadmaster—as Fasil had learned while watching the operation at the Superdome. The pilot hovers over the cargo. He is guided by the belly-man, who lies on the floor back in the fuselage, peering straight down at the cargo and talking to the pilot via a headset.

The loadmaster is on the ground. He attaches the cargo hook to the load. The men in the aircraft cannot close the hook by remote control. It must be done on the ground. In an emergency, the pilot can drop the load instantly by pressing a red button on the control stick. Fasil learned this in conversation with the pilot during a brief break in the lifting. The pilot had been pleasant enough—a black man with clear, wide-set eyes behind his sunglasses. It was possible that this man, introduced to a fellow pilot, might allow Awad to go up with him on a lift. A fine opportunity for Awad to further familiarize himself with the cockpit. Fasil hoped Awad was personable.

On Super Bowl Sunday he would shoot the pilot immediately, and any of the ground crew that got in the way. Awad and Dahlia would man the helicopter, with Fasil on the ground as loadmaster. Dahlia would see to it that the craft was positioned correctly over the stadium and, while Awad still waited for the order to drop the nacelle, she would simply touch it off under the helicopter. Fasil had no doubt that Dahlia would go through with it.

He worried about the red drop button though. It must be rendered inoperative. If Awad, through nervousness, actually dropped the device, the effect would be ruined. It was never designed to be dropped. A lashing on the cargo hook would do it. The hook must be lashed tight at the last second before the lift, when Awad could not see what was going on beneath the helicopter. Fasil could not trust some imported front-fighter to take care of this detail. For this reason, he himself must be the loadmaster.

The risk was acceptable. He would have much more cover than he would have had at Lakefront Airport with the blimp. He would be facing unarmed construction workers rather than airport police. When the big bang came, Fasil intended to be driving toward the city limits, toward Houston and a plane to Mexico City.

Awad would believe to the last that Fasil was waiting for him in a car in Audubon Park beyond the stadium.

Here was the garage, set back from the street just as Dahlia described. Once inside with the door closed, Fasil opened the rear of the truck. All was in order. He tried the engine on the forklift. It started instantly. Well and good. As soon as Awad arrived and his arrangements were complete, it would be time to call Dahlia, tell her to kill the American and come to New Orleans.

CHAPTER
23

LANDER MOANED ONCE and moved in the hospital bed. Dahlia Iyad put aside the New Orleans street map she was studying and rose stiffly. Her foot was asleep. She hobbled to the bedside and put her hand on Lander's forehead. The skin was hot. She sponged his temples and cheeks with a cool cloth, and when his breathing settled into a steady wheeze and rattle she returned to her chair under the reading lamp.

A curious change came over Dahlia each time she went to the bedside. Sitting in her chair with the map, thinking about New Orleans, she could look at Lander with the steady, cool gaze of a cat, a look in which there were many possibilities, all determined solely by her need. At his bedside, her face was warm and full of concern. Both expressions were genuine. No man ever had a kinder, deadlier nurse than Dahlia Iyad.

She had slept on a cot in the New Jersey hospital room for four nights. She could not leave him for fear he would rave about the mission. And he had raved, but it was about Vietnam and persons she did not know. And about Margaret. For one entire evening he had repeated, "Jergens, you were right."

She did not know if his mind was gone. She knew she had twelve days until the strike. If she could salvage him, she would do it. If not—well, either way he would die. One way was no worse than the other.

She knew Fasil was in a hurry. But hurrying is dangerous. If Lander was unable to fly and Fasil's alternate arrangements did not suit her, she would eliminate Fasil, she decided. The bomb was too valuable to waste in a hastily contrived operation. It was far more valuable than Fasil. She would never forgive him for trying to get out of the actual operation in New Orleans. His weaseling had not been the result of a failure of nerve, as was the case with the Japanese she shot before the Lod airport strike. It was a result of personal ambition, and that was much worse.

"Try, Michael," she whispered. "Try very hard."

Early on the morning of January 1, federal agents and local police fanned out to the airports that ringed New Orleans—Houma, Thibodaux, Slidell, Hammond, Greater St. Tammany, Gulfport, Stennis International, and Bogalusa. All morning long their reports filtered in. No one had seen Fasil or the woman.

Corley, Kabakov, and Moshevsky worked New Orleans International and New Orleans Lakefront airports with no success. It was a glum drive back toward town. Corley, checking by radio, was told that all reports from Customs at entry points around the country and all reports from Interpol were negative. There had been no sign of the Libyan pilot.

"The bastard could be going anywhere," Corley said as he accelerated onto the expressway.

Kabakov stared out the window in sour silence. Only Moshevsky was unconcerned. Having attended the late-late show at the Hotsy-Totsy Club on Bourbon Street the previous evening instead of retiring, he was asleep on the back seat.

They had turned on Poydras toward the federal building when, like a great bird flushed from hiding, the helicopter rose above the surrounding buildings to hover over the Superdome, a heavy square object slung close under its belly.

"Hey. Hey. Hey, David," Corley said. He leaned over the wheel to look up through the windshield and slammed on his brakes. The car behind them honked angrily and pulled around them on the right, the driver's mouth working behind his window.

Kabakov's heart leaped when he saw the machine, and it was still pounding. He knew it was too early for the strike, he could see now that the object hanging under the big helicopter was a piece of machinery, but the image fit the imprint in his mind too well.

The landing pad was on the east side of the Superdome. Corley parked the car a hundred yards away, beside a stack of girders.

"If Fasil is watching this place, he'd better not recognize you," Corley said. "I'll get us a couple of hardhats." He disappeared into the construction site and returned in minutes with three yellow plastic helmets with goggles.

"Take the field glasses and move up into the dome, where that opening overlooks the pad," Kabakov told

Moshevsky. "Keep out of the sunlight and sweep the windows across the street, anywhere high, and the perimeter of the loading area here."

Moshevsky was moving as he spoke the last word.

The ground crew trundled another load onto the pad, and the helicopter, rocking gently, began its descent to pick it up. Kabakov went into the construction shack at the edge of the pad and watched through the window. The loadmaster was shielding his eyes from the sun with his hand and talking into a small radio as Corley approached him.

"Ask the chopper to come down, please," Corley said. He cupped his badge so only the loadmaster could see it. The loadmaster glanced at the badge and then at Corley's face.

"What is it?"

"Would you ask him to come down?"

The loadmaster spoke into the radio and yelled at the ground crew. They rolled the big refrigeration pump off the pad and turned their faces away from the blowing dust as the machine gingerly touched down. The loadmaster made a cutting motion with his hand across his wrist and beckoned. The big rotor slowed and began to droop.

The pilot swung himself out and dropped to the ground in one motion. He wore a Marine flight suit, weathered until it was almost white at the knees and elbows. "What is it, Maginty?"

"This guy wants to talk to you," the loadmaster said.

The pilot looked at Corley's ID. Kabakov could detect no expression on his dark brown face.

"Can we go in the shack? You too, Mr. Maginty," Corley said.

"Yeah," the loadmaster said. "But look, this egg-beater costs the company $500 an hour, can we sort of hurry this up?"

In the littered construction shack, Corley took out the picture of Fasil. "Have you—"

"Why don't you introduce yourselves first," the pilot said. "That's polite, and it'll only cost Maginty here $12 worth of time."

"Sam Corley."

"David Kabakov."

"I'm Lamar Jackson." He shook their hands solemnly.

"It's a matter of national security," Corley said. Kabakov thought he detected a glint of amusement in the pilot's eyes at Corley's tone. "Have you seen this man?"

Jackson's eyebrows raised as he looked at the picture. "Yeah, three or four days ago, while you were rigging the sling on that elevator hoist, Maginty. Who is he anyway?"

"He's a fugitive. We want him."

"Well, stick around. He said he was coming back."

"He did?"

"Yeah. How did you guys know to look here?"

"You've got what he wants," Corley said. "A helicopter."

"What for?"

"To hurt a lot of people with. When is he coming back?"

"He didn't say. I didn't pay too much attention to

him to tell you the truth. He was kind of a creepy guy, you know, coming on friendly. What did he do? I mean you say he's bad news—"

"He is a psychopath and a killer, a political fanatic," Kabakov said. "He has committed a number of murders. He was going to kill you and take your helicopter when the time came. Tell us what happened."

"Oh, Christ," Maginty said. He mopped his face with a handkerchief. "I don't like this." He looked quickly out the door of the shack, as though he expected the maniac momentarily.

Jackson shook his head like a man making sure he is really awake, but when he spoke his voice was calm. "He was standing by the pad when I came over here for a cup of coffee. I didn't particularly notice him, because a lot of people like to watch the thing, you know. Then he started asking me about it, how you make a lift and all, what the model designation was. He asked if he could look inside. I said he could look in through the side door of the fuselage, but he shouldn't touch anything."

"And he looked?"

"Yeah, and let me see, he asked how you go back and forth from the cargo bay to the cockpit. I told him it's awkward, you have to lift one of the seats in the cockpit. I remember I thought it was a funny question. People usually ask, like, how much will it pick up and don't I get scared it will fall. Then he told me he had a brother who flies choppers and how his brother would love to see it."

"Did he ask you if you work on Sundays?"

"I was getting to that. This dude asked me three

times if we were going to work through the rest of the
holidays and I kept telling him yeah, yeah. I had to go
back to work, and he made a point of shaking hands
and all."

"He asked you your name?" Kabakov asked.

"Yes."

"And where you are from?"

"Right."

Instinctively, Kabakov liked Jackson. He looked like
a man with good nerves. It would take good nerves to
do Jackson's job. He also looked as though he could be
very tough when he needed to be.

"You were a Marine pilot?" Kabakov asked.

"Right."

"Vietnam?"

"Thirty-eight missions. Then I got shot up a little
and I was 'ree-tired' until the end of the hitch."

"Mr. Jackson, we need your help."

"To catch this guy?"

"Yes," Kabakov said. "We want to follow him when
he leaves here after his next visit. He'll just come and
bring his fake brother and look around. He mustn't be
alarmed while he's here. We have to follow him for a
little while before we take him. So we need your cooperation."

"Um-hum. Well, it so happens I need your help too.
Let me see your credentials, Mr. FBI." He was looking
at Kabakov, but Corley handed over his identification.
The pilot picked up the telephone.

"The number is—"

"I'll get the number, Mr. Corley."

"You can ask for—"

"I can ask for the head dick in charge," Jackson said.

The New Orleans office of the FBI confirmed Corley's identity.

"Now," Jackson said, hanging up the telephone, "you wanted to know if Crazy Person asked me where I'm from. That means him locating my family if I'm not mistaken. Like to coerce me."

"It would occur to him, yes. If it was necessary," Kabakov said.

"Well, I'll tell you. You want me to help you by playing it straight when the man shows up again?"

"You'll be covered all the time. We just want to follow him when he leaves," Corley said.

"How do you know his next call won't be time for the shit to go down?"

"Because he'll bring his pilot to look at the chopper in advance. We know the day he plans to strike."

"Um-hum. I'll do that. But, in five minutes I'm going to call my wife in Orlando. I want her to tell me there is a government car parked out front containing the baddest four dudes she has *ever* seen. Do you follow me?"

"Let me use your telephone," Corley said.

The round-the-clock stakeout at the helipad stretched on for days. Corley, Kabakov, and Moshevsky were there during working hours. A three-man team of FBI agents took over when the helicopter was secured for the night. Fasil did not come.

Each day Jackson arrived cheerful and ready to go, though he complained about the pair of federal agents that stayed with him during off-duty hours. He said they cramped his style.

Once in the evening he had a drink with Kabakov and Rachel at the Royal Orleans, his two bodyguards sitting at the next table dry and glum. Jackson had been a lot of places and had seen a lot of things, and Kabakov liked him better than most of the Americans he had met.

Maginty was another matter. Kabakov wished they had avoided bringing Maginty into it. The strain was telling on the loadmaster. He was jumpy and irritable.

On the morning of January 4 rain delayed the lifting, and Jackson came into the construction shack for coffee.

"What is that piece you've got back there?" he asked Moshevsky.

"A Galil." Moshevsky had ordered the new type of automatic assault rifle from Israel at Kabakov's indulgence. He removed the clip and the round from the chamber and passed it to Jackson. Moshevsky pointed out the bottle opener built into the bipod, a feature he found of particular interest.

"We used to carry an AK-47 in the chopper in Nam," Jackson said. "Somebody took it off a Cong. I liked it better than an M-16."

Maginty came into the shack, saw the weapon, and backed out again. Kabakov decided to tell Moshevsky to keep the rifle out of sight. There was no point in spooking Maginty any further.

"But to tell you the truth. I don't like any of these things," Jackson was saying. "You know a lot of guys jerk off with guns—I don't mean *you*, that's your business-but you show me a man that just loves a piece and I'll—"

Corley's radio interrupted Jackson. "Jay Seven, Jay Seven."

"Jay Seven, go ahead."

"New York advises subject Mayfly cleared JFK customs at 0940 Eastern Standard. Has reservation on Delta 704 to New Orleans, arriving 12:30 Central Standard." Mayfly was the code name assigned Abdel Awad.

"Roger, Jay Seven out. Son of a bitch, Kabakov, he's coming! He'll lead us to Fasil and the plastic and the woman."

Kabakov gave a sigh of relief. It was the first hard evidence that he was on the right track, that the Super Bowl was the target. "I hope we can separate them from the plastic before we take them. Otherwise there will be a very loud noise."

"So today's the day," Jackson said. There was no alarm in his voice. He was steady.

"I don't know," Kabakov said. "Maybe today, maybe tomorrow. Tomorrow is Sunday. He'll want to see you working on Sunday. We'll see."

Three hours and 45 minutes later Abdel Awad got off a Delta jet at New Orleans International Airport. He was carrying a small suitcase. In the line of passengers behind him was a large, middle-aged man in a gray business suit. For an instant the eyes of the man in gray met those of Corley, who was waiting across the corridor. The big man looked briefly at Awad's back, then looked away.

Corley, carrying a suitcase, trailed the debarking

passengers toward the lobby. He was not watching Awad, he was looking at the crowd waiting to greet the new arrivals. He was looking for Fasil, looking for the woman.

But Awad clearly was not looking for anyone. He went down the escalator and walked outside, where he hesitated near the line of passengers waiting for limousines.

Corley slid into the car with Kabakov and Moshevsky. Kabakov appeared to be reading a newspaper. It had been agreed that he would lie low in the event that Awad had seen his picture in a briefing.

"That's Howard, the big guy," Corley said. "Howard will stay with him if he takes the limo. If he takes a cab, Howard will finger it for the guys in the radio cars."

Awad took a taxi. Howard walked behind it and stopped to blow his nose.

It was a pleasure to watch the trailing operation. Three cars and a pickup truck were used, none staying immediately behind the taxi for more than a few minutes on the long drive into the city. When it was clear that the taxi was stopping at the Marriott Hotel, one of the chase cars shot around to the side entrance and an agent was near the registration desk before Awad came to claim his reservation.

The agent by the desk walked quickly to the elevator bank. "Six-eleven," he said as he passed the man standing under the potted palm. The agent under the tree entered the elevator. He was on the sixth floor when Awad followed the bellhop to his room.

In half an hour the FBI had the room next door and

an agent at the switchboard. Awad received no calls, and he did not come down. At 8 P.M. he ordered a steak sent to his room. An agent delivered it and received a quarter tip, which he held by the edges all the way back downstairs where the coin was finger-printed. The vigil went on all night.

Sunday morning, January 5, was chill and overcast. Moshevsky poured strong Cajun coffee and passed a cup to Kabakov, a cup to Corley. Through the thin walls of the construction shack they could hear the rotor blades of the big helicopter blatting the air as it made another lift.

It had been against Kabakov's instincts to leave the hotel where Awad was staying, but common sense told him this was the place to wait. He could not perform close surveillance without running the risk of being seen by Awad, or by Fasil when he showed up. The surveillance at the hotel, under the direct control of the New Orleans Agent In Charge, was as good as Kabakov had ever seen. There was no question in Kabakov's mind that they would come here to the helicopter before they went to the bomb. Awad could change the load to fit the chopper, but he could not change the chopper to fit the load—he had to see the helicopter first.

This was the place of greatest peril. The Arabs would be on foot in this vast tangle of building supplies and they would be dealing with civilians, two of whom knew they were dangerous. At least Maginty wasn't here and that was a boon, Kabakov thought. In the six days of the stakeout, Maginty had called in sick twice and had been late on two other days.

Corley's radio growled. He fiddled with the squelch knob.

"Unit One, Unit Four." That was the team on the sixth floor of the Marriott, calling the Agent In Charge.

"Go ahead, Four."

"Mayfly left his room, heading for the elevators."

"Roger Four. Five, you got that?"

"Five standing by." A minute passed.

"Unit One, Unit Five. He's passing through the lobby now." The voice on the radio was muffled, and Kabakov guessed the agent in the lobby was speaking into a buttonhole microphone.

Kabakov stared at the radio, a muscle in his jaw twitching. If Awad headed for another part of the city, he could join the hunt in minutes. Faintly on the radio he heard the swoosh of the revolving door, then street noises as the agent followed Awad outside the Marriott.

"One, this is Five. He's walking west on Decatur." A long pause. "One, he's going into the Bienville House."

"Three, cover the back."

"Roger."

An hour passed and Awad did not emerge. Kabakov thought about all the rooms in which he had waited. He had forgotten how sick and tired a man gets of a stakeout room. There was no conversation. Kabakov stared out the window. Corley looked at the radio. Moshevsky examined something he had removed from his ear.

"Unit One, Unit Five. He's coming out. Roach is with him." Kabakov took a deep breath and let it out slowly. "Roach" was Muhammad Fasil.

Five was still talking. "They're taking a taxi. Cab number four seven five eight. Louisiana commercial license four seven eight Juliett Lima. Mobile Twelve has—" A second message broke in.

"Unit Twelve, we've got him. He's turning west on Magazine."

"Roger Twelve."

Kabakov went to the window. He could see the ground crew adjusting a harness on the next load, one of them acting as loadmaster.

"One, Unit Twelve, he's turning north on Poydras. Looks like he's coming to you, Jay Seven."

"This is Jay Seven, Roger Twelve."

Corley remained in the construction shack while Kabakov and Moshevsky took up positions outside, Kabakov in the back of a truck, concealed by a canvas curtain, Moshevsky in a Port-O-San portable toilet with a peephole in the door. The three of them formed a triangle around the helicopter pad.

"Jay Seven, Jay Seven, Unit Twelve. Subjects are at Poydras and Rampart, proceeding north."

Corley waited until Jackson in the helicopter was clear of the roof, settling toward the ground, then spoke to him on the aircraft frequency. "You're going to have company. Take a break in about five minutes."

"Roger." Jackson's voice was calm.

"Jay Seven, this is Mobile Twelve. They're across the street from you, getting out of the taxi."

"Roger."

Kabakov had never seen Fasil before, and now he watched him through a crack in the curtain as though he were some exotic form of wildlife. The monster of Munich. Six thousand miles was a long chase.

The camera case, he thought. *That's where you have the gun. I should have gotten you in Beirut.*

Fasil and Awad stood beside a stack of crates at the side of the pad, watching the helicopter. They were closest to Moshevsky, but out of his line of vision. They were talking. Awad said something and Fasil nodded his head. Awad turned and tried the door of Moshevsky's hideout. It was hooked. He went into the next Port-O-San in the line and after a moment returned to Fasil.

The helicopter settled to the ground, and they turned their faces away from the dust. Jackson swung down from the cockpit and walked toward the ground crew's water cooler.

Kabakov was glad to see that he moved slowly and naturally. He drew a cup of water and then appeared to notice Fasil for the first time, acknowledging his presence with a casual wave.

That's good, Kabakov thought, that's good.

Fasil and Awad walked over to Jackson. Fasil was introducing Awad. They shook hands. Jackson was nodding his head. They walked toward the helicopter, talking animatedly, Awad making the hand gestures that mark all pilots' shop talk. Awad leaned into the fuselage door and looked around. He asked a question. Jackson appeared to hesitate. He looked around as though checking on the whereabouts of the boss, then nodded. Awad scrambled into the cockpit.

Kabakov was not worried about Awad trying to take the helicopter—he knew Jackson had a fuse from the ignition in his pocket. Jackson joined Awad in the cockpit. Fasil looked around the pad, alert but calm. Two minutes passed. Jackson and Awad climbed down again. Jackson was shaking his head and pointing to his watch.

It was going well, Kabakov thought. As expected, Awad had asked to go up on a lift. Jackson had told him he couldn't take him up during working hours for insurance reasons, but that later in the week, before the boss showed up for work in the morning, perhaps he could arrange it.

They were all shaking hands again. Now they would go to the plastic.

Maginty came around the corner of the construction shack, rummaging in his lunch pail. He was in the center of the pad when he saw Fasil and froze in his tracks.

Kabakov's lips moved soundlessly as he swore. *Oh, no. Get out of there, you son of a bitch.*

Maginty's face was pale, and his mouth hung open. Fasil was looking at him now. Jackson smiled broadly. *Jackson will save it. He'll save it,* Kabakov thought.

Jackson's voice was louder. Moshevsky could hear him. "Excuse me a minute, fellas. Hey, Maginty, you decided to show up, baby. It's about time."

Maginty seemed paralyzed.

"Drinking that bug juice and laying out all night, you look awful, man." Jackson was turning him around to walk him to the construction shack when Maginty said quite clearly, "Where are the police?"

Fasil barked at Awad and sprinted for the edge of the pad, his hand in the camera case.

Corley was screaming into his radio. "Bust 'em. Bust 'em, goddammit, bust 'em."

Kabakov snatched back the curtain. "Freeze, Fasil."

Fasil fired at him, the magnum knocking a fist-sized hole in the truck bed. Fasil was running hard, dodging between piles of building materials, Kabakov 20 yards behind him.

Awad started after Fasil, but Moshevsky, bursting out of his hiding place, caught him and without breaking stride slammed him to the ground with a blow at the base of his skull, then ran hard after Kabakov and Fasil. Awad tried to rise, but Jackson and Corley were on him.

Fasil ran toward the Superdome. Twice he stopped to fire at Kabakov. Kabakov felt the wind of the second one on his face as he dived for cover.

Fasil sprinted across the clear space between the stacks of materials and the yawning door of the Superdome, Kabakov laying a burst from his submachine gun in the dirt ahead of him. "Halt! *Andek!*"

Fasil did not hesitate as the grit kicked up by the bullets stung his legs. He disappeared into the Superdome.

Kabakov heard a challenge and a shot as he ran to the entrance. FBI agents were coming from the other way, through the dome. He hoped they had not killed Fasil.

Kabakov dived through the entrance and dropped behind a pallet stacked with window frames. The upper levels of the vast, shadowy chamber glowed with the lights of the construction crews. Kabakov could see the yellow helmets as the men peered down at the floor. Three pistol shots echoed through the dome. Then he heard the heavier blast of Fasil's magnum. He crawled around the end of the pallet.

There were the FBI agents, two of them, crouched behind a portable generating unit on the open floor. Thirty yards beyond them at an angle in the wall was a breast-high stack of sacked cement. One of the agents fired, and dust flew off the top tier of bags.

Running low and hard, Kabakov crossed the floor toward the agents. A flash of movement behind the breastwork, Kabakov was diving, rolling, hearing the magnum roar, and then he was behind the generator. Blood trickled down his forearm where a flying chip of concrete had stung him.

"Is he hit?" Kabakov asked.

"I don't think so," an agent replied.

Fasil was hemmed in. His breastwork of cement protected him from the front, and the angle of the bare concrete wall protected his flanks. Thirty yards of open floor separated his position from Kabakov and the agents behind the generator.

Fasil could not escape. The trick would be in taking him alive and forcing him to tell where the plastic was hidden. Taking Fasil alive would be like trying to grab a rattlesnake by the head.

The Arab fired once. The bullet slammed into the generator engine, releasing a steady trickle of water. Kabakov fired four shots to cover Moshevsky, charging across the floor to join him.

"Corley's getting gas and smoke," Moshevsky said.

The voice from behind the cement bag barricade had a weird lilt. "Why don't you come and get me, Major Kabakov? How many of you will die trying to take me alive, do you suppose? You'll never do it. Come, come, Major. I have something for you."

Peering through a space in the machine that shielded him, Kabakov studied Fasil's position. He had to work fast. He was afraid Fasil would kill himself rather than wait for the gas. There was only one feature that might be useful. A large metal fire extinguisher was clipped to the wall beside the place where Fasil was hidden. Fasil must be very near it. All right. Do it. Don't think about it anymore. He gave Moshevsky brief instructions and cut off his objection with a single shake of his head. Kabakov poised like a sprinter at the end of the generator.

Moshevsky raised his automatic rifle and laid down a terrific volume of fire across the top of Fasil's breastwork. Kabakov was running now, bent under the hail of bullets, hard for the cement bags. He crouched outside the breastwork beneath the sheet of covering fire; he tensed and, without looking back at Moshevsky, made a cutting motion with his hand. Instantly a new burst from the Galil and the fire extinguisher exploded over Fasil in a great burst of foam, Kabakov diving over the bulwark, into the spray, on top of Fasil, slick with the chemical. Fasil's face full of it, the gun going off deafeningly beside Kabakov's neck. Kabakov had the wrist of the gun hand, snapping his head from side to side to avoid a finger strike at his eyes, and with his free hand broke Fasil's collarbone on both sides. Fasil writhed out from under him, and as he tried to rise

Kabakov caught him with an elbow in the diaphragm that laid him back on the ground.

Moshevsky was here now, raising Fasil's head and pulling his jaw and tongue forward to be sure his air passage was clear. The snake was taken.

Corley heard the screaming as he ran into the Superdome with a teargas gun. It was coming from behind the stack of cement, where two FBI agents stood uncertainly, Moshevsky facing them, full of menace.

Corley found Kabakov sitting on Fasil, his face an inch from the Arab's. "Where is it, Fasil? Where is it, Fasil?" He was flexing the fractures in Fasil's collarbones. Corley could hear the grating noise. "Where's the plastic?"

Corley's revolver was in his hand. He pressed the muzzle to the bridge of Kabakov's nose. "Stop it, Kabakov. God damn you, stop it."

Kabakov spoke, but not to Corley. "Don't shoot him, Moshevsky." He looked up at Corley. "This is the only chance we'll have to find it. You don't have to make a case against Fasil."

"We'll interrogate him. Take your hands off him."

Three heartbeats later: "All right. You'd better read to him from the card in your wallet."

Kabakov stood. Unsteady, splattered with fire extinguisher foam, he leaned against the rough concrete wall, and his stomach heaved. Watching him, Corley felt sick as well, but he was not angry anymore. Corley did not like the way Moshevsky was looking at him. He had his duty to do. He took a radio from one of the FBI agents. "This is Jay Seven. Get an ambulance in the east entrance of the Superdome." He looked down at

Fasil, moaning on the ground. Fasil's eyes were open. "You are under arrest. You have the right to remain silent," Corley began heavily.

Fasil was held on charges of illegal entry and conspiracy to violate customs regulations. Awad was held for illegal entry. The embassy of the United Arab Republic arranged for them to be represented by a New Orleans law firm. Neither Arab said anything. Corley hammered at Fasil for hours Sunday night in the prison infirmary and received nothing but a mocking stare. Fasil's lawyer withdrew from the case when he heard the nature of the questions. He was replaced by a Legal Aid attorney. Fasil paid no attention to either lawyer. He seemed content to wait.

Corley dumped the contents of a manila envelope on a desk in the FBI office. "This is all Fasil had on him."

Kabakov poked through the pile. There was a wallet, an envelope containing $2,500 in cash, an open airline ticket to Mexico City, Fasil's fake credentials and passport, assorted change, room keys from the YMCA and the Bienville House, and two other keys.

"His room is clean," Corley said. "A few clothes. Awad's luggage is clean as a whistle. We're working on tracing Fasil's gun, but I think he brought it in with him. One of the holes in the *Leticia* was a magnum."

"He hasn't said anything?"

"No." By tacit agreement, Corley and Kabakov had not referred to their angry clash in the Superdome again, but for a moment they both thought about it.

"Have you threatened Fasil with immediate extradition to Israel to stand trial for Munich?"

"I've threatened him with everything."

"What about sodium pentathol or hallucinogens?"

"Can't do it, David. Look, I have a pretty good idea of what Dr. Bauman probably has in her purse. That's why I haven't let you in to see Fasil."

"No, you're wrong. She wouldn't do that. She wouldn't drug him."

"But I expect you asked her."

Kabakov did not reply.

"These keys are for two Master padlocks," Corley said. "There are no padlocks in Fasil's luggage or in Awad's. Fasil has locked up something. If the bomb is big, and it would have to be big if it's in a single charge or even two charges, then it's probably in a truck, or close to a truck. That means a garage, a locked garage.

"We're having 500 of these keys made. They'll be issued to patrolmen with instructions to try every padlock on their beats. When one clicks open, the patrolman is to lay back and call for us.

"I know what's bothering you. Two keys come with each new padlock, right?"

"Yes," Kabakov said. "Somebody has got the other set of keys."

CHAPTER
24

"DAHLIA? ARE YOU HERE?" The room was very dark.

"Yes, Michael. Right here."

He felt her hand on his arm. "Have I been asleep?"

"You've slept for two hours. It's one A.M."

"Turn on the light. I want to see your face."

"All right. Here it is. The same old face."

He held her face in his hands, gently rubbing his thumbs in the soft hollows beneath her cheekbones. It had been three days since his fever broke. He was getting 250 milligrams of Erythromycin four times a day. It was working, but slowly.

"Let's see if I can walk."

"We should wait—"

"I want to know *now* if I can walk. Help me up." He sat on the side of the hospital bed. "Okay, here we go." He put his arm around her shoulders. She held him by the waist. He stood and took a shaky step. "Dizzy," he said. "Keep going."

She felt him trembling. "Let's go back to the bed, Michael."

"Nope. I can make the chair." He sank back in the chair and fought down a wave of nausea and dizziness. He looked at her and smiled weakly. "That's eight steps. From the bus to the cockpit won't be more than fifty-five. This is January fifth, no, the sixth, it's after midnight. We've got five and a half days. We'll make it."

"I never doubted it, Michael."

"Yes, you did. You doubt it now. You'd be a fool not to doubt it. Help me back to bed."

He slept until mid-morning, and he was able to eat breakfast. It was time to tell him.

"Michael, I'm afraid something is wrong with Fasil."

"When did you talk to him last?"

"Tuesday, the second. He called to say the truck was safe in the garage. He was scheduled to call again last night. He didn't." She had not mentioned the Libyan pilot to Lander. She never would.

"You think he's caught, don't you?"

"He wouldn't miss a call. If he hasn't called by to-morrow night, then he's taken."

"If he was caught away from the garage, what would he be carrying to give it away?"

"Nothing but his set of keys. I burned the rent receipt as soon as I got it. He never even had that. He had nothing that would identify us. If he had anything, and he was caught, the police would be here now."

"What about the hospital telephone number?"

"Only in his head. He picked pay telephones at random to call here."

"We'll go on then. Either the plastic is still there, or it's not. The loading will be harder with just the two of us, but we can do it if we're quick. Have you got the reservations?"

"Yes, at the Fairmont. I didn't ask if the blimp crew was there, I was afraid—"

"That's all right. The crew has always stayed there when we flew New Orleans. They'll do it again this time. Let's walk a little."

"I'm supposed to call the Aldrich office again this afternoon and give them your condition." She had introduced herself on the telephone as Lander's sister when she reported him ill.

"Say I've still got the flu and I'm out for at least a week and a half. They'll keep Farley on the schedule as chief pilot and Simmons as second officer. You remember what Farley looks like? You only saw him once, when we flew the night-sign run over Shea."

"I remember."

"He's in some of the pictures at the house, if you want to look at him again."

"Tomorrow," she said. "I'll go to the house tomorrow. You must be sick of this dress." She had bought underclothing at a shop across the street from the hospital, had bathed in Lander's bathroom. Otherwise, she had not left his side. She laid her head on Lander's chest. He smiled and rubbed the back of her neck.

I can't hear him bubbling, she thought. *His chest is clear.*

CHAPTER
25

THE PRESENCE OF Fasil and Awad in New Orleans left no doubt in the minds of the FBI and the Secret Service that the Arabs had planned to blow up the Super Bowl. The authorities believed that with the capture of Fasil and Awad the prime threat to the Super Bowl was blunted, but they knew they still faced a dangerous situation.

Two persons known to be at least peripherally involved in the plot—the woman and the American—were still at large. Neither had been identified, although the officers had a likeness of the woman. Worse, more than a half-ton of high explosive was cached somewhere, probably in the New Orleans area.

In the first few hours after the arrests, Corley half-expected a shattering blast somewhere in the city, or a threatening telephone call demanding Fasil's release as the price of the guerrillas not detonating the bomb in a crowded area. Neither occurred.

New Orleans' 1,300-man police force passed the duplicate padlock keys from shift to shift. The instructions to try them on warehouses and garages were repeated at every roll call. But New Orleans has a small police force for its size, and it is a city of many doors. Throughout the week the search went on, amid the Super Bowl ballyhoo and the crowds that swelled as the big weekend approached.

The crowd coming in for the Super Bowl was different from the Sugar Bowl group that preceded them. This crowd was more diversified in origin, the clothes were smarter. The restaurants found their customers less relaxed and more demanding. Money always flows freely in New Orleans, but now there was more of it to flow. The lines outside Galatoire's and Antoine's and the Court of Two Sisters stretched for half a block, and music spilled into the streets of the French Quarter all night long.

Standing-room tickets had been sold, bringing the total expected attendance at the Super Bowl to 84,000. With the fans came the gamblers, the thieves, and the whores. The police were busy.

Kabakov went to the airport on Thursday and watched the arrival of the Washington Redskins and the Miami Dolphins. Itchy in the crowd, remembering how the Israeli athletes had died at the Munich airport, he scanned the faces of the fans and paid little attention to the players as they came off their planes, waving to the cheering crowd.

Once Kabakov went to see Muhammad Fasil.

He stood at the foot of Fasil's bed in the infirmary and stared at the Arab for five minutes. Corley and two very large FBI agents were with him.

Finally Kabakov spoke. "Fasil, if you leave American custody you are a dead man. The Americans can extradite you to Israel to stand trial for Munich, and you will hang within the week. I would be happy to see it.

"But if you tell where the plastic is hidden, they'll convict you here on a smuggling charge and you will serve some time. Five years, maybe a little more. I'm sure you believe Israel will be gone by then and will be no threat to you. It won't be gone, but I'm sure you believe it will. Consider that."

Fasil's eyes were narrowed into slits. His head jerked and a stream of spittle flew at Kabakov, speckling the front of his shirt. The effort was painful for Fasil, strapped in his shoulder braces, and he grimaced and lay back on his pillow. Corley moved forward, but Kabakov had not stirred. The Israeli stared at Fasil a moment longer, then turned and left the room.

The expected decision came from the White House at midnight Friday. Barring further developments, the Super Bowl would be played on schedule.

On Saturday morning, January 11, Earl Biggs and Jack Renfro of the Secret Service held a final briefing at New Orleans FBI headquarters. Attending were 30 Secret Service agents, who would supplement the squad traveling with the President, 40 agents of the FBI, and Kabakov.

Renfro stood before a huge diagram of Tulane Stadium. "The stadium will be swept for explosives again beginning at 1600 today," he said. "The search will be completed by midnight, at which time the stadium will be sealed. Carson, your search team is ready." It was not a question.

"Ready."

"You will also have six men with the sniffer at the President's box for a last-minute sweep at 1340 tomorrow."

"Right. They've been briefed."

Renfro turned to the diagram on the wall behind him. "Once the possibility of concealed explosives in the stadium is eliminated, an attack could take two forms. The guerrillas could try to bring in the explosive in a vehicle, or they could settle for coming in with as much as they can conceal on their bodies.

"Vehicles first." He picked up his pointer. "Roadblocks will be prepared here at Willow Street on both sides of the stadium and at Johnson, Esther, Barret, Story, and Delord. Hickory will be blocked where it crosses Audubon. These are *positive* roadblocks that will stop a vehicle at high speed. I don't want to see anybody standing beside a sawhorse waving down traffic. The roadblocks will close tight as soon as the stadium is filled."

An agent raised his hand.

"Yeah."

"TV is bitching about the midnight setup rule. They'll have the color van set up this afternoon, but they want access throughout the night."

"Tough tit," Renfro said. "Tell them no. After midnight nobody comes in. At 10 A.M. Sunday the camera crews can take their places. Nobody carries anything. Where's the FAA?"

"Here," said a balding young man. "Considering

the persons already in custody, the use of an aircraft is considered highly unlikely." He spoke as though he were reading a report. "Both airports have been checked thoroughly for hidden ordnance." The young man hesitated, choosing between "however" and "nonetheless." He decided on "however." "However. No private aircraft will take off from New Orleans International or Lakefront during the time the stadium is filled, with the exception of charter and cargo flights which have already been cleared individually by us.

"Commercial flights remain on schedule. New Orleans police will man both airports in the event someone should try to commandeer an aircraft."

"Okay," Renfro said. "The Air Force advises no unidentified aircraft will get into the New Orleans area. They're standing by as they did on December 31. Naturally, they would have to solve that kind of problem well outside the city. The perimeter they are establishing has a 150-mile radius. We'll have a chopper up to watch the crowd.

"Now, about infiltration of the stadium. We have announcements on the media requesting ticketholders to show up one and one-half hours before game time," Renfro said. "Some of them will, some won't. They will have to pass through the metal detectors provided by the airlines before they enter the stadium. That's you, Fullilove. Are your people checked out on the equipment?"

"We're ready."

"The ones who arrive late will be mad if standing in line at the metal detector makes them miss the kickoff, but that's tough. Major Kabakov, do you have any suggestions?"

"I do." Kabakov went to the front of the room.

"Regarding metal detectors and personal searches: No terrorist is going to wait until he's in a metal detector with the bell going off to go for his gun. Watch the line approaching the detector. A man with a gun will be looking around for an alternate way in. He'll be looking from policeman to policeman. Maybe his head won't move, but his eyes will. If you decide someone in the line is suspect, get him from both sides suddenly. Don't give any warning. Once he knows his cover is about to be blown, he'll kill as many as he can before he goes down." Kabakov thought the officers might resent being told their business. He didn't care.

"If possible, there should be a grenade sump at every gate. A circle of sandbags will do; a hole with sandbags around it is better. A grenade rolling on the ground in a crowd is hard to get to. What's worse is to get to it and have no place to put it. The fragmentation grenades they use usually have a five-second fuse. They will be attached to the guerrilla's clothing by the pin. Don't pull a grenade off him. Kill him or control his hands first. Then take your time removing his grenades.

"If he is wounded and down, and you cannot get to him instantly and control his hands, shoot him again. In the head. He may be carrying a satchel charge, and he'll set it off if you give him time." Kabakov saw expressions of distaste on some of the faces. He did not care.

"Gunfire at one gate *must not* distract the men at another. That's the time to watch your own area of responsibility. Once it starts in one position, it will start elsewhere.

"There's one other thing. One of them is a woman, as you know." Kabakov looked down for a moment and cleared his throat. When he spoke again his voice was louder. "In Beirut once, I looked at her as a woman rather than as a guerrilla. That's one reason we are in this position today. Don't make the same mistake."

The room was very still when Kabakov sat down.

"One backup team is on each side of the stadium," Renfro said. "They will respond to any alarm. Do not leave your position. Pick up your ID tabs at this desk after the meeting. Any questions?" Renfro looked over the group. His eyes had the finish of black Teflon. "Carry on, gentlemen."

Tulane Stadium late on the eve of the Super Bowl was lit and quiet. The stadium's great spaces seemed to suck up the small noises of the search. Fog rolling off the Mississippi River a mile away swirled under the banks of floodlights.

Kabakov and Moshevsky stood at the top of the stands, their cigars glowing bright in the shadowed press box. They had been silent for half an hour.

"They could still pack it in, some of it," Moshevsky said finally. "Under their clothes. If they weren't carrying batteries or sidearms it wouldn't show on the metal detectors."

"No."

"Even if there are only two of them, it would be enough to make a big mess."

Kabakov said nothing.

"There's nothing we could do about that," Moshevsky said. Kabakov's cigar brightened in a series of angry puffs. Moshevsky decided to shut up.

"Tomorrow I want you with the backup team on the west side," Kabakov said. "I've spoken to Renfro. They'll expect you."

"Yes, sir."

"If they come with a truck, get in the back fast and get the detonators out. Each team has a man assigned to do that, but see to it yourself as well."

"If the back is canvas, it might be good to cut through the side going in. A grenade could be wired to the tailgate."

Kabakov nodded. "Mention that to the team leader as soon as you form up. Rachel is letting out the seams in a flak jacket for you. I don't like them either, but I want you to have it on. If shooting starts, you'd better look like the rest of them."

"Yes, sir."

"Corley will pick you up at 8:45. If you are in the Hotsy-Totsy Club after 1 A.M. tonight, I'll know it."

"Yes, sir."

Midnight in New Orleans, the neon lights on Bourbon Street smeared on the misty air. The Aldrich blimp hung over the Mississippi River Bridge, above the fog, Farley at the controls. Great letters rippled down the airship's sides in lights. "DON'T FORGET, HIRE THE VET."

In a room two floors above Farley's at the Fairmont Hotel, Dahlia Iyad shook down a thermometer and put it in Michael Lander's mouth. Lander had been exhausted by the trip from New Jersey. In order to avoid New Orleans International Airport, where Dahlia might be recognized, they had flown to Baton Rouge and come to New Orleans in a rented car with Lander stretched out on the back seat. Now he was pale, but his eyes were clear. She checked the thermometer. Normal.

"You'd better go see about the truck," he said.

"It's there or it's not, Michael. If you want me to check it, of course I will, but the less I'm seen on the street—"

"You're right. It's there or it's not. Is my uniform all right?"

"I hung it up. It looks fine."

She ordered hot milk from room service and gave it to Lander with a mild sedative. In half an hour, he dropped off to sleep. Dahlia Iyad did not sleep. In Lander's weakened condition, she must fly with him tomorrow on the bomb run, even if it meant leaving a section of the nacelle behind. She could help him with the elevator wheel, and she could handle the detonation. It was necessary.

Knowing that she would die tomorrow, she wept quietly for a half hour, wept for herself. And then, deliberately, she summoned the painful memories of the refugee camp. She went through her mother's final agonies, the thin woman, old at 35, writhing in the ragged tent. Dahlia was ten, and she could do nothing but keep the flies off her mother's face. There were so many suffering. Her own life was nothing, nothing. Soon she was calm again, but she did not sleep.

———

At the Royal Orleans, Rachel Bauman sat at the dresser brushing her hair. Kabakov lay on the bed, smoking and watching her. He liked to watch the light shimmer on her hair as she brushed it. He liked the tiny hollows that appeared along her spine as she arched her back and shook her hair over her shoulders.

"How long will you stay after tomorrow, David?" She was watching him in the mirror.

"Until we get the plastic."

"What about the other two, the woman and the American?"

"I don't know. They'll get the woman eventually. She can't do a great deal without the plastic. When we get it, I'll have to take Fasil back to stand trial for Munich."

She wasn't looking at him anymore.

"Rachel?"

"Yes."

"Israel needs psychiatrists, you know? You'd be astounded at the number of crazy Jews. Christians, too, in the summertime. I know an Arab in Jerusalem who sells them fragments of the True Cross, which he obtains by breaking up—"

"We'll have to talk about that when you are not so distracted, and you can be more explicit."

"We'll talk about it at Antoine's tomorrow night. Now that's enough talking and hairbrushing, or shall I be more explicit?"

The lights were out in the rooms at the Royal Orleans and the Fairmont. And around them both was the old city. New Orleans has seen it all before.

CHAPTER

26

ON SUNDAY, JANUARY 12, the red sun rising silhouetted the New Orleans skyline in fire. Michael Lander woke early. He had been dreaming of the whales, and for a moment he could not remember where he was. Then he remembered, totally and all at once. Dahlia was in a chair, her head back, watching him through half-closed eyes.

He rose carefully and went to the window. Streaks of pink and gold lay along the east-west streets. Above the ground mist he could see the lightening sky. "It's going to be clear," he said. He dialed the airport weather service. A northeast wind at 15 knots, gusting to 20. That was good. A tailwind from the Lakefront Airport to the stadium. Wide open, he could get better than 60 knots out of the blimp.

"Can you rest a little longer, Michael?"

He was pale. She knew that he did not have much strength. Perhaps he would have enough.

The blimp was always airborne at least an hour before game time to allow the TV technicians to make final adjustments and to let the fans see the airship as they arrived. Lander would have to fly that long before he came back for the bomb.

"I'll rest," he said. "The flight crew call will be at noon. Farley flew last night, so he'll sleep in, but he'll be leaving his room well before noon to eat."

"I know, Michael. I'll take care of it."

"I'd feel better if you had a gun." They could not risk carrying firearms on the flight to Baton Rouge. The small arms were in the truck with the explosive.

"It's all right. I can do it all right. You can depend on me."

"I know it," he said. "I can depend on you."

Corley, Kabakov, and Moshevsky set out for the stadium at 9 A.M. The streets around the Royal Orleans were filled with people, pale from last night's celebrations, wandering the French Quarter with their hangovers out of some sense of duty, a grim determination to see the sights. Paper cups and bar napkins blew down Bourbon Street in the damp wind.

Corley had to drive slowly until they were clear of the Quarter. He was irritable. He had neglected to get himself a hotel reservation while the getting was good, and he had slept badly in an FBI agent's guest room. The breakfast he had been served by the agent's wife was pointedly light. Kabakov appeared to have slept and breakfasted well, adding to Corley's irritation. He was further annoyed by the smell of a cantaloupe Moshevsky was eating in the back of the car.

Kabakov shifted in his seat. He clanked against the door handle.

"What the hell was that?"

"My dentures are loose," Kabakov said.

"Very funny."

Kabakov flipped back his coat, revealing the stubby barrel of the Uzi submachine gun slung under his arm.

"What's Moshevsky carrying, a bazooka?"

"I have a cantaloupe launcher," came the voice from the back seat.

Corley shrugged his shoulders. He could not understand Moshevsky easily at the best of times and not at all when his mouth was full.

They arrived at the stadium at 9:30. The streets that would not be used as the stadium filled were already blocked. The vehicles and barriers that would seal off the stadium when the game began were in place on the grass beside the main traffic arteries. Ten ambulances were parked close to the southeast gate. Only outbound emergency vehicles would be allowed through the blockade. Secret servicemen were already in place on the roofs along Audubon Avenue overlooking the track where the President's helicopter would land.

They were as ready as they could get.

It was curious to see sandbag emplacements beside the quiet streets. Some of the FBI agents were reminded of the Ole Miss campus in 1963.

At 9 A.M., Dahlia Iyad called room service in the Fairmont and ordered three breakfasts to be delivered to the room. While she was waiting for them, she took a pair of long scissors and a roll of friction tape from

her bag. She removed the screw holding the scissors together and put a slender, three-inch bolt through the
screw hole in one half of the scissors, binding it in place
with the tape. Then she taped the entire handle of the
scissor and slipped it up her sleeve.

The breakfasts arrived at 9:20 A.M.

"You go ahead, Michael, while it's hot," Dahlia
said. "I'll be back in a minute." She took a breakfast
tray to the elevator and descended two floors.

Farley's voice sounded sleepy as he answered her
knock.

"Mr. Farley?"

"Yes."

"Your breakfast."

"I didn't order any breakfast."

"Compliments of the hotel. The whole crew is getting them. I'll take it away if you don't want it."

"No, I'll take it. Just a minute."

Farley, hair tousled and wearing only his trousers,
let her into the room. If someone had been passing in
the hall they might have heard the beginning of a
scream, abruptly cut off. A minute later, Dahlia slipped
outside again. She placed the "Do Not Disturb" sign
on the doorknob and went back upstairs to breakfast.

There was one more piece of business to be settled.
Dahlia waited until she and Lander had finished eating.
They were lying on the bed together. She was holding
Lander's mangled hand.

"Michael, you know I want very much to fly with
you. Don't you think it would be better?"

"I can do it. There's no need."

"I want to help you. I want to be with you. I want to see it."

"You wouldn't see much. You'll hear it wherever you go from the airport."

"I'd never get out of the airport anyway, Michael. You know the weight won't make any difference now. It's 70 degrees outside and the aircraft has been standing in the sun all morning. Of course if you can't get it up—"

"I can get it up. We'll have superheat."

"May I, Michael? We've come a long way."

He rolled over and looked into her face. There were red pillow marks on his cheek. "You'll have to get the shot bags out of the back of the gondola fast. The ones beneath the back seat. We can trim it up when we're off. You can go."

She held him very close and they did not talk anymore.

At 11:30 Lander rose and Dahlia helped him dress. His cheeks were hollow, but the tanning lotion she had used on his face helped disguise the pallor. At 11:50 she took a syringe of Novacaine from her medical kit. She rolled up Lander's sleeve and deadened a small patch on his forearm. Then she took out another, smaller hypodermic syringe. It was a flexible plastic squeeze tube with a needle attached, and it was filled with a 30 milligram solution of Ritalin.

"You may feel talkative after you use this, Michael. Very up. You'll have to compensate for that. Don't use it unless you feel yourself losing strength."

"All right, just put it on."

She inserted the needle in the deadened patch on his

forearm and taped the small syringe firmly in place, flat on his arm. On either side of the squeeze tube was a short length of pencil to keep the tube from being squeezed by accident. "Just feel through your sleeve and press the tube with your thumb when you need it."

"I know, I know."

She kissed him on the forehead. "If I shouldn't make it to the airport with the truck, if they are waiting for me—"

"I'll just drop the blimp into the stadium," he said. "It will mash quite a few. But don't think about the bad possibilities. We've been lucky so far, right?"

"You have been very clever so far."

"I'll see you at the airport at 2:15."

She walked him to the elevator, and then she returned to the room and sat on the bed. It was not yet time to go for the truck.

Lander spotted the blimp crew standing near the desk in the lobby. There was Simmons, Farley's co-pilot, and two network cameramen. He walked over, exerting himself to put on a brisk manner.

I'll rest in the bus, he thought.

"My God, it's Mike," Simmons said. "I thought you were out sick. Where's Farley? We called his room. We were waiting for him."

"Farley had a rough night. Some drunk girl stuck her finger in his eye."

"Jesus."

"He's all right, but he's getting it looked at. I fly today."

"When did you get in?"

"This morning. That bastard Farley called me at 4 A.M. Let's go, we're late now."

"You don't look too good, Mike."

"I look better than you do. Let's go."

At the Lakefront Airport gate, the driver could not find his vehicle pass and they all had to show their credentials. Three squad cars were parked near the tower.

The blimp, 225 feet of silver, red, and blue, rested in a grassy triangle between the runways. Unlike the airplanes squatting on the ground before the hangars, the airship gave the impression of flight even when at rest. Poised lightly on its single wheel, nose against the mooring mast, it pointed to the northeast like a giant weathervane. Near it were the big bus that transported the ground crew and the tractor-trailer that housed the mobile maintenance shop. The vehicles and the men were dwarfed by the silver airship.

Vickers, the crew chief, wiped his hands on a rag. "Glad you're back, Captain Lander. She's ready."

"Thank you." Lander began the traditional walkaround inspection. Everything was in order, as he knew it would be. The blimp was clean. He had always liked the cleanliness of the blimp. "You guys ready?" he called.

Lander and Simmons ran down the rest of the preflight checklist in the gondola.

Vickers was berating the two TV cameramen. "Captain Video, will you and your assistant kindly get your asses in that gondola so we can weigh off?"

The ground crew took hold of the handrail around the gondola and bounced the airship on its landing wheel. Vickers removed several of the 25-pound bags of shot that hung from the rail. The crew bounced the airship again.

"She's just a hair heavy. That's good." Vickers liked the blimp to take off heavy; fuel consumption would lighten it later.

"Where are the Cokes? Have we got the Cokes?" Simmons said. He thought they would be airborne for at least three hours, possibly longer. "Yeah, here they are."

"Take it, Simmons," Lander said.

"Okay." Simmons slid into the single pilot's seat on the left side of the gondola. He waved through the windshield. The crewmen at the mooring mast tripped the release, and eight men on the nose ropes pulled the blimp around. "Here we go." Simmons rolled back the elevator wheel, pushed in the throttles, and the great airship rose at a steep angle.

Lander leaned back in the passenger seat beside the pilot. The flight to the stadium, with the tailwind, took nine and a half minutes. Lander figured that, wide open, it could be done in a shade over seven minutes, if the wind held.

Beneath them, a solid stream of traffic jammed the expressway near the Tulane exit.

"Some of those people are gonna miss the kickoff," Simmons said.

"Yeah, I expect so," Lander said. They would all miss half time, he thought. It was 1:10 P.M. He had almost an hour to wait.

Dahlia Iyad got out of the taxi near the Galvez Street wharf and walked quickly down the block toward the garage. The bomb was there, or it was not. The police were waiting or they were not. She had not noticed before how cracked and tilted the sidewalk was. She looked at the cracks as she walked along. A group of small children were playing stickball in the street. The batter, no more than three and a half feet tall, whistled at her as she went by.

A police car made the players scatter and passed Dahlia at 15 miles an hour. She turned her face away from it as though she were looking for an address. The squad car turned at the next corner. She fished in her purse for the keys and walked up the alley to the garage. Here were the locks. She opened them and slipped inside, closing the door behind her. It was semi-dark in the garage. A few shafts of sunshine came in through nailholes in the walls. The truck appeared undisturbed.

She climbed into the back and switched on the dim light. There was a thin film of dust on the nacelle. It was all right. If the place were staked out, they would never have let her get to the bomb. She changed into a pair of coveralls marked with the initials of the television network and stripped the vinyl panels off the sides of the truck, revealing the network emblem in bright colors.

She found the checklist taped to the nacelle. She read it over quickly. First the detonators. She removed them from their packing and, reaching into the middle of the nacelle, she slid them into place, one in the exact center of each side of the charge. The wires from the detonators plugged into the wiring harness with its lead-in to the airship's power supply. Now the fuse and its deto-nator were plugged into place.

She cut all the rope lashings except two. Check the bag for Lander. One .38 caliber revolver with silencer, one pair of cable cutters, both in a paper sack. Her Schmeisser machine pistol with six extra clips and an AK-47 automatic rifle with clips were in a duffle bag.

Getting out, she laid the Schmeisser on the floor of the truck cab and covered it with a blanket. There was dust on the truck seat. She took a handkerchief from her purse and wiped it carefully. She tucked her hair into a Big Apple cap.

1:50. Time to go. She swung open the garage doors and drove outside, blinking in the sunshine, and left the truck idling as she closed the garage doors.

Driving toward the airport, she had an odd, happy feeling of falling, falling.

Kabakov watched from the command post at the stadium as the river of people poured in through the southeast gate. They were so well dressed and well fed, unaware of the trouble they were causing him.

There was some grumbling when lines formed at the metal detectors, and louder complaints when now and then a fan was asked to dump the contents of his pock-ets in a plastic dishpan. Standing with Kabakov were the members of the east side trouble squad, ten men in flak jackets, heavily armed. He walked outside, away from the crackle of radios, and watched the stadium fill up. Already the bands were thumping away, the music becoming less distorted as more and more bodies baffled the echoes off the stands. By 1:45 most of the spectators were in their seats. The roadblocks closed.

Eight hundred feet above the stadium, the TV crew in the blimp was conferring by radio with the director in the big television van parked behind the stands. The "NBS Sports Spectacular" was to open with a shot of the stadium from the blimp, with the network logo and the title superimposed on it. In the van, facing 12 television screens, the director was not satisfied.

"Hey, Simmons," the cameraman said, "now he wants it from the other end, the north end with Tulane in the background, can you do that?"

"You bet." The blimp wheeled majestically northward.

"Okay, that's good, that's good." The cameraman had it nicely framed, the bright green field, solidly banked with 84,000 people, the stadium wreathed with flags that snapped in the wind.

Lander could see the police helicopter darting like a dragonfly around the perimeter of the stadium.

"Tower to Nora One Zero."

Simmons picked up the microphone. "Nora One Zero, go ahead."

"Traffic in your area one mile northwest and approaching," the air controller said. "Give him plenty of room."

"Roger. I see him. Nora One Zero out."

Simmons pointed and Lander saw a military helicopter approaching at 600 feet. "It's the Prez. Take off your hat," Simmons said. He wheeled the airship away from the north end of the stadium.

Lander watched as the landing marker was deployed on the track.

"They want a shot of the arrival," the cameraman's assistant said. "Can you get us broadside to him?"

"That's fine," the cameraman said. Through his long lens, 86 million people saw the President's helicopter touch down. The President stepped out and walked quickly into the stadium and out of sight.

In the TV van, the director snapped "Take Two." Across the country and around the world, the audience saw the President striding along the sideline to his box.

Looking down, Lander could see him again now, a husky blond figure in a knot of men, his arms raised to the crowd and the crowd rising to their feet in a wave as he passed.

Kabakov heard the roar that greeted the President. He had never seen the man, and he was curious. He restrained the impulse to go and look at him. His place was here, near the command post, where he would be instantly alerted to trouble.

"I'll take it, Simmons, you watch the kickoff," Lander said. They switched places. Lander was tired already, and the elevator wheel seemed heavy under his hand.

On the field, they were "re-enacting the toss" for the benefit of the television audience. Now the teams were lined up for the kickoff.

Lander glanced at Simmons. His head was out the side window. Lander reached forward and pushed the fuel mixture lever for the port engine. He made the mixture just lean enough to make the engine overheat.

In minutes the temperature gauge was well into the

red. Lander eased the fuel mixture back to normal. "Gentlemen, we've got a little problem." Lander had Simmons' instant attention. He tapped the temperature gauge.

"Now what the hell!" Simmons said. He climbed across the gondola and peered at the port engine over the shoulders of the TV crew. "She's not streaming any oil."

"What?" the cameraman said.

"Port engine's hot. Let me get past you here." He reached into the rear compartment and brought out a fire extinguisher.

"Hey, it's not burning, is it?" The cameraman and his assistant were very serious, as Lander knew they would be.

"No, hell no," Simmons said. "We have to get the extinguisher out, it's SOP."

Lander feathered the engine. He was heading away from the stadium now, to the northeast, to the airfield. "We'll let Vickers take a look at it," he said.

"Did you call him already?"

"While you were in the back." Lander had mumbled into his microphone all right, but he had not pressed the transmit button.

He was following U.S. 10, the Superdome below him on the right and the fairgrounds with its oval track on the left. Bucking the headwind on a single engine was slow going. All the better coming back, Lander thought. He was over the Pontchartrain Golf Course now, and he could see the airfield spread out in front of him. There was the truck, approaching the airport gate. Dahlia had made it.

From the cab of the truck, Dahlia could see the airship coming. She was a few seconds early. There was a
policeman at the gate. She held the blue vehicle pass
out the window and he waved her through. She cruised
slowly along the road flanking the field.

The ground crew saw the airship now, and they
stirred around the bus and the tractor-trailer. Lander
wanted them to be in a hurry. At 300 feet he thumbed
the button on his microphone. "All right, I'm coming
in 175 heavy, give it plenty of room."

"Nora One Zero, what's up? Why didn't you say
you were coming, Mike?" It was Vickers' voice.

"I did," Lander said. *Let him wonder.* The ground
crew were running to their stations. "I'm coming to the
mast crosswind and I want the wheel chocked. Don't
let her swing to the wind, Vickers. I've got a small
problem with the port engine, a *small* problem. It's
nothing, but I want the port engine downwind from
the ship. I *do not* want a flap. Do you understand?"

Vickers understood. Lander did not want the crash
trucks howling down the field.

Dahlia Iyad waited to drive across the runway. The
tower was giving her a red light. She watched as the
blimp touched down, bounced, touched again, the
ground crew grabbing the ropes that trailed from the
nose. They had it under control now.

The tower light flashed green. She drove across the
runway and parked behind the tractor-trailer, out of
sight of the crew milling around the blimp. In a second
the tailgate was down, the ramp in place. She grabbed
the paper bag containing the gun and the cable cutters
and ran around the tractor-trailer to the blimp. The

crew paid no attention to her. Vickers opened the cowling on the port engine. Dahlia passed the bag to Lander
through the window of the gondola and ran back to
her truck.

Lander turned to the TV crew. "Stretch your legs,
it'll be a minute."

They scrambled out and he followed them.

Lander walked to the bus and immediately returned
to the blimp. "Hey, Vickers, Lakehurst is on the horn
for you."

"Oh, my ass—All right, Frankie, take a look in here,
but don't change nothin' until I get back." He trotted
toward the bus. Lander went in behind him. Vickers
had just picked up the radio telephone when Lander
shot him in the back of the head. Now the ground crew
had no leader. As Lander stepped off the bus he heard
the putt-putt of the forklift. Dahlia was in the saddle,
swinging around the rear of the tractor-trailer. The
crew, puzzled at the sight of the big nacelle, made room
for the forklift. She eased forward, sliding the long nacelle under the gondola. She raised the fork six inches
and it was in place.

"What's going on, what's this?" the man at the engine said. Dahlia ignored him. She flipped the two front
clamps around the handrail. Four more to go.

"Vickers said get the shot bags off," Lander yelled.

"He said *what*?"

"Get the shot bags off. Move it!"

"What is this, Mike? I never saw this."

"Vickers will explain it. TV time costs $175,000 a
minute, now get your ass in gear. The network wants
this thing." Two crewmen unclipped the shot bags as

Dahlia finished fastening the nacelle. She backed the forklift away. The crew was confused. Something was wrong. This big nacelle with its network markings had never been tested on the blimp.

Lander went to the port engine and looked in. Nothing had been removed. He shut the cowling.

Here came the TV cameraman. "NBS? What *is* that thing? That's not ours—"

"The director will explain it, call him from the bus." Lander climbed into his seat and started the engines. The crew skipped back, startled. Dahlia was already inside the gondola with the cable cutters. No time to unscrew anything. The TV equipment had to go before the blimp would fly.

The cameraman saw her cutting the equipment loose. "Hey! Don't do that." He scrambled into the gondola. Lander turned in his seat and shot the cameraman in the back. A startled crewman's face in the door. The men closest to the blimp were backing away now. Dahlia unclamped the camera.

"Chock and mast now!" Lander yelled.

Dahlia jumped to the ground, she had the Schmeisser out. The crewmen were backing away, some of them turning to run. She pulled the chock away from the wheel and, as the blimp swung to the wind, she ran to the mast and uncoupled it. The nose boom must come out of the socket in the mast. It must. The blimp was swinging. The men had fled the nose ropes. The wind would do it, would twist the blimp free. She heard a siren. A squad car was screaming across the runway.

The nose was free, but the blimp was still weighted

with the body of the cameraman and the TV equipment. She swung into the gondola. The transmitter went first, smashing to the ground. The camera followed it.

The squad car was coming head on with the blimp, its lights flashing. Lander slammed the throttles forward and the great ship started to roll. Dahlia was struggling with the body of the cameraman. His leg was under Lander's seat. The blimp bounced once and settled again. It reared like a prehistoric animal. The squad car was 40 yards away, its doors opening. Lander dumped most of his fuel. The blimp rose heavily.

Dahlia leaned out of the gondola and fired her Schmeisser at the squad car, star fractures appearing across its windshield, the blimp rising, a policeman out of the car, blood on his shirt, drawing his gun, looking up into her face as the blimp passed over. A blast from the machine pistol cut him down, and Dahlia kicked the cameraman's body out the door to fall spread-eagled on the hood of the patrol car. The blimp surged upward. Other squad cars were coming now, growing smaller beneath them, their doors opening. She heard a "thock" against the gas bag. They were firing. She aimed a burst at the nearest police car, saw dust kick up around it. Lander had the blimp at 50 degrees, engines screaming. Up and up and out of pistol range.

The fuse and the wires! Dahlia lay on the bloody floor of the gondola, and hanging outside she could reach them.

Lander was nodding at the controls, near collapse. She reached over his shoulder and pressed the syringe beneath his sleeve. In a second his head was up again.

He checked the cabin light switch. It was off. "Hook it up."

She pried the cover off the cabin light, removed the bulb and plugged in the wires to the bomb. The fuse, to be used if the electrical system failed, must be secured around a seat bracket near the rear of the gondola. Dahlia had trouble tying the knot as the fuse became slippery with the cameraman's blood.

The airspeed indicator said 60 knots. They would be at the Super Bowl in six minutes.

Corley and Kabakov sprinted to Corley's car at the first confused report of shooting at the airfield. They were howling up Interstate 10 when the report was augmented.

"Unknown persons shooting from the Aldrich blimp," the radio said. "Two officers down. Ground crew advises a device is attached to the aircraft."

"They got the blimp!" Corley said, pounding the seat beside him. "That's your other pilot." They could see the airship over the skyline now, growing larger by the second. Corley was on the radio to the stadium. "Get the President out!" he was yelling.

Kabakov fought the rage and frustration, the shock, the impossibility of it. He was caught, helpless, on the expressway between the stadium and the airport. He must think, must think, must think. They were passing the Superdome now. Then he was shaking Corley's shoulder. "Jackson," Kabakov said. "Lamar Jackson. The chopper. Drive this son of a bitch."

They were past the exit ramp, and Corley turned across three lanes of traffic, tires smoking, and shot the wrong way down the entrance ramp, a car was coming, big in their faces, swerving over, a rocking sideswipe and they were down into Howard Avenue beside the Superdome. A screaming turn around the huge building and they slammed to a stop. Kabakov ran to the pad, startling the stakeout team still on duty.

Jackson was descending from the roof to pick up a bundle of conduit. Kabakov ran to the loadmaster, a man he did not know.

"Get him down. Get him down."

The blimp was almost even with the Superdome now, moving fast just out of range. It was two miles from the packed stadium.

Corley came from the car. He had left the trunk open. He was carrying an M-16 automatic rifle.

The chopper settled down, Kabakov ducking as he ran in under the rotor. He scrambled up to the cockpit window. Jackson put his hand behind his ear.

"They got the Aldrich blimp," Kabakov was pointing upward. "We've got to go up. We've got to go up."

Jackson looked up at the blimp. He swallowed. There was a strange, set expression in his face. "Are you hijacking me?"

"I'm asking you. Please."

Jackson closed his eyes for a second. "Get in. Get the belly man out. I won't be responsible for him."

Kabakov and Corley pulled out the startled belly man and climbed inside the cargo bay. The helicopter leaped into the air with a great blatting of its blades. Kabakov went forward and pushed up the empty co-pilot's seat.

"We can—"

"Listen," Jackson said. "Are you gonna bust 'em or talk to them?"

"Bust 'em."

"All right. If we can catch them, I'll come in above them, they can't see above them in that thing. You gonna shoot the gas bag? No time for it to leak much."

Kabakov shook his head. "They might set it off on the way down. We'll try to knock out the gondola."

Jackson nodded. "I'll come in above them. When you're ready, I'll drop down beside them. This thing won't take a lot of hits and fly. You be ready. Talk to me on the headset."

The helicopter was doing 110 knots, gaining fast, but the blimp had a big lead. It would be very close.

"If we knock out the pilot, the wind will still carry it over the stadium," Jackson said.

"What about the hook? Could we hold him with the hook, pull him somewhere?"

"How could we hook on? The damn thing is slick. We can try if there's time—hey, there go the cops."

Ahead of them they could see the police helicopter rising to meet the blimp.

"Not from below," Jackson was yelling. "Don't get close—" Even as he spoke the little police helicopter staggered under a blast of gunfire and fell off to the side, its rotor flailing wildly, and plunged downward.

Jackson could see the movements of the airship's rudder as the great fin passed under him. He was over the blimp and the stadium was sliding beneath them. Time for one pass. Kabakov and Corley braced themselves in the fuselage door.

Lander felt the rotor blast on the blimp's skin, heard

the helicopter engine. He touched Dahlia and jerked his thumb upward. "Get me ten more seconds," he said.

She put a fresh clip in the Schmeisser.

Jackson's voice in Kabakov's earphones, "Hang on."

The helicopter dropped in a stomach-lifting swoop down the blimp's right side. Kabakov heard the first bullets hit the belly of the helicopter and then he and Corley were firing, hot shell casings spattering from the automatic weapons, glass flying from the gondola. Metal was ringing all around Kabakov. The helicopter lurched and rose. Corley was hit, blood spreading on his trousers at the thigh.

Jackson, his forehead slashed by the glass in his riddled cockpit, mopped away the blood that had poured into his eyes.

All the windows were out of the gondola and the instrument panel was shattered, sparks flying. Dahlia lay on the floor, she did not move.

Lander, hit in the shoulder and the leg, saw the blimp losing altitude. The airship was sinking, but they could still clear the stadium wall. It was coming, it was under him, and a floor of faces was looking up. He had his hand on the firing switch. Now. He flipped the switch. Nothing. The backup switch. Nothing. The circuits were blasted away. The fuse. He dragged himself out of the pilot's seat, his lighter in his hand, and used his good arm and leg to crawl toward the fuse at the rear of the gondola, as the blimp drifted between the solid banks of people.

The hook trailed beneath the helicopter on a 30-foot cable. Jackson dropped until the hook slipped over the blimp's slick skin. The only opening was the space between the rudder and the fin beneath the rudder hinge. Kabakov was coaching Jackson, and they got it close, close, but the hook was too thick.

They were stampeding in the stadium. Kabakov looked around him desperately and he saw, coiled in a clip on the wall, a length of three-quarter-inch nylon rope with a snap shackle in each end. In the half second he stared at it, he knew with an awful certainty what he had to do.

From the ground, Moshevsky watched, his eyes bulging, fists clenched as the figure appeared, sliding spiderlike down the cable beneath the helicopter. He snatched the field glasses from an agent beside him, but he knew before he looked. It was Kabakov. He could see the rotor blast tearing at Kabakov as he slid down the greasy cable. A rope was tied around his waist. They were over Moshevsky now. Straining back to see, Moshevsky fell on his rear and never stopped watching.

Kabakov had his foot in the hook. Corley's face was visible in the opening in the belly of the chopper. He was talking in the headset. The hook slid down, Kabakov was beside the fin, no! The fin was rising, swinging. It hit Kabakov and knocked him away, he was swinging back, passing the length of rope between the rudder and the fin, beneath the top rudder hinge, snapping it in a loop through the hook, one arm waving, and the helicopter strained upward, the cable hardening along Kabakov's body like a steel bar.

Lander, crawling along the blood-slick floor of the

gondola toward the fuse, felt the floor tilt sharply. He
was sliding and scrabbled for a handhold on the floor.

The helicopter clawed the air. The tail of the blimp
was up at 50 degrees now, the nose bumping against
the football field. The spectators screaming, running,
the exits jammed as they fought to get out. Lander
could hear their cries all around him. He strained
toward the fuse, lighter in hand.

The nose of the blimp dragged up the stands, the
crowd scattering before it. It caught on the flag-poles at
the top of the stadium, and lurched over, clear and
moving over the houses toward the river, the helicopter's engine screaming. Corley, looking down, could
see Kabakov standing on the fin, holding onto the
cable.

"We'll make the river, we'll make the river," Jackson said over and over, as the temperature gauge
climbed into the red. His thumb was poised over the
red drop button.

Lander heaved himself the final foot up the slanting
floor and thumbed his lighter.

Moshevsky tore his way to the top of the stands.
The helicopter, the blimp, the man standing on the fin,
hung over the river for one instant, fixed forever in
Moshevsky's mind, and then they were gone in a blinding flash of light and a Doomsday crack that flattened
him on the shuddering stands. Shrapnel slashed the
trees beside the river as the blast uprooted them, and
the water, whipped to foam, was blown out in a great
basin that filled again with a roar of its own, the water
rising in a mountainous cone into the smoke. And sec-

onds later, far downriver, spent shrapnel pocked the water like hail and rattled off the iron hulls of ships.

Miles away, finishing a late lunch at the Top of the Mart overlooking the city, Rachel saw the flash. She rose, and then the tall building trembled, the windows shattered, and she was on her back, glass still falling and, looking up at the underside of the table, she knew. She struggled to her feet. A woman sat on the floor beside her, mouth hanging open.

Rachel looked at her. "He's dead," Rachel said.

The final casualty list totaled 512. At the stadium 14 were trampled to death in the exits, 52 suffered fractures in the struggle to escape, and the rest had cuts and bruises. Among those cut and bruised was the President of the United States. His injuries were suffered when 10 Secret Service men piled on top of him. In the town, 116 persons received minor injuries from flying glass, as windows were blasted in.

At noon on the following day, Rachel Bauman and Robert Moshevsky stood on a small pier on the north bank of the Mississippi River. They had been there for hours, watching the police boats drag the bottom. The dragging had gone on all night. In the first few hours, the grapnels had brought up a few charred pieces of metal from the helicopter. Since then, there was nothing.

The pier on which they stood was riddled and splintered with shrapnel. A large dead catfish bumped against it in the current. The fish was punched full of holes.

Moshevsky remained impassive. His eyes never left

the police boats. Beside him on the pier was his canvas suitcase, for in three hours he would take Muhammad Fasil back to Israel to stand trial for the Munich massacre. The El Al jet that was coming for them also contained 14 Israeli commandos. It was felt that they would provide a suitable buffer between Moshevsky and his prisoner on the long flight home.

Rachel's face was swollen, and her eyes were red and dry. She had cried herself out on the bed in the Royal Orleans, fingers locked in a shirt of Kabakov's that reeked of his cigars.

The wind was cold off the river. Moshevsky put his jacket around Rachel. It hung below her knees.

Finally, the lead boat sounded a single long blast. The police fleet pulled in their empty grapnels and started downstream. Now there was only the river, moving in a solid piece toward the sea. Rachel heard a strange, strangled sound from Moshevsky, and he turned his face away. She pressed her cheek against his chest and reached her arms as far around him as they would go and patted him, feeling the hot tears falling in her hair. Then she took his hand and led him up the bank as she would lead a child.

ribs as a treat. She said that Dixie got rib bones regularly. It was not unusual. It was, in fact, her usual treat for special occasions. She had never had a problem before. She had told the truth when I had asked her whether she had given Dixie anything unusual to eat.

Before she left, she handed me a small object wrapped in brown paper. It was the bone. I put it in a jar and set it up on the shelf in room 2, beside the giant stone that had filled Guido the tiny Pomeranian's entire bladder, and beside the rogue's gallery of pickled parasites. Dixie's bone was there to remind me that I should always ask, "Could she have eaten anything other than dog food?" rather than "Did you feed her something unusual?" It was also there to remind me to tell people that Charles Schultz, bless his soul, did the dog-owning public a grave disservice by depicting Snoopy powering through a stack of bones like they were Pringles. But then Snoopy is clearly a magical dog. When your dog starts fighting the Red Baron and decorating Christmas trees, we can talk about feeding him bones. Until then, know this: bones can be so dangerous, especially pork and poultry.

To be honest, the bone in the jar was kind of gross, so I understand why it's gone. And I remember these things anyway.

P.S.
Some of you reading this will protest that the dog you had growing up on the farm ate nothing but pork and chicken

bones and lived to be 103. Or something like that. This was likely the same dog who never saw a vet, not even once in his unnaturally long life, and the same dog who ran 20 miles through a blizzard to get help when grandpa got his arm stuck in the snowblower. All I can say to you is that I guess they don't make dogs like they used to.

P.P.S.
A small but measurable percentage of you will now have the *Welcome Back, Kotter* theme looping through your brain for the next two days. No, there's really no need to thank me.

RASCAL RABBIT FOUR

As a rule, I change the names of patients and clients when writing about them, but from time to time, for a variety of reasons, I don't. This time it's because the name Rascal Rabbit Four still makes me smile every time I think of it, and his story wouldn't be the same without his name. On a side note, the owners wrote "four" with Roman numerals, but "IV" would be confusing in a medical setting. Rascal Rabbit Four was a little white male toy poodle and he was called that because he was the fourth little white male toy poodle named Rascal Rabbit the Sezniks had owned.

Earl and Dolly Seznik must have been a hot couple back in the day. Well into her eighties, Dolly still wore short skirts, high heels and candy apple-red lipstick, while Earl styled his grey hair into a lavish pompadour and often wore a jaunty scarf. They drove to the clinic in a white convertible Cadillac Eldorado with Rascal Rabbit Four on Dolly's lap, tongue lolling and long ears flapping in the breeze as he stuck his head out the side, delighted to be going for a car ride, even if it was to the vet. The other three Rascal Rabbits were before my time, but I was told that the Sezniks had not originally added a number to the name. They were apparently so unprepared to cope with the loss of the first Rascal Rabbit that they decided to get another dog that looked as similar as possible, to name him Rascal Rabbit and to carry on as if nothing had happened. They were eventually gently persuaded that this might be confusing, so they added the ordinal.

The Sezniks' predicament was brought to mind the other day when I read an article about pet cloning. Things have progressed quickly since Dolly the sheep was cloned in 1996, in what at the time was a startling breakthrough. The process has since been perfected and no longer presents any important technical hurdles. Now there are several companies offering to clone your dog or cat. While the price is coming down, it is still not something most people would consider a bargain, with dog clones costing around $50,000 and cats a little less. Horses can also be cloned for $85,000. But for the sake of argument, let's say that the expense doesn't seem ludicrous and that you can afford this. You were planning on buying a sailboat anyway, but you figure you'll get more pleasure out of a dog that is just like your favourite old pal. Fair enough. The problem, however, comes in the "just like" part. A clone is not a perpetually identical copy. Think about identical human twins. They are clones of each other. The process is different, but the genetic outcome is the same. If you know any twins, you will know that they are almost indistinguishable from each other, but only almost. DNA is a tricky little molecule and the same genes may express themselves differently in different individuals. This is the basis of the science of epigenetics, the complex study of which I have inelegantly summarized in that single sentence. Look it up if you want to know more, but for the purposes of this discussion, the takeaway is that clones, or twins, may have the same DNA, but they will not be identical in every way. And that's just appearance. Personality will diverge even more because it is also dependent on random things that happen to you over the course of your life. Those little differences may or may not matter to you, but for many people it is akin to looking at a famous painting with one detail off — say Mona Lisa's eyes are suddenly green instead of brown — and although the painting is substantially the same, you cannot stop thinking about the difference.

One of the most famous owners of cloned dogs is Barbra Streisand. In 2017 Samantha, Streisand's beloved

Coton du Tuléar (similar to a Bichon Frisé, if you're unfamiliar), died and she decided to have her cloned. She even had her cloned twice to be on the safe side. Now that Miss Scarlet and Miss Violet — named after the colours of the doggie dresses she put on them to tell them apart — are full grown, they are each the absolute spitting image of Samantha. Yet, in a recent interview, Ms. Streisand hinted at what I would consider to be a deal-breaking problem. Whether it is due to epigenetics or other random factors, there are subtle differences between the two new dogs and the old one. And these subtle differences, like Mona Lisa's eyes, threaten to become a pebble in the mind's shoe. The entire endeavour demands that you constantly compare old and new, original and clone, beloved and not-quite-yet-beloved. Of course, one always compares regardless, but when something is meant to be identical, these comparisons can become far more fraught. I think it would seem uncanny to me, like an alien bodysnatching that was not quite completely successful. But maybe that's just me. Maybe 99% the same isn't a problem because it falls short of 100%; maybe it's a solution because it blows 80% out of the water. However, if the shelters are full and that 80% desperately needs a home, perhaps there's another angle to consider as well.

The Sezniks had a different take on this debate. They told me more than once that Rascal Rabbit Four was the best one. In fact, they felt that each one was an improvement over the last, so that each time they were grateful not to have chanced on a carbon copy. Four was the ultimate

Rascal Rabbit as, sadly, there was to be no Rascal Rabbit Five. By the time Four died the Sezniks were not in a position to get another dog. Earl died shortly after, and Dolly developed dementia. They had a good long run, though, those two, or should I say, those six. I really miss them.

FIDO VERSUS THE WORLD
URBAN WILDLIFE ENCOUNTERS
IN THREE PARTS

PART ONE: SPRAYED

Before I even saw him, I could smell Brownie. The whole clinic could smell Brownie. Probably the neighbours could smell Brownie. Maybe even the people driving by on Portage Avenue could smell Brownie. But Brownie didn't care. He was still the same old happy, tail-wagging chocolate Lab we loved, at least until he came in and made everyone go, "Oh my God! What is that smell? Is that skunk?"

Yes, it was. Brownie had been skunked. He may not have cared but his owner was in a state of some distress. She kept apologizing for bringing him in, but she didn't want him in the house and he had met the skunk in the yard, so she didn't want him there either, at least until she was sure that it was safe, and it was a hot summer day, so she couldn't leave him in the car. The only place left to go was the clinic, where she was desperately hoping we could help. We did have Skunk-Off in stock, so a brave vet tech put on a large smock and led Brownie, tail still wagging, to a distant room to apply it. Brownie was lucky because he hadn't gotten it in the eyes, where it can be quite irritating, and he was lucky because he was up to date on rabies vaccine and it didn't look like he had actually come into direct contact with the skunk. Skunks are the most common carriers of rabies in Manitoba.

Now some of you, especially those of my generation and older, will be thinking about all those classic television shows where skunked dogs were bathed in tomato juice. Don't do it. First of all, it is easily more expensive than an enzymatic cleaner; secondly, it is ridiculously messy; and thirdly, it doesn't actually work. It only seems to work because of something called olfactory fatigue whereby your nose is overwhelmed by the combined tomato-skunk stench and calls it quits. Anyone else encountering the dog will still smell the skunk until their nose packs it in too. And then the competing tomato smell wears off and you have a stinky pink dog. If you really need a home remedy, the recipe you'll see online for 3% peroxide, baking soda and dishwashing soap does work. (Just search "skunk spray peroxide recipe" for detailed instructions.)

On the plus side you and your dog have been exposed to a marvel of nature. Skunks can spray three metres from their little anal sac nozzles, their spray odour can be detected up to five kilometres away, and it only takes ten parts per billion to make a stink. So, mix a little wonder into your horror.

PART TWO: POKED

In porcupine country, every clinic has these. In the city perhaps only one or two, but in rural areas probably quite a few. I'm talking about "quill dogs." We call them that because there appears to be a circuit in the canine brain that is dedicated to solving "The Mystery of the Spiky Beast." You would think that getting a face full of quills would be a deterrent to approaching the Spiky Beast again, and that's certainly what the Beast intends, but to a quill dog this is just a mystery that needs to be solved. A puzzle that needs to be figured out. An enigmatic opponent who needs to be bested. And this mystery is almost never solved. The Spiky Beast almost always makes a getaway.

The practical consequence of all this is that these quill dogs will present again and again to the vet to have the quills removed. This is rarely medically serious, but it is often a significant nuisance. On the rare occasions where it is serious, it is because a quill has gotten in the eye, or deep in the throat. In even rarer occasions, they can migrate deeper into the body. Usually, though, it's just a matter of giving the poor bewildered dog an anaesthetic and painstakingly searching for the quills. Once you find them, they're easy to remove. "Once you find them . . ." Please do not be upset if your vet has missed a few quills! Ones that have broken off at the surface can be very difficult to find. And please do not consider this a DIY project — you will miss far more if your dog is not sedated or anaesthetized, and it will be painful.

On the upside, porcupine quills are coated in an antibiotic substance. We will still often prescribe an antibiotic as a precaution but getting quilled leads to far less infection than you might expect. You might wonder why the porcupine is being so kind to others. It's not. It's being kind to itself because the animal most commonly poked by a porcupine is the porcupine itself, when it accidentally falls out of a tree! This is more common than you might think. Porcupines are not especially elegant creatures.

And before we move on to Part Three, I want to dispel a porcupine myth. They cannot shoot or even toss their quills. What they can do is jump very quickly towards their opponent and then lash out with their tail before jumping away again. Still not elegant, but lightning fast.

PART THREE: CHOMPED

As the saying goes, there's a first time for everything. And I suspect that this may also be the last time I'll see something like this. Mrs. Bernard brought in Duffy, her beautiful golden retriever, after he had fought with a beaver and lost. He had a set of perfectly chisel-shaped puncture wounds on his paw. Yes, a beaver. Yes, fighting with a retriever and losing. And yes, right here in the city of Winnipeg.

So, let's unpack that.

Last thing first. Winnipeg is a city of rivers and streams, and beavers are actually quite plentiful here. They keep to themselves, though, and I suspect that the majority of Winnipeggers have never seen one, but if they walk their dogs near these rivers and streams, their dogs have almost certainly smelled them and been intrigued. Well, Duffy was intrigued. He was intrigued enough to dive into the creek and investigate the source of that smell.

This brings me to the next thing: beavers and fighting. There is a general prejudice about beavers that they are amiable but dull-witted. People have a cartoon image of a good-natured, hard-working, basically passive animal going about its business without paying attention to much else. Well, they are hard-working, but they are as mentally sharp as any rodent and they are only amiable, good-natured and passive if you leave them alone. Duffy did not leave the beaver alone. The beaver tried to swim away, but Duffy followed until they got close to the lodge, when the beaver decided to stop and make a stand. It whipped around and chomped the surprised dog on the paw. It was a one-sided fight. Duffy may have intended to bite the beaver, but quickly changed his mind and splashed back to his shocked owner.

In 2013 a beaver attacked a 60-year-old fisherman in Belarus. The bite severed an artery and the man died. Kind of gives you new respect for our supposedly comical national animal.

ORBIT'S OFF DAY

Orbit didn't eat his breakfast this morning. This is like saying the sky was purple with green polka dots this morning. In other words, it's something that never happens. Essentially impossible. Or so I thought. Orbit is my seven-year-old Shetland sheepdog and his mealtimes are like the tides in the sea, an unstoppable force of nature. At least unstoppable until it stopped. I was so confused by this bizarre turn of events that at first I just stared at him, bewildered, while he stared back at me, presumably equally bewildered. Then I stuck his bowl right under his nose and made every kind of encouraging noise I could think of. When that didn't work, I took kibble into my hand and pretended to eat it, saying, "Nom, nom, nom, mmm, so good!" Yes, I did. Orbit looked at me blankly. I don't think he was judging me, but he wasn't persuaded.

At this point a conversation began between my emotions and my intellect.

Emotions: "Oh my God! He's not eating! He never misses a meal! Never! What's wrong?"

Intellect: "Settle down. Your patients do this all the time and you tell the clients not to worry if it's just a meal or two. Probably a stomach bug."

Emotions: "I remember now, he barfed yesterday too! Oh my God!"

Intellect: "Yeah, yeah, whatever. That goes with a stomach bug too. No big deal."

Emotions: "But it could be something bad, couldn't it? Something really, really bad! We should take him with us to the clinic. We should run some blood and take some x-rays. Maybe do an ultrasound. Just to be safe, right?!"

Intellect: "Are you serious? You're really starting to sound like a wacky paranoid client."

Emotions: "But he looks so sad and worried!"

Intellect: "You're projecting. To me he just looks confused because we keep staring at him."

Emotions: "He could die! I'd miss him so much!"

Intellect: "Don't be a freak. He's not going to die. Not today anyway. Let's offer him a treat and see what he does."

I left the room and came back with a small piece of freeze-dried liver, his absolute favourite. He sniffed it and then happily ate it.

Intellect: "See, you goof, he's fine. He's just having an off day."

Emotions: "But remember when you put Buddy to sleep the other day? Remember? He took liver treats right up to a few minutes before he died! And he had cancer! Cancer! And it all started with vomiting and eating less, didn't it?"

Intellect: "Good grief, get a grip. Buddy had loads of other symptoms. Orbit does not have cancer. I told you, he's just having an off day. Like a bug or something. Other than the one vomit yesterday, the appetite today and being a little quieter, he's normal, right? No more vomiting, still wants to go for his walks, still greets us, taking treats . . ."

Emotions: "Yeah, I guess."

Intellect: "So, let's give it another day or two. If his appetite isn't back after 48 hours, or he develops other symptoms, we'll take him in. Sound good?"

Emotions: "OK, but you'd better be right, buster, because if you're wrong, I'll never forgive you and I'll never trust you again. Not ever."

I tell this story to illustrate that I get it. Pet owners sometimes feel silly bringing their animals in when they're having an off day, but their intellect is trained to teach elementary school, or calculate taxes, or fix computers, and not to diagnose sick pets. Consequently, it makes total sense that their emotions are going to have the edge and will occasionally (often?) be able to wrestle their intellect to the ground. So, there's no need to feel silly. And you know what? Sometimes emotions are right and sometimes intellect is out to lunch.

In this case, intellect was right. Orbit was just having an off day.

MONTY'S STORY

Little gets a veterinarian's attention faster than a person running in the door screaming, "Please help me! My dog collapsed in the parking lot! I think he's dead!"

One of my colleagues and two of our nurses jumped up and ran out to help. A minute later they came back in carrying a medium-sized mixed-breed dog on a stretcher. His name was Monty Jacobs and, while he was not dead, he was clearly in trouble. His breathing was laboured and his gums were pale. Mrs. Jacobs was freaking out. My colleague is a very calm person and she was able to reassure her that we would do our best to stabilize Monty and get to the bottom of whatever was going on as quickly as possible.

Sure enough, 15 minutes later we had a chest x-ray. The heart looked enormous.

"Oh no, it's another right atrial hemangio," I said when I was asked to look at it. I was referring to a common cancer that can cause bleeding on the outer surface of the heart. The blood becomes trapped under the pericardium — the membrane that wraps around the heart — which causes the entire heart shadow to appear enlarged on an x-ray.

"Do you have time to do an ultrasound?" my colleague asked.

"Yeah, I can squeeze it in. Sadly for the dog, it's going to be quick as these are really easy to see."

But I was wrong. It was not quick, and Monty did not have a bleeding cancer. Monty had dilated cardiomyopathy. Dilated cardi . . . what? I'll break it down for you. "Dilated" means what you think it means — stretched out. "Cardio" means heart, "myo" means muscle and "pathy" means disease. Put it all together and you have a disease of the heart muscle causing it to become so weak that it becomes baggy and stretched out.

This made no sense. We only see DCM (the easier-to-remember abbreviation) in a small handful of breeds, because it is a genetically determined disease. Monty was maybe terrier, mixed with maybe husky, mixed with maybe German shepherd, mixed with maybe . . . who knows? A classic "Heinz 57." I was stalling for time by describing some of the less important things on the screen before getting to the inevitable "why" question, when suddenly a little (metaphorical) bell rang inside my head. Bing.

I turned to the owner and asked, "What do you feed Monty?" She named a brand of food I hadn't heard of before and said that it was grain-free. Now I knew.

Two years ago reports began to bubble up of dogs developing something that looked like DCM but which did not fit the usual breed profile. Individual private practitioners did not detect a pattern because they would only see one or two cases, but cardiologists did see a pattern. All of these dogs had been on grain-free diets from "boutique" brands.

To expand on this a little, by "boutique" we mean relatively small-batch foods produced by companies that do not have a certified animal nutritionist on staff and who are not able to do proper scientific feeding trials. Their grain-free diets are enormously popular at the moment. I have no hesitation in saying that these diets are a fad built on two fallacies. The first fallacy is that allergies to grains are common. In fact, allergies to grains are quite rare in dogs. Moreover, when there is a grain allergy it is usually to a single type of grain, such as wheat, not to all grains. The second fallacy is that dogs are essentially wolves and therefore should not eat grains. Your dog is no more a wolf than you are a Neanderthal (mind you, I'm making an assumption about you). We now know that evolution works much faster than we used to think it did. A lot has changed in dog, and human, biology since those good old wolf and Neanderthal days.

The problem with taking the grains out is that dogs do need a source of carbohydrates, so these companies have replaced the grains with legumes such as green peas, lentils and chickpeas. A handful of peas makes a healthy treat for your dog, but as a major component of his diet it's a problem. The exact mechanism is not entirely clear, but it seems to have something to do with the fact that legumes have protein in addition to carbs and the exact ratio of amino acids in that protein creates issues for dog's hearts.

We expect that only a small number of grain-free diets are involved; however, that list is growing so we cannot yet be sure that any specific grain-free diet is safe. So, although there may be some fine grain-free diets, at this time we have to recommend that you feed a traditional diet from a well-established company that has a solid footing in nutritional science. Ask your veterinarian for a list of these companies. And please don't panic if you are feeding a boutique grain-free diet; this problem is not that common, but you really should talk to your veterinarian about switching. And please don't feel guilty either; many of the boutique grain-free diets are particularly good at marketing in a way that appeals to our desire to do the right thing.

There are good drugs for DCM and most patients can be stabilized if it is caught early enough, but the terrible thing is that there may be no warning signs. Monty had just been a little weaker for a few days prior to the collapse, and had been breathing a little harder. This is typical. We expect that by changing his diet we can stop further heart damage from occurring and we hope that maybe some of the damage can even be reversed.

I have seen dozens more cases since Monty. Several tragically didn't survive, one of them dying right in front of me, but Monty is doing well. And he likes the new food.

DOGS GETTING HIGH

Ralph was certainly not himself. It was hard to tell how he actually felt, but the old German shepherd was barely able to walk, stumbling and swaying each time he tried to take a step. And his eyes had a glassy, far-away look.

"His arthritis is so much worse today!" Mrs. Sorensen said, clearly upset and worried.

Although he was obviously having trouble getting up and walking, this did not look at all like arthritis symptoms.

"Have you been giving him anything for the arthritis?" I asked, a suspicion beginning to form.

"He gets his glucosamine and fish oil, and then recently I started to give him a little CBD oil. Just a little, Doctor."

Suspicion confirmed — Ralph was stoned.

In theory this shouldn't happen with CBD, also called cannabidiol, because in theory the oil should not contain any THC, the psychoactive component of cannabis. But that's just in theory.

In a couple of years, CBD has gone from a "what's that" obscurity to an everyday conversation with pet owners. Quite literally every day. I have been in practice long enough to have seen this phenomenon before. Just in recent memory vitamin E, echinacea and coconut oil have all had their moment in the sun as potential panaceas. The internet age spreads the word so much faster while amplifying the most improbable stories. In each case these remedies did not end up curing cancer, reversing kidney disease or noticeably "boosting the immune system," but each did end up finding a place in the array of options for some specific conditions in some specific patients. It's just a much smaller place than the enthusiasts had hoped for. If only medicine were so simple!

And so it will be for CBD oil. The range of disorders that people want to try it on their pets for is breathtaking, but the best evidence we have is that it might be useful for four things: epilepsy, anxiety, nausea and, yes, arthritic pain. There are some problems, though.

The first problem is that the research is lacking. There is a lot of work being done right now, though, so hopefully we'll have some more clarity soon, but for the time being everything we know is based on anecdote and extrapolation from humans. There are plenty of examples in other areas of medicine where anecdotes and extrapolations have misled us, so some caution is warranted.

The second problem, as illustrated by Ralph's experience, is that quality control and regulation are also lacking. Contamination with THC is not that rare. I haven't seen numbers on that, but I did see another stoned dog with the same story soon after Ralph. Some reports also indicate that the majority of commercially available CBD oil is contaminated with pesticides and other troubling substances. Google "contaminated CBD" if you're in the mood to be alarmed. When tested, some of the products contain either very little or even no CBD oil at all. Moreover, all of this can vary from batch to batch, so just because Aunt Marge's corgi is like a pup again after three drops of "Doctor Good Earth's All Natural Holistic Small-Batch Artisanal CBD Oil," that doesn't mean that your dog will have the same experience.

Patience, people. My own dog is epileptic, and I'll probably try CBD, but only once the science is in and the quality is truly assured (i.e., not just recommended by the dude with the man-bun at the health food store). If your dog suffers from epilepsy, crippling anxiety, chronic nausea or arthritic pain and you feel like you can't be patient because nothing else has worked, please check with your vet first before winging it with CBD. New information is coming out regularly.

Ralph was better after about a day. Mrs. Sorensen is going to be patient now.

THREE AND A SPARE

"See that bright white line? That's normal bone." I was showing Jasper's x-ray to the Folsoms. "Then see here?" I pointed to an area of the humerus that was both wider and fuzzier looking, as if someone had smudged the picture with a cheap eraser. "This is abnormal bone. I'm really sorry, but I'm afraid this looks like bone cancer."

Mr. and Mrs. Folsom said nothing for a moment while Jasper, a slender seven-year-old yellow Lab cross, wagged his tail and looked up at them.

Then Mr. Folsom said in a flat, very controlled voice, "So, he's done then. You're sure?"

"We should do a biopsy to be sure because it could be something else, but I doubt it. I'm sorry, I know that this must be a terrible shock for you. If the biopsy confirms cancer, I will recommend amputation and . . ."

Mr. Folsom cut me off, "No way. We're not doing that. We can't let him suffer."

Mrs. Folsom put her hand on his arm to shush him and turned to me, "We'll talk about it, Doctor. Let's get the biopsy first and then we'll see."

So, this is what we did. Within a week we had the diagnosis confirmed — osteosarcoma, malignant bone cancer. We also did a series of tests to check for visible metastases or spread of the cancer to other parts of the body. Finally, some good news — these tests were negative. The Folsoms wanted to come down to discuss the options in person, with their teenage kids present.

After introductions, plus cookies for Jasper, I began, "If Jasper were my dog I would amputate. He is still young enough and healthy enough that he is a good candidate. Without amputation he is at a high risk of breaking that leg because the cancer has weakened the bone so much. If we do nothing his life expectancy at this point is about six to eight weeks on average."

"Is that it? Just six to eight weeks?" their daughter asked.

"Yes, that's the average, some shorter, some longer, but none very much longer. This is why I want you to think about amputation. That immediately gets rid of the pain and obviously eliminates the risk of a fracture. With surgery plus chemotherapy the average jumps to almost a year, with 20% of dogs living longer than two years. And a year is a really long time in a dog's life. Also, chemo is usually much gentler in dogs and has far fewer side effects than in people."

"But how's he going to manage on three legs?" Mr. Folsom asked, his arms crossed, his expression clearly skeptical.

"That's the beauty of being a dog or cat. They do so well on three legs! You'd be amazed. In 28 years, I honestly have never had anyone come back later and say that they regretted doing it. Obviously, we have to make sure that his three remaining legs are in good shape, but otherwise it's just not a barrier."

"It's like he has three and a spare!" the daughter said. Mr. Folsom was staring straight ahead.

Exactly. I couldn't have put it better myself. Three and a spare. It can be such a hard procedure to convince people to do, but it's one of the ones that brings the most obvious and immediate benefit to the patient. It's helpful not just for scenarios like Jasper's, but also for some complicated fractures. I liken it to pulling a bad tooth. At that point the tooth is just a liability. It no longer provides benefit, only pain and risk.

Clearly this is not for every dog or cat with bone cancer. I don't want any of you who may have been through something like this and chose not to amputate to feel bad about your decision. The age of the pet can be a significant factor. For every year beyond middle age the decision becomes more complicated. And the bigger the dog, the faster they age. Also, as I mentioned, the other legs need to be healthy, and if it is cancer, it must not have spread. And finally, to be honest, I wish it didn't have to be about the money, but sometimes it has to be. Surgery plus chemo runs into the thousands.

Incidentally, this general principle of being able to remove prominent parts of the body to benefit the patient goes for the eyes too. In some cases of glaucoma, which is high fluid pressure in the eyeball, the medication stops working and the eyeball painfully swells. At that point it is a liability, like a rotten tooth, or a cancerous leg. People are sometimes aghast when we recommend removing the eye (a procedure called enucleation), but just like with amputation, once the owners get over the psychological hurdle, nobody ever regrets having the eye removed. Nobody.

This is one of the beautiful things about animals. They have very little in the way of body image hang-ups. They just do not seem to care how many teeth or eyes or legs they have. Terry Fox would be proud.

As I'm sure you guessed, three of the Folsoms ultimately out-voted the fourth and they opted for surgery. Jasper, being an above-average dog in a lot of other ways, lived an above-average length of time. He had 16 good months of tearing around on three legs chasing squirrels in the park before we had to let him go. They swore he was just as fast as he had been on four legs. He was definitely just as happy.

MR. BARKY BARKERSON

My own dog is a beautiful Shetland sheepdog named Orbit. In common with many dogs he also has a number of nicknames: Orbers, Orbie, Orbiedo, the Fluffmeister, Shithead and, more recently, Mr. Barky Barkerson because, in common with many Shetland sheepdogs, he has learned to bark. He didn't bark much at first, but you could tell he was often thinking about it. My wife, Lorraine, and I, both being veterinarians and knowing the breed, were very careful to discourage barking. Some people make the mistake of trying to train their dog only to bark when a stranger comes to the door. Perhaps they'll succeed, but more often than not, once a dog is allowed to bark for one reason, they will find justifications for barking for a dozen other reasons. "That leaf, it could have been a threat! Never trust a leaf." Or, "OK, now I know that that noise was just a figment of my imagination, but it could have been the start of a barbarian invasion!" We did not allow Orbit to bark for any reason, but this was like trying to keep the lid on a jar of nitroglycerin. You just know it's going to blow someday. (Yes, yes, I know that nitroglycerin doesn't come in jars and that if it did, keeping the lid on would be the least of your worries, but you get the picture.)

That someday was one evening when a group of four of my friends showed up, hammered loudly on our front door and then waltzed in before I could get to the door, startling Orbit and rearranging four of his five neurons (I said he was beautiful, I didn't say he was smart). He began to bark furiously at them and since that day he has barked whenever there is a knock on the door. Not only does he bark whenever there is a knock on the door, but he also barks whenever he *thinks* there is a knock on the door. This encompasses a breathtakingly wide array of knock-like sounds associated with cooking, cleaning and life in general. After years of counselling people to avoid letting their dogs bark, here I was with a dog that barked like a deranged fool when I so much as accidentally hit the side of a saucepan with a wooden spoon.

So, the problem is clear, but what's the solution? Dogs are like humans in that acquiring a bad habit is the easiest thing in the world to do, but unacquiring it is an entirely different matter. Unjust, isn't it? It takes a lot of work and it takes a lot of time. At its most basic level you want to negatively reinforce the bad behaviour and positively reinforce the good. Now, before I go on, I should emphasize that negative reinforcement is not the first choice for most behaviours in dogs. For example, when you're housetraining a puppy, you ignore the bad behaviour (and positively reinforce the good), and when you're trying to stop a dog from chewing your shoes, you redirect away from the bad behaviour (and positively reinforce the good). In most cases ignoring or redirecting is the way to go. But ignoring does not work for barking, and in Orbit's case, redirecting did not work either. He was that dedicated to his task. A workaholic barker.

In theory this all sounds simple enough, but the real trick is that you have to do it consistently. For a barker, the positive is easy enough. If ever someone knocks on our door and Orbit doesn't bark, he gets rewards and lavish praise. This doesn't happen very often. The negative reinforcement is tougher, though. I recommend a squirt gun or a plant mister accompanied by a firm "No." Squirt him in the face each time he barks and say no in as gruff a tone as you can muster. The problem is the consistency. The barking is self-reinforcing, meaning each time he barks he feels even more like barking the next time, so if you only squirt him one out of three times, the barking is winning two to one. Practically speaking, this means having squirt guns or bottles placed all around the house so that one is always at hand. Or I suppose you can keep one in a holster, but you might feel self-conscious answering the door like that. Regardless, you will have to do it a thousand times in row to be effective. It's exhausting.

Incidentally, if your dog is one of those weirdos who likes being squirted in the face, you'll have to find something else he doesn't like, such as a blast from an athletic whistle. And I don't recommend the bark collars. The ones that spray citronella had potential when they were first released, but I found that many dogs just learned to tolerate the citronella spritz. The collar does have the advantage that you do not need to be home for it provide negative reinforcement, but if you can do the spraying with water you can control the dose, as it were, to get the desired effect. The first few times Orbit ended up with a dripping wet face before he stopped barking, but now we often just have to reach for the bottle for him to squint his eyes, lower his head and, yes, stop barking.

I wish I could end the story there. Unambiguous success. Clever veterinarian triumphs over foolish barking dog. But life is rarely so simple. Recall that I said that consistency was key. Too often I can't find a squirt bottle at that moment, or my hands are full, or I'm not near enough to where he is, or . . . insert a dozen other excuses. In short, we are not consistent. He barks less, but still too much. However, should the barbarian invasion actually come, we'll have ample warning. There's always an upside.

FLAT FACE

You see them everywhere now. I'm sure I'm seeing three or four times as many in my practice as I used to. Statistics in the UK indicate a rise of anywhere from 96% to 3,104% (!) in the last decade, depending on the specific breed in this group. There's one on the cover of my first book and one of my partners recently got one. I'm talking about flat-faced dogs, what we technically call the brachycephalic breeds (which translates as "short head," which I suppose is accurate when you look at them from the side), such as English bulldogs, French bulldogs, boxers, pugs and Boston terriers. Many breeds have had their moment in the sun. In the '60s and '70s German shepherds and cocker spaniels were much more popular than they are now. More recently golden retrievers have been the cool breed. And now it's the turn of the brachycephalics.

Let me start by saying that I love these dogs. Of course, I love all dogs (more or less), but I especially love these as patients as they have a higher probability of being sweet and good-tempered. Note, I wrote "higher probability," not "certainty." There is never a guarantee, and when a flat-faced dog goes rogue, look out — that short snout can be very difficult to put a muzzle on! But mostly they are easy to work with and consequently also make trustworthy family pets, which in part explains their popularity.

But. You knew there'd be a but, didn't you? But this mostly pleasant temperament needs to be weighed against the plethora of health issues that are common with these breeds. Yes, truly a plethora. This is important to underline because people will counter that all breeds have their issues and that their cousin has a Heinz 57 mutt and he has issues too! Again, this is a question of probabilities, of loading the dice, of stacking the deck. Brachycephalics have a longer list of potential issues than most dogs and, in some cases, they have a higher probability of being unlucky enough to turn these potential issues into actual issues. As a very general rule of thumb, the less a dog looks like their original ancestor (picture something between a dingo and a wolf), the more health problems it's likely to have.

What kind of issues are we talking about here? It should be self-evident that squishing a dog's snout flat could result in breathing problems. And it does. Most of these dogs snore, which some people might even consider charming, but the snoring is evidence of air struggling to get through a narrower passage. Often the roof the mouth has been pushed back so far that it extends into the airway. The resulting obstruction can be severe enough that surgery is required. Excessively narrowed nostrils are also commonly operated on. These dogs are also more prone to cancer and although there are certainly genetic factors at play that are independent of the anatomy of their heads, there is also some evidence that chronic low oxygen levels may contribute. So, that's the breathing. Then there are the teeth. They have the same number of teeth as a dog with a regular muzzle but jammed into a much smaller space. Severe dental disease is routine. And then there's the skin. All those cute folds around the pushed-in nose are vulnerable to skin disease, as debris and oil and tears can't get out and air can't get in. And there's the eyes — more prominent eyes become diseased and injured more frequently. And the narrow hips, which are perversely part of the "breed standard" for some of these, and can make C-sections almost mandatory.

I have only listed the common issues. There are more. Unsuspecting owners are caught off guard and overwhelmed by this so frequently that flat-faced dogs are greatly overrepresented among purebreds abandoned at humane societies and rescue centres.

Honestly, it's so bad that the British Small Animal Veterinary Association (BSAVA) has joined with scientists, animal welfare organizations and breed organizations to form the Brachycephalic Working Group. Its aim is to reduce the popularity of the breeds. Why would breeders be involved in such a thing? With careful breeding by dedicated and knowledgeable people, some of these problems can be reduced in severity and probability, but when a breed becomes popular, amateurs get on the bandwagon. These amateurs may be motivated by a new-found love for the breed, or they may be in it purely for the money: these dogs currently sell for about three times what less popular breeds sell for. Regardless of the motivation, the result of amateur breeding is an increase in genetically based issues because of a lack of skill, knowledge and investment in testing and screening. This is obviously not good for the breed, let alone the poor individual animals afflicted, so the professional breeders are important members of this working group.

One of the first actions taken by the group was to write an open letter to the media and the advertising industry asking them not to use these breeds in their programs and promotional materials. Most of you know the effect movies like *101 Dalmatians*, or *Beethoven*, or *Turner & Hooch* had on the popularity of their featured breeds. The effect is real, and it is strong. Brachycephalics are showing up everywhere and this is driving demand and careless breeding. And I am to blame too, in my tiny little way. As I mentioned, my first book, *The Accidental Veterinarian*, featured an adorable French bulldog on the cover. I thought nothing of it at the time.

All that being said, I still smile when one of these dogs comes in. I know that chances are pretty high that I'm going to get a doggie smile and a slobbery, snorty, enthusiastic greeting.

SHOES CLUES

Research indicates that facial expressions in dogs are not always just reflex outer signs of inner emotion, but that sometimes they are conscious attempts to communicate with us. In other words, that sad-puppy-begging expression is a deliberately thought out effort to wheedle that bit of toast crust from you and is not just a helpless sagging of the facial features. You probably already knew this, but you have probably given in to it anyway, thus positively reinforcing the ploy. It doesn't matter that we know we are being manipulated; we are often helpless to resist.

I am no different. Orbit (my seven-year-old Shetland sheepdog, if you haven't been paying attention) knows exactly how to look at me to get what he wants. It doesn't always work, but it works often enough that it is definitely worth his while trying. Sometimes, however, his facial expressions are clearly just a reflex. This is the case with the shoe disappointment. Whenever I go to the front door, Orbit comes running. He sleeps through all sorts of other noises, but my footsteps in the direction of the front door consistently wake him, wherever he might be in the house. He rushes up to me, tail wagging, eyes bright and hopeful, doggie smile on his lips. Then he sits down and waits to see which shoes or boots I select. He does this because his second favourite thing in life, after eating begged toast crusts, banana chunks and carrot slices, is going for walks. Like many dogs, he has a seemingly limitless capacity for walks. He waits to see which shoes or boots I select because he has learned that only some of them are associated with walks. If I don't put one of these pairs on, he makes a "harrumph" snort that sounds very much like an expression of disgust and then turns heel and leaves the front hall. However, if I do put on walking shoes or boots, he becomes excited and happy again. But he continues watching my face carefully, because he has also learned that occasionally I put on these shoes or boots and then, inexplicably, don't take him for a walk. So, when this happens and I don't say the "w-a-l-k" word, he looks genuinely sad and disappointed. This is no longer a begging kind of sad, but his real, heartfelt emotion, pitifully on display. Many of you will agree with me — there is nothing we do on a regular basis that is as heartbreaking as leaving our dog behind when he was expecting to be taken along.

Watching how Orbit so obviously analyzes my footwear selection made me wonder about how dogs generally try to understand us. For sure they know some words. At one extreme, there's the famous border collie Chaser, who apparently understood 1,022 words. At the other end there are dogs who struggle to understand one or two. To be sure, in most cases this is just a lack of training rather than a reflection of their intelligence, but the bottom line is that spoken language has limitations when we are trying to communicate with our dogs. What else, then? They certainly pay close attention to our body language, our gestures and what we're actually doing, as in Orbit's focus on what I put on my feet. That is why when I have a fearful patient, I am careful to move slowly, avoid eye contact and, when possible, approach the dog from the side. And, tone of voice is key. Admit it, you have at some point in your life said something like, "You're a shithead!" to your dog, in a happy, sing-song voice, and found it hilarious that he responded with a big smile and a wagging tail, seeming to agree, "Yes, I am a shithead!" Understanding this concept is important when dealing with behavioural issues — use a louder, deeper, gruffer tone when you are disciplining your own dog, but use a quieter, higher, gentler tone when dealing with a nervous dog you don't know as well.

I love watching my patients watching me. They are often scanning for clues. Is the guy in the white coat reaching for the treat jar? Or is he reaching for those pointy things in the drawer? Some are very attuned to my routine and from their own expressions I can tell that they know what's next. Some nervous dogs won't take a treat until the end of the visit. The astonishing thing is that they seem to know exactly when that is. I haven't opened the door yet or said good-bye or anything obvious like that, but these dogs pick up on something in my voice or actions that tells them that they can relax now, that the guy in the white coat has done his worst and is finished.

The subject of communication between different species is fascinating. Who has not dreamed of being Dr. Dolittle for a day and being able to literally talk to the animals? Or to have a "Babel fish," like in *The Hitchhiker's Guide to the Galaxy*? But alas, we will continue to have to make do with a handful of words and with trying to read each other's clues, including choice of footwear (although if you're an optimist, look up the "dog translator app" online — it claims to be able to convert barks to English and vice versa).

BONJOUR, MONSIEUR POISSON

I am picturing two different reactions to the essay title. Most of you are puzzled. "Hello, Mister Fish?" In French? But some of my friends, colleagues and staff are rolling their eyes and groaning lightly. Oh no, he's going to talk about Poisson clumping. *Again*.

I freely admit that I am fond of the concept of Poisson clumping and what it explains. Perhaps excessively fond. But to my mind, understanding it is key to understanding many things that happen in medicine, and in life.

The 19th-century French mathematician Simeon Denis Poisson first described what is now called the Poisson Distribution and which, yes, includes the aforementioned Poisson clumping. He recognized, and described mathematically, that random events are not distributed evenly, but rather will be scattered with a variety of spaces and clusters, or clumps. In other words, randomly. Duh. But not so duh for most people, as intuitively we seem to believe that random events should be more evenly spaced. This intuition is wrong, but it is powerful. As soon as random events begin to clump together, we start to read patterns into them. This is our deeply ingrained human tendency, dating back to when we were nervous naked apes trying to survive amongst much more powerful predatory creatures. It was much safer to over-interpret a potential pattern then to under-interpret it.

Take a handful of coins and toss them across the floor. See how some cluster? This is Poisson clumping. How about those shapes we see in clouds? Or how about the lucky streaks people sometimes have at the slot machines? Or when you roll four sixes in a row? Poisson clumping, Poisson clumping, Poisson clumping and Poisson clumping again.

That's all very interesting Philipp, but we do[...]
your books to learn about statistical theory. Where[...]
animals in this story?

Don't worry, I'm getting to them.

As I mentioned near the beginning, once we get a [...]
on how prevalent Poisson clumping is, we begin to be[...]
understand some otherwise mysterious medical events, f[...]
people and for animals.

Mr. and Mrs. Kobayashi were great people and won-derful pet owners. They had brought a long series of dogs to the clinic over the decades and were quite elderly by the time I started seeing them. They both had a great sense of humour and were always all smiles, so it was a pleasure to work with them. They were also fantas-tic pet owners, always following our advice, and always focused on doing what was the very best for their dogs, at times to their own detriment. They were the kind of pet owners who prompted the staff to say that when they died, they wanted to be reincarnated as one of the Kobayashis' dogs. Consequently, it was even harder than usual to have to give them bad news. We were in the darkened ultrasound room and I was scanning their little terrier mix's abdomen. Patches had been eating less and losing weight.

"Do you see that area there?" I pointed to something that I'm sure just looked like bad television reception circa 1955 to them, but I always felt obliged to at least try to show what I was talking about.

"Yes, doctor, what is that?" Mrs. Kobayashi said quietly.

"I'm really so sorry, but I think that that's a cancerous tumour. It makes sense with his history and other test results too."

We discussed the pros and cons of trying to biopsy (mostly cons) and the possible treatment options (no realistic ones). After this was done, I said I was very sorry again and they thanked me, and then three of us sat in silence for a long moment, while Patches stared at the door.

Then Mr. Kobayashi spoke. "Doctor, why does this keep happening to us? This is our third dog in a row with cancer. What are we doing wrong?"

"That's really terrible. I had forgotten that you've been through this before. There is little that is certain in medicine, but I am certain about this — you are not doing anything wrong. In fact, you are doing everything right. Patches and the others have great lives with you and every aspect of their health that is under your control is great too. But most cancers are not really under your control. Even when you eliminate all the obvious risk factors, it's still a common disease. You can reduce the risk sometimes, but you can't take it to zero. It's mostly random and random events will cluster. Three dogs with cancer in a row is one of those random clusters. It's just plain old heartbreaking rotten luck. I'm so sorry."

No, I did not say Poisson clumping. I learned early on to stick to plain language, although the temptation to sound smart by using obscure expressions is overwhelming at times. They said that they understood this explanation, but I'm sure in their hearts they still wondered. And you

know, sometimes a pattern is significant. Sometimes the dice really are loaded. The trick is in not assuming that they are. Be alert, but don't be paranoid. Ultimately this is the power of science, and more specifically, the power of medical science. It gives us a way to analyze apparent patterns.

Many people at the Kobayashis' age would think twice about getting another dog, especially after the heartbreak of losing three to cancer, but after a few months I was delighted to see them in the waiting room again with a beautiful little puppy. I'd like to think that they came around to believing in the randomness of clusters, but honestly, it's more likely that they put all of that out of their minds and focused on the joy of having a new puppy in the house again.

THE BALANCE OF RESPONSIBILITIES

As a veterinarian in private practice you end up having to balance responsibilities to a number of different parties. You have responsibilities to the patient, to the client, to the community, to the profession, to the practice, to your staff, to your family and, of course, to yourself. When the day is good and the sky is bright and we have a song in our hearts and the world is as it should be, all these responsibilities are in alignment with each other and it's not something we need to think about.

Thankfully this is often the case, but sometimes it is not.

Sometimes we find ourselves in situations where two or more of these responsibilities are in conflict. Most commonly this arises when the client disagrees with our advice regarding the treatment of their pet. Unless the client's decision amounts to animal abuse, there is little we can do. Our legal responsibility to the client to follow their instructions trumps our moral responsibility to the patient to do what we feel is in their best interests. This is, of course, a sad and frustrating bind to be in, but most veterinarians are used to it. It is easiest to bear when it happens because of real financial limitations. Short of giving the service away (and this does happen), there's nothing anyone can do about it. It is hardest to bear when the client is absolutely able to follow the advice, but chooses not to. Sometimes this is due to stubborn ignorance, and sometimes it is for more surprising reasons. Take the case of Marty Bigelow.

Marty was a scruffy and hairy little eight-year-old terrier mix who had, in the past few months, progressively become less hairy as his fur fell out and failed to grow back. He was still scruffy in appearance because the remaining fur stood straight out — as if he had just emerged from a hot-air drier — but if you looked closely you could see he was becoming bald underneath. He was also beginning to drink more water and urinate more. The diagnosis was not challenging. In fact, if you do a web search for "dog drinking more losing fur" you will get the right answer. It goes without saying that I am not suggesting that Google replaces medical testing; that answer was simply the most probable and, in this case, it also happened to be right. Tests needed to be run to confirm the suspicion, but yes, Marty had Cushing's Disease, more technically known as hyper-adrenocorticism (translation: overactive adrenal gland). Cushing's comes in two flavours. The more common is the benign form where a little nodule in the pituitary gland at the base of the brain overproduces a hormone that stimulates the adrenal glands (there are two — right and left) to enlarge and in turn overproduce their own hormones. It's these hormones, especially cortisol, known as the stress hormone, that result in the symptoms. The rarer and more worrisome form is due to a cancer developing in one of the adrenal glands, enlarging it and also overproducing hormones, but potentially also threatening the life of the patient. The best way to tell the difference between these two forms is with ultrasound, which is where I came in.

Marty had been a colleague's case up until this point and I had not met the Bigelows before. They were neatly dressed and groomed, were in what appeared to be early middle age and were very polite and friendly. They quickly gave me the impression of being ideal clients — intelligent, curious and motivated to do the very best for Marty. They clearly loved the little scruffmonster.

With Marty in position on his side and, after my apologies, some of the remaining fur having been shaved, I quickly established that the left adrenal gland was more or less normal in appearance. This was worrisome. In the common, benign flavour of Cushing's both glands should be equally enlarged. Either he didn't have Cushing's after all, or he had a cancerous right gland. We gently repositioned Marty, shaved a little more after apologizing again, and had a look. Unfortunately my suspicion was correct — his right adrenal gland was enormous and misshapen. Marty had an adrenal tumour. Moreover, it was very closely attached to the caudal vena cava, a major blood vessel that pipes blood from the abdomen back towards the heart. There was good news too, though. Although this was clearly a tumour and cancerous, there was no evidence of metastatic spread. Surgical removal had a good chance of being curative. Given the location, tucked under the right kidney (incidentally, that's what adrenal means — *ad renal*, "near the kidney"), and so intimate with the vena cava, this was not a job for a general practitioner: this was a job for a specialist. Happily, we have an excellent surgical specialist in Winnipeg. I explained all this to the Bigelows and, although alarmed at the diagnosis, they were relieved that the chance of a cure was high. The cost didn't matter. Marty was their baby and as long as this was the right thing to do, they would do it. And it was the right thing to do. I just had to email the specialist to confirm the details. We shook hands and they left smiling. Marty was going to be alright.

The next day, after I heard back from the surgeon, I called the Bigelows to let them know what he had said and to obtain the confirmation from them to go ahead and book the procedure.

"So, it's good news. The surgeon confirmed that the chance of success is very high. The only wrinkle is that he is booking a month ahead now, so we may want to think about a referral to the veterinary college in Saskatoon. That said, these tend to be quite slow growing and also quite slow to metastasize, so it isn't an emergency situation."

"OK, thank you, Doctor. I'll talk to my wife and let you know this evening which way we want to go."

"Great. Either way seems reasonable to me. The advantage of the veterinary college is that they have a proper ICU and board-certified anaesthetists there, but the procedure has been done many times in Winnipeg too. We can certainly provide a very safe anaesthesia and do any needed blood transfusions here just as well as they can."

There was an odd silence for a long moment.

"Blood transfusion? Is that necessary?"

"Um, yes, often it is, because of how close that big vein is. The surgeon said 80% of them need transfusions, but don't worry, it's completely routine these days and the dogs do really well with it!"

"Oh, I'm sorry, but we won't permit that. Our beliefs do not allow for blood transfusions for ourselves, or for our pets."

Now it was my turn to be silent for a moment. This was a new one.

I gathered my thoughts and steadied my voice, "OK. I guess surgery is off the table then. It's not fair to Marty to take such a high risk of dying from blood loss, nor is it fair to the staff to have to watch that. There is a drug we can use instead to try to shrink the tumour. It won't be a cure, but it should offer a good quality of life for a while."

The conversation petered out somewhat from there. Mr. Bigelow had been very taken aback that a transfusion would likely be necessary, and I had been very taken aback that this would be a deal-breaker. Both of us were stunned.

This was honestly a really tough one. They were such smart and good-hearted people, and the religious belief that guided their decision was deeply and sincerely held. Yet it was also manifestly contrary to Marty's best interest. There have been many times when owners have declined this kind of surgery because they couldn't afford it, or because they felt their pet was too old, or because, frankly, they just didn't think it was worth it, but this was the first time someone had declined for religious reasons. Although it amounted to the same thing for the dog, it felt different to me.

In human children the courts have overruled parents and have ordered life-saving blood transfusions. It was deemed that society's responsibility to safeguard the child's welfare trumped society's responsibility to respect the religious beliefs of the parent. Pets are property under law, so there is no similar societal responsibility to safeguard, beyond the protections against outright cruelty. Moreover, in Marty's case, as mentioned before, plenty of people chose not to go ahead for all sorts of legitimate reasons. But what if it had been an emergency and he had been rushed in, bleeding profusely after being hit by a car? What if his other injuries weren't too bad, but only a blood transfusion would save his life? What if they refused then? We'd be obliged to put him to sleep before he could bleed to death. Or, if it were somehow possible to do so, would we secretly transfuse him? Would we put our responsibility to the patient ahead of our responsibility to the client, the profession and society not to break the law?

I like to think I know the answer to that question.

ZOONOSES

No, not the noses of zoo animals, but the diseases that can spread from animals to humans. It comes from the Greek *zoo-* ("of animals") and *nosos* ("disease"), whereas the nose on your face gets its name from ancient Anglo-Saxon roots. Coincidence.

Zoonoses have been on my mind because of two items in the news recently. One is at the top of every news feed right now and the other you'd have to scroll some distance to find, and only on certain sites.

The first is the coronavirus causing COVID-19.

Some strains of coronavirus can be considered zoonotic. The current one, for example, is thought to have originated in wildlife, possibly bats or pangolins. Middle Eastern Respiratory Syndrome (MERS) is another coronavirus, and it jumped from camels to people. Severe Acute Respiratory

Syndrome (SARS) was also a coronavirus, and it seems to have been passed from civets (a cat-like creature).

And now I have shocking news for you. Are you ready? Dogs get coronavirus too. Quite frequently, in fact. This is common enough knowledge — vet clinics have seen a surge in requests for canine coronavirus vaccination since the recent outbreak hit the news. Yes, we do have a vaccine, but we rarely use it. We rarely use it because canine coronavirus is a very mild disease, at worst causing diarrhea, mostly in puppies. It has nothing to do with SARS, MERS or COVID-19, other than belonging in the same very general family of viruses. Being afraid of canine coronavirus because other strains are potentially lethal is like being afraid of garter snakes because cobras and rattlesnakes can kill you. For sure, some people are afraid of all snakes, but they (hopefully) understand that this is an irrational phobia, not a rational basis for decision-making. Ditto for viruses. I get it if you're germophobic, but don't panic as a result. Your dog's diarrhea will not kill you. It might be the end of your carpet, but not of you.

The other zoonosis in the news is more bizarre. A woman in Alberta was diagnosed with a rare and aggressive liver cancer. In a surgical "Hail Mary" pass, the doctors planned to remove a large part of her liver and a number of nearby tissues. Then the surprise. It was not cancer, it was a parasite. It was a zoonotic tapeworm called *Echinococcus multilocularis*. Creepy, eh? This worm has been around for millennia, but in parts of the world, including western and northern Canada, it may be on the increase. Nobody knows for sure where this woman contracted it, but normally it's through canid feces. *Canid*, not necessarily *canine*. But possibly. *Echinococcus* cycles between a definitive host, usually a coyote, wolf or fox, and an intermediate host, usually a rodent. The adult worm sets up shop in the intestines of the definitive host, shedding eggs in the feces for the intermediate host to ingest. The eggs then hatch into larvae, which migrate and form cysts somewhere in the intermediate host, perhaps in the liver, waiting to be eaten by the definitive host and thus completing one of nature's more disturbing circles of life (cue Elton John).

Now read back over the third-to-last sentence in the paragraph above. Note the use of the word "usually" twice. The definitive host is *usually* a coyote, wolf or fox, but it could be a dog if the dog eats rodents. And the intermediate host is *usually* a rodent, but it could be a human if the human snuggles with their rodent-eating dog and then goes to eat a corned beef on rye sandwich without washing their hands first. To be clear, it doesn't have to be corned beef on rye, or any sandwich at all, but I'm sure you sorted that out for yourself. I was just trying to create a more memorable mental image. So, if you suspect your dog of eating rodents, you should mention it to your vet (we don't always ask, although I think we will be doing so more often now) because there are effective deworming medications for this, and you should always wash your hands before eating. I know that I am preaching to the choir in the COVID-19 era. Well, now you have one more reason to keep up the habit after the pandemic passes.

This is still very rare, so please don't panic. However, while no concern whatsoever is warranted for canine coronavirus, some mild attentive concern is appropriate for *Echinococcus*. This frontier between human medicine and veterinary medicine is fascinating. One list I saw had 64 different zoonoses on it, from African sleeping sickness (from cattle via tsetse flies) to Zika fever (from primates via mosquitoes), and while most are tropical and passed through insect vectors from their animal hosts, some move directly from your pet to you. Of these, only rabies is fatal, and it is very rare here because of vaccination. Everything else, from ringworm (incidentally, not a worm and not always in a ring — "rashfungus" would be a better name) to scabies to giardia, is not especially common or especially serious, unless you have a weakened immune system.

In closing, I have to wonder, if camels at the zoo with MERS sneezed on you, would that be a zoonosis from zoo noses? (Sorry.)

ALIEN

Missy was a classic "northern special" — a shepherd husky mix from a remote northern community. The complete absence of access to veterinary services in these communities, many of which can only be reached by air, means that very few dogs are spayed or neutered. Consequently an endless supply of puppies is produced for a very limited supply of potential homes. Packs of semi-feral dogs have become a significant public health hazard in some areas. Until spay and neuter programs can consistently be provided, a partial solution is the rescue of litters of puppies by organizations which then try to find homes for them in the south. Missy was one of these puppies. She had black and tan German shepherd markings, but also the classic curled tail that gave her away as a northern husky mix. She was a very sweet dog with soulful brown eyes and an enthusiasm for strangers that is not very common in these rescues, who often have reason to fear people.

I had seen Missy for her booster vaccines and then at the age of six months it was time to spay her. Despite all her positive qualities, I doubt that I would remember Missy now if the spay hadn't taken a surprising turn. I have seen tens of thousands of dogs in my career, and performed thousands of surgeries, so, as I'm sure you understand, the individual patients and procedures mostly blur together. But not Missy.

Routine surgeries like spays and neuters remind me a little of the adage about war being hours of boredom punctuated by moments of terror. I know the common perception of surgery is that it is somehow exciting, and I suppose some surgery is quite exciting, but as small animal veterinarians, 90% of what we do is remove ovaries, testicles and lumps. Thrills are hard to come by in those procedures. I suppose "hours of boredom" is overstating matters, because one does have to remain alert and pay careful attention; true boredom would be dangerous. "Moments of terror" is apt, however. Little is as terrifying as the sudden development of a life-threatening complication. Happily, the sudden development in Missy's surgery was not life-threatening, but until my brain got into gear, I felt, if not terror, then at least shock and a tinge of horror. She was safely under general anaesthesia and I had made my incision in the abdomen and was beginning to look for the uterus when I saw it.

Something was slowly moving between her abdominal organs.

🐾 *Squeamish readers are advised to skip the rest of this story and move on to the next one, which I promise has no content that will produce nightmares or trigger undesirable phobic reactions. To complete this story these readers are invited to imagine that what I saw moving between Missy's abdominal organs was merely a trick of the light causing little rainbows to appear in there. Moreover, imagine that at that exact moment the radio was playing Israel Kamakawiwo'ole's powerful ukulele rendition of "Somewhere over the Rainbow." It was a very special moment. In this case, please replace "Alien" in the chapter title with "Rainbows."*

"Wha . . . ?" I exclaimed to the tech monitoring the anaesthetic.

"What's up?" she asked cheerfully, not looking up from her monitoring chart.

"I . . . I don't know. But I think I just saw something move between the mesenteries there."

"Something? What kind of something?" She stood up to look at the incision.

There it was again. About the thickness of the small bowel, but brick red and definitely moving on its own and not just passively with Missy's breaths or pulse.

"That! Did you see that?! That's what's moving! What the . . ."

"Oh my God! I saw it too! *What is that?*"

"I don't . . ." But before I could properly express my confusion and ignorance I was interrupted by events. The something that was moving suddenly poked its head up. Like a periscope. A red periscope peering up from the tan and pale-pink bowels and membranes. Like an alien abomination from a horror sci-fi movie.

The tech screamed.

My mouth fell open.

People came running.

The thing popped its head back down and disappeared.

Now, I used the word "head" advisedly. It was the front end of a tubular object that showed every sign of being a living thing, so "head."

Then my brain restarted.

If this is alive and it is inside my patient it is, by definition, an internal parasite (or the result of an extremely elaborate prank). But what kind of internal parasite is so freaking large? *Dioctophyme renale* is so freaking large. Of course. It made perfect sense. I almost slapped my forehead to emphasize the drama of the "aha" moment, but that would have broken sterility, so I stopped myself.

"It's a kidney worm! Cool!"

Kidney worm? Yes, kidney worm. But this one was not in the kidney. I will explain.

These worms have a life cycle that takes them through freshwater fish. Dogs in remote northern communities sometimes eat scraps of raw fish containing the worm's larvae. These then migrate from the dog's intestines to the liver, where they mature into adults. The adult worms migrate out of the liver to the kidneys, usually the right kidney as that's the first one they encounter. There they grow and reproduce, shedding eggs into the urine. The eggs make their way into the water and ultimately into other fish, thus completing the cycle. This usually destroys the right kidney, but the patient does not feel this, so there are often no symptoms other than blood in the urine. Missy's worm had made a mistake and missed the kidneys, ending up wandering aimlessly (and pointlessly) around the abdominal cavity. If there had also been worms in the right kidney, we could have removed the kidney, as you can live quite happily with one kidney. In Missy's case it was just a matter of hauling the worm out, making sure there were no others, checking the kidneys and then proceeding with the spay.

You might have noticed that I wrote "hauling" the worm out. The word choice was deliberate. These are among the largest parasites known to medical science. Missy's worm was almost a metre long, so it just kept coming and coming as I tugged on it. There was more screaming. Yes, a metre, as in 100 centimetres, or just over three feet. And it was as thick as my middle finger. I still have it, pickled in a jar, so that I can do a little dramatic show-and-tell when I'm in a playful mood and we're talking about fishing. Incidentally, cooking destroys the larvae. Also, it only lives in freshwater fish, so there's no need to panic about sushi. Interestingly, though, archeologists have found *D. renale* eggs in fossilized human poop from 3000 BCE. Our ancestors apparently learned about cooking lake fish the hard way.

IT'S THE DOG, I SWEAR

Ranger, an elderly black lab, lay obediently on his right side on the ultrasound table while I performed the abdominal scan. The room was quiet and dark but for a soft glow from the ultrasound screen. Ranger's owner was at his head, stroking him, and a tech was beside the owner, gently holding Ranger's legs, although the dog was so calm that it probably wasn't necessary. Then it hit. A wave of intense odour suddenly filled the room. It was incredibly pungent and impossible to ignore. It was as if someone had — inexplicably — carefully inserted something dead and rancid into each of my nostrils.

"It's the dog, I swear!" the owner said, laughing. Ranger had, as the polite phrase puts it, "broken wind." Had he ever. We all did loud stage coughs and in the semi-dark I could see the tech waving a hand in front of her face, trying to dispel the cloud. She was closest to the source.

Who among us dog people does not recognize this scenario? Who has not hastened to point at the dog when heads turn and noses wrinkle? To be fair, it often is the dog, as they are a farty bunch. In Ranger's case we had additional evidence: on the ultrasound I could see a significant amount of gas in his large intestine.

"Good news! There's more to come!" I cheerfully announced and pointed at the screen. Veterinarians and clinic staff are more or less immune to bad smells and so, apparently, was Ranger's owner, so it was safe for me to be jovial about it. You do have to judge your audience carefully, though.

But why? Why are dogs such a farty bunch? There are two main reasons: gulping and fermenting. Let's tackle fermenting first.

Fermentation is the process by which microorganisms in an anaerobic environment (i.e., one with no oxygen) break down larger molecules into smaller molecules, often releasing gas molecules in the process. When bread rises or beer bubbles, it's because of the gas produced by yeast fermenting the grains. In the case of Ranger's large intestine, it's bacteria fermenting food molecules that weren't fully digested higher up in the small intestine. It's impossible to know specifically which food molecules were fermenting, but (as in humans) peas, beans, dairy products, complex carbohydrates and high-fibre ingredients are at the top of the list. The list is really long, though, so if the gas is a problem, the best first step is to switch to a new food that's as different in its ingredients as possible. And when I say "problem," I don't just mean from a human olfactory comfort standpoint. I also mean from a canine abdominal comfort standpoint. I routinely have patients referred to me for abdominal ultrasound because of vague pain symptoms. Usually the referring doctor is trying to rule out a tumour, but often I end up finding excessive gas. Pardon me for asking a personal question, but have you ever had bad gas cramps? Gas is either embarrassing or funny or both until you have gas cramps, and then you no longer care about the embarrassment and it sure isn't funny anymore.

The second major source of gas is gulping and this, in turn, happens for two different reasons. The first is that some dogs simply eat too fast and swallow a lot of air in the process. Correction — most dogs simply eat too fast. Humans are more likely to burp up swallowed air because of our vertical anatomy, but in dogs it tends to cruise on into the digestive system and pick up poopy odour molecules on its way to the rear exit. If you're concerned about this you can try a "slow feed" bowl, which will typically have a hump in the middle, forcing the dog to chase his food around the resulting doughnut. I have also heard of people scattering kibble across a cookie sheet to achieve a similar slow-down. The other reason for gulping is anatomy. Dogs with squishy faces such as boxers, pugs, Boston terriers and bulldogs often have very narrow nasal passages, so they are forced to mouth breathe and consequently can swallow a lot of air.

While fermenting and gulping account for most doggie flatulence, gas can occasionally also be related to disease in the digestive system, so please do mention it to your veterinarian, especially if there has been a sudden increase in the amount of gas.

And what about cats? With the exception of cats who are given too much milk, farting is unusual in this species. Their diets usually contain far fewer fermentable ingredients and although they can eat quite quickly, they do not generally gulp with the same wild "eating like nobody's watching" abandon as the average food-crazed dog.

Before we leave this fascinating subject, I'll give you a few nuggets of trivia for the next time conversation lags at a dinner party:

- The scientific study of flatulence is called flatology. This is pronounced with a long "a" as in "slate" or "fate." So now you can add flatologist to the list of career ambitions for eight-year-old boys.

- Dog farts objectively smell worse because of dogs' higher protein diets. Protein digestion can produce sulfur-containing amino acids that mix with the fermented gas to produce an especially fetid smell.
- In 2001 the Waltham Centre for Pet Nutrition in England performed a study which involved fitting the subject dogs with special fart suits, allowing nutritionists to collect the gas and analyze the sulfur content. I am 100% serious. Google "dog fart suit" if you don't believe me. There are pictures too.
- The average human produces 476 to 1491 millilitres of fumes per day, divided over 8 to 20 . . . er . . . events. As the dog fart suit does not measure volumes, we sadly do not have this data for dogs, but as I have outlined, they are a farty bunch. Even accounting for smaller size, we are talking about a lot of gas.
- Although the exceptions are hilarious, most dog flatulence is silent. The reason for the difference with humans is anatomical. In deference to my more sensitive readers I will not expand on this. Yes, believe it or not, even I have my limits.

Ranger's ultrasound was ultimately normal. He had no tumours, or anything else of concern, and the amount of gas was not unexpected for an old lab. He was just slowing down, which was also not unexpected for an old lab.

RAW

Your mother was right. Or at least she was right about this one thing — wash your hands. Wash your hands frequently, but especially before you eat. You may have a general sense that this a good idea because of "germs" that could otherwise go from your hands to your stomach and cause trouble that way, but I'm going to give you a specific and — consider yourself forewarned — somewhat horrifying rationale for hand-washing if you are a pet owner.

For this warning to make sense, you are going to have to accept a disturbing fact — your pet licks his butt. Even if you haven't observed this behaviour, I can assure you that it happens. Guaranteed. Some animals are simply secretive butt lickers. The butt licking transfers fecal bacteria not only onto their tongues, but generally onto their muzzles. From the muzzle it doesn't take long for those bacteria to move throughout the animal's fur. Then you pet him and then, well, you get the picture. So, wash your hands. This is pretty much common sense, I suppose, but where the issue departs from what is commonly known, and where it gets interesting, is when you are feeding a raw diet to your pet, and especially your dog (less is known about cats and raw diets).

So, here's another thing your mother, or father for that matter, might have taught you about hygiene — always wash your hands thoroughly before and after handling raw meat, especially chicken and ground beef. Consequently, if you are feeding your dog one of the recently trendy raw diets, I'm confident that you've been washing your hands after handling that raw chicken or ground beef. Right? You know all about *Salmonella* and *E. coli* risks. Right? I'm sure you know a lot, but I'm willing to bet that you don't know this: *Salmonella* and *E. coli* in the raw meat can go right through your dog's digestive system and come out in their poop. Now that you know this, go back and re-read the preceding paragraph. Yes, that *Salmonella* and *E. coli* is likely on their fur too. You might object and say that your dog isn't getting sick from the food, so those batches of raw diet must be safe.

<insert gameshow wrong-answer buzzer noise>

Dogs are fairly resistant to *Salmonella* and *E. coli* and frequently have no symptoms whatsoever. You, on the other hand, are not fairly resistant to *Salmonella* and *E. coli*. Therefore, if you are feeding a raw diet to your dog, it is especially important that you wash your hands before eating. In fact, given how much we touch our faces (3,000 times a day, according to one study), you should be washing your hands after every cuddling session with your dog. You may have already gotten sick this way and didn't know it, because many illnesses that people call "stomach flu" are in fact foodborne infections from exposure to fecal bacteria. The symptoms can be the same. It's just that with *Salmonella* and *E. coli* from raw diets passing through your dog, you could get much sicker.

And the horrifying news doesn't stop there. Because of the amount and type of antibiotics used in raising the animals used to produce pet food, these bacteria often have increased antibiotic resistance. There was an interesting study showing that dogs with urinary tract infections who also happened to be fed raw diets were more likely to have antibiotic-resistant infections.

So, those are the downsides of feeding a raw diet, but what about the benefits? Many people do report that their pets like the food, so for picky eaters there may be a palatability benefit. Some also report improved coat and skin condition, and even resolution of allergies. With respect to the latter I can state categorically that cooked versus raw has no impact on allergies. If your dog is allergic to chicken, for example, the immune system does not care whether it's raw or cooked or organic or free range or whatever — it's still chicken at the immunological level. When allergies have improved it's because something changed in the ingredients when you switched from the previous food to the raw diet. The same goes for any other improvements — you have changed foods, perhaps to a diet that is generally better quality, but that has nothing to do with whether the food was cooked or raw. You could get the same benefit from finding the right non-raw diet, which is often a trial-and-error process.

"But wolves don't cook their food," you object. No, they don't. Nor does any animal. Nor did humans before about one and a half million years ago. Humans are a hugely successful species — to the detriment of the planet, it must be said — and at least some of that success is a result of learning to tame fire and cook food. Cooking kills bacteria and partially pre-digests food to make the nutrients more accessible. Have you ever looked at one of the human raw diets out there? You have to eat a much larger volume of food to get the same nutrition. The greatly improved health and lifespan of our pets, mirroring our own, have many causes, but one of them is the improved nutrition we can now offer.

Even if raw diets did offer benefits to your dog that could not be matched by any cooked diet, your dog still has to live with you, he still poops, he still licks his butt and you still sometimes forget to wash your hands.

Think about it.

THE ULTIMATE TERROR

This happens at least once a day in most small animal clinics: a waiting room full of people and pets will be treated to the high decibel sounds of a dog shrieking from somewhere in the back of the clinic, in a manner suggesting that one of its limbs is being sawn off without the benefit of anaesthesia. The pets in the waiting room all develop

"OMG" facial expressions, as do some of the people. The staff have learned to quickly explain that this is not what it seems.

"Buddy is just having his nails trimmed and he sure doesn't like it!"

Nervous laughter follows.

I will confess to never having been in a nail salon, but when I walk by them, I cannot ever recall hearing the customers screaming. Maybe they also have a special soundproof room in the back for that, but more likely it simply doesn't hurt, even when someone else does it to us. So, what gives with dogs?

The first problem is that while dog nail anatomy is similar to ours, it is not identical. In humans, what's called the nail plate, or the pink part, is cleanly and clearly defined as separate from what's called the free edge, or the white part. Under the nail plate is the nail bed, and everyone knows that touching that hurts like the dickens (is that still an expression?). In dogs, the nail bed runs inside the equivalent of the free edge, tapering gradually to a point, like a cone within a cone. The nail bed is called the quick in dogs and it also hurts like the dickens if it's touched. Because the quick is partially inside the bit you want to cut, you have to look very carefully to avoid it. And if the dog's nails are black, you have to have a decent grasp of nail anatomy to be able to make a safe guess. Consequently, many dogs have had a bad experience during nail trimming. One such bad experience is often enough to sour them on the idea for life.

The clever among you — which is all of you of course, I didn't mean to suggest otherwise — will note that even some innocent little puppies and some dogs who have definitely never had their nails cut too short also hate having it done, so something else must be going on. There are two something elses. One something else is that many dogs hate being restrained. Try this little experiment — go pet your dog. What happened? He hopefully wagged his tail and looked pleased. Now hug your dog. How did he look then? Probably tense and worried. Dogs, as a rule (I know someone is going to write to me immediately about an exception), do not like being held tightly for any reason. The other something else is that many dogs simply dislike having their feet handled, period, regardless of what the intent of the handling is. How would you feel about having your feet grabbed and handled without understanding why?

The problem is hopefully clear now, so what's the solution? For dogs who are already nail-trim shriekers, it's tough. Going very slowly and gently is always a good idea. Only do a few nails at a time and back off as soon he looks upset. Making it a bad experience is not going to help for the next time! Give him lots of treats and rewards, even reserving special ones for nail trims. You can also consider gradually filing them down or using a Dremel tool. And if he's upset before you can cut even a single nail, or get out the Dremel, then perhaps check with your veterinarian. Some dogs are better with clinic staff than their owners and, of course, we have access to happy drugs if need be. There's nothing wrong with using a mild anti-anxiety medication to avoid turning the nail trim into a high-stress rodeo.

With puppies, on the other hand, you have a golden opportunity to prevent problems. Remember what they say about an ounce of prevention. Right from the very beginning you should be handling the puppy's paws and nails daily. Make it a fun and positive experience, again using treats and rewards. Have the nail trimmers nearby in his sight while you're doing this. After a week or two, put the nail trimmers in your hand during these handling sessions, but don't cut any nails yet, just let him see them, sniff them and feel them touching his feet. Then, when everyone seems ready, trim one nail. That's it, just one! Follow with lavish praise and rewards again. I think you get the idea. Slow and gentle and easy and gradual and, when possible, fun! For a detailed description of where and how short to cut, Google "dog nail anatomy." The first few hits give good information.

I wish you the very best of luck. The dogs who hate their nails being trimmed may be shrieking on the outside, but the staff who have to do it are shrieking on the inside. Making this easier would be a classic win-win.

THE MYSTERIOUS CASE OF THE
BALDING POODLE

Myrna was a white miniature poodle and she was a beautiful dog. She was beautiful and well behaved and generally quite healthy. Moreover, her owner, Mrs. Wilson, was an intelligent and charming woman, who was good at asking questions and also good at listening to answers. This combination of ideal pet and ideal owner can really make my day, and it makes me want to be helpful and get things right. Of course, of course, I always want to be helpful and get things right, but let's just say that I *especially* want to be helpful and get things right for pets like Myrna and people like Mrs. Wilson.

This had always been a piece of cake because Myrna was, as I mentioned, generally quite healthy. It's not difficult to appear knowledgeable and competent in the care of a healthy patient. This is like being a good driver on a smooth, empty highway. So long as you don't fall asleep, nothing bad will happen. Then one day, we left the highway and took off at high speed down a dirt road dropping into a canyon.

"She's losing her fur," Mrs. Wilson explained, pointing out bald areas on either side of Myrna's back.

"I see, hmm . . . Is she itchy?" I asked.

"No, I have never seen her scratch, and I'm pretty sure she doesn't do it secretly."

See? She was a smart client. She knew that not seeing a pet scratch doesn't mean that they're not doing it when you're not looking. Some animals seem to know that you disapprove and will deliberately wait until you're out of the room.

"I think you're right. There are no marks or lesions at all on her skin. In fact, it doesn't even look inflamed." I was looking carefully with a magnifier and strong light while Myrna stood there, not moving, politely waiting for the treat she knew would come after the exam.

"So, what could it be?"

"How is her health otherwise? Is she eating, drinking, pooping and peeing normally?"

"Yes, totally normal. It's just the missing fur, and I think the bald areas are spreading."

"Well, non-itchy symmetrical fur loss is almost always hormonal. And by hormonal I don't mean sex hormones, because she's spayed of course, but hormones from glands like the thyroid and adrenal. With both of those problems they usually have other symptoms, but as we like to say — the dogs don't read the textbooks! There are always exceptions. We'll have to run some tests."

"Of course, whatever you need to do."

We first submitted blood for a thyroid panel. It came back normal. Then we had Myrna come in for a couple of hours for an adrenal function test, to rule out Cushing's Disease. Mrs. Wilson and I had convinced ourselves that this was the ticket because it is common in poodles. Again, however, the test came back normal. I stared at this result hard for a long moment before picking up the phone to call Mrs. Wilson. What was I going to say? What else could it be?

"Hi! Well, we've got Myrna's Cushing's test back and, to my surprise, it's negative." Thinking on my feet, I went on, "But these tests are never 100% accurate, so it's possible that it's a false negative. Before running another test to confirm, though, I think it would be a good idea for Myrna to see the veterinary dermatologist. We don't have one in Manitoba, but one comes from Ontario a couple times a year to hold a clinic here. I recommend we sign Myrna up to see him."

"Yes, that makes sense. I do have one question, though."

"Sure."

"I use an estrogen cream and put it on my forearms every day. Myrna often snuggles in my arms. Could that be doing anything?"

If this were a cartoon, a big, bright, yellow lightbulb would now be drawn above my head. Bing! That's it!

"Um, yes . . . I'll check, but I think so. She's pretty small, so it wouldn't take much to have an effect. Estrogen is definitely a hormone!"

I checked and sure enough, there are multiple reports in the literature of this. There are even cases of puppies as young as two months of age going into heat because of exposure to estrogen cream used by post-menopausal women. The normal age to go into heat is after six months, so this is like four-year-old girls having their period. I had never heard of this issue before. Even after 30 years in practice, the old adage regarding learning something new every day applies. Often the "something new" is pointless trivia, but here was something useful and actually pretty cool. I felt bad about not having asked the right questions at the outset (although, what's the right way to ask a woman whether she uses estrogen cream . . . ?), but I felt good that this was easy to fix. Mrs. Wilson switched to applying the cream to the back of her neck. Soon Myrna would be beautiful again, and regardless she remained well behaved and healthy, which is of course much more important anyway.

TZU-HSI ROLLS THE DICE

In every veterinarian's mental cabinet is a drawer marked "Horrors." We rarely open this drawer. Why would we? There are plenty of far more appealing drawers to open, ones labeled "Fluffy Kittens" and "Thank-You Cards" and "Pets Cured." And we know that "Horrors" does not contain spine-tingling fun, but rather it is full of the worst-case scenarios we all eventually encounter. There are many of them. It is a big drawer. At the top is a patient dying in surgery. You cannot even peek into this drawer without seeing that. Usually you just slam it shut right then. But if you are feeling brave, you inch it open a little further and see the discouragingly long list of potential misdiagnoses, the accompanying list of poorly chosen treatments, the letter from the Peer Review Committee, the letter from the clinic inspector, the frothing-at-the-mouth negative online review, the dog attacking another dog in the waiting room, the client slipping on the ice at the front door, the staff backing into a client's car in the parking lot, the fatal drug reaction, the . . . Yikes! Now you definitely slam the drawer shut. But as you do, out of the corner of your eye you catch a glimpse of a patient escaping the clinic. Shudder. Now there is a true horror.

Tzu-Hsi Fenwick was a middle-aged female Pekinese who had been hospitalized. I don't remember the specific reason. History buffs may recognize her name as being that of the last Empress of China. The pronunciation of her name was very close to Suzie, but Mrs. Fenwick made sure that you only made that mistake once. Most of the staff were afraid of Mrs. Fenwick. She looked and dressed like an old hippie, but she had none of the cliché happy hippie chill. Mrs. Fenwick was famous for her sharp tongue, her habit of taking out tiny reading glasses to read every line of an invoice aloud and her habit of staring at you without blinking as if she were trying to see right through your skull. I can't recall ever seeing her smile, but I grew to respect her as she genuinely had the best interests of her dogs at heart and, if I took care to explain things in enough detail, she always followed my advice.

Tzu-Hsi was steadily getting better, but I still wanted her hospitalized for the weekend. I recommended transferring her to the 24-hour emergency clinic as we did not have staff on continuously through the weekend, but Mrs. Fenwick had had a couple of apparently quite heated run-ins with the emergency doctors and refused to go back there. Leanne, one of our pre-veterinary students, was assigned to go in a few times on the Sunday to check on Tzu-Hsi, give the dog her meds and take her out for a pee. I also planned to pop in once to assess her and it so happened that my wife, Lorraine, who is also a vet, came along as we were passing through that part of town together on our way to an errand. As we pulled into the parking lot Leanne ran up to us, her face flushed, breathing hard.

"Oh my God! I'm so glad you're here!" She bent down and put her hands on her knees, trying to catch her breath. "It's Tzu-Hsi! She escaped!"

"Escaped? How?" I asked as I climbed out of the car as quickly as I could.

"I was taking her out to pee and she wriggled out of her collar! She has no neck! Oh my God! I'm so sorry! And of all the people, Mrs. Fenwick! She's going to freak out if we don't catch her!"

"It's OK, we'll catch her. Where did you last see her?"

"Down the lane, that way, towards Ainsley. She's so fast! She'd stop, let me get close and then she'd bolt away again."

We fanned out to try to encircle the area where Leanne thought Tzu-Hsi was. Sure enough, the little Peke was under a shrub just a few houses up Ainsley Street, panting and eyeing us warily.

"Hi Tzu-Hsi," I said softly, crouching down and extending my hand as if I had a treat in it, although having come directly from the car, I didn't. She cocked her head slightly and I thought that perhaps she recognized me. I hoped that this was a good thing. Many patients are afraid of me, but Tzu-Hsi had always liked me, or at least liked the treats I gave her. "OK, you guys, stay back a bit," I said, waving my free hand at the other two. I crept closer to the dog, all the while quietly promising her treats. She appeared to relax. This was going to be a piece of cake. Philipp saves the day.

You know where this is going.

I was an arm's length away from Tzu-Hsi and a second away from scooping her up when she rocketed off, exactly as Leanne had described. One instant she's motionless and calm, the next second she's a blur of flying legs and flapping ears.

The blur was headed for Portage Avenue.

For those of you unfamiliar with Winnipeg, Portage is the main east-west artery. It is part of the Trans-Canada Highway system and it is eight lanes of more or less solid metal moving at 60 to 80 kilometres an hour. And it was only a block away.

"Leanne, you go after her and Lorraine and I will loop right and try to cut her off before she gets onto Portage!"

Off we ran. The dog, the student and the two veterinarians. Each one running as fast as they possibly could. Tzu-Hsi was at Portage before we could reach her or cut her off. There she paused for a split second and I imagined her rolling the dice in her mind. Should she chance it? If she did and she made it, there'd be no way we could follow fast enough and she'd be free! And if she didn't make it, well, like her Chinese namesake she was bold and confident, so I doubt she thought that likely. And like her Chinese namesake she was also wrong.

For a horrifying couple of seconds we waved our arms and shouted and tried to stop traffic, while the little dog darted around speeding, honking cars with an almost supernatural finesse, like a highly skilled basketball player weaving down the court. Then her luck ran out and she was hit. Brakes squealed, Leanne screamed, I screamed, Lorraine screamed, a bunch of other people screamed, and Leanne ran out and scooped her up. Without stopping to explain anything to anyone we raced into the clinic with the limp dog. Her gums were very pale, and her heart was faint and erratic. She was in shock.

Lorraine may not always believe this, but in many ways, she is the better veterinarian. Thank whatever cosmic twist of fate placed Lorraine there at that moment, but she was immediately able to get an intravenous catheter into a vein that I could not see. She did it on the first try. This saved Tzu-Hsi's life. Leanne's relief was intense. She had to sit down as she felt faint from the release of the pent-up stress. The poor dog was still quite banged up, including a broken leg that would need fixing, but she was going to live. What was not clear was whether I was going to live after having to call Mrs. Fenwick and explain what happened.

As a direct result of Tzu-Hsi's adventure we changed the collars we used when walking dogs, and we haven't had another escape since. Leanne ultimately got into vet school, graduated and is now a partner at my clinic. And Mrs. Fenwick? She shocked me by being completely reasonable and understanding on the phone, just grateful that Tzu-Hsi was going to be OK. However, whenever Tzu-Hsi became ill through her long life, Mrs. Fenwick would insist that it was somehow connected to the accident, suggesting that we should cover the costs. We did so gladly.

PART TWO

CATS

BEHOLD, THE MIGHTY HUNTER

Kristi wrinkled her nose when she described what she had seen. "There's, like, little gross white things in his litter box." The neatly dressed young woman was holding Tange, short for Tangerine, on her lap. Tange was a very large orange male tabby. "I thought it was rice, but then they wriggled! Eww! So gross!"

"Yes, that would be alarming," I allowed. I smiled at Tange. He looked supremely relaxed, purring like an outboard motor as Kristi stroked him. "Does Tange go outside?" I asked.

"No, we never let him out. Our last cat got killed by a car. Tange is my baby."

This was a surprise. I expected him to be an outdoor cat. Then I had an idea. "Any chance you have mice in your house?"

"Yes, we do! My boyfriend wants to put out poison, but I said no way. And Tange is a great hunter, so he gets most of them, I think. I don't like seeing that because sometimes he plays with them first. My cruel, beautiful little boy," she said this warmly, tickling his ears.

"Then those wriggly white things are tapeworm segments. They are gross, but they're not really a big health risk and they don't go to humans. You have to eat a mouse or another rodent to get them. And they're really easy to treat."

"OK, that's a relief. I thought they were maggots eating out his insides or something!"

There really are only two common types of worms seen in small animal practice — tapeworms, whose shed segments look like grains of rice, and roundworms which, if you'll forgive another food analogy, look like spaghetti. The latter are usually only seen in puppies and kittens and the former only in hunters, generally cats, although the occasional dog has been known to enjoy a rodent snack as well.

The hunting instinct in cats is remarkable. Most house cats only get to exercise this instinct with the odd unlucky insect, but it is a marvel to behold. I can't tell you the number of times someone has told me that their kitten, who has been inside since birth, successfully stalked, pounced on, killed and then — to the collective disgust of the family — ate a moth, its wings still flapping feebly as the kitten munched proudly. It's totally hardwired. To paraphrase an old aphorism, "You can take the cat out of the wild, but you can't take the wild out of the cat."

I love the story one client once told me about their Siamese at the other end of the age spectrum. I don't recall that cat's name, but apparently it was 20 or 21 years old, toothless, declawed (yes, the bad old days) and half blind, yet it still caught birds with great regularity. This is either a testament to the depth and power of that hunting instinct, or a testament to the stupidity of the average bird. Or both.

This brings me to a very serious point. While the hunting of rodents by cats is arguably beneficial (not for the rodent mind you) and is likely the reason cats were originally domesticated, the hunting of birds by cats is an under-recognized apocalypse. Scientists recently estimated that cats kill an absolutely shocking 100 to 350 million birds a year in Canada. If you're reading this in the US, the estimate is 1.4 to 3.7 *billion* birds. This makes cats the leading cause of death for birds, especially the smaller songbirds. A little more than half of these killings are by feral cats, but people's lovely, gentle housecats, such as Tange, are a major factor. There are many reasons to keep your cat indoors and that discussion is beyond the scope of this essay, but unless you watch him every second he's out there, you should assume that your cat kills birds, possibly endangered songbirds, when he goes out, even if it's just in your yard for a short while. The price of his pleasure is too high.

I'll close with an anecdote that is both funny and gross, as is the case with many veterinary anecdotes. The first cat my family had was a big black and white boy named Mook. We lived on an acreage just outside of Saskatoon where Mook would hunt all manner of rodents and, yes, birds. With respect to the latter, he had a perverse fondness for the most colourful ones, such as the bluebirds and goldfinches. But I've already made my point about bird hunting. His other favourite prey were pocket gophers. While a lot of his hunting was merely for sport, he appeared to love the taste of pocket gopher. In fact, he appeared to love the taste of the entire pocket gopher, fur and bones and organs and all, with one specific exception. We always knew when Mook had dispatched and consumed one of his favourites because afterwards we would find a small, teardrop-shaped, dark-green object on the front step. It was the gallbladder. With surgical precision he would somehow excise this and set it aside. Too bitter, one presumes.

I suppose that's mostly gross and only a little bit funny, but you've got to admit that it's impressive. Tange was impressive in his own way. Mook used to fight like a crazed warthog when we tried to give him his deworming pill, but Tange took it like it was mouse-flavoured candy. This was a more practical way to impress me.

THE SHOEMAKER'S CHILDREN

A few months ago my wife, who as I've mentioned is also a veterinarian, and I began noticing that Gabi, our 11-year-old little black and white cat, was becoming even more aggressive about stealing food. I say "even more" because our three cats and one dog are an unruly, barely trained lot who climb on tables and surf countertops with impunity. OK, impunity is an exaggeration because we do shout at them, but this is apparently just a bunch of monkey noise as far as they're concerned.

One day I caught Gabi trying to take Orbit's food from right under his nose, something I couldn't imagine her doing. Nor could Orbit. He was clearly confused. As I shooed Gabi away, I noticed that she was getting skinnier, despite the mealtime banditry. I noticed this, but I didn't pay attention to it. An important distinction.

Now those of you with some knowledge of cat diseases are beginning to go, "hmm . . ." However, Lorraine and I, despite having considerably more than "some" knowledge of cat diseases, did not go, "hmm . . ." We just shrugged and didn't make much of the changes. She seemed fine otherwise.

Fortunately Gabi was due to have some dental work done, so I took her into the clinic for that. I was ordering routine pre-anaesthetic bloodwork for her when the penny finally dropped. Seeing her in a clinical setting caused a sudden shift in my perspective. I asked them to run a thyroid level as well. Yup. Our cat was hyperthyroid and had probably been hyperthyroid for several months, displaying textbook symptoms right under our noses.

Most of you will be familiar with the proverb regarding the shoemaker's children. The shoemaker is so focused on making beautiful shoes for his customers that he doesn't notice that his own family is shoeless. It's not quite that extreme for most veterinarians, most of the time, but at times the shoemaker's children phenomenon is quite real and it is downright embarrassing.

This is an interesting subject (I hope . . .) because, when faced with a difficult decision, many clients will ask us what we would do for our own pets. This is a fair question. In fact, when I first started out in practice, I didn't have any pets of my own, but in giving advice I had "if this was my mother's pet" as a mantra to guide me. I can obviously only speak for myself and I may well be a freakish outlier, but despite that mantra I have to confess that I do sometimes treat my own pets differently from my clients' pets. Often worse, as in Gabi's story, but sometimes better too. Maybe it's instructive to see where I deviate, so I've made a list:

- I never stop vaccinating due to age, because immune function can decline, and I never worry about reactions because they are so rare, but I am not good at keeping to an exact vaccine schedule. Thorough, annual exams are important, though, as pets age five to seven human-equivalent years for every calendar year. If the experience with Gabi has taught me anything, it's that I need to do this religiously for my own pets and not rely on those casual assessments that may or may not occur because I happen to live with them.

- The moment I finally recognize that something is wrong with one of my animals, I run every test that might conceivably be helpful. With clients we're often concerned about the cost of running lots of tests, but we should give them the option of doing more than the minimum if they can afford it and want the peace of mind.

- When one of my pets is deathly ill, I am tempted to try heroics, and have in at least one case done more than was in retrospect sensible to do. I think we do a better job counselling our clients on end-of-life decisions than we do for ourselves.

- My family feeds more treats and "people food" than I recommend, so I understand what those soft brown eyes and purring leg rubs can do to a person's willpower. This is not an excuse, though — you can and should be stronger willed than me!

- Ditto for brushing their teeth. We don't do it and I really do know we should, and I really do believe in the benefits of it. But it's supposed to be my kids' job. That's my excuse and I'm sticking to it.

Gabi is on medication for her hyperthyroidism now, and is doing well, so no harm done. But it was a valuable lesson and one that I hope I will actually remember next time! But I might not. Just being honest here.

IT'S A HELL NEW WORLD

When my daughter Isabel was little, she wrote a short book called "Cat School." The first chapter was entitled, "Kitten Chaos — It's a Hell New World." Yes, she spelled "chaos" correctly, but was hilariously off with her attempt at "whole." Yet weirdly she was also unintentionally perceptive.

For a long time we had one dog and two cats. The two cats got along with each other well, united in their hatred of the dog, and the dog generally stayed out of their way, so it was a reasonably balanced little domestic ecosystem. Then Lillie arrived.

It's a hell new world.

Lillie is an incredibly beautiful little Siamese cross and she is also the living embodiment of Leo Tolstoy's wise maxim "It is amazing how complete is the delusion that beauty is goodness." Lillie is badness, pure badness. From the very first day these few small ounces of cuddly fluff launched a terror campaign of such energy and ferocity that everyone

— the cats, the dog, the kids, Lorraine and me — was caught completely unprepared. She moves so quickly that she appears to teleport. One second I am eating my dinner peacefully, the next second Lillie's face is in my plate. Toss her off the table and instantly she is back. Again. And again. And again. One second Gabi is grooming herself peacefully, the next second Lillie is on top of her, biting her ears. One second Orbit is munching his breakfast, the next second Lillie is in his bowl and he is looking up me, mournfully. One second a picture is on the wall, the next second it is on the floor. One second a vase is . . . well, you get the idea.

As the modern internet people say, O. . . M . . . G . . . So, Lorraine and I are both veterinarians and between us we have 56 years of experience. Yesiree. For those combined 56 years we have given all sorts of calm, reasoned, sage advice to pet owners in similar straits. I am here right now to confess that none of this advice has worked in my own home. At least not yet. Doors are being kept shut to provide refuges to the other cats, distracting cat toys are being accumulated at a manic pace, kids are being coached to keep Lillie occupied, but it's still a demented circus around here. Probably the smartest suggestion we got was to get a second kitten to occupy the first. Intellectually I know that this would likely help, but I tell you, psychologically, it feels like we would be pulling the pin on a second grenade after stupidly doing so once already. Not. Happening.

So, to bring this full circle, why did we get a kitten at all? Some of you have heard me advise that having two cats is ideal and that three or more is pretty dicey, so what gives? We got her for Isabel. Isabel went from being that happy little girl, singing to herself and writing wacky stories, to being a teenager laid low by crippling anxiety and depression. She missed so much school that the year was a wash-out. It's the last thing I expected and it's the hardest thing to watch. The sense of helplessness is immense. And then Lillie came into Lorraine's clinic from a rescue shelter. Any other time I would have said no. Any other time. But Isabel was at her very lowest and the only spark I had seen in her in weeks was when she saw Lillie's picture.

And despite all her kitteny badness, Isabel loves her, really, really loves her.

This isn't a tidy, heartstring-pulling story where the kitten saves the girl. If only depression were so simple. Isabel still has many bad days, but you know, there are some good ones now too. Is Lillie responsible for any of this possible progress? I have no idea. For the rest of us it's still a hell new world, but for Isabel, hopefully perhaps the first steps to a whole new one.

CATURDAY

The downside of the whole nine lives situation with cats is that when they have run through all nine and have come to the natural end of their lives and no longer find any pleasure in their daily routine, they tend not to just pass away peacefully in their sleep. They tend to need to come into the clinic to be given that final gentle nudge into the great beyond. Cats are that tough. Consequently, we see a lot of really ancient, really skinny, really creaky cats come in for euthanasia. Often they are accompanied by entire families, sometimes including older teenagers who have never known life without that cat.

It's been a long time since I've had to say goodbye to my own cat, but after the last old cat euthanasia at the clinic — an 18-year-old tortie named Kitten — it's been on my mind. Kitten reminded me a lot of our oldest cat, Lucy, also a tortie. I recalled that Caturday would soon be upon us. Lucy was a stray and we have no idea when exactly she was born, so making an educated guess we assigned her birthday to the first of March. Gabi, the second oldest cat, has her birthday in September (we think), but the newest beast, Lillie, was probably also born in early March. It was then that we decided to make the first Saturday in March "Caturday" to mark both Lucy and Lillie's birthday. This Caturday Lucy will be 13 and will be officially an old cat. Not ancient by any means, but old. Old enough that I look at her a little differently.

I came home after Kitten's euthanasia, made myself a mug of tea and sat in my usual spot on my usual couch. Lucy was sleeping on the other couch but stirred when I sat down. She looked over at me, stretched, leapt down and made her way over, purring loudly. Oh yes, she can definitely still leap. In fact, there's nothing about her that would hint at her age except for the fact that she has become thin. She was always the fat cat — the fat boss cat who would prowl about the house, keeping the other pets in line, handing out swats and issuing hisses as she deemed necessary and appropriate. But in the last couple of months, she has very gradually become thinner. She seems healthy enough in every other respect and she is still just as bossy with the other animals, but the other change is that she has become friendlier to me. She was never unfriendly, but she always favoured Isabel and Lorraine. However, the arrival of Lillie (aka the Hellbeast, aka the FK — I'll let you figure that one out) resulted in a slow-motion shuffling of loyalties. From the start, Lillie was Isabel's kitten. Lucy still wanted to be with Isabel, but she could not be in the same room with Lillie, so after a few months of cats screaming at other cats, she stopped trying as hard. In the meantime, Gabi — the "middle cat" — cemented her position as Lorraine's cat.

Enter me. I don't mind being third string.

I petted Lucy absentmindedly while checking my emails. My thoughts then drifted to how she was snuggling. She never used to do that, at least not with me. It made me think of Kato, the cat Lorraine had when she was a student. Kato was a Siamese cross and was named for Inspector Clouseau's sidekick in the old Pink Panther movies. Like her film character counterpart, she would ambush you with frightening savagery at the most unexpected moments. I learned to enter Lorraine's place with extreme caution. When we moved in together it was to a pet-free apartment and Kato went to live with Lorraine's parents. It was only much later, when we had a house and Lorraine's parents had passed on, that Kato came back to live with us. By this point she was very old and she was a completely changed cat. No more ambushes. No more savagery. In her old age Kato had become mellow and affectionate. Letting her go when her time finally came tore our hearts out.

Lucy, having apparently had enough snuggling, stretched and sat up, looking about her. Lillie had entered the far side of the room. Lucy tensed and jumped down. As she stalked towards Lillie, I took note for the first time how boney her hips were. Contrary to the shoemaker's children principle, Lucy had had a full check-up and blood tests within the last year, but a lot can change quickly in an old cat, so I knew I had better watch her carefully. Old cats need special attention and special love.

My grandfather lived to the age of 93. Shortly after he died, I was talking to one of my uncles. I don't recall exactly what I said, but I must have implied that it is easier to let go when the deceased is very old. I may not remember what I said, but I do remember my uncle's reply very clearly:

"Philipp, just because someone is very old doesn't mean that you love them less. In fact, the older they are, the longer they have been part of your life and it is possible that you love them even more."

Happy Caturday, Lucy, my old cat.

CAT BARF

Who among us cat owners has not regretted walking barefoot through the house in the dark? For the rest of you, I will leave the cause of that regret to your imaginations. (There is a hint in the essay title.)

The simple truth is that cats barf. For those of you who

have non-barfy cats, let me assure you that you are part of a happy minority. The question, then, is why do cats barf? Why more than us or dogs, or really any other species you care to name? And why in the most inconvenient locations? I have some answers for the first question, but sadly none for the last. I'm afraid that after reading this you will still have to remain attuned to that distinctive "hrrck, hrrck, hrrck" sound so that you can sprint to wherever Tigger is, pluck him up off the carpet and place him on the tiles before he finishes his emesis.

Broadly speaking, cats barf for two different reasons. The first is specific — hair issues. The second is general —

health issues. To call hair an "issue" is a stretch. Grooming is a natural and healthy activity for cats, and the rasp-like nature of their tongues ensures that they will swallow a lot of hair in the process. Most of this hair passes through the digestive system and gets pooped out, but some of it accumulates in the stomach. Hair cannot be digested, but it does become stickier the longer it remains in the stomach, so gradually the swallowed hairs bunch up and, voilà, Tigger has a hairball! How often this happens depends on how vigorously the cat grooms herself and how long her fur is. Some random factors regarding the function of the digestive system are at play too. In the worst-case scenario of a heavy groomer with long fur and a jumpy stomach, hacking up a hairball can be normal even up to once weekly. Roughly once or twice monthly is more common, though. If this is distressing to you (believe me, it is not distressing to the cat: they bring up hairballs as casually as you and I change channels on the TV), then excellent hairball remedies are available. There are numerous foods and treats that claim to control hairballs. They do so with additional fibre, which helps to move the hair through the system. This appears to be helpful for mild problems, but I haven't found it to be very effective for the more enthusiastic hairball producers. Better is the hairball paste sold under a variety of brand names. It looks kind of like a tube of toothpaste and is usually flavoured with malt or tuna. The active ingredient is white petrolatum, also known as petroleum jelly or Vaseline. This may sound nasty, but it is entirely tasteless and inert, and it is not absorbed into the bloodstream. It passes through the way it went in, picking up hair along the way. Generally, about a half a teaspoon — enough to cover the end of your index finger — once a week is enough, although occasionally you may need to give it daily until things settle down.

Two more points about hairballs before we move on. The first is that hair "ball" is a misnomer. They are usually more tubular, or cigar shaped, having been molded by the esophagus (food tube) on their exciting journey out of the body. In fact, they are often mistaken for poop. The brave among you can feel free to use the sniff test to determine which is which. The second point is that you should not assume that, just because hair comes out when your cat barfs, hair must be the culprit. Many cats often have some hair in their stomachs, so even if they are vomiting for other reasons, you may see hair, or even full-on hairballs. This brings me to the other category of issue that results in vomiting: health.

I haven't counted, but my best guess is that there are at least a hundred health reasons for a cat to vomit. It is a very non-specific symptom. And given that the bar for vomiting seems to be set very low in cats, almost any internal disease you care to name could have vomiting as one of its symptoms. Consequently, there's not much point in exploring the subject in depth here. What I *can* tell you about, however, is how to decide that it's time to consult your veterinarian about the puking. If any of these happen, you should make an appointment:

1. vomiting that is accompanied by a reduction in appetite or energy, a change in thirst or urination or a change in the character of the stool;
2. chronic vomiting that occurs, on average, more than once a week;
3. chronic vomiting when there is also weight loss;
4. vomiting that appears to be due to hairballs, but which remedies do not seem reduce (they are rarely 100% effective, so some vomiting is still expected).

If it's none of these and if there is just the occasional hairball, then all I can tell you is wear slippers or sandals at night (socks aren't good enough).

GEORGE

George was one of my favourite patients and Mrs. Mackintosh was one of my favourite clients. This was many years ago, not long after I started in practice, and Mrs. Mackintosh was one of the first clients who began asking to see me specifically. One of my bosses had been there for more than 30 years and his clientele was extremely loyal. My other boss was the first full-time female veterinarian in the practice, and she had rapidly built a following based on her more modern approach and the fact that some animals are less fearful around a gentle woman than a boisterous man. Not that all women are gentle or that all men are boisterous, but that was the situation at Birchwood. In any case, even though I was kept busy, it was not easy to attract regular clients and I was immensely pleased by the vote of confidence that Mrs. Mackintosh gave me.

Mrs. Mackintosh was an elderly lady with a soft Scottish accent and a seemingly limitless supply of cat-themed sweaters. I suspected that she had been a war bride, but in those days, I felt compelled to employ a rather narrowly defined version of professionalism and it didn't occur to me to ask any personal questions. George was a young orange male tabby. Mrs. Mackintosh explained that he had been named George after her father. Give her age, I reasoned that George Mackintosh Senior must have been born in the 19th century back in Scotland. I smiled at the thought of how he would have reacted to knowing that a cat would be named after him, 100 years later, in Canada.

Orange tabbies tend to be big and they tend to be friendly. George was both, in spades. He was an enormous teddy-bear of love. Examining him was a challenge because he constantly wanted to head-butt my hand or rub against my arm, and he purred so loudly I swear the table shook from it. I loved this cat. He was perhaps the first patient I really bonded with. Consequently, it was with special concern that I listened to Mrs. Mackintosh describe his symptoms to me on the phone, one grey November day.

"The wee fellow hasn't eaten a thing in two days! Not even his favourite — tuna from the can."

George was hardly a "wee fellow," but I let that slide as the tone of her voice was full of concern.

"How is his drinking and urination?"

"Terrible, Doctor. He's not doing any of either."

This concerned me enough that I asked her to come in with George that afternoon.

When George arrived, he still purred, but he did not have the energy to head-butt or rub up against my arm. He was dehydrated and his breath was very foul. It smelled like an unclean urinal. I had a sinking feeling.

"OK, we're going to run some blood tests. I'm worried about his kidneys. We'll hook him up on intravenous fluids while we wait for the results."

"Please do whatever you need to do."

The test results confirmed my suspicion. His kidneys were in appalling condition. He had something called anuric acute renal failure. This means that his kidneys had suddenly shut down and had done so with such severity that they were no longer able to make any urine at all. This might not surprise some readers, as people often assume that a lack of urine production is a common sign of kidney failure, but in fact, it is almost always the opposite. Usually as kidneys fail they actually produce more urine because their ability to concentrate the urine and conserve water for the body is impaired. It is only in the very last stage that they stop making urine. Why this should happen to George, who was only five years old, baffled me. I explained this to Mrs. Mackintosh.

"Is there anything we can do for him? Is there anything at all?" she asked after I was done. She was a tough lady, but her eyes were red, and her voice was quavering.

"Yes, let's keep him on the IV for 48 hours and see if we can kick-start the kidneys. And let's do a few more tests and try to find the cause."

I don't know how good she was at picking up on body language, but I know that I did not really believe what I had just said. I could not face telling her the truth that there was no hope and that finding the cause would not actually be helpful. George needed a kidney transplant, and that was just not possible. Certainly not in Winnipeg in the early 1990s. After saying this I talked myself into thinking that perhaps there was just the slenderest hope of recovery. Maybe the tests had been wrong.

The tests were not wrong. George stayed in hospital on aggressive IV for the two days. He purred whenever Mrs. Mackintosh visited him and whenever I handled him for examination or treatment, but he otherwise looked so sad. This was not the George we knew, and he was becoming less so by the hour. By the second day I had my answer. He had been poisoned by anti-freeze. Often we can see the characteristic crystals produced by anti-freeze on the urine test, but for some reason these were absent or had been missed. Instead we saw on x-ray that his kidneys had essentially turned to solid stone. There was truly no hope and he was suffering. He died peacefully in Mrs. Mackintosh's arms as I infused an overdose of barbiturate into the IV line. We both cried.

We never did find out whether the poisoning was deliberate or accidental. George did like to roam to the neighbours', but everybody loved him. Mrs. Mackintosh preferred to assume that it was accidental. Anti-freeze is sweet, and irresistible to cats and dogs.

Two weeks later Mrs. Mackintosh was back in the clinic. She had a kitten with her. It was an orange one again, but this time a female. She called it Anne, after her mother.

HERPES!

"Yay! It's a kitten!" I exclaimed as I entered the exam room. This is my standard greeting in these situations. The sentiment is quite genuine as there are very few days that are not made better by a kitten visit. Kittens hardly ever have something seriously wrong with them and kittens are almost always cute, or good for comic relief, or both.

"His name is Bernard," the young woman said brightly while holding out a small clump of squirming black and white fur. She was in her mid to late teens, I guessed, and she had been snuggling Bernard against her grey hoodie.

"Well, hello, Bernard," I said, as I bent down to greet him. Bernard looked me squarely in the eye and hissed. Is there anything more adorable than a tiny creature trying to make itself look fierce? Just so long as the tiny creature doesn't proceed to bite you, it is very adorable. And Bernard did not bite, he just hissed some more and took a couple of swipes at me with his paws. Kitten nails are needle sharp, so his adorableness went down a notch in my estimation, but overall, I was still happy to be seeing a kitten.

"I can see why you brought him in," I said as I peered at his eyes, which were rimmed with crusted discharge. "How long have you had him?"

"I just got him two days ago from the rescue shelter. They said he had a cold but was getting better. This morning his eyes were stuck shut."

"How's he feeling otherwise? How's his appetite and energy?"

"Great! He's got lots of energy and he's eating really well."

I asked a few more questions about his symptoms and then proceeded to examine him, to the extent that he permitted it. It is a mistake to think that small animals are easier to handle than large ones. There is a sweet spot in the small-golden-retriever size range, and the further you get away from that in either direction, the harder it gets.

"His eyes are infected and it's secondary to the same cold virus he had at the shelter," I explained after I had finished the exam and handed him back to her. He hissed at me again from her lap.

"A cold in the eye?" she asked.

"Yes, you could say that. We most commonly get our colds in our noses and throats, while cats get them in their noses and eyes. There are lots of different cat cold viruses, or upper respiratory viruses, as well call them, but I think this might be herpes."

Sometimes this diagnosis causes a reaction, but it didn't. The young woman just smiled and nodded while trying to hold on to Bernard, who was determined to make a break for it and explore the room.

"It's probably better if you don't let him go as these viruses are quite contagious and it'll be easier to sanitize the room after if he doesn't get into every corner! I'm going to prescribe some drops and then we should recheck him in a couple weeks. Occasionally this can become chronic, in which case we'll need a different strategy. And please call if he goes off his food or seems to get worse in any way in the meantime."

We chatted about a few other aspects of his care, said goodbye and I went on to my next appointment, quickly forgetting about Bernard.

The next morning one of the receptionists snagged me on my way to my desk. "Sorry to bug you before you've even got your coat off, Philipp, but please call Mr. Fowler back right away. He's called twice already this morning and he's really mad!"

"Mr. Fowler? Who's that?"

"He's the dad of the girl who brought that kitten in yesterday. You know, the one with upper resp."

"Oh, OK. I wonder what he's upset about?"

"No idea, but he was actually shouting on the phone. Said he needed to talk to 'that dammed vet' right now."

"Great."

"Good luck," she said with a wink.

I took a deep breath and tried to replay the visit in my mind. Usually people are mad about the charges, but I didn't think it had been expensive. There was just the kitten exam and the eye drops. Weird. Oh well, there's no point in stewing or speculating. Best just to get it over with. I picked up the phone and dialed.

"Good morning, may I please speak to Mr. Fowler?" I asked, hoping that the good cheer in my voice didn't seem too forced.

"This is he."

"Hi, it's Dr. Philipp Schott at Birchwood. I understand you had a concern about your daughter's visit with Bernard yesterday?"

"Thank you for calling. Now maybe you can tell me why you let her go home with that kitten?" His tone was cold and hard.

"Sorry? There must be a misunderstanding. He's really not that sick. There was no reason to keep him."

There was a brief pause and then his voice exploded over the line, "That is not what I'm taking about! I'm talking about the diagnosis! How dare you allow my 17-year-old daughter to keep a kitten who has herpes!"

Facepalm.

"Oh no! I'm so sorry! I see what your concern is now. It's not that kind of herpes, sir! I should have explained that to your daughter. It's a big family of viruses and the cat ones don't go to people and they are not . . . um . . . they are not . . . sexual."

Lesson learned. I now either just stick to "cold virus," or I explain very carefully what I mean when I say herpes. I hope Bernard is doing well. I never did see them again.

DOING THE NIP

We try to be good members of the community and as such have put up a dog-shaped bicycle rack in front of the clinic, landscaped an area to the side with shady trees and a picnic bench, and put in several planters and flower-beds. Aside from some minor irritants, such as when our bedding plants were stolen (who does such a thing?), this has been enjoyable. The enjoyment was, however, primarily for the humans and not for the animals who, after all, really should be our main focus. That was the case until the day a client offered to plant catnip for us. She said that she had "hundreds" of catnip plants in her yard and wanted to spread the joy. The clinic faces south, and catnip loves the sun, so the catnip was going to thrive there. Her idea was

that clients could pick some for their cats as a reward for having come to the vet. I had no good argument against this, so within days we became a fresh, natural, catnip dispensary. Then soon after the questions began:

"I don't want my cat on drugs, is it like getting stoned?"

"Will he become addicted?"

"What will he do if I suddenly cut him off?"

"Is it bad for him?"

"Can she OD on it?"

"Why does it make her so weird?"

"Why doesn't it work on my cat?"

"Is it free?"

Um. No, no, nothing, no, no, olfactory receptor stimulation, genetics, yes. That's the short version. The long version is pretty interesting, though, so read on.

Catnip, *Nepeta cataria*, is in the mint family and contains a volatile oil in its leaves called nepetalactone. This compound is released into the air when the leaves are crushed or bruised, and it then binds to receptors inside the cat's nasal passage where it activates their internal opioid system, releasing endorphins, like a more intense version of a runner's high. It also stimulates nerves leading to amygdala and hypothalamus in the brain, where strong emotional and even sexual responses are mediated. Consequently, affected cats behave a little like they're in heat, regardless of their gender. In addition, they drool and rub on the nip, possibly to try to release more nepetalactone. The effect usually lasts about ten minutes, after which they're immune to its charms for approximately half an hour. No long-term tolerance is established, though, so for an individual cat, the response is pretty much the same every time they're exposed.

Wild cats such as tigers, lynx, lions and leopards also respond to catnip. This makes it likely that there is an evolutionary advantage to this otherwise goofy-looking behaviour. We had no idea what that advantage might be until this year, when a group of Japanese scientists discovered that nepetalactone is a powerful mosquito repellant. Early work is underway to investigate its use as such for humans, although the researchers caution that it would be unwise to anoint oneself in nepetalactone while hiking in cougar, lion or tiger country. Indeed.

About 70% of cats respond to catnip, with the remaining 30% not affected at all. It's very much an either/or proposition. Imagine what the non-responders think of the drooling, rolling, meowing majority. "Flakes." "Losers." The difference is purely genetic. Interestingly, kittens don't respond until roughly six months of age.

And of course, humans don't respond either, although not for lack of trying. People have often attempted to use it as a marijuana substitute with, according to science, any perceived similarity being purely imaginary. Some Indigenous people have used catnip as a colic remedy in babies.

Other plants can have a catnip-like effect in some cats, especially those that don't respond to catnip itself. These include valerian root, silver vine and honeysuckle wood.

Eventually the catnip plants all died because we're good at keeping animals alive, not plants. We didn't replace them, but catnip-infused fleecy knots are very popular after a stressful vet visit. We keep a bowl of them on the front counter. It's safe, it's legal, it's not addictive (no, Tigger is not going to rob gas stations to feed his habit) and it makes most cats briefly very happy. What's not to love about that?

BRRT

When I first moved to Winnipeg, I worked a few shifts at the emergency clinic, and it was on one of those shifts that, on an unusually slow Sunday morning, a technician tapped me on the shoulder.

"Philipp, your aunt just came in with a cat."

"My aunt? That's not possible. All my aunts are in Germany." Vet clinics in general get more than their share of wacky clients, but the emergency clinic seemed to have special magnetic powers for them. Clearly, my "aunt" was one of them. I had had a few people claiming to be my friend, presumably in the hope of obtaining special consideration, but never before had someone claimed to be my relative. This was going to be good.

"That's what she says! She seems nice. Can you see her cat now?"

"Yeah, sure, why not?"

It was Lorraine's Aunt Nettie. In those days Lorraine and I weren't yet living together, so calling herself my aunt was a stretch, but Nettie was a warm-hearted and inclusive person. She had a three-and-a-half legged grey tabby with her. Yes, three *and a half*. His left front leg was a stump, ending just below the elbow. Ah. I remembered. This was Bert. Lorraine had told me about him.

Bert had come into her clinic as a stray. His left front paw had been caught in a trap and was beyond salvation. Given that he didn't have a home and given that the shelters were all full and given that a fair bit of work would be needed to deal with the mangled foot, the consensus was that the poor little guy should be relieved of his suffering and euthanized. This was a tough decision to make, but objectively the right one. The cat's good leg was shaved, the vein was located, and Lorraine was preparing to inject the euthanasia solution when Bert butted his head against her hand and made a loud "brrt!" sound.

She couldn't do it. Most of the time veterinarians will swallow hard and soldier on, but sometimes it's just not possible. This was one of those times. She sighed and sat back, wondering what to do next. The cat kept head-butting her and saying, "brrt, brrt." Then she thought of her Aunt Nettie. Nettie was a cat lady, but not of the crazy variety. Maybe Nettie had room for just one more cat. She did. And she had a name for him right away — Bert, because of those "brrt, brrt" noises he loved to make.

So, back to the emergency clinic. Nettie had brought Bert in because she wanted his stump checked. Lorraine had done the amputation a couple of weeks prior and everything had been going well, but Nettie was concerned with how it looked today.

True to form, Bert said "brrt" and head-butted me as I carefully inspected the stump. The stitches had recently been removed and everything looked pretty good, except for a bit of redness at the tip. It didn't look infected, though.

"Is this what you mean, Nettie? The redness?"

"Yes, I wanted to make sure that was OK."

"I think it's OK. Watch for swelling or discharge or if it gets even redder. Give Lorraine a call if that happens, but it's fine for now. How's he doing otherwise?"

"He's doing great! It only took a day and he was king of the house!"

"Oh? Chasing the others around on three legs, is he?"

"Not only chasing but catching! He catches them, pins them down with the good leg and then starts thumping them with his stump!"

Now I knew why the stump was a little red.

Nettie died recently. She had become very elderly and had developed dementia. Bert had long since passed, but I'm told that the last time Nettie smiled was when her cat Missy was brought to the hospital to see her.

THE THREE Fs

Most of you will have heard of the "fight or flight response." If something happens that the animal — or person — perceives as a threat, there is a cascade of nervous system and stress hormone events along the hypothalamic-pituitary-adrenal axis (reading that out loud is an excellent sobriety test). The end effect is that the threatened-feeling individual has dilated pupils to take in more light, a pounding heart to supply more blood to the muscles and a cessation of non-vital functions such as digestion, so that all resources are directed to dealing with the potential crisis. The individual is instantly primed to fight the threat or flee the threat. There is a third "f" word, however (no, not that one!): freeze. And thank goodness that when my patients perceive me as a threat, they are far more likely to freeze than to fight. Fleeing is probably somewhere between freezing and fighting.

Consequently, it's quite common for a frightened cat to be rigid on the exam table, refusing to look at me or even consciously admit to itself that I exist. Ditto for dogs under their owner's chairs. Yet they still have the dilated pupils and high heart rate indicating that that hypothalamic-pituitary-adrenal axis has been fully activated. What, then, is the purpose of all that preparation, if all you're going to do is freeze? Why not be relaxed and save your energy if you're just going to sit there and try to convince everyone that you're not actually there? "Cat? What cat? I don't see a cat." I think the best way to look at the freeze response is to see it as pre-flee. You can poke and prod a lot of frozen patients quite vigorously and they remain frozen, but I think most of them have a limit beyond which they would flee, or possibly even "fight" (i.e., bite your finger off). Their body has decided that it is best, while frozen, to remain in a state of maximal readiness for when that limit is reached. Although freezing is admittedly convenient for some parts of the physical examination, I do feel bad for these poor, stressed-out creatures. I have taken courses in what's known as "Fear-Free" veterinary medicine, and have even become certified as a Fear-Free Practitioner, but for some animals the concept of a fear-free vet visit is like the concept of a fear-free haunted house visit for some people. There is no such thing.

That's freezing, and fighting I have written about in my first book, so what about fleeing? While there are quite a few comical stories to relate regarding cats skittering at high speed around corners while vet techs dive at them only to dramatically miss, screaming, "Close the doors! CLOSE THE DOORS!," most of these stories involve pets who are losing their minds with fear, so the comedy is tainted. Instead I will relate a story that does not involve a real animal, although it does involve real fear — real fear in the staff. Let me explain.

There may be some of you who believe that when veterinarians and their staff are not busy healing animals, they are sitting around and earnestly talking about how to heal animals. To be sure, there is a fair bit of that, but we are human, and we also gossip, goof off, joke and play pranks. The staff are wise to me now, but for several years in a row I was able to get away with some excellent (if I do say so myself) April Fool's Day pranks. There was the year I turned refried beans into a very convincing facsimile of diarrhea. There's probably no need to go into detail about that. Or there was the year when I managed to persuade my colleague that a disgruntled and grief-stricken hamster owner was going to sue him unless he participated in an interpretive dance at the hamster's memorial.

I had to think of a way to top that the next year. Fortunately April 1 fell on a Monday and fortunately I was the doctor on duty the preceding Saturday. This was fortunate because it allowed me to create a fake patient after everyone else had left on Saturday (we're closed Sundays). I recruited my daughter to come with me and bring one of her more realistic plush-toy cats. I made a file and wrote the cat up on the treatment white board as a hospitalized patient. Then Isabel and I set up a cage with a blanket over the bars, which is what we do when there is a very anxious cat that we want to give quiet and privacy. On the cage card I wrote in big red letters, "Caution! Lunges and bites! Escape risk!!" Then we left the cage door open a crack and went back into the main treatment room. I got a stepladder and climbed up to shift one of the ceiling tiles aside. Isabel, giggling, handed me her cat which I placed up there and then slid the ceiling tile mostly back into place, leaving just enough open to allow a small part of the toy's convincing tail to peek out.

Monday morning was great. I made sure I was there when the first staff arrived. They hadn't been in on Saturday, so the deception of the fake patient was easier to pull off.

"Oh my God, that crazy cat they kept over the weekend got loose!"

I nodded gravely and emphasized how dangerous that cat was when it was frightened. Then someone spotted the tail. They all knew the story of the cat at another clinic who had spent weeks living in the ceiling, evading all attempts to entice or trap it. They knew they might have only one chance to catch it before it fled deeper into more inaccessible parts of the ceiling. While the others stood in a wary perimeter with big towels at the ready, one of them quietly got the step ladder, donned the big leather gauntlets, climbed up towards the tail and . . .

I was briefly the most hated man in Winnipeg.

BLIZZARD

Snow-themed names are, for entirely obvious reasons, popular for white cats. I have seen a lot of Snowballs, a lot of Snowys, a few Snowflakes and a Winter or two, but only one Blizzard. Mrs. Carver demonstrated spooky prescience when she named her adorable little white furball after the most fearsome and deadly snow-related phenomenon. In my almost 30 years in practice I have seen more than a few wild cats, but Blizzard was the king of them all. He may have been adorable at home, but in the clinic he was like a white wolverine on acid. Fortunately Mrs. Carver was as good-natured as her cat was foul-tempered. She was a very small, elderly woman with a stooped back and twinkle in her eyes. "Oh Blizzard," she would chuckle as the staff armed themselves with welder's gloves and heavy towels.

Usually Blizzard's annual visits included only the most perfunctory of examinations. He would scream and howl and swat and hiss while the aforementioned heavily armoured staff would attempt to gingerly manoeuvre him into a position where I could at least see parts of his body. Palpating or closely examining any part of him was entirely out of the question. Fortunately he always seemed very healthy. *Even a little too healthy*, I would think to myself in my more sarcastic moments. Mrs. Carver was a very observant owner, so she also provided a good history. Sometimes a good history and distant observation of the patient is all you get. And it was good enough until one day she brought him in reporting that he had been acting funny. Before my inner sarcasm kicked in regarding what constituted "acting funny" for Blizzard, she went on to describe him being slow, wobbly and a bit out of it. He was none of those things at that moment in the exam room, but come to think of it, the intensity of his loathing of me and desire to remove my face did seem to have dialed down slightly, from, say, an 11 to a 10. And when he screamed at me, I noticed something odd. His gums, tongue and the roof of his mouth were all a deep brick red. Certainly his blood pressure would be way up and that would have an influence on his colour, but this was different. I didn't know what to make of it, or how to connect it to his symptoms, so I resigned myself to taking a blood sample. Or, to be more accurate, directing the unfortunate staff to take a blood sample.

At that time, we had a student named Tim working for us who was trying to get into veterinary school. He functioned as an assistant to the veterinary technologists and was excellent at collecting blood samples. I explained the situation to Tim and warned him that he would need help. Often, we'll sedate patients like this, but as Blizzard had something very mysterious wrong with him, it was not clear what sort of sedative would be safe, so we'd have to try without first. The technologists were all tied up and I was running behind in my appointments, but my colleague Bob was free, so he volunteered to give Tim a hand. That was one of the great things about Bob — even though he was the senior doctor, he did not consider anything to be beneath him, be it emptying the garbage, cleaning a kennel or restraining the most fractious cat in the practice while the student collected the blood sample. Or attempted to collect the blood sample. If this ever becomes a movie or a TV series, this is the point where ominous music should be played. And as further foreshadowing I will point out that Blizzard was all-white, Tim was wearing a white lab coat and Bob was wearing a pale-blue doctor's jacket.

I had to dive into my next appointment, but I could hear the cat shrieking and the people shouting from the other side of the clinic. My next client and I smiled at each other weakly.

"Unhappy cat?" the client ventured.

"You could say that, yes."

Fortunately this appointment was just a routine vaccine booster, so I was able to wrap up quickly and dart to the back to see what was going on. Apparently Blizzard had squirmed out of Bob's grasp when Tim handed him over, and the two of them had chased him across the treatment room, blankets in hand, while the rest of the staff sprang out of the way, closing doors that might have offered an escape. The waiting room was full, so I can only imagine the scene if Blizzard had gotten into there — a screeching white missile, swatting at anything that got in its way. Ultimately, they managed to corner Blizzard and get a big towel over him. Bob decided that they should take him into the x-ray room to try to get the sample there, as it is small, quiet and away from the busy part of the clinic. So, Bob hauled Blizzard, wrestling like a demon under the blanket, into the x-ray room, with Tim running ahead to open the door, while the rest of the staff looked on with a mixture of horror and apprehension.

There was silence for a couple of long minutes and then a hellish commotion erupted from inside the x-ray room. Nobody dared to open the door, lest they accidentally let Blizzard out. Then suddenly there was silence again and the three of them emerged. Bob was covered in blood, Tim was covered in blood, and what one could see of Blizzard from under the blanket was covered in blood. It was Bob's blood and Tim's blood, splattered like a Jackson Pollock special Halloween canvas. The inside of the x-ray room was unspeakable. But they got the sample. Blizzard's blood was there too, contained in a little vial.

Some diseases you see weekly, some monthly, some once a year and some every few years. And then there are the once-in-a-career diseases. Blizzard had one of those. The blood sample showed that he had twice as many red blood cells as he should have. This is called polycythemia and it is the opposite of anemia. It causes the blood to become thick and sludgy, slowing its flow through the brain and resulting in Blizzard's odd neurological symptoms. Sometimes this is due to a tumour in a kidney, which produces excessive erythropoietin, the hormone that stimulates red blood cell production, and sometimes it is what is known as primary polycythemia, or polycythemia vera, where because of a genetic defect the bone marrow is simply too active. We decided Blizzard's relative youth meant that he probably had the latter. Moreover, the testing to identify it conclusively was out of Mrs. Carver's price range, and anyway, she said that she wouldn't treat a cancer if it was there.

The objective then was to focus on Blizzard's quality of life by getting his red blood cell count down. The only way I could think of doing that was phlebotomy, meaning drawing large amounts of blood out on a regular basis, kind of like the leech approach 200 years ago, but using science and a needle. Incidentally, a cat would groom a leech off right away, in case you're wondering. This approach was apparently tried experimentally. Once. I was talking about Blizzard's phlebotomy to a group of us, including Tim, who immediately said, "I'm off that day." Realizing that I hadn't mentioned a specific day, he added, "Whatever day Blizzard comes in for that, I know I'm off then."

At this point I have to give credit to another of my colleagues, Barb. She mentioned that she had heard about a drug called hydroxyurea at a conference. It might work for polycythemia vera. This was before the days of the veterinary databases on the internet and when textbooks were usually a few years out of date, so new knowledge came to us randomly through conferences, journals and conversations with colleagues. Hyroxyurea did not always work and there were some potentially serious side effects, but given the laughability of phlebotomy as a regular treatment for Blizzard, we decided to try it. And you know what, it worked. We went on symptoms rather than trying to test his blood again, but Mrs. Carver reported that after a few weeks he was back to normal. When I saw him, and he screamed his customary screams at me, his gums were back to the regular bright pink.

Blizzard went on to live several years. I'm the last person left working at Birchwood who remembers Blizzard. Bob has sadly passed on and in the 20 years since, the rest of the staff has turned over. Tim went on to become a veterinarian and works across town. I bet he remembers Blizzard too.

HIS FAVOURITE SPOT

"Can you please do it in his favourite spot?" This was the first thing the young woman said to me when she greeted me at the door. She was tall and thin and dressed all in black. It was obvious that she had been crying. I was there to euthanize her cat, Reginald. Euthanasia is one of the most common reasons for someone to request a house call. It makes sense, especially for animals who hate coming to the vet. As much as possible their last moments should be peaceful and free of fear. Clearly, however, having a stranger come to the door was also a cause of fear, as Reginald was nowhere to be seen.

"Yes, he always bolts when anyone other than me is here."

The woman and I set about looking for him. She lived in the upper floor of an old mansion. I don't know whether it was originally this way or had been renovated to remove walls, but the space was vast, with the room I had entered appearing to serve as living room, dining room and kitchen. It was full of beautiful details such as wainscoting and carved door lintels, but I was too preoccupied to take much notice. The room was also very dark, and it had countless nooks and crannies that could potentially conceal Reginald. The medical record indicated that he was a small cat and it is astonishing what sort of spaces a determined small cat can wedge himself into. We scouted about silently, often crouching and looking under things, sometimes opening cabinet doors if they were already partly ajar. No Reginald.

Then the woman smiled and said, "I know where he is. He's a clever boy. I bet he has already gone to his favourite spot. He never goes there when he's trying to hide from strangers, so I didn't think to look there, but he knows it's his time now and that that's where he should be."

I just nodded in response and watched as she walked over to the old black cast-iron radiator against the far wall. Sure enough, there was Reginald. As I mentioned, it was dark in the room, but I could just make out two yellow eyes and some whiskers under the radiator. The woman made some cooing noises and reached under to stroke Reginald. It was absolutely silent in the room so I could hear him purring in response.

"He loves it there, especially now that he is so old and so thin."

"I don't recall, how old is he exactly?"

"Twenty-three last October. I've had him since I was five. I brought him with me when I moved out of my parents.' We've been together forever."

I recalled from his records that Reginald hadn't gotten the memo regarding nine lives and had helped himself to a dozen or more. But it was time now. He had just about every chronic old cat disease you would care to name, and now he apparently hadn't eaten in three days.

"I can't imagine how hard this is for you, but you are doing the right thing," I said, feeling a bit lame for resorting to a cliché, but it was a completely appropriate one.

"Thank you for saying that. I hope I am."

"You absolutely are."

"Can you please do it there, Doctor? He's peaceful and happy in his favourite spot."

What was I going to say? I should have said no. Perhaps if I'd had a technologist with me to help it would have been more realistic, but at the time I was doing a locum for a practice where the owner chortled at the idea. "I always go by myself!" he said. "Besides, we can't spare any staff." *Oh well, how bad could it be?* I thought.

I had no idea it could be this bad.

At his age and in his condition, Reginald would have tiny, terrible veins; it was dark, he was under the radiator, I had no help . . . what could go wrong? There should be a word for a situation that is simultaneously terrifying, comical and sad. Tragicomic comes close, but it doesn't address the intense dread I felt that this could all easily go horribly sideways. I had visions of Reginald rocketing about the room with a needle still in his leg, the owner screaming, the cat screaming . . .

"I'll try. We'll just take it one step at a time."

I prepared my syringe of euthanasia solution and sat down on the floor beside the radiator. Reginald looked tense, but he didn't bolt. I suppose it was his favourite spot after all. I spoke softly to him and waited until he showed signs of beginning to relax. Slowly his ears came up and slowly the tension in his body appeared to ease a tiny bit. Normally I would sedate first, but to do so would mean dragging him out, as I needed access to loose skin or muscle for that. All I could see or potentially reach was his face and his two front legs. There's no way he or his owner would tolerate a dragging.

OK, deep breath.

I very cautiously reached under the radiator and began to stroke Reginald's left elbow. He flinched at first but permitted the stroking. It probably helped that his owner was beside me now, talking to him. After a few minutes of this I reached for the tourniquet with my other hand and slid it towards his left paw.

"Is that necessary?" the woman asked.

"Yes, yes, it is, I'm afraid."

Step by slow step I pushed the tourniquet up to his elbow and then gently tightened it. So far, astonishingly, so good. Now to find the vein. I shaved a bit of fur with the portable clippers, again astonished that it went off without a hitch, and applied a bit of alcohol to highlight the vein. Then I peered closely at his foreleg. Where was the vein? The woman was now sobbing quietly beside me.

Deep breath. Look again.

There. A faint purplish thread.

There was no way I was going to hit that. I prepared my "sometimes it's not possible to find a vein and we have to sedate to the point of unconsciousness and inject internally" (meaning the heart) speech, not knowing how I could possibly say that to this person.

I picked up my syringe and took another very deep breath. I remembered an instructor in vet school whose mantra was "see the vein, be the vein." This doesn't actually make any sense. "Be the vein"? Really? But I suppose the idea is to focus your mind. Kind of like Luke Skywalker.

The needle went into the vein.

Reginald was so ill that he was gone after half the usual dose. I struggled mightily to stop myself from showing any sign of relief, let alone loudly exclaiming "Yay!" Luck is an exceptionally powerful force in our lives.

Although we didn't know each other the woman hugged me. I asked if she would like some more time before I took his body. She said no, so I wrapped Reginald in a towel and left, feeling another blend of contradictory emotions which there should be a word for.

PART THREE

VETS

THE LETTER

Psychologists call them "flashbulb memories." These are the memories of dramatic events that are preserved in our minds in great detail, as if caught in an old-fashioned camera's flashbulb. That first plane crashing into the World Trade Center on September 11, 2001, is probably the most common modern flashbulb memory based on a news event. Most people over the age of 30 can clearly bring to mind the scene around them when they first found out. In our personal lives it's marriage proposals, the birth of children and news of the death of a family member that create flashbulb memories. And for veterinarians, it's getting the letter. Yes, *the* letter. The acceptance letter to veterinary college, in my case the Western College of Veterinary Medicine in Saskatoon. Maybe these days it's a text message, though.

It's May of 1986 and I'm standing in Dr. Bruce Murphy's endocrinology laboratory on the second floor of the biology building at the University of Saskatchewan. I'm pipetting mink serum into tiny vials while sitting on a stool halfway along the middle workbench when the phone on the far wall, beside the walk-in freezer, rings.

"Philipp, it's your mom!"

My mom never phones me at work. Never. Either a grandparent has died, or the letter arrived.

I set down the pipette and trotted over to the phone. Bruce used to call me "Flying Phil" because I never seemed to walk anywhere.

"Yes, Mom?" I keep my tone even.

"There's a letter for you from the veterinary college!"

It's the letter! Or, more accurately, it's a letter.

"Is it thick or thin?"

"Thin. Is that good or bad?"

Bad bad bad, I think. *Shit, it's thin.*

"Um, neither I guess. Go ahead, open it."

Ripping sounds at her end of the line. Panicky breathing sounds at my end. Long pause and then . . .

"You've been accepted!"

I got it! It was *the* letter! It's hard to describe how this feels. Like winning the lottery (although I have never done that). Like getting an Oscar (never done that either). Like having your marriage proposal accepted (did that one!). Elation. Validation. Magic. In one instant your previously murky future suddenly comes into crystalline focus. And this coming from someone who decided to become a veterinarian only three years prior. Imagine how this feels for all the people who have wanted to become a veterinarian from before they even knew the word.

I'll put aside the false modesty and admit that any doubt was just due to neurotic anxiety rather than a rational analysis of the odds. As Bruce put it before my interview, I could go in there naked, throwing ice cream at them, and I would still get in. That's literally what he said — naked, throwing ice cream. In part this was because I was from Saskatchewan, which had more vet school seats per capita than any of the other provinces served by the college. Moreover, admission was based mostly on marks and I had very good marks. I would never have admitted it then, but I'm happy to admit now that school was "my thing." I may have swum like an epileptic spider and sung like a scalded baboon, and my social life may have been limited to Friday night Dungeons & Dragons sessions, but by gosh, I could whip off an essay or demolish an exam like nobody's business.

A third ace up my sleeve was the fact that I had told them in the interview that I intended to go into research and teaching, rather than practice. In the mid-1980s there was a strong movement towards getting more people with combined Doctor of Veterinary Medicine (DVM) degrees and PhDs working in the veterinary colleges, rather than just PhDs, so they were very keen on candidates like me. The reason it didn't quite work out that way is another story, but back then, that was definitely my plan. At the end of the interview one of the professors said, "See you in the fall!" So, it could reasonably have been viewed as "in the bag," yet I was genuinely nervous waiting for the letter.

The numbers vary quite wildly from school to school and year to year, but a commonly accepted figure is that only 12% of applicants to veterinary college are accepted. I have one colleague who applied seven times before getting in. If your marks are in the grey zone everything will depend on who you are competing against in a given year, so he kept rolling the dice until he got lucky one year. Or the interview committee was just tired of talking to him. He became an excellent veterinarian by the way.

Which brings me to my final point. High marks may be needed to get into veterinary college, but they do not in any way predict what kind of a veterinarian you're going to be. Two out of the top three students in my graduating class did not succeed as veterinarians. And when I hire a new vet, I never look at their marks. Then why are high marks needed to get in? In part it's because the academic program is so rigorous that they want to make sure you can cope with it, and in part it's because they need a semi-objective basis for admission to protect themselves against accusations of subjective bias. The interview is mostly just to assess your emotional stability and sanity (with the bar apparently being set below naked ice cream throwing).

I wish I had kept that letter. Maybe admission to veterinary college was a foregone conclusion, but getting that letter was a major milestone in my life and it was the starting gun for a wild ride, no other part of which has been a foregone conclusion. Far from it.

AN HOUR SPENT SITTING AT A FORK IN THE ROAD

2:00 p.m., Friday January 13, 1989.

I had promised him I would call with my decision by 3:00 p.m. at the very latest. I had exactly one hour left, and I felt no closer to making up my mind than when the problem had first been presented a month ago. My brain was beginning to whir uselessly like my rusted-out Honda Civic stuck in a snowdrift, spinning its wheels, just polishing the snow to smooth ice under the tires. A lot of noise, a lot of vibration, a faint burning smell, but no forward motion.

To remove myself from all possible distractions I headed up to the mezzanine level of the library at the veterinary college. This was the home of obscure, unread journals and a clutch of spartan study carrels. Nobody else was up there. I picked out a carrel and proceeded to stare at the bare wood partitions in the hope of clearing my mind and coming to a decision.

Nope. No decision. Just more whirring and wheel spinning and, to extend the Honda metaphor, now also regular puffs of black smoke.

Aargh! 2:20 p.m.! Only 40 minutes left!

The decision was just, at one level, about my summer job for the four months between third year and fourth year at vet school. But at another level it was about my entire career and working future. This was the problem. Summer job decision? Easy. Done it many times before. Entire career and working future decision? Not so easy. Even the decision to enter vet school wasn't as hard, as it had offered a wide range of career options, including my original plan of going into research and teaching. But with this decision I could feel the funneling and burning of bridges beginning in earnest, and it was freaking me out.

2:40 p.m.

The choice was between a job offer at the Veterinary Infectious Disease Organisation (VIDO), where I would assist in cutting-edge research and make contacts with scientists and their postgraduate programs, and a job offer at the small animal clinic at the veterinary college, where I would gain practical experience in a clinic setting and get to know my instructors for fourth year. I hadn't yet worked in a clinic and felt profoundly unready for fourth year, which was very clinically oriented. Almost all of my classmates had worked in vet clinics before, often for years. But VIDO was an incredible opportunity for someone who was focused on a research career. My mind began flipping back and forth, like putting the car into forward and reverse, forwards and reverse, forward and . . .

2:55 p.m.

I continued to stare at the partition. My heart rate was high, and my palms were damp with sweat. People, especially at that age, can sometimes attach far too much importance to decisions they need to make and get far too stressed about them, but all these years later when I look back at that moment, it is even more clear now that it was an absolutely key decision — easily one of the three or four decisions I have made in my life that have had the most profound long-term impact. The stress was unhelpful, but understandable. I needed a couple of minutes to walk to the phone (pre-cellphone days) and, as I took those steps, I still did not know what I was going to say.

3:00 p.m.

I called the director of VIDO and declined the offer. You've already guessed this outcome, but I sure hadn't. I can't recall a conscious decision having been made. It was as if my subconscious mind directed my mouth.

The summer at the veterinary college small animal clinic was a fantastic experience and, after fourth year, I followed my future wife to Winnipeg and began to work in a private practice, temporarily, I said . . .

MANY CREATURES GREAT AND SMALL

No, not all, but many. I am of course referring to James Herriot's masterpiece of veterinary literature. For those of you too young to know this, Herriot was easily the most famous and beloved veterinarian of the 20th century. Incidentally, as a matter of trivia, *All Creatures Great and Small* is the title of a compilation of his first two books and part of a third. His original books had titles like *If Only They Could Talk*, *Let Sleeping Vets Lie* and, curiously, *Vets Might Fly*. However, *All Creatures Great and Small* was then also taken as the title of the hit BBC television series based on the stories, so that is how we now largely remember his work.

Herriot is emblematic of an era when all veterinarians truly treated, or at least attempted to treat, "all creatures." This era is slowly winding down. I have only a handful of colleagues who still practice in the Herriot way, if we can call it that. The great majority of us have significantly narrowed the spectrum of creatures we'll see. This is surprising news to some people. I still regularly get asked whether or not I treat farm animals, even though my clinic is in the middle of a city of three quarters of a million people. I'm not sure what their mental picture of my waiting room is (dog, dog, cat, cow, gerbil, cat, donkey, turkey . . . ?), but

I do know that the old notions of what a veterinarian does are remarkably tenacious in the public's imagination.

An important reason why practice has evolved towards species specialization is the colossal amount of knowledge required to achieve a reasonable level of clinical competence in multiple species. The amount of available knowledge is ballooning rapidly as research progresses, so to achieve this competence is now a far more challenging prospect than it was when James Herriot graduated in 1939. That said, few of us see only one species, and many of us still see a substantial range. But not "all." I treat nine species on a regular basis and have seen at least another twenty occasionally. The truth is that, other than in emergency situations, so long as you have a solid grounding in the basic principles of veterinary medicine and surgery, you can look the specific stuff up and deal with it on an as needed basis. Consequently, from that perspective, it would not be such a leap for me to take on a cow or a chicken. Just one or two more creatures out of the close to thirty. But I don't, because of another important reason this species specialization has occurred: the divide in how we value what we call companion animals and what we call food-producing animals. The veterinary approach and the mindset are very different for these two groups, and are becoming ever more so as farms become larger, more sophisticated and more specialized themselves.

My favourite class in my final year in vet school was what they called "field services." This meant getting in the school's station wagon (fake wood paneling! cassette tape deck! funky smell!) with an intern or resident and a couple classmates, and then bombing off down gravel roads in rural Saskatchewan to go on farm calls. While there were certainly moments of high stress, overall, this was a far less intense experience than being in the small animal clinic. The farmers were almost all welcoming, friendly and grateful, and the pace was reasonably relaxed. When the weather was good it was an absolute delight to be out in a paddock under the gentle spring sun and feel the wind in your face while watching the animals milling about. It's difficult to overstate the contrast to the severe fluorescent lights, the jarring blare of the intercom and the omnipresent sense of barely constrained panic that dominated our days back at the school's teaching hospital. At moments like that I would permit myself a brief Herriotesque reverie, but then, as often as not, the less bucolic side of farm animal practice would intrude. Farms are businesses. Moreover, they are businesses that often operate on the thinnest of margins, or, in some years, even at a loss. Consequently, that cow we are examining, as much as the farmer may be emotionally bonded to her, has a dollar value that can be calculated to the penny. People may joke about how little their dog is worth in economic terms, but rarely do they make decisions on that basis. Farmers would not be farming for long if they didn't make most of the decisions on that basis.

There are still hobby farms and smaller diversified family farms that blur these lines, but a lot of animal agriculture is evolving to a scale where most of the veterinarian's interactions are now with the herd or the flock, rather than with the individual animals. Unless the individual is valuable breeding stock, the farmers often deal with the minor ailments and injuries themselves. Farm animals unfortunate enough to be afflicted by something more serious are frequently sent for slaughter rather than treated, as it may not make economic sense to call the vet out for just one animal. The veterinarian's role in the largest corporate farms is more as a resource for preventative health and to deal with disease outbreaks among multiple animals. Some of my colleagues thrive in this growing sector, but for me, being what is essentially an agricultural consultant is almost as remote from my skills, my knowledge, my interests and my life as being an orthodontist or a long-haul truck driver. When people ask that question about whether I treat farm animals, I often joke in response that I am now more qualified to look at human children than cows or pigs. I am only partly joking.

I will state without fear of contradiction that ours is the most diverse of professions. Among my graduating class alone there is a breathtaking range. One of my classmates is a fish vet. He flies in a floatplane to remote salmon farms in British Columbia. Here the watchword is not herd health or flock health, but school health. Keeping with the wet patients, another classmate is a lobster pathologist on the east coast. Yes, you read that correctly, and no, it's not a punch line to an alarming seafood joke. Yet another classmate is a veterinary neurologist in California and one more does a lot of rehab work with eagles and owls. There is also a classmate who works in government biosafety regulation, two that teach at university, at least one that supervises meat inspection and one that specializes in racehorses. Most of us, however, are either pet vets or farm animal vets. And then, finally, there are those who have followed in James Herriot's footsteps and can claim to see all creatures with equal skill and enthusiasm, whether great or small. Although I doubt they have ever seen a lobster or a salmon. At least not in a professional capacity.

THE EXPERIMENTAL VETERINARIAN

That's right, gentle readers, I experiment on your pets. Some of you are narrowing your eyes, nodding and thinking, *I knew it!*, while others are already rounding up buckets of tar and bags of feathers, but hopefully the majority of you will have merely sighed, or groaned lightly, in recognition of the fact that I used a deliberately provocative but misleading title as a hook. It's a lame writer's trick, but I think I'm permitted one or two per book.

In fact, the title does have a legitimate origin. I was sitting around with my friend Al, riffing on titles that rhymed with *The Accidental Veterinarian* for my next collection of stories. *Occidental, Continental, Sentimental, Incremental, Incidental, Excremental* and *Transcendental* were all rejected before we landed on *Experimental*. Turning this over in my mind I realized that it was actually kind of apt. I don't experiment in the sense of performing procedures strictly for the purposes of learning, nor do I wantonly give unproven treatments that may have harmful effects, but I do, like all veterinarians, go out on a limb and "try stuff" more often than human physicians. We experiment, gently.

Pharmaceutical companies alone spent $160 billion dollars worldwide on human health research last year.

If you include government, university and other non-pharmaceutical private spending, total medical research expenditure exceeds a trillion dollars. The equivalent veterinary research budgets are a drop in this ocean of cash, and even that drop is weighted very heavily towards the health concerns of animal agriculture. So for pets, we're talking about a droplet within a drop. It is entirely proper and right that we value human health and life more highly, so I'm not making an argument here. I'm just pointing out that our knowledge of animal diseases is patchy and thin in places. In human medicine evidenced-based medicine (EBM) is a big deal. It's an approach that relies on consistent use of the strongest research data, rather than on instinct, experience, outdated training or weaker studies. Sometimes we can apply EBM to veterinary practice, but more often we're looking at studies that were performed with six beagles in Kansas in 1984, or possibly no studies at all. In these cases, we often extrapolate from the human side. Fortunately humans and my patients are medically far more similar to each other than they are different, so this often works OK, but we are also often stuck just trying stuff — "gently experimenting," if you will.

The other force that pushes us to experiment is what I will cautiously refer to as the funding model for veterinary medicine. In most wealthy countries human medical costs are paid for by governments or insurance, but while a small number of my patients do have private insurance, the great majority do not, and clients are paying out of their pockets. This means that there are often limits on which tests we can run, leaving us with a tentative diagnosis, rather than a confirmed diagnosis, far more often than in humans. A tentative diagnosis means a tentative treatment. A common conversation starts with: "Mrs. Smith, I think Buddy has disease 'x,' so we're going to try medicine 'y.' There's no harm if I'm wrong, but if I am, we'll have to do more tests or try medicine 'z' instead." This is essentially a mini-experiment. A single such mini-experiment does not provide generally applicable information because whether Buddy gets better or not might just be a coincidence. However, if I try medicine "y" for disease "x" in multiple patients over the years and they seem to get better more often than they would have on their own, then I've done a more proper experiment. This is not an experiment that could be published, as there are no controls or rigorously followed protocols, nor did I do this with the thought in my mind that I was conducting an experiment. I was merely doing my best to help my patients, but by such means the practice of pet medicine gradually advances. Sometimes the real science eventually supports what we've been doing on our own; sometimes it doesn't.

Inevitably the experimentation will give way to more EBM, but in the meantime, take heart that not only are we trying to help Buddy, but in doing so, sometimes we are also learning things that will help future Buddies.

MONEY IS NO OBJECT

Mr. Rogers was very friendly, charming even, as he introduced his dog Frodo to me. Frodo was a short, middle-aged, slightly pudgy Lab cross, while Mr. Rogers was also short, middle-aged and slightly pudgy. He had a big smile and a firm handshake, and was impeccably dressed in business attire, having just come from work. He told me that he had taken Frodo to several other veterinarians and had been dissatisfied, either with their bedside manner or with their recommendations. He had heard such great things about me that he was very optimistic that he had finally found the right doctor for his best friend. Sometimes clients who hop from clinic to clinic end up being difficult and demanding, but Mr. Rogers was a genuinely nice guy, who I had to assume had stumbled on the couple of bad apples in our otherwise very good local veterinary community. He didn't say which clinics he had been to before and I felt awkward asking. With the pleasantries out of the way, I asked him what his concern with Frodo was.

"He's been limping on that left hind leg for a couple weeks. The other vets told me he needs surgery on his knee, but I want another opinion."

I bent down and, after a liver treat and couple of pats,

got Frodo to stand four-square while I slowly manipulated each of the joints in the left hind leg. The knee, which we call the stifle in dogs, was swollen and had the telltale laxity that confirmed a tear in the cranial cruciate ligament, known as the anterior cruciate ligament in humans, or ACL. The ligament prevents the femur (thigh bone) from slipping forward over the top of the tibia (shin bone), so when it is torn the leg becomes unstable. I checked the rest of Frodo over and then explained the issue to Mr. Rogers. I told him that surgery was going to be necessary.

"OK, that's what the others said too, but I trust you, so I want you to do the surgery."

"No, you don't!" I chuckled. "I have no experience or training with that kind of surgery. One of my partners can perform an older procedure involving creating a new artificial ligament, or we can get a specialist in who does a new procedure in which he rebuilds the top of the tibia. His procedure, called a TPLO, has a higher success rate and a faster recovery time, but it is more expensive."

(Incidentally, this was a few years ago and we no longer offer the older procedure as the TPLO has proven to be so much better.)

Mr. Rogers smiled at me and patted Frodo on the head. "Dr. Schott, money is no object. I just want the very best for this guy. Book the specialist please."

On the appointed day, when he was dropping Frodo off for the surgery, Mr. Rogers made a point of waiting so that he could catch me between appointments and thank me personally for arranging everything. He mentioned that he had consented to the optional pre-anaesthetic bloodwork because, again, money was no object.

Surgery went very smoothly. When it was time to pick Frodo up, Mr. Rogers asked to see me privately before the paperwork was processed at the front desk. He was not his normal ebullient self. He looked distressed and was having trouble meeting my eyes.

"I am so embarrassed, Dr. Schott," he stammered.

"It's OK, what's wrong?"

"I never do this. I am a very proud person, so believe me this is tough for me to say, but I can't pay you today."

"Oh?"

"My ex screwed up on depositing the alimony cheques and they suddenly went through today. I'm tapped out until Friday, but I can definitely pay you in full then. One hundred percent. Even with interest if you need. I'm so sorry."

What could I do? It was a Monday and I couldn't hold Frodo until Friday. Besides, he was obviously really upset. The poor guy. I could only imagine how humiliating it must be to have to beg for credit. I told him it was OK, but that he would have to fill out a credit application form. I asked if he had anything at all he could put down on the account, but apparently, he had absolutely nothing. I wasn't worried, though.

I blame my upbringing for making me naïve. I had a good childhood. My family was stable, my neighbourhood was safe and everyone I encountered was trustworthy. It is, of course, a good thing to trust people, as life without trust would be sad and stressful, but us naïve, trusting types have to be prepared to be proven wrong from time to time.

Mr. Rogers proved me wrong. He did not come in on Friday and the number we used to contact him on the day of surgery was no longer in service. None of his other numbers were in service. His place of employment, listed on the credit application form, had never heard of him. Letters were returned marked "wrong address." In the meantime, we had to pay the specialist surgeon out of pocket, as he charges us and we pass his charge on to the client, plus our fees for anaesthesia, x-rays, meds, hospital care and so on. We're talking about a substantial amount of money. TPLOs are among the most expensive procedures routinely performed in our hospital. I have no idea where Frodo's staples were taken out and what story he told the vet there. I imagine he told them something similar to what he told me. I imagine one of my colleagues felt flattered and happy to get such a good new client.

Because of people like Mr. Rogers our policies have changed, and we are not supposed to extend credit anymore. Instead we direct people to commercial veterinary credit providers. I often think of the sign at my mechanic's that states, "My banker doesn't change oil, so we don't cash cheques or extend credit." That encapsulates the problem. Each business has a specialized skillset at its disposal. Veterinarians are very good at preventing, diagnosing and treating illnesses in pets. Veterinarians are quite terrible at assessing someone's credit worthiness. The problem, though, is that some people really are desperately poor and do not qualify for credit from any source. Consequently, and contrary to policy, we still sometimes end up doing it, even though we really have no way of knowing who is truly needy and who is the next Mr. Rogers. Last year we had around $12,000 in unpaid accounts, of which $8,000 were more than 90 days overdue and therefore unlikely ever to be recovered.

"Money is no object." It turns out that that can be true for two completely different reasons.

INCOMING

A number of metaphors have been used to describe veterinary practice, but when it is busy the most enduring one is the battlefield metaphor. I'm sure that people in the human medical field will recognize this as well. I want to be very careful, though, and point out that this metaphor does have limitations; chief among them is that it should not be taken to imply that the patients and the clients are the enemy. They are not the enemy, but more like civilians caught in the crossfire, with the enemy simply being "circumstances." (OK, most of the time they are not the enemy. . . .) It's more that the metaphor gives a flavour of what it's like to try to function at a high level of competence in an environment of chaos, noise, confusion, bad smells and occasional random unpleasantness.

And if the practice can be like a battlefield, it is the receptionists who stand at the front lines. When clients start surging through the doors and all the telephone lines are ringing and the doctors are standing around, getting in the way, and the dogs are competitively peeing on the welcome mat, and the couriers are waving documents to sign, and the computer system is malevolently generating random errors, then, at those times, to be a receptionist must feel like it feels for soldiers advancing through fire, hearing mortar rounds whistling towards them . . . "Incoming!"

To be fair, it can be just as stressful and busy at these times for the doctors and the veterinary technicians, but there are important differences. The doctors and techs can withdraw into quieter places to work with patients and clients one-on-one. More importantly, the doctors benefit enormously from one key thing: the client's respect. This makes all the difference. I know that the great majority of clients are decent and sensitive people who do respect the receptionists, but sadly, sometimes it doesn't show. And when it doesn't show, it can really hurt the receptionists, who are just trying their best to do their jobs and often don't have the power to change things for the clients. Society is gradually evolving in the right direction, but some old habits persist, and one of these old habits is to automatically — and probably unconsciously — assign more respect to the person in the lab coat with the title and a series of initials after their name than to the person in scrubs sitting behind the reception counter who you call by their first name.

Specifically, how does this manifest itself? The classic scenario is where the receptionist warns the doctor that the client is really angry about something, having just been yelled at by them, and then when the doctor and client are in the exam room together the client is sweet and polite to the doctor. The reverse also occurs, where the doctor says something upsetting to the client in the exam room, like recommending an expensive procedure, and the client nods and smiles and then leaves the room and, once the doctor is out of earshot, proceeds to freak out at the receptionist about what a rip-off the recommendation is.

I am not suggesting that clients freak out at the doctors instead, but I am suggesting that they refrain from doing so at the receptionists. As in all other areas of life, the best approach when you're angry is to take a few deep breaths, calm down and then politely and respectfully address the concern. But I don't mean to lecture any of you on manners — if you are reading this, I expect you are not one of the shouters or freaker-outers. I have seen receptionists in tears after these encounters and I have had some threaten to quit. I have had to fire a couple of clients over the years when this sort of behaviour really got out of hand. Yup, I can do that.

Other than basic human decency, why do receptionists deserve respect? They deserve respect because of what they do. Not only is there management of the battlefield, as described above, when there is so much "incoming." There is also management of the doctor's needs ("Can you print this? . . . "Can you fill this prescription?" . . . "Can you call so-and-so?" . . . "What's that weird smell in room 2?" etc.), and mastery of a remarkable range of skills. Some receptionists have college training in the field, but many do not. Even for those that do, the training is often in generic medical reception, and not specific to the veterinary environment. There is a complex (and capricious) computer system, terminology galore, arcane practice protocols, animal handling and, of course, basic veterinary knowledge. Imagine how daunting it is to have to triage every phone call. Is this person's concern serious enough to warrant an immediate squeeze-in appointment? A later appointment? A return call from the doctor? Or just advice I can give as a receptionist? And imagine the stress of treating something as urgent that isn't and having the doctor complain that it put them behind, and, conversely, the stress of not treating something as urgent enough and having the patient suffer. It is all a bit of a high-wire balancing act.

High wire over a battlefield . . . ? Sorry for mixing my metaphors. Whatever it is, we are so very lucky in my clinic to have a group of receptionists who do this so well that they make it look easy. It is not easy. Please respect them for it.

Thank you, Cheryl and Tara and Amber and Cam and Kyla and Lisa! We in the officer's tents and on the sidelines salute you on the front lines!

EAT THE FROG

How do you eat a frog? I know this sounds like a trick question, but, in fact, it's a philosophical one. Let's assume for the purposes of this discussion that the frog in question lived a marvellous, fulfilled life and died peacefully, surrounded by his loved ones. Additionally, let's assume that you have no choice. You must eat the frog. And finally, let's assume that you are not a habitual frog eater and that the thought of eating a frog fills you with dread and horror. How do you do it? Think about it while you read this story.

I arrived at work a few minutes early, hung up my coat, sat at my desk and woke up my computer. The first program I open is always our office management software which, on a series of tabs, has the schedule, messages, medical records, prescriptions and so forth. I started with my schedule. It looked like a unicorn had vomited on it. Green colour-coding for patients already waiting, orange for ones still coming, purple for ones in hospital, blue for ultrasounds, red for euthanasias, yellow for squeeze-ins . . .

Sigh.

I then clicked on the messages tab. There were about eight or nine. I scanned down the list quickly, relieved that none seemed urgent, until I got to the last one.

Please call Judy Finkelman ASAP — very angry. Says she was misquoted and that it killed her dog. Non-client.

Sigh.

Really? A non-client needs a call ASAP when I've got all this other stuff going on? And the complaint is bizarre. How does a misquote kill a dog?

Sigh.

I pushed my chair back and walked quickly up to the reception desk.

"Good morning! Who took the call from Ms. Finkelman?"

"Oh my God, her. Yeah, that was me," one of the receptionists groaned.

"Do you know what this is about? Is it really that urgent?"

"Well, she claims she called here to find out what we would charge for a pyometra spay and that someone told her it would be $3,000 and because she couldn't afford that she surrendered her dog to the Humane Society and they euthanized it." (A pyometra is an infected uterus.)

"That makes no sense. Nobody would quote that. I suppose it could go up to $1,000 in some situations, but not $3,000."

"Yeah, totally. Of course, she doesn't know who she spoke to, but the kicker is that she called back after her dog was gone and asked again and got the real quote. She says she could have afforded that, so it's our fault her dog is dead. She was screaming at me!"

"She's got to have some mental health issues. I feel bad for her, but I really don't want to call her. What's the point? She'll say she was quoted $3,000 and I'll say that's not possible."

"Please call her, Philipp. She's called a few times already and is just getting angrier! She wants to have a long conversation with somebody in charge. She says she's going to go on social media and tell everyone what horrible people we are."

Sigh.

"OK, I'll call her as soon as I can."

Although it was a busy morning, at various intervals clients came late, or I finished an appointment faster than scheduled, so I had time to make a few phone calls. I plucked the low hanging fruit first, the simple calls to assure someone that, yes, it's normal for puppies to eat their poo, or, no, you don't have to bring Freckles in because she sneezed once. Each time I opened the message tab, however, I eyed the frog with growing apprehension. I pride myself on my ability to be calm when people I'm dealing with are losing their heads, but I still don't enjoy being screamed at or trying to stick-handle a conversation around barriers of irrationality.

Then it was lunch time and I was fully caught up. This was unusual. Normally I have a lot of files to write in, or case research to do, or phone calls to make. This time the files were up to date, there was no pressing research and there was only one phone message left. I stared at the number on the screen and willed myself to pick up the phone. Then I remembered that someone had brought cookies, so I went to the staff room to check those out. Upon returning to my desk I noticed that there was some junk mail that I hadn't opened, so I took care of that. Then I refreshed my message list to see if anything new had come in.

There was nothing new.

There was only the frog.

It was at that moment that I remembered the wisdom about how one should deal with a situation like this — how one should eat a frog.

This is how you do it: eat it immediately and with as few bites as you can possibly manage. Get the damned thing over with. You are going to have to eat it for real eventually, so why eat it in your mind for hours or days before? Why prolong the experience? Anticipation is a double-edged sword — great for vacations and other good things in life, but really terrible for frog eating.

I dialed and the phone rang. The interval between rings was exceptionally long. I focused on keeping my breathing slow and even. Eventually it went to voice mail. I left a message that I hoped was both positive and serious sounding.

I never heard back.

VETS GONE BAD

I recently participated in a brief Facebook conversation with some of my colleagues about the highest rated program on *National Geographic Wild*. I have not seen it, but I have certainly heard and read a lot about it. I may have the name wrong, but it's something like *The Appalling Dr. Pol*.

ECW Press lawyers: "You can't say that! You know it's not called that. We'll get sued!"

Me: "Come on, get real. Hardly anyone will read this."

People appear to love this guy despite the fact that he is manifestly a quack.

Lawyers: "OMG!"

You would be hard pressed to find a veterinarian who feels otherwise. But I'm not going to talk about the show or the details of his practice. I only mention him because his story is a useful illustration of the weakness of the professional disciplinary process.

One of the hats I wear is that of Chair of the Peer Review Committee (PRC) of the Manitoba Veterinary Medical Association (MVMA). I've been Chair since 2011 and sat on the PRC as a committee member reviewing complaints for about ten years before that. Veterinary medicine is like most other professions in that it has been accorded the right to self-govern and self-regulate. The reason professions are permitted to do this is that the government recognizes that only those who actually do the work are in a position to determine what is appropriate and what is not, and which errors are avoidable and which are not. Lay people are also appointed to the PRC to make sure that the public interest is kept in mind and that it doesn't evolve into an "old boys' and girls' club."

It's an interesting job but it's also a stressful job. Standing in judgment of your peers can feel like an onerous responsibility at times. A more subtle stress, though, comes from the knowledge that the worst offenders are getting away with it and that we are only seeing a skewed sample. This is because the process is necessarily complaint driven. Clinics are inspected for equipment, record keeping, sanitation, etc., but nobody swoops in and looks over your shoulder to see how you are handling a case. There aren't the resources to do so and it would be pointless because, under observation, you would of course be on your best behaviour. The legislation states that for the PRC to investigate a complaint it must receive the complaint in writing. That's it, that's all. So, we sit and wait for letters to arrive; our hands are otherwise tied.

Think for a moment about your GP. Are they "good"? If so, how are you assessing that? Do you know enough about medicine to understand what is proper medical practice and what is not? Honestly? No, more likely, when you say that your doctor is good, you are saying that they are nice, and listens to you, and seems to care, and doesn't keep you waiting too long, etc. You have no real idea if the right test has been run, and even if it was, no idea of whether it was interpreted correctly or not. Your doctor could easily be incompetent, and it would be very difficult for you to tell. Consequently, you probably would not complain about your doctor to the College of Physicians and Surgeons, even if you had a poor health outcome. However, if you encountered a rude doctor with terrible bedside manner and had that same poor outcome, chances are higher that you would complain, even if they did everything right and the bad outcome was due to bad luck.

And so it is with veterinary medicine too. In all the complaints I have seen, the great majority have been due to poor communication by the veterinarian rather than poor skills or knowledge. Those of my colleagues who are a little more awkward around people, or perhaps are short tempered, but are objectively quite competent, attract far more complaints than those who are charming and charismatic but are objectively less competent.

The good news, though, is that given enough time, eventually the charming quacks trip up badly enough or often enough to unmask themselves, and professional discipline can take action. As Churchill said regarding democracy, it's the worst system, except for all the others.

Dr. Pol has finally been sanctioned by the Michigan Board of Veterinary Medicine.

SURGERY FOR DUMMIES

When I came up with this essay title, I thought it was cute and absurd. The "For Dummies" series of books may have a breathtaking range, from *ASVAB for Dummies* ("Armed Services Vocational Aptitude Battery" — yeah, I have no idea either) to *Zoho for Dummies*, which is apparently a suite of cloud computing applications, but surely there would be no *Surgery for Dummies*. Ha ha, right? Well . . . it turns out that there is *Weight Loss Surgery for Dummies*, as well as *Cosmetic Surgery for Dummies*. One hopes these are written for the patients, not the surgeons.

I decided to stick with "Surgery for Dummies," even though it now seems slightly less cute and absurd. My point was to highlight that there is no great mystery to surgery. A lot of surgery is much simpler than you might have thought. For many lay people, surgery may seem like the pinnacle of a veterinarian's (or medical doctor's) specialized skill and knowledge, but I'm here to tell you that I could easily teach any of you the basics of the majority of the surgeries we do, and that I could teach them with lessons that would fit on an index card. A small index card.

Basically, most surgery can be boiled down to one of two processes — either you are removing something, or you are repairing something. The latter can be far more complex, but it accounts for less than 10% of surgeries in a general practice. Most of the time you are removing something and that is usually not terribly complex. You could be removing testicles (neuter), ovaries and uterus (spay), a lump, a foreign object or a bladder stone, to give the most common examples. Here are the steps:

(NB: We are assuming the patient is already appropriately anaesthetized.)

1. Use a scalpel to cut a straight line in the best place to find the thing you want to remove. Avoid cutting through blood vessels, but if you have to, tie them off with suture so they don't bleed.
2. Find the thing you want to remove.
3. Identify the blood supply to this thing and tie it off.
4. Remove the thing.
5. Sew up the cut or cuts you made. Depending on how deep the cut was, you may need to sew a few separate layers.

That's it. If you cut and paste those five steps, they'll fit on an index card.

If you have to cut into an organ to find "the thing," for example a foreign object in the stomach or a stone in the bladder, step 3 will be slightly different:

3. Cut into the organ containing the thing in the same manner as step 1.

And the sewing is really just that — sewing. The thread (suture) may be special and we usually tie the knots using instruments, but the knots themselves are often just square knots. It's not hard.

All that being said, there are two very important additional factors to consider before you dive into this. OK, three if you count the fact that you need a license. And you should count that.

The first factor is that in order to "find the thing" and "identify the blood supply," and all that stuff, you do need to know the anatomy. Surgery is basically applied anatomy. (And, by the way, medicine is basically applied physiology.) Anatomy may seem complicated, but it's really just a lot of memorization. It helps to have a good visual memory, but it's not essential. And honestly, to perform a spay, for example, you don't need to know the anatomy of the brain or the elbow or the lungs — just the abdomen. Even there you don't need to know the name and location of every blood vessel running into the liver, you mostly just need to know what hangs out in the same neighbourhood as the ovaries and uterus. Also, as soon as you start doing it, remembering becomes easier and easier, as anatomy is something concrete that you can hold in your hands and see (unlike, say, the names of prime ministers you might have been forced to memorize in history).

This leads me directly to the second aspect, which is that it takes practice to become good at this. Duh. But this applies to veterinarians too! Regardless of how thoroughly a veterinary student has memorized the anatomy and the five points on my index card (or whatever notes they have from their surgery lectures), it will take them a ridiculously long time to perform their first spay. And they will be terrified, and they will have to ask questions and get help, and they will not be confident. At least one hopes that they will not be confident, because they shouldn't be, not yet. One of my classmates even fainted during their first surgery. Whump — hit the floor. They went on to become a fine surgeon. Eventually. With practice.

So, learn the anatomy, keep the index card handy and practice, practice, practice under the supervision of someone who can swoop in should things go sideways, or should you pass out. And then you too can be a surgeon. (But don't forget the part about needing a veterinary license.)

DR. GOLIATH, DVM

It may be a cliché to say so, but change is inevitable. In few aspects of life is this as true as it is in the world of work. Every job and every profession is changing, and the pace of that change is accelerating. In veterinary medicine we have seen great technological change and we have seen an enormous change in our understanding of many diseases. We have also seen the profession change from being male dominated to female dominated in a single generation. These changes are evident to most pet owners, but here I want to talk about an equally important change that is occurring behind the scenes. I want to talk to you about the creeping corporate takeover of veterinary medicine.

Practice groups consisting of locally owned hospitals with a few satellite clinics have been around for a long time, and the larger ones may blur the lines with corporate practice, but I'm not talking about them here. What I'm talking about started in 1986, when Veterinary Centers of America (now Veterinary Clinics of America, or VCA) was founded in California and began buying private practices and practice groups across North America one by one. VCA now owns more than 800 animal hospitals in 43 states and 5 provinces, and operates approximately 1000 (!) more under its Banfield brand name, which it acquired in a 2017 merger. VCA is a publicly traded company listed on the NASDAQ stock exchange (under the cloyingly cute stock symbol "WOOF"). Other corporations include National Veterinary Associates, with over 400 clinics, and Vet Strategy with close to 100 clinics.

Winnipeg is always the last place for any trend to hit. We were the last to get Starbucks and the last for the microbrewery revolution, and we are the last major market to be targeted by corporate veterinary medicine. Up until very recently all the practices in Winnipeg were locally and privately owned. Then four years ago a large corporation began to buy clinics, and now owns seven and is eager to buy more.

Change can be good, change can be bad, and change can be just change. On the good side corporations bring deep pockets to the profession, making it easier to upgrade to the newest technology and to present sparkling, professionally decorated practices. But with ample respect and affection for my colleagues who now work for corporate, I am going to argue that this particular change is, on balance, bad for the profession.

The fundamental problem is that large corporations exist solely to make money. Of course, small private practices also have to make money, but the difference is that if my clinic has a bad year financially, we tell ourselves that it was bad luck, or the weather, or the economy, and we'll hope for a better year next year. We answer only to ourselves, not to shareholders or investors. In contrast, if revenue drops in a corporate practice, management from Los Angeles or Toronto or wherever will put pressure on the veterinarians they employ to meet quotas — or else. Some corporations track remarkably specific metrics. For example, in the US one looks at the number of x-rays a veterinarian should take relative to the amount of respiratory disease they see. The corporations do not dictate the management of specific cases — that would actually be illegal — but they will set general benchmarks for numbers of specific tests and procedures, and they certainly make specific financial goals clear to their employees. On the one hand more tests can be "good medicine" and, as in the above example, it can be hard to argue against precautionary "just in case" x-rays for a cough, but on the other hand this does diminish a vet's freedom to use their professional judgment and make sensible decisions without having to worry about what management is going to say about their numbers at the end of the quarter.

Another problem is vertical integration. Mars Corporation has recently bought a controlling interest in VCA. Mars is massive. It had $33 billion in sales in 2015, and only a fraction of that was from chocolate bars. It is now the world's largest provider of pet health products and services. In addition to VCA it owns Royal Canin food, with their prescription diet line, and a whole series of non-prescription pet food brands, including Pedigree, Whiskas, Eukanuba, IAMS, Nutro and more. It also owns the largest chain of veterinary specialty and emergency centres, the second largest veterinary laboratory company, one of the largest veterinary ultrasound companies, and the number-one canine DNA analysis company. Oh, and a chain of 130 boarding and doggie daycare facilities. All that's missing from their portfolio is a pharmaceutical company. The fear here is that veterinarians will increasingly be required to use only products and services under the same corporate umbrella, rather than picking and choosing from all the options based on their professional judgment of their patient's needs. I mostly love Royal Canin foods, but only mostly. I would not tolerate being told that it is the only prescription diet I can offer my patients.

At the end of the day the important relationship is the one between you and your pet and your veterinarian. Who your veterinarian works for is hopefully not all that relevant. It's just sad for us within the profession to see the freedom and independence we enjoyed being gradually eroded. And it's sad to think about the coming generations of veterinarians who will have less opportunity to enjoy the sense of pride that comes with owning your own practice and making all your own decisions.

Before leaving this subject, I should explain how these corporations have been able to buy clinics. Obviously, there must be willing sellers. There must be veterinarians who see this as something that is more good than bad. Of course, there are. In part this happens because the large veterinary corporations can offer older veterinarians a relatively straightforward way to ease into retirement. Moreover, they are able to make these offers very generous. I am fortunate in that I have younger veterinarians working for me who are keen and financially able to buy into the practice, so when my time comes, I will be able to sell to them without any trouble. This is not the case in every practice. Sometimes willing buyers are just not that easy to find. Sometimes junior veterinarians prefer not to take on the responsibilities of ownership and management. Corporate practice therefore fills a previously unmet need and some of my colleagues are grateful for that. And as much as I might personally wish for it to be otherwise, veterinary medicine is ultimately not immune to the laws of economics.

THE CURIOUS TALE OF THE
RESTAURANT NEXT DOOR

The Marigold restaurant recently closed its doors after 50 years of being our neighbour. It was bittersweet news. On the one hand, it's hard to see iconic businesses and institutions close, but on the other hand, to be honest, I was never really very fond of their style of North American Chinese food, with its dayglow pink sauces and its anatomically improbable chicken balls. Moreover, their Friday lunch buffet often caused problems: large van-loads of Marigold enthusiasts from the country, in town for a day of shopping, would clog our parking lot, either in defiance or in ignorance of our signs.

Perhaps our signs needed to be larger, because whenever I think of the Marigold restaurant, I think of one incident in particular. This might have been 15 or so years ago and it was a Friday in the summer. It was a reasonably busy day at the clinic when a nervous-looking middle-aged couple came in through the back door. The clinic is relatively long and narrow, with the parking lot out back and the front facing a busy street, so it was not unusual for people to try to come in that way. We generally keep the back door locked, because it can be crowded and chaotic in that part of the clinic, and it's not really meant for through-traffic, but sometimes we forget. That day we forgot.

The couple walked slowly past the grooming area, and past the kennel areas full of dogs and cats, and through the treatment room with staff in scrubs scuttling about and pets on stainless steel tables and various machines going "ping." They walked past all of this and made their way to the reception counter at the front of the clinic. There they stopped and the man smiled shyly at the receptionist, cleared his throat and quietly asked a question.

He asked, "Is this the Marigold restaurant?"

I'll let that sink in for a moment.

"Is this the Marigold restaurant?"

The most astonishing part isn't that they would walk into Birchwood thinking it was the Marigold. The back of the clinic and the back of the restaurant look pretty similar, I suppose. And sometimes your brain just blanks out signs. I get that. It's probably happened a few times before and people just giggled at their error and made a quick about-face.

And the most astonishing part isn't even that, after seeing everything they had just seen, and hearing everything they had just heard, and smelling everything they had just smelled, they would think that this could possibly be a restaurant. That's really astonishing, but it is not, in fact, the most astonishing part. These looked like trusting, innocent and, dare I say it, unsophisticated folk.

No, the most astonishing part is that after everything

they had seen, heard and smelled, they were still hungry and apparently still interested enough to ask that question!

The Marigold is being replaced by a funeral home, so the parking will only get worse. And I sincerely hope that it doesn't generate any funny stories.

THE 80%

Yesterday was International Women's Day, so I thought I'd take a moment to point out a fact that you might not have noticed or considered: no other profession has experienced as great a shift in gender balance as veterinary medicine.

In 1970 barely 10% of veterinary school students were female; now more than 80% are. And the trendline is continuing upwards. In some schools, it's 90%. In contrast, medical school is still 50% male, as is law school, and dental school is 62% male. The 50/50 crossover point for veterinary medicine occurred in the mid-1980s. My own school, the Western College of Veterinary Medicine in Saskatoon, was ahead of the curve, and my first-year class in 1986 was already about 70% women.

In 1970 a tiny number of practising veterinarians in Canada were women; now 60% are. These women are on average ten years younger than their male colleagues, so this number will steadily rise as the men retire and are replaced by the 80% of graduates who are female. In the span of a half century the profession has gone from being overwhelmingly male to being overwhelming female.

Why is this? Part of the answer lies in the changing nature of the work. Over the same time period as the gender shift, the profession experienced a parallel shift from rural- and farm-animal oriented to urban- and companion-animal oriented. The fact that women continue to bear the primary responsibility for childcare in many families makes the more regular and predictable hours of the latter much more accessible and attractive. Farm practice can be 24 hours a day, 7 days a week at times, with hours and hours on the road away from home. But that factor alone should have only lifted barriers and given more equal opportunity to women, not pushed them to a predominant position. Why have they shot past the 50/50 equilibrium one might otherwise have predicted?

It's complicated. One factor is that competition to get a spot in veterinary school is ferocious, more ferocious than for any other profession, and young women are increasingly in a better position to win that competition. Women now dominate in academics, often occupying the top rungs in the lists of the best students in any given class. The reason for this is beyond the scope of this essay, but there are innumerable articles on the subject and, if you read one, you'll see that the falling academic performance of young men is the cause of much hand-wringing.

Another factor is that veterinary medicine pays less well and is perhaps less prestigious than many of the other professions. This is a terrible statement about the state of gender relations in our society, but women historically have accepted lower pay and men historically have been encouraged to seek prestige. These things are changing, but some ingrained cultural norms will take a long time to truly fade away.

And finally, veterinary medicine requires more empathy than any other profession. If you are reading this, then you already know why this is true. Again, this is likely more a statement about our culture than anything else, as I don't think I am any less empathetic than my female colleagues, but perhaps I am less concerned about those subtle cultural signals. This is not to absolutely deny the influence of biology. In a survey of very anxious dogs, seven out of ten preferred a female veterinarian. Something about men's deeper voices and harder features freaks them out. (I'm joking, of course. To the researcher's endless frustration, the dogs were unable or unwilling to answer the questions. But the observation is generally true.)

None of this is black and white; it is just tendencies and trends. But look where those tendencies and trends have brought us. When I think back to when I graduated in 1990, it's astonishing how things have changed. Even though I looked like I was 12 years old, I was male, so I was immediately assumed to be the doctor, whereas many of my female classmates struggled for years with reactions along the lines of "When is the real doctor coming in?"

Veterinary medicine has changed, and it is thriving like never before. I'll let you draw your own conclusions.

VET VET

"Veterinarian" is an odd word. The five syllables are difficult for many people to fully enunciate, often resulting in "vet'narian": and the fact that it is a noun, not an adjective, appears to baffle some people as well. Veterinary is the associated adjective, yet I often hear the expression "veterinarian hospital." That, my dear readers, would be a specific hospital for ill veterinarians, which would be kind of cool, but also kind of weird. The abbreviation can also cause confusion. More than once when I have said that I am a "vet," the listener has assumed I meant military veteran. The similarity between the words "veteran" and "veterinarian" is a coincidence. The former comes from the Latin "*vetus*," meaning old, whereas the latter appears to come from the Latin "*veterinum*," referring to beasts of burden. I say "appears to," because this is just a best guess. There is a gap of more than 1,000 years between Latin falling out of common use and the first appearance of the word "veterinarian" in the context of someone treating animal diseases.

Given this coincidence, there arises the mildly amusing homonym of the "vet vet," i.e., the veteran veterinarian, or veterinary veteran. Here I don't mean an old vet (veterinarian) who has spent decades in the trenches of clinical practice, but a military veteran who may have spent time in actual trenches and who is also a veterinarian. The Royal Army Veterinary Corps in the UK was established in 1796 following a public outcry regarding the suffering and death of British cavalry horses. Currently it has about 30 veterinary officers, primarily looking after search-and-rescue and explosive-detection dogs. Two of these officers were killed in the recent conflict in Afghanistan. In the US, the Army Veterinary Corps is substantially larger, employing 700 veterinarians who not only treat military dogs, but also work in the fields of food safety, biosecurity and disaster relief, as well as providing veterinary services for pets owned by military personnel. Sadly, the Royal Canadian Army Veterinary Corps (RCAVC) was disbanded in 1940, but not before becoming responsible for one of the more moving memorials in the Canadian Parliament buildings.

The Memorial Chamber in the Peace Tower is where the Books of Remembrance are kept, listing all the people who have died in the service of Canada. It is a solemn and sacred space. To the surprise of many, above the entrance to this chamber are carved the images of several animals: a reindeer, a mule, a carrier pigeon, a horse, a dog, a canary and a mouse. This is accompanied by the inscription "The tunnelers' friends, the humble beasts that served and died." ("Tunnelers" refers to the men in the trenches of World War One.) The roles of the mule, carrier pigeon, horse and dog are obvious, but the other animals less so. It turns out that canaries and mice were kept as early warning systems for the presence of poison gas. The reindeer remain mysterious, although there was apparently a Canadian Siberian Expeditionary Force in 1918, so it's possible that there's a connection there.

Despite the relatively small size and brief existence of the RCAVC, it did produce one veteran who is arguably Canada's most famous veterinarian. In 1915 Winnipeg veterinarian Major Harry Colebourn rescued an orphaned black bear cub in White River, Ontario, naming her Winnie after his hometown. He was on his way to serve on the Western Front with the RCAVC. Winnie served as a regimental mascot while they were still training in England, but she had no place in an active war zone. Harry donated her to the London Zoo, where, a few years later, A. A. Milne and his son, Christopher Robin, would visit her frequently. You know the rest of that story. After the war Major Colebourn returned to Winnipeg, where he opened a private practice before going into government work in 1926 when his health began to decline as a long-term consequence of having been gassed during the war. He continued to treat animals part-time out of his home at 600 Corydon Avenue until he died in 1947. There are statues of Colebourn with Winnie in both the Winnipeg and London zoos.

So, Major Colebourn was the quintessential vet vet. As his post-war practice was predominantly focused on small animals, you could also say that he was a pet vet vet. And if you met him outside on a particularly rainy day, he would have been a wet pet vet vet. Forgive me, but sometimes I find myself helpless against these impulses.

PET 911

There isn't one. No doubt some people call 911 when they have a pet health emergency on their hands, but I don't know what the operators tell them beyond "call your vet." The real "911" for such emergencies is obviously your veterinary clinic's phone number. If your clinic is not open, it should have information on the answering machine regarding who you should contact when they're closed: sometimes an on-call veterinarian and sometimes an emergency hospital that your clinic refers to.

You probably knew all this already, but it never hurts to cover the basics. Now that I know that you know what to do when there is an emergency, we can move on to the more interesting question of what actually constitutes an emergency.

Fortunately true emergencies are much less common in pets than in humans. If you look at the eight most common emergencies in people — chest pain, stroke symptoms, accidents, choking, abdominal pain, seizures and shortness of breath — really only the last two are at all common and easy to recognize in pets. They do get abdominal pain, but it's harder to tell and is fortunately less often life-threatening (no appendix in there to burst). Dogs and cats rarely have strokes and even more rarely have "heart attacks." In fact, coronary artery disease is unknown in our pets. Yes, they do get other kinds of heart diseases, but these tend to be chronic and do not often result in a sudden worsening constituting an emergency. True choking (i.e., not coughing or gagging that sounds like choking) is also less common than you might think. And pets do have accidents, but far less frequently than people, maybe because they don't drink or drive or ski or cycle or take showers or clean their guns or play with matches or rewire their homes or try to create viral videos . . .

As an aside, when I started in practice in the early 1990s, "HBC" was a fairly regular emergency presentation. This had nothing to do with the Hudson's Bay Company, but is rather our abbreviation for "hit by car." These days far more dogs are on leash and far more cats are kept indoors, so we may only have a handful of HBCs a year. Similarly, "BDLD" is on the decline. Can't guess? "Big dog — little dog." This is a traumatic dog fight injury where the size and strength differential leads to serious wounds in the "LD." We still see this, but people generally seem to be more aware of dog behaviour (generally — not universally), and again, more dogs are on leash. That being said, the increasing popularity of off-leash dog parks is preventing BDLD from declining as quickly as HBC. Cat fights are far less common than they once were, though. (We do not have a cool acronym for those.)

So now that you know what not to worry too much about, what should you worry about? When should you call "Pet 911"? The American Veterinary Medical Association has provided a useful list. I will summarize an amended version here:

1. Severe bleeding or bleeding that doesn't stop within five minutes.
2. Choking, difficulty breathing, or nonstop coughing and gagging.
3. Inability to urinate or obvious pain associated with urinating.
4. Eye injuries.
5. You suspect or know your pet has eaten something poisonous such as anti-freeze, xylitol (in sugar-free gum), chocolate, grapes, rodent poison, etc.
6. Seizures and/or staggering.
7. Fractured bones, severe lameness or inability to move leg(s).
8. Obvious signs of pain or extreme anxiety.
9. Heat stress or heatstroke.
10. Severe vomiting — more than two major bouts in a 24-hour period, or combined with obvious illness or any of the other problems listed here.
11. Refusal to drink for 24 hours or more.
12. Unconsciousness.

I worked in an emergency clinic for a little while after I graduated, which is a story unto itself, and I can tell you that 90% of what called and came in was not on that list. But that's absolutely OK. A good emergency service provides peace of mind. They can often triage on the phone to decide whether your pet needs to be seen or not. Consequently, I can give you a greatly simplified list of when to call:

1. Your pet appears to be in distress (or, conversely, very lethargic).
2. You are in distress about something regarding your pet.

Don't hesitate to call. You're not bothering someone. It's their job to help and they are happy to do it. Unless you are drunk and it's 2:00 a.m. and you want to ask why your cat is staring at the wall (true story). Then reconsider.

VETS ABROAD

We've just returned from vacation overseas and although we saw loads of animals (mostly sheep if you're interested in trying to guess where we were), happily none of them were visibly ill or injured, so we were able to comprehensively disengage our veterinary brains. That is not always the case. Over the years, in various countries, Lorraine and I have tried to help goats with infected udders and cats who were bleeding internally. However, the most memorable vet abroad episode occurred 20 years ago in the Philippines, when Leeann insisted we spay her dogs on her kitchen table. I will elaborate.

Lorraine and I had found our way to a little island called Malapacao, off Palawan in the southwest corner of the Philippines. This was a tropical paradise straight from the tourist posters and, in fact, the view from our beach was used as the cover photo of the Lonely Planet guide to the Philippines. But it was very quiet there because it was hard to get to and there was only one place to stay, a resort consisting of a cluster of thatched huts run by an older Australian woman named Leeann. A polite one-word description for Leeann would be "eccentric." To begin with, she regularly practised naked yoga on the beach near our hut. This is not nearly as cool as it sounds, and it probably doesn't sound all that cool. Also, she had strict no alcohol and no smoking policies. The latter wasn't a problem for us or for the only other guests, John and Jesse, a couple from New York City (fun guys — one a Pulitzer Prize–winning journalist and the other a fashion show producer), but it was a problem for a number of people who attempted to come and were consequently turned away. In fact, we got really good at spotting them as their boats approached the beach. Middle-aged dude in a speedo with a paunch: probably a smoker. Cool. We liked this because Leeann let us have the "premium" huts at the regular price so long as nobody else came who wanted them.

The no alcohol was an issue, though. Leeann would make her "Malapacao Special" virgin punch for us every evening before the group dinner, but it so desperately needed a kick.

We quickly found a workaround.

Malapacao is a saddle-shaped island with dramatic limestone cliffs to the east and west, Leeann's postcard beach to the north and then, over the jungle-clad saddle, a little Filipino fishing village to the south, only a 15-minute walk away. One of us would sneak over with John or Jesse and buy a bottle of the local hooch, small enough to slip into a pocket in our shorts, so we could quickly spike the drinks while Leeann rambled on about chakras or cosmic vibrations or whatever. Dinner was a heck of a lot more fun this way.

This is where we begin to approach the veterinary portion of the story for you, patient readers, because the same village supplied not only liquor, but also randy male dogs (so drugs and sex, only the rock and roll was missing).

Leeann had two lovely female dogs. They were the classic "beach dogs" one sees the world over — lean, lanky, short fur, curly tails, a bit wary but ultimately super pleased to receive kind human attention. And they were not spayed. There were no veterinary services anywhere nearby. As soon as Leeann found out that we were veterinarians, her already unnaturally lit eyes became even brighter.

"You can spay the girls for me!"

I laughed and took another sip from my drink.

"No, really, I mean it! What do you need?"

"No, Leeann, it's just not possible. A spay involves abdominal surgery so we need general anaesthetic and sterile conditions, as well as all the surgical tools."

I was going to change the conversation, but Leeann persisted.

"No problem. I have connections on the main island. It's the Philippines. I can get anything you need. Anything. Just give me the list." She pulled out a pad of paper and a pencil and looked at me eagerly.

"Ha, no! Really, we use gas anaesthetic which involves complicated equipment, although . . ." I began to waver a little," . . . I suppose injectable anaesthetic might be possible . . ."

Lorraine shook her head vigorously. I looked at the two dogs and their giant nipples and deep-chested shape, and considered that these would be tough spays even at home. I know that some of my colleagues are guffawing now (I'm looking at you, Colleen and Jonas), as you have probably done spays in Mexico using a Swiss Army knife, a headlamp and some dodgy expired ketamine for anaesthesia, but Lorraine and I were (are) spoiled and soft. There was no way we were going to do this.

"But it's just so risky, Leeann. You love these girls. You don't want to take that chance. In addition to the considerable anaesthetic risks, there's the fact that we can't sterilize the equipment or create clean enough conditions here."

At this point Lucas, the cook, flashed one of his enormous smiles and chimed in, "No problem! I clean the kitchen table very well, Mr. Philipp!" He made a vigorous wiping motion with his right hand.

The argument went back and forth for a while, but we were determined not to attempt a tropical kitchen spay. We felt bad, though, so when we returned to Canada, I bought a large tub of a medication that can work as an oral contraceptive in dogs and shipped it to her. I never heard back. To this day, 20 years later, I still sometimes wonder whether we could have pulled off those kitchen spays after all.

Incidentally, I just Googled Malapacao and Leeann is still there and is still as eccentric as ever.

FIDDLING WITH THE DIALS

I remember clearly the first time it happened. It was about two years ago, and a good client who I had known for a long time told me that she had heard I was retiring. I was touched that she looked concerned but was disconcerted by the question. Since then I have been asked at least half a dozen times about my alleged imminent retirement.

First things first, I am not retiring soon. Quite aside from any question about how long I want to work, the plain mathematical fact is that I am very unlikely to be able to afford it for a good while yet. If I retire now, we are moving into a trailer and the kids, and possibly the pets, will have to find jobs. Also, I am only 55 years old! Yes, that's right, I said "only."

At first, I was quite taken aback by these rumours, thinking that they related to my grey hair and my admittedly at times somewhat haggard appearance. It honestly feels like no time elapsed between the last time I looked too young to be a doctor and the first time I was asked whether I qualified for a senior's discount at Shoppers Drug Mart (to be fair to myself, the clerk was so young that I'm sure anyone over 30 looked impossibly ancient to him). From Doogie Howser to Marcus Welby overnight. And before anyone makes any snide remarks, no, I am too young to have watched *Marcus Welby, MD* on TV — I just happen to know who he is.

But when I calmed down, I realized it probably wasn't my appearance so much as it was my schedule. Four years ago, I cut back to three days a week. At the same time, I adjusted the shifts so that in those three days I work 70% of full-time. I had gone to working four days a week a long time ago and back then the transition from five to four hardly attracted any comment, but at three I seem to have crossed a line. Now it looked to some like I was beginning the process of easing my way out of practice.

That, however, is not the case.

The reason has far more to do with my work-life balance than with my career trajectory. When I worked four days a week, the one day off was designated for errands, appointments, housework and childcare. Although both children are now teenagers, both have some special needs that require additional attention. Consequently, this day off is as busy as my workdays. I took the additional day off to have a day to pursue other interests, such as writing, and to go for long walks, and to have delicious stretches of unscheduled, unplanned hours. I am well aware that a "me day" like this is a luxury that few people can enjoy, and I am very grateful for it. And this finally brings me to my point. My point is that one of the great beauties of veterinary medicine as a career choice is the freedom to choose your hours and thereby also, to a limited extent, choose your income.

It's like there are two linked dials: one for hours and one for income, and in many multi-doctor, small animal practices you have the ability to fiddle with these dials. You want to work less? You turn the hours dial down and the income dial turns down automatically. You want to earn more? You turn the income dial up and the hours dial turns up automatically. In theory, if you could afford it, you could work as little as eight hours a week or, if you could survive it, as many as 80. Not many people have that sort of freedom. To be accurate, though, some veterinarians don't either. In smaller practices you may be forced to work full-time just to be able to keep all the shifts covered, and for many large animal veterinarians, freedom and flexibility, or lack thereof, is tied to the dramatic seasonality of the practice. But many of us now work in practices where flexible scheduling is possible. For those wanting to start a family this can be very attractive (so long as the spouse earns enough . . .). And for those grey-hairs like me, who want to do the things they put off for decades but don't want to (or can't) leave the profession, this can be very attractive too.

ALARMED

One of the very many things they don't teach you about in vet school is security. When you operate a veterinary clinic, you are operating a business that handles quite a bit of cash and that stores drugs that have significant street value. Because this is all new to you, you rely on whatever system your predecessor or mentor had in place and you rely on the professionals, such as the alarm company and your local police department. Usually this works just fine. Usually.

Sadly, however, and in common with most businesses, the biggest risk of loss from theft in a vet hospital is from your own employees. If any of my current employees are reading this, relax! We have a good group of people right now and have for a few years. All of you guys have earned my trust. But there was a time when I handed out trust like candy on Halloween.

There was a time when large amounts of ketamine kept disappearing. It's known on the street as "vitamin k," "special k" or "kit-kat." Users are apparently seeking a floating sensation and pleasant hallucinations, but when they misjudge the dose, they can end up having a terrifying near-death experience, which is colourfully referred to as the "k-hole." It goes without saying that taking the risk of visiting the "k-hole" is a profoundly bad idea. We couldn't prove who the culprit was, but the person we most strongly suspected soon left of their own accord and the ketamine stopped disappearing. We've since beefed up monitoring the dispensing of all the "controlled drugs."

Then there was the time when we hired a new receptionist and within a week gave her a key and all the safe and alarm codes. You know where this story is going . . . One Saturday morning the first staff arrived to find the back door not only unlocked, but slightly ajar. They chuckled about their sloppy colleagues and thought nothing more of it until someone noticed that the safe was wide open. Wide open and empty. Had we been broken into? Had last night's staff forgotten not only to lock the door, but also to set the alarm? Then the third clue. The new receptionist was scheduled to work that morning and hadn't shown up. Let's call her Becky because I've never had anyone named Becky work for me. One of the staff called Becky's number. Her boyfriend answered. He said that she hadn't come home the night before and then, after a brief pause, asked if anything was missing from the clinic. The staff member told him that, why yes, cash and drugs were missing, how did he know?! He just laughed and said that he guessed Becky had fallen off the wagon, again.

The staff called me at home to explain what had happened. After I hung up, I remembered that Becky had Facebook friended me a few days prior. I don't go on Facebook all that often, so I hadn't looked at her profile and timeline yet. It was eye-opening, to say the least. There was picture after picture of people flashing gang signs and there was post after post praising Becky for her progress in Cocaine Anonymous. Oh.

The police were of course unable to recover any of the stolen drugs or cash.

Although "inside jobs" represent most crime in a veterinary hospital, break-ins do occasionally occur. Of course, we have a monitored alarm system in place, with the doors wired and motion sensors in the main open areas. The arrangement is that the alarm company will first telephone a "key holder" and ask how they should proceed. As this is an annoying job, the "key holder" position is rotated between the partners and senior staff who live close to the clinic. On the night I want to tell you about, I was the lucky individual. The phone rang at 3:00 a.m., which is the worst time for that happen. If I had to go down to the clinic, there would be no way to get back to sleep. The alarm company representative said that the motion detector had gone off in the reception area. I said that it must be a false alarm as the door alarms hadn't gone off. The representative countered that sometimes alarms fail and, moreover, that thieves could enter through a window or a weak point on the roof, so they strongly recommended I go down to have a look. I recalled that Dr. Clark had told me about a break-in in the 1970s through an old skylight in one of the wards that he subsequently had sealed up, so the roof idea didn't seem so outlandish after all. The representative then asked whether or not I would like the police to meet me there, and I said yes, please.

The police were already there by the time I arrived. The young officer met me by the back door.

"Good evening, sir, I've checked the perimeter and there's no sign of forced entry."

"Good. But I suppose there's the possibility of someone coming through the old skylight in the roof, isn't there?" The officer just smiled and nodded, so I went on, "So, I suppose you're going to go in now and check?"

"I'd prefer it if you went in first, sir."

"Me?"

"If there's a vicious dog loose in there, it's better if you deal with it." He was grinning broadly. I was too polite and restrained to say what I thought. What I thought was that this guy was close to half my age and close to twice my muscle power. Plus — need I point this out? — he had a gun. Maybe I was better trained to deal with a loose dog, but what if there was really a thief in there? Aren't cops supposed to be brave? Aren't they supposed to be heroes? This was an absurd situation! I thought all these things, but what I actually did was unlock the door and cautiously go inside. The officer stayed just outside the door until I called back to say that the place seemed empty. Then he slowly came in, big flashlight at the ready. It occurred to me that an escaped dog would not hide, but a cornered thief might. But no dogs and no thieves, just a piece of paper on the floor. As far as we could tell, it seemed that the ventilation system had blown a piece of paper off of a counter at just the right angle to set off the motion detector. The cop was amused. I was not.

It's been a long time since the last false alarm, but next time I'm going to have a longer conversation with the police officer first.

DOCTOR OF VETERINARY M . . . ?

A number of years ago we were visiting old friends in the US when we were introduced to some people our friends knew at a dinner party. I'm used to hearing a variety of cute, not so cute and outright horrifying pet stories when people find out what I do for a living, but I was not prepared for what followed when one of these people button-holed me.

"So, you're a vet?" he said, smiling a big white smile and shaking my hand a little too firmly.

"Yes, a small animal vet."

"That's a funny coincidence! I just took Sadie, our Lab, to the vet yesterday. She had something going on with her skin and he recommended this test and that test and the other test and then when I saw the estimate for all this,

I just about shit myself! Three hundred bucks! Can you believe it?"

I could believe it and was beginning to open my mouth to reply but he barrelled ahead. "Three hundred smackers! So, you know what I asked him?"

I shook my head.

"I asked him what DVM stood for! And then I told him that it didn't look to me like the 'M' was for medicine! It looked to me like the 'M' was for marketing! 'A Doctor of Veterinary Marketing is what you are,' I said!"

I chuckled weakly and began furtively looking around for Lorraine or my friends.

"But I'm sure you're the real deal, Phil — a true Doctor of Veterinary *Medicine*!" my new acquaintance said, using the tone people adopt when they say "present company excepted" after proclaiming that all men are pigs or something like that. I smiled and pushed the conversation into a less irritating direction.

I couldn't get his comments out of my head, though, as they felt so unjust. Perhaps some of my colleagues have become masters of marketing, but almost every veterinarian I have ever worked with has had problems recommending enough tests and procedures, not problems recommending too many. The profession attracts sensitive people, and sensitive people feel bad when somebody is upset by anything, including a bill. I swear that one client complaining about the costs has a ripple effect on what you recommend for the next ten clients, or more. This is aided by the fact that there is a big grey zone when it comes to which tests, procedures and treatments to recommend. On one end of the spectrum there are the things that are absolutely essential minimums for a given case, and every vet recommends those, and at the other end of the spectrum are the truly unnecessary things that very few vets recommend, but in between are a multitude of judgment calls. The more you are burned by angry clients, the more you may err on the side of recommending less. We are not taught marketing in vet school, or really much of anything related to business matters at all. We can be hopelessly inept at that unpleasant part of our jobs. Calling it "marketing" makes it even worse by putting a hucksterish spin on what is necessary for the good health of our patients — we need to be comfortable trying to persuade people to act in the best interests of their pets. But it's tough.

Equally tough, and equally missing from most of our education, is the third "M": management. This is yet another thing that we sensitive pet doctors do not have a natural aptitude for. We need to be able to manage staff and most of us have got no idea how to go about doing that. Some large practices have office managers who are responsible for this, but in many cases it's the veterinarians who own the practice looking after HR. Just this weekend I fielded a barrage of emails that boiled down to employees gossiping about each other and being mean.

Sigh.

For years my management philosophy could be boiled down to "be nice." I figured that, if I was nice to the employees, this would set the tone and then they'd be nice to each other and general happiness and good times would ensue. No such luck. Somebody is always measuring the niceness and calculating who is getting more and who is getting less and who is deserving more and who is deserving less.

Sigh.

Consequently, I am trying harder to leaven the "be nice" with a little more "be strict" and "be tough." Ironically, my kids consider me a strict parent, so it should be in me somewhere to be able to pull it off. Employees are not children, though, so what is effective at home will not necessarily be effective when applied to 20 adults with widely ranging personalities interacting in a complex and stressful work environment.

But I am not discouraged. OK, I'm a little bit discouraged after this weekend, but only a little bit. I flatter myself that I am a true Doctor of Veterinary Medicine and I will continue to work on becoming a better Doctor of Veterinary Management. For better or worse, however, I think I will always be a poor Doctor of Veterinary Marketing.

COLONOSCOPY AND LIVER TREATS

I'm sure you're wondering how colonoscopy and liver treats relate to each other, and if you've formulated a guess, I can almost guarantee you that it's wrong.

Let's start with the liver treats. I've written before about how the rapid advancements in medical science and in the role of veterinary technologists have dramatically changed veterinary practice, but I'm here to tell you that nothing has had a greater impact on my day-to-day life as a small animal veterinarian than the advent of the freeze-dried liver treats.

There are all sorts of good reasons for wanting my patients to like me. It makes my job more fun, it makes my job safer and it makes my patients dread seeing me less, which in turn means that my clients are more likely to bring them in when they should. And the best way to get them to like me is with food. This is trickier with cats, where fewer than half accept treats, regardless of the quality, but with dogs, if you have the right treat, 90% will take it and ask for more. We used to have terrible treats. They were the veterinary equivalent of the pediatrician handing out sticks of broccoli as a reward to the children coming to her office. Some dogs didn't care, but enough did that we decided to try to find something else. Something else that was at least respectably healthy. Fresh bacon would have been popular too, but obviously there would have been issues with that. Enter the freeze-dried liver treat. They are literally little chunks of dry liver. If you look carefully you can see the veins and stuff. I don't recommend you do. Dogs act as if they've just seen the face of God the first time they are given one of these. Dogs don't just like me now, they love me. I hand them out when I come into the room, I hand them out as I do things like injections and, most importantly, I hand them out at the end of the visit.

Why "most importantly"? This is where colonoscopy comes in. Bear with me. In 1996 the Nobel Prize–winning behavioural psychologist Daniel Kahneman and his colleague Ziv Carmon demonstrated what is called the "peak-end rule" using colonoscopy as an example. This rule states that people (and presumably animals) judge the quality of a remembered experience primarily by its peak, or most intense moment, and by how it ends, rather than by an aggregate or average of the entire experience.

To demonstrate this, they divided human colonoscopy patients into two groups. The first group was subjected to the standard colonoscopy experience. The second group was given the identical colonoscopy with one key difference — at the end of the procedure, the tip of the colonoscope was allowed to linger for three minutes longer and then slowly withdrawn. The second group subjectively evaluated their experience as significantly less unpleasant, even though it lasted longer. More colonoscopy was actually preferred! Why? It was less unpleasant because although the peak of the experience was the same, the end was better. Apparently, leaving the scope to sit for a few minutes felt better than having it jostling around right up to the end. This has practical implications because the patients in the second group were more likely to agree to subsequent colonoscopies when recommended. (Incidentally, this experiment also begs important questions about sedation protocols wherever this was done, but never mind.)

So, gentle readers, this is why the little mints and chocolates at the end of a restaurant meal are so important. Tips apparently increase on average by 14% when these are given. You may not even be conscious of it, but your feelings about the meal are most heavily influenced by the peak (the most memorable moment) and by the last part. Just like a colonoscopy. And I'm betting Rover feels the same way about his visit to my clinic. Even if he doesn't remember for next time, at least he's happier for that moment. That's worth something too.

TWO HOLES

My education at the Western College of Veterinary Medicine in Saskatoon was marvellous. The amount of knowledge that was imparted in those four years was far beyond what I thought could be possible. The average human brain is about 1.2 litres in volume, or two and a half tall cans of beer. *How does it all fit?* All that histology, pathology, embryology, anatomy, physiology, pharmacology, microbiology, immunology, dermatology, ophthalmology, surgery, oncology, cardiology, internal medicine, anaesthesiology, critical care, neurology, exotics, gastroenterology . . . need I go on? You get the idea. It makes no sense. I can only assume that a bunch of other stuff gets pitched. Come to think of it, there are some pretty long blank periods in my memory from my late teens and early twenties before vet school. Given what one does at that age, though, there may be other reasons for those blanks.

In any case, we learned an astonishing amount, but of course it is not possible to teach everything, so there were some gaps. I've mentioned elsewhere that there was no education whatsoever regarding business management, despite the fact that vet clinics — whether we like it or not (the answer is not) — are in fact small businesses.

And our entire dental education consisted of one lecture given by a surgeon who clearly thought it was beneath him to be forced by administration to talk about — shudder — teeth, despite the fact that dentistry is a major part of small animal practice. But business and dentistry were known gaps. We knew that if we were interested, upon graduation we'd have to seek training in these areas on our own. Fine, no problem. The real problem was with the unknown gaps that lay in wait for us like well-concealed landmines. I stepped on my first such landmine within a couple weeks of graduation.

A curious feature of the veterinary emergency clinics in Winnipeg in the 1990s was that they were partly, or sometimes mostly, staffed by new graduates. This was curious because it is in an emergency setting that you most need to rely on experience and instinct. There is often no time to look something up or check with a colleague. In fact late at night you were often on your own anyway, so the latter wasn't even an option. The problem was that it was very difficult to persuade experienced vets to work those kinds of hours when there were plenty of regular day jobs available to them. For a new graduate, however, it was an excellent way to get a lot of experience quickly. Also, it paid far better than a regular job, so you could rapidly dispose of your student loans. The analogy of learning to swim by jumping directly into the deep end comes to mind. And in fact, there were some drownings. The schedule was littered with the names of young veterinarians who worked one or two shifts and then said, "No way."

Me? I learned to dog paddle after a few dozen shifts and then refused any others, once I had steady daytime work and the financial situation was no longer as dire.

One of my early emergency shifts was on a Saturday afternoon when the senior veterinarian was also on duty. Let's call him Dave because, well, that was his name and I don't think he'll mind. I had already worked one harrowing night shift on my own, so I was really pleased to have the back-up.

The technician came up to me with a clipboard and said, "Philipp, can you go into room 2? There's a lady in there with her little dog who has a history of bleeding from the bum."

"Sure, I'll be right there." I was relieved. I assumed the blood would be connected to an intestinal issue and I had enjoyed gastroenterology in school. Perhaps it was hemorrhagic gastroenteritis? I had not seen a case yet, but I could clearly picture the relevant page in the internal medicine textbook. I have a visual memory, sometimes even photographic.

The little Maltese was named Sandy. (Aside: why do white dogs seem to especially like to bleed?) The owner, a middle-aged woman with expensive-looking hair and long, lacquered red nails was clearly distressed. I assumed my most reassuring doctor manner, which was tricky because I looked like I was 14 years old, and lifted Sandy's tail. The owner looked away. Sandy's entire hind end was red. I soaked a stack of gauze sponges with peroxide and began to clean the blood away. Slowly a shocking picture began to emerge from the mess. Sandy had two holes! One was presumably the anus, but the other . . . ? A second anus? No, ridiculous idea Schott! What about those perianal fistulas we learned about in soft tissue surgery? But I thought they were mostly just in German shepherds. I was flummoxed.

"What's wrong with Sandy, Doctor? Is it serious?" the owner asked. I realized that I had been staring at the dog's anus for a long time without saying anything, which was probably beginning to alarm her.

"Ah yes, well, it is complicated," I began, and then seeing her eyes widen with fear, "but don't worry! It's certainly not serious!" (Was this true?) "I'm going to consult with my colleague, and we'll have a plan to fix up Sandy right away! Don't worry!"

She looked very worried.

I backed out of the room, smiling and nodding like a fool, and then as soon as I closed the door behind me, I turned around and sprinted down the hall to find Dave.

"What's up?" he inquired.

"Dave, this little dog has . . . I don't know, but it looks like it has two anuses!" (Or would that be ani? I'm not too sure. Fortunately there is usually little need to pluralize anus.)

To his credit, Dave neither burst out laughing, nor did he fire me on the spot. Instead he smiled and asked me to explain exactly what I had found. Once I had done so he chuckled, "Philipp, that is a ruptured anal gland abscess. Treat it like any other abscess anywhere else and you'll be fine."

Anal gland abscess? Anal glands (or more technically accurate, anal sacs) had been a gap in our education. The dermatology instructor assumed internal medicine would cover it, and vice versa. Moreover, my only pet equipped with these glands, our cat Mook, never had trouble with them, so I was barely even aware they existed, let alone that they could become impacted, become infected or abscess. I had no idea.

More such landmines were discovered in the coming months and even years, but none as embarrassing as the dog with the two holes.

BUSY NIGHT

I heard it again the other day. I hadn't heard it in several years. I was at a small business office when the telephone behind the reception desk rang. My stomach clenched, my heart began to race and my palms became sweaty. I wondered if the receptionist noticed anything. You see, that office still had an old Nortel business telephone, the kind that was ubiquitous in veterinary clinics the 1980s and '90s. Those Nortel sets had a distinctive ringtone that inhabits my nightmares to this day.

To understand why, I have to take you back to the months after I graduated from veterinary school in 1990.

As I have mentioned before, in those early days I worked some emergency shifts to make money and gain experience. There were two emergency clinics back then. Dave's clinic was in the previous story and it was the larger and more sophisticated of the two. The other was smaller and usually quieter, which was a good thing for a new graduate, but it also had some distinct disadvantages. One was that you slept on a couch in the staff lounge. The other was that there was no telephone or intercom at the front door. Late night arrivals just rang the buzzer or pounded on the door.

On the night in question I had just done the 2:00 a.m. treatments for the one patient we had staying overnight, Bilbo, a friendly diabetic cat. His next treatment wasn't scheduled until 6:00 a.m., so there was an opportunity to try to get a little sleep. The phone very rarely rang after midnight. If you think about it, who's paying attention to their pet's medical needs at that hour of the night?

Who indeed.

I zipped myself into my sleeping bag — made necessary by all the dog hair on the couch and the fact that the air conditioning was always set to frigid — and closed my eyes. I was asleep in minutes.

The phone's ringer was at the loudest setting possible. During the day this made sense, as there is so much competing noise. At night it is a sonic drill to the centre of your brain. And when you're asleep, it's a sonic drill to the centre of your dream. I don't recall what I was dreaming about, but the phone ringing became a fire alarm in my dream. I woke up in a panic and tried to leap out of bed. I tried. I was zipped up in my sleeping bag, so I thrashed about and then rolled off the couch, hitting the floor with a thud like a giant fish landing on a trawler's deck.

It was the phone, not the fire alarm. And the phone was still ringing. It was somehow even louder now.

The zipper was stuck, so I wriggled out of the sleeping bag, stood up and stumbled to the phone, glancing at the red LEDs of the clock radio as I did so. 3:10 a.m.

I steadied myself, took a couple deep breaths, and picked up the phone, "Hello, Dr. Schott speaking. How may I help you?"

"Hi, yeah, thanks." It was a young man's voice. He sounded remarkably crisp for 3:10 in the morning. "So, my dog, Bernie, he needs these eye drops four times a day, and I give them six and six and noon and midnight."

"OK."

"But I was out late and just got home, so I don't know if I should give the drops now or skip them, or if I do give them now whether I should give the 6 a.m. ones later, or if . . ."

He was probably still talking, but my brain was making dead car battery sounds.

Then a hellish noise erupted from the front of the clinic. Someone was pressing the buzzer repeatedly, hammering on the glass, and yelling.

"I'm sorry, sir, but I'm going to have to put you on hold for a moment." I stared at the function buttons beside the keypad. This should have been the easiest part of the night, but somehow it wasn't. Little stickers marked the purpose of each of the buttons and the ink had faded. I guessed which one was the hold button.

I guessed wrong.

A dial tone followed.

I didn't have time to worry about this because the noise from the front had gotten even louder. I was worried that they, whoever they were, were going to break the glass. I jammed my arms into the sleeves of my lab coat, grabbed a stethoscope and sprinted to the lobby.

The phone began ringing again.

Two young women were standing at the door and both were yelling. One was hitting the door with her fists.

I ignored the phone and opened the door.

"I broke him!" the shorter one wailed. She was in high heels, fishnet stockings, a black miniskirt and a sheer blouse. It looked like she had her hands in a black hand-warmer muff, but that turned out to be a small Pomeranian. The taller girl was similarly dressed.

"Oh dear," was all I could muster.

"Are you the doctor?" the taller girl demanded. She was chewing gum and kept making loud smacking sounds as she stared at me.

"Yes, I'm Dr. Schott. Come on in, please, and we'll see what's going on."

"You look like you're in high school," she said as they stepped past me. I was used to this. I just smiled in response. The phone was still ringing. The tall girl kept popping her chewing gum.

Hoping the phone would stop ringing, I led them into the exam room and asked the short girl to put her dog on the exam table.

"So, what's his name?"

"Brando. He's my baby, and I broke him!" She began to cry, causing her mascara to smear.

"What happened?"

"We just got home from work and I picked him up to give him a hug and then my pager went off and I dropped him!" She was crying loudly now.

I looked at Brando. It was hard to see his legs because he was so fluffy, but I could tell he was standing on three legs with his right hind leg held up. He was tiny, perhaps four pounds at the most. It was certainly possible that he had broken his leg. I stepped towards him. He gave me a look that said, "I don't know you, but I know your type and I don't like your type." He began to growl. He looked like a malevolent black powder puff.

The phone was still ringing in the other room.

The short girl was still crying.

The tall girl was still chewing gum and staring at me with a look that said, "I don't know you, but I know your type and I don't like your type."

"I think I'll need to put a muzzle on the little guy, just so that everybody's safe!" I said in a ridiculous sing-song voice.

The tall girl snorted and rolled her eyes. The short girl kept crying.

The muzzling went better than I had feared it might and, to my immense relief, I was quickly able to determine that Brando had not broken his leg. Rather, he had locked his kneecap out of joint. Small dogs, especially Pomeranians, commonly have what is called a luxating patella, or loose kneecap. Usually it just pops in at and out on its own without giving the dog much trouble, but in rare cases it can lock out of joint, especially if the dog is tense. And Brando was tense. Very tense.

I explained what was going on and with a simple, painless manoeuvre was able to put the kneecap back in place. I was proud of myself. From zero to hero in 30 seconds.

"That's all? Are you really sure?" the tall girl asked. "What's this going to cost her?"

Nope, still a zero.

"It doesn't matter," the other one said. "My baby's all better!" She scooped Brando back up and gave him a hug before handing him to her friend.

Brando glared at me.

Her friend glared at me.

The phone was still ringing.

I told her what the cost of the exam was, plus the after-midnight charge (to which the tall girl muttered "fucking rip-off"). Brando's owner was flustered and emptied her tiny clutch purse onto the counter, spilling out a large roll of twenties, lipstick, condoms and a pager. She peeled off the required amount and waved away the change I offered her.

After they left, I sat and rubbed my face for a long moment before picking up the phone.

"Busy night? So, like I was saying, Bernie gets these drops and I should mention he also has this skin condition that I give him pills for, but the vet said that wouldn't interfere with the drops, but anyway his eye is looking a bit better, but I feel bad about missing that midnight dose, so I want to know what to do about that, and I while I've got you on the phone I do have some more questions about the skin, and . . ."

While he was talking, I found the ringer volume dial.

"I'm sorry, sir, I'm going to have to put you on hold again."

A PRIEST, A RABBI AND A VET
WALK INTO A BAR

No, it's not a joke. Sorry to mislead you. Instead, I'm setting you up for a discussion of correlation versus causation. Isn't that a lot more fun anyway? Don't answer that.

Of all the many aspects of medicine — veterinary or human — that befuddle and mislead people, one of the most important is the confusion that arises when two or more things happen at the same time but are not caused by each other. They are coincidences. But people don't trust the concept of coincidence. It sounds suspicious. It sounds like a dodge.

For example, let's say you watch a priest, a rabbi and a vet walk into a bar. You're a detective and you're sitting in your car outside, trying to look nonchalant. You've heard that the vet might be mixed up in some shady stuff, so you're trailing him. (Just to be clear, this is pure fiction.) A half hour later the priest and the rabbi burst out of the bar and jog to the curb. The priest immediately hails a passing cab, and they're gone in a flash. You wait for the vet to emerge, but he doesn't. Normally you would go into the bar to check the situation out, but you're not welcome in there and, in any case, you're worried the vet would recognize you. After a couple of hours he still hasn't emerged, so you take a chance and poke your head inside. No vet. The barman tells you to take off and claims not to know anything about the vet. He must have given you the slip and snuck out the back. The next morning you read in the news that the vet was found dead in the washroom of the bar. The cause of death was listed as unknown, pending autopsy. You immediately pick up the phone and call your contact at the police. You know what happened — the priest and the rabbi did it.

What do you think? Are you right about the priest and the rabbi? There certainly is a correlation and there are lots of reasons to be suspicious. Unfortunately for your detective career, though, the autopsy report comes back showing that the vet had a heart attack. And questioning of the priest and rabbi revealed that they hurried out before anything happened to the vet, because they had gotten so engrossed in telling the vet funny pet stories that they lost track of time and almost missed a special interfaith charity poker tournament they were supposed to host.

Nice story, Philipp, but what does this have to do with veterinary medicine? Everything. That's what. Let's say the bar is your pet's body and three things happen at the same time, like a new bag of food (the priest), a vaccination (the rabbi) and sudden blindness (the dead vet), to pick a perfectly random example. Some people will jump to the conclusion that the food or the vaccine caused the blindness, even though there is no mechanism to explain either. Blindness probably seems like an obvious coincidence to you, but what about if the dead vet represents diarrhea instead? A new bag of food or a vaccine could conceivably cause diarrhea (especially the food), but does this prove it? Nope. It's just a correlation, nothing more. Diarrhea has hundreds of causes and coincidences happen all the time. We usually need the equivalent of an autopsy, in other words some tests, to prove causation.

Thank you for wading through that. Make sense? It's a really important concept. Correlation is not necessarily causation. Sometimes it is, but often it isn't. As a reward, here are two real animal-related "walks into a bar" jokes:

> A man walks into a bar and says to the bartender, "Hey, will you give me a free beer if I show you something so incredible that I promise you've never even imagined it could be possible?"

The bartender says, "Yeah, sure, but it had better be pretty damned incredible."

The man reaches into his jacket and pulls out a hamster. He puts the hamster on the bar. It runs to the end of the bar, jumps high in the air, turns a perfect triple-axel, and then lands on the piano. The hamster dances across the keys, playing Mozart's "Eine kleine Nachtmusik" like a trained concert pianist. The bartender says, "Wow! That really was incredible! Here's your beer!"

The man drinks his beer and, when he's done, says, "Can I have another free beer if I show you something else, just as incredible, which I know you've never ever seen or imagined before?"

"If it's as amazing as that hamster, then absolutely!"

So, the man reaches into his jacket again and this time pulls out a small green frog. He puts the frog down on the bar, and it immediately begins to sing "My Heart Will Go On." His voice is beautiful. A crowd of astonished people gather.

When the frog is finished, one of the onlookers says, "That was phenomenal! I'll give you $1,000 for that frog."

The first man says, "A grand? It's a deal!" and sells the guy his frog. The bartender shakes his head as he's giving the man his second free beer and says, "It's not any of my business, buddy, but that was one-of-a-kind singing frog. Why would you sell him for only $1,000? He could have earned you millions!"

The man replies, "Ha! Don't worry. The hamster's a pianist and a ventriloquist."

And the second one:

A horse walks into a bar and the bartender asks, "Why the long face?" The horse does not reply because it is a horse. It cannot speak English and only understands simple equestrian commands. It becomes very confused and upset by all the noise in the room and starts to gallop around the bar, knocking over tables and chairs, smashing glasses, until it finally finds its way back out.

THANK YOU FOR SAYING THANK YOU

Dear Client,

It may not always seem that way when I'm in my confident professional mode, but I can be socially awkward at times. Sometimes I don't have a good instinctive grasp of the social norms. My kids are on the autism spectrum, so perhaps I have a little touch of that as well. The one social norm that continues to confuse me is whether one ever says thank you for being thanked. Taken to an extreme, this could obviously spiral out of control.

"Thank you!"

"Thank you for saying thank you!"

"Well, thank you for saying thank you to my thank you . . ."

Ridiculous, right? Best nipped in the bud after that first thank you. But that doesn't sit entirely right with me either. This is why I am writing this open letter. To all of you who have sent me thank-you cards, and thank-you emails, and bottles of wine, and cookies or chocolates, and framed photographs of your pets, and other tokens of gratitude — to all of you I say a very sincere and heartfelt thank you. I am thanking you for thanking me. If this is socially inappropriate, so be it. It's how I feel.

If you, the reader of this letter, have sent me one of those cards, you should know that I have kept it, no matter how long ago you sent it. I have kept all of them. I have a large drawer full of thank-you cards. One day I will count them, but there are hundreds and hundreds. Sometimes when I'm feeling down about work, I'll just pull that drawer open and look at them all stacked in there and I will feel better. Occasionally I'll even pull an old one out and reread it, even though this will sometimes be bittersweet: people usually send me a thank-you card after I have put a pet to sleep, although I know that they are not thanking me specifically for that service, but rather for the care throughout their pet's life. But the sweet far outweighs the bitter. Time does heal many (although perhaps not all) wounds, and as time goes on I will mostly smile at the memory of your pet and I will think about the relationship you and I have as people. As I have often said, veterinary medicine is not an animal business that happens to involve people, but rather it is a people business that happens to involve animals. And it is people like you who keep me in it.

Veterinarians are often sensitive people. It is a highly complex job, which means that things sometimes do not go as planned, so criticism, disappointment, annoyance and even anger from clients is inevitable. As sensitive people we take this to heart. We really take this deeply to heart, so a sharp word from an upset client can fester in our minds for a very long time. We should be able to just shrug it off, but it's not easy. The only true antidotes are our own confidence that we're doing the best we can, and the thank yous from clients like you that remind us that what we do is actually appreciated by so many people. If only the patients could express their gratitude as well it would be perfect, but the fact that you did so is good enough.

So, thank you for saying thank you. You have no idea how much it means to me.

Sincerely,
Dr. Philipp Schott, BSc, DVM

P.S. Please do not feel bad if you're reading this and are realizing that you meant to send a thank-you card but never got around to it. Don't worry! In no way do I expect to be thanked, nor do I notice when I haven't been. And I totally get it. Even though I feel grateful for all sorts of professionals and other people who keep my life on track, I am terrible at remembering to thank them. Thanking really is such a tricky business.

EVERYTHING YOU WANTED TO KNOW ABOUT EUTHANASIA BUT WERE AFRAID TO ASK

I imagine that many people didn't make it past the title, and that's OK. This essay is not intended for everyone, but I do want to have something on the record regarding this. It's a heartbreaking subject, but it's an important one. I understand that it could be too disturbing or emotional for some readers, and that others would just rather not know. Have no fear — if you're in either category you can happily skip this piece and move forward to the next one instead.

There is a general rule that for every person who asks a question, there are ten others who have the same question but did not want to ask. I have no idea where this little bit of folk wisdom came from, but it strikes me as roughly true for many situations. When it comes to euthanasia. however, and because of the intense emotions involved, I think the ratio is closer to a hundred to one.

Here, then, are the questions I have been asked:

Does it always work?

Yes, it does. It's poignant to consider that while veterinarians spend their careers trying to save lives, the one service they provide that is absolutely guaranteed to be effective is ending life.

Why do you sedate first?

Not everyone sedates their euthanasia patients first, but I almost always do. To begin with, I want to make sure that the pet is not picking up on everyone's emotions at the end. They are often very attuned to this and can become frightened, especially in a vet office. Secondly, especially in ill patients, finding a good vein for the euthanasia injection is not always that quick. Sedation can go under the skin, but euthanasia needs to be in a solid and reliable vein. I don't want the patient to become anxious if we're taking a few moments to secure a good vein, nor do I want them to move while we're injecting the euthanasia solution.

How fast is sedation?

It varies quite a bit, but usually ten minutes or so. We wait until they are woozy and unaware. Some individuals will become fully unconscious with the sedation alone.

How does the euthanasia drug work?

We use an overdose of an injectable anaesthetic. It's in the barbiturate class, therefore similar to some sleeping pills or the anaesthetic you might have had to get your wisdom teeth out a few decades back (safer drugs are used now, you'll be pleased to hear). We use such a high dose that all parts of the brain fall asleep — first the parts that keep a patient conscious and thinking, and then the parts that control breathing and the heartbeat. Because it is an anaesthetic the sensation is like that of falling rapidly asleep.

And how fast is this?

Very fast. Once we get a vein it can go very quickly. Depending on the size of the patient it may take a few seconds to inject the entire dose, but they are always completely unconscious before the injection is even done and have often stopped breathing as well.

Why do you put alcohol on the vein?

I hadn't considered how this looked until a client asked, "Why are you sterilizing that when he's going to be dead in a minute anyway?" Good question, but I'm not sterilizing it. Alcohol helps make the vein stand out better.

Are there ever any bad reactions?

The great majority of the time everything goes smoothly. The sedation we use can sometimes briefly sting a little as it goes in, but very soon after they start to feel good. And on the odd occasion the pet can seem disoriented while the sedation is kicking in, but this passes quickly. Bad reactions to the euthanasia itself are extremely rare and usually take the form of vocalizing. This is very distressing to the owner, but the pet already has enough drug in their system that they're not really aware of what is happening, or in control of the sounds they're making. And again, it's extremely rare. They do sometimes take a couple of deep breaths at the end, though, when they're already fully unconscious.

Why don't they close their eyes?

When you die all your muscles relax, including those in your eyelids. Eyelid muscles have to contract to close. Incidentally, bowel and bladder muscles can relax too, so sometimes they will release these as they die. Pets are of course completely unaware of this.

What happens to the body now?

The crematorium doesn't pick up every day, so in most cases the body will be kept in a dedicated freezer until they come. You are probably going in a special fridge for a short while after you die, so it's really very similar.

How do I know that the ashes I get back are from my pet?

We trust the crematorium. We know the operators well and we have all had our own pets cremated there. You are also welcome to visit the facility and even take your pet's remains there yourself.

You're not going to do experiments on him now, are you?

No. The fact that I have actually been asked this more than once underlines how little some people understand about science, let alone professional ethics. Not only is the very idea repugnant, but there are honestly no useful "experiments" that can be done in this scenario.

Can I donate his body to science?

In rare instances, maybe. Every now and then there's an odd case where we might learn something from the results of an autopsy. While this is not really "donating his body to science," it's the same kind of idea. We would never do so without asking permission first, though. As we often feel too awkward to ask, autopsies usually only get done when a client suggests it themselves.

Do you ever get used to having to euthanize people's pets?

No. Never. My heart breaks a little every time.

LOVE

"I've been spending the nights with him on the living room floor, where he has his favourite blanket. I keep worrying he's going to stop breathing, so I'm not sleeping much. I know his time is coming soon. I didn't want to bring him today because I'm so worried you're going to say I have

to put him down." Mrs. Gagnon's eyes were red rimmed, and her voice trembled as she said this.

I looked down at Edwin, an elderly, black cocker spaniel. He was wheezing a bit, but at first glance he did not appear to be on his last legs. I crouched on the floor and offered him a liver treat, which he happily took, wagging his little stubby tail. As I dug around in the treat jar to get another one, I thought about Mr. Wilson, who had taken the day off work to sit with his cat Parsnip while he was being treated for complications from diabetes. Parsnip would be in all day and Mr. Wilson would be there the whole day too, reading a little, patting Parsnip and generally just being there with him. I thought about Mr. Wilson because Mrs. Gagnon reminded me of him. She reminded me of him because they were both here for the same reason: love.

I am in a very privileged profession. What other professionals are you primarily motivated to visit because of love? Family doctor? No. Lawyer? Ha. Accountant? Double ha. Dentist? Triple ha. The list goes on. In fact, the only other similar profession I can think of is pediatrics. I have often joked with my kids' pediatrician that I practise furry, four-legged pediatrics, or he practises hairless, two-legged veterinary medicine. For sure many veterinary clients (and parents of children?) are also motivated by a sense of duty, a desire to do the right thing or even feelings of guilt, but the basic driver is usually love.

This is where the conversation can become awkward around people who don't have pets. Love? Really? Isn't that a bit overblown? Too sentimental? A sign that they are lacking human love? No, no and no. Forgive me if I am, as the saying goes, preaching to the choir, but the following is for the benefit of the occasional non-pet owner (can I call them Muggles?) who stumbles on this book and thinks, *WTF*.

Part of the problem is language. English is a wonderful, rich and expressive language, but it has some gaps. We have an exhaustive list of words to choose from when it comes to describing and naming objects, but rather fewer when it comes to relationships and emotions. Think, for example, about the word "uncle." In English this can describe your parent's brother, or it can describe the random dude your parent's sister was briefly married to. It can even sometimes describe an older male family friend. There are many languages that have distinct titles for each of these but may not have separate words for all the different kinds of car shapes or shoe styles or couch configurations that we do. I'll let you draw your own conclusions regarding what this says about our culture.

In any case, so it is with the word love. There should be more words to describe all the kinds of love. Does your love for your parents feel the same as the love you feel for your spouse? Or your children? Or your siblings or best friends? They are all closely related emotions, but they are not the exact same. So it is with the love many people feel for their pets. If we're stuck with this one word, "love," then it has to be big and it has to be inclusive. Comparisons between the different flavours of love are not useful. Sure, in a *Sophie's Choice* nightmare scenario all of you would choose to save your child at the price of losing your dog or cat (or almost all of you . . . most of the time . . .), but that is never a real-life choice.

With respect to it being sentimental, yeah, I suppose it can be. So what? Isn't the appreciation of much of what makes life worth living often somewhat sentimental? Good music, movies, art and literature all make use of emotional responses to draw you in and involve you. Loving and appreciating the company of a pet is broadly similar. Can you imagine a world where sentiment was banished, and everything had to be cold and practical?

And as to the love people feel for their animals indicating the need to fill a void, this has been amply proven false for the majority of cases. There certainly are many lonely people who find solace in the company of their pets, but pet owners represent the widest cross-section of society, including many of the most gregarious and outgoing "people people." In fact, my experience has been that the more capacity a person has to love an animal, the more capacity they often have to love people too.

Both Edwin and Parsnip did OK. I won't say that it was the power of love that made them better, but it certainly didn't hurt.

> "We can judge the heart of a man by his treatment of animals."
>
> — *Emmanuel Kant*

PART FOUR

OTHER BEASTS

THE SECOND DUCK

I have seen two ducks in my career and both ducks merit stories. That's a story-to-patient ratio of 1:1, which puts ducks ahead of all the other species I have had the pleasure of seeing more than once. That's how cool ducks are. I suspect that goats would also generate a high story-to-patient ratio, but sadly my career path has taken me well away from goats. More's the pity.

The first duck was named Puddles, a white farm duck who waddled into the clinic (with his owner) for regular check-ups. His story was in my last collection and it remains one of the most popular. As I said, ducks are cool. This second duck was named Jake, and he was in many ways the opposite of Puddles. While Puddles was supremely relaxed in the clinic, Jake was terrified. While Puddles was surprisingly large, Jake was surprisingly small. And while Puddles was pure, plain white, Jake's feathers were all the shimmering dark green of a mallard's head, and his bill and feet were jet black. Jake was an East Indies duck and he was stunning to behold. I had never seen such a beautiful duck. In fact, I had never imagined such a beautiful duck could exist.

Jake's owner, Mr. Bolton, was a quiet, polite man about my age. He seemed every bit the average suburban dad, right from the way he dressed (t-shirt, jeans) to what he drove (minivan), until you found out that he had a duck fetish. And I mean fetish in a wholesome way, not in some sexual way. While other suburban dads tended to their lush backyard lawns or their patio barbecue set-ups, Mr. Bolton had apparently turned his entire backyard into an elaborate duck habitat. He showed me pictures. These ducks had it good. As Jake's appearance suggested, these were not just any ducks, these were "fancy ducks." And I mean "fancy" in the technical sense, and not just "deluxe" or "elegant." There is, apparently, a whole subculture of duck fanciers out there, as there are guinea pig fanciers, pigeon fanciers and goldfish fanciers, and they breed striking-looking ducks to qualify as "fancy" in the duck show world. The East Indies duck turns out to have nothing to do with the actual geographic East Indies, but was rather was an exotic name dreamed up by a past duck fancier for his exotic-looking creation. Mr. Bolton had several East Indies ducks and also a few Mandarin ducks — eye-catching purple-, teal-, orange- and cream-coloured feathered confections. These seemed excessively garish, though, beside the thoroughly posh East Indies ducks.

Mr. Bolton had brought Jake to me because the country vet he normally dealt with for his ducks was starting to come across as dismissive and unsympathetic. He apparently viewed Jake and his friends through the livestock lens rather than the pet lens, and was not interested in spending the time required for the latter approach. I don't recall who this vet was, and it's entirely possible that Mr. Bolton's assessment was unfair and that he was perhaps being overly sensitive to something the vet said, but regardless, Mr. Bolton wanted to try a pet vet. The fact that I had only seen one duck before didn't phase him.

After the initial introductions and greetings, I asked Mr. Bolton what his concern with Jake was. Jake was an anxious duck, so he was in a crate on the floor beside his owner, only his dark green head and shining little black eyes visible.

"It's his penis."

It was becoming a little clearer why Mr. Bolton didn't want to see the country vet about this.

"Oh? What's wrong with it?"

"Jake's a great breeder. Very enthusiastic. I think he injured it because it's really swollen and won't go back in."

Sometimes my job is boring and routine, and sometimes it isn't, and when it isn't it can take some truly odd turns.

"OK, well, let's have a look."

Mr. Bolton crouched down, opened the crate and very gingerly lifted Jake out, all the while making soft cooing noises. Jake was even more spectacular up close and in person (in duck?) than I had anticipated from the photos. The way the light caught those gleaming emerald feathers was breathtaking, especially contrasted with his jet-black bill, eyes and feet. Those were not the only black parts. His penis was black, too, and it was hanging down, like a morose little sausage. Normally their penises are corkscrew-shaped (no, I'm not making this up), but the swelling had eliminated the twists.

"Oh my" was the best I could muster. I got a light and a magnifier and had a closer look. Jake was very quiet and didn't struggle, but he was also very tense. Not surprising, I suppose. A swollen black duck penis is probably gross enough for most readers, so I won't describe it in more detail, but suffice to say that after careful inspection of said swollen black duck penis I concluded that poor Jake was suffering from balanitis, which is an infection of the penis. "I think it's infected," I told Mr. Bolton, "but honestly I don't know much about this, so let me double check the literature before we decide on a plan."

I excused myself from the exam room and went into the office, where I logged on to the Veterinary Information Network, a subscription service that has an absolutely massive database of opinion, data and case reports on every conceivable veterinary scenario. I typed "duck balanitis" into the search bar. Zero hits. Apparently, this was not a conceivable veterinary scenario. I then went to Google. This was a bad idea. I'm so naïve. In any case, I do not recommend you use it for any duck penis–related searches. So, I resorted to a fundamental veterinary tool — extrapolation. If this were a dog, I would use antibiotics and anti-inflammatories and advise the owner on regular gentle cleaning at home. I thought there might be a wacky duck-specific angle to consider, but if there was, I had no way of knowing.

A week later Mr. Bolton phoned to let me know that the penis was still enlarged and protruding, but perhaps less so, and Jake seemed happier. I asked him to call again in another week, as by that point the meds would be finished. He did, and the report was the same — some improvement, but not cured. I decided to try a different antibiotic and I re-crossed my fingers. Over the following weeks we went through several rounds of this and the answer was always the same. Eventually Mr. Bolton and I agreed that management of Jake's balanitis was the best we could hope for. A cure seemed out of reach. Evidently there was some unknowable, wacky, duck-specific angle at play after all. The ultimate solution would have been a phallectomy. I'll let you work out for yourself what that means. Nobody, including Jake, one presumes, thought that that was a good idea. He could no longer be Jake the Drake, stud duck extraordinaire, but he was reasonably happy for the rest of his days. Sometimes reasonably happy is the best we can hope for. Actually, often it is the best we can hope for.

BEE MED

One of the most fascinating aspects of this profession is the range of creatures veterinarians treat. I have cared for animals as small as a hummingbird and as large as a bull moose, although I will confess that both were while I was still in vet school. In my own pet practice, the range is somewhat more restricted, let's say from mice to mastiffs. But my colleagues out there will attend to the full spectrum, from bees to whales. Whales, OK, you can probably picture that. Sort of. But bees? Surely, I must be exaggerating or joking. I am not.

I am aware of at least three conferences this year that featured sessions on honey bee medicine. The Honey Bee Veterinary Consortium now has 345 American veterinarians listed in its database and there is also a British Bee Veterinary Association with a cool website (britishbeevets .com), as well as a Veterinary Invertebrate Society. The latter appears to be more focused on spiders and lobsters, but it is certainly interested in anything which creepeth or crawleth or buzzeth.

OK, you can get the obvious jokes out of the way now. You must have a very tiny x-ray machine! It must be hard to give it a pill without getting stung! How do you take its temperature?! Ha ha. Nope, nope and nope. Bee medicine is like the medicine of many other food-producing animals and is directed towards diagnosis and treatment of large groups rather than individuals. Dead bees are tested and then, if appropriate, something is prescribed for the entire swarm.

What has changed recently and made this something more than an obscure reference buried deep in the veterinary literature is a change in the laws governing antibiotics. In the past couple of years, the regulatory authorities in both the US and Canada have begun to require a veterinary prescription for most antibiotic use in bees. And a veterinary prescription requires a valid "veterinarian–client–patient" relationship. Yes, the vet will have to have a relationship with the bee (bees). They will have to see them and make a diagnosis before anything is prescribed. This is because beekeepers were in the past able to buy the antibiotics over the counter; misuse, largely due to lack of knowledge and training rather than actual negligence, has led to antibiotic resistance and residues appearing in the honey.

So now vets will have to learn about "varroa mites" and "acarine mites" and "nosema fungus" and "small hive beetles" and "Israeli acute paralysis virus" and "black queen cell virus" and the wonderfully medieval-sounding "chalkbrood" and "foulbrood," among many other bee ailments.

Foulbrood, a highly infectious bacterial disease that kills bee larvae, now affects about 25% of hives in Canada and is the main reason for antibiotic use. With correct diagnosis and careful prescription of appropriate antibiotics at the appropriate doses and times, this can be managed better than it has been in the past. Veterinarians to the rescue! Other veterinarians, though — I'll stick to my mice and my mastiffs, and most of what's in between.

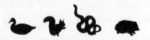

THE LIFE AND TIMES OF HANK RAMIREZ

Hank Ramirez lived a long, full life punctuated by adventure and surrounded by love. Given the relative nature of time and how subjectively its speed of passage is felt, I'm sure that in his admittedly minuscule mind he lived the equivalent of 100 human years. We don't know where or exactly when he was born and we don't know who his parents were, but every aspect of his subsequent life was lavishly documented by his companion and guardian, a ten-year-old girl. It is astonishing that something weighing only 45 grams could live such a rich life. And it is perhaps astonishing to some that something weighing only 45 grams could be loved so deeply and loved so truly.

Hank Ramirez was a teddy bear hamster.

His full name was actually Hank Ramirez Penner, as he was owned by the precocious Chloe Penner. I say precocious because the first time she brought Hank Ramirez in she was in the exam room by herself. Her parents had decided that as he was Chloe's hamster she should be fully in charge of his medical care, so they sat out in the waiting room. (I think they still paid the bills, though.) To be frank, sometimes this type of arrangement is irritating to the veterinarian as it can effectively double some of our work when we have to repeat everything to the parents later. But not in Chloe's case. She was attentive and sharp and clearly capable of following my advice. Such as it was. Really, she was fully on top of things, so on that first visit when Hank Ramirez was brought in for a check-up, my role was primarily to confirm for her that she was doing everything correctly. She showed me pictures of his cage, from which sprouted an elaborate network of clear plastic pipes leading to various chambers, including, if memory serves, one made to look like a little space capsule. Hank Ramirez was going to have a good life.

At this point I should offer up a confession. I love all types of patients. I do not favour dogs over cats (or vice versa), or rabbits over guinea pigs, or budgies over canaries, nor do I shy away from snakes or rats or hedgehogs or ferrets, to name just a few that sometimes elicit bias. But I was long a secret hamster skeptic. It's funny because my wife had hamsters when she was young whereas I had a gerbil, so we would sometimes engage in spirited hamster versus gerbil debates. I felt I had solid facts on my side. And I had been bitten by more hamsters than all other rodent species put together, so that might have biased me a little as well. But then Hank Ramirez came along. He did not bite. He was clean. And he was cool. This was a hamster I actually looked forward to seeing.

Normally hamsters do not go to the vet. There are no vaccines for them, and we do not need (or even want) to spay or neuter them. Moreover, they are really pretty rugged, so not all that much tends to go wrong in their short lives. But perhaps the most common reason that they don't go to the vet is that unfortunately many people view spending money on their medical care as silly, putting them more in the goldfish category of pet than in the dog and cat category. I wonder why this is. Is it because hamsters are cheap to acquire? But then so are many dogs and cats (and heck, human children come into the world free). Is it because they are so small? If so, then does that mean that Great Danes deserve more care than Chihuahuas? Is it because of that *Simpsons* episode where the buff veterinarian (accurate) tries to a revive a hamster with defibrillator paddles (inaccurate) and then, when that fails, tosses the hamster through a basketball hoop set over a wastepaper basket (inaccurate)? Or is it because they are loved less? I suppose that must be it. But that was happily not the case for Hank Ramirez.

I think I saw Hank Ramirez five times in his three years. Once for the initial visit, twice for annual check-ups and twice for medical reasons. The first of those was for what is referred to as "wet tail." "Wet tail" is a euphemism. The tail is not wet with water, it is wet with liquid poo. Much like diarrhea in every other species, "wet tail" is not a single specific disease but rather a symptom that has a range of causes. These little creatures can dehydrate quickly, so it can be serious, but fortunately Hank Ramirez revived right away when we sorted out why it was happening. Hamster tummies can be quite finnicky and although Chloe was feeding him all the right foods in the right balance, her family was guilty of sneaking him too many treats on the sly. Everybody wanted to be Hank Ramirez's best friend (or second-best friend after Chloe). A little bit of apple from time to time is great, but three people giving him a little bit of apple every day was a case of too much of a good thing.

The second time I saw him sick was when Chloe brought him in with what she thought was a tumour on his face. She was clearly really upset but trying hard to be brave. Hank Ramirez had an enormous irregularly shaped lump in his right cheek, and he had stopped eating. Hamsters are prone to cancer, but this was not a cancer. When I palpated the lump and pried his tiny mouth open to peer inside, I was as surprised by what I found as Chloe was. He had somehow filled his right cheek pouch so full of food that it had become impacted and bulged out to roughly equal the size of the rest of his head. And because he had jammed unshelled sunflower seeds in there it felt very odd and lumpy on the outside. We both knew that hamsters had large cheek pouches but had no idea that they were this large or that food could get so badly stuck in there. The solution was gratifyingly simple. I simply turned the pouch inside out like the pocket in your jeans. He was weak enough that he let me do this without anaesthetic.

I know you're expecting a sad ending, but the cheek pouch incident isn't it. Hank Ramirez bounced back yet again. Just like with wet tail. Just like when he did an EVA* from his capsule and was found three days later in the heating ducts. Just like when the Penners got a cat and the cat knocked over his cage. Eventually Father Time caught up with him and he died peacefully in his bed at the ripe old age of three and one-third years. I found this out when Chloe came in with Edna von Trapp, a new young female hamster. Edna von Trapp had an evil glint in her eye and proceeded to bite me savagely at every opportunity, thus proving, in case proof was needed, that hamsters are not interchangeable. There are a lot of stories of parents sneaking out to the pet store without telling their children to get a look-alike replacement when a hamster dies. I suspect that the child almost always knows, even if they don't let on. Sort of like a Santa or Easter Bunny scenario. And Chloe definitely would have known.

---

* Extra-vehicular activity. It's an outer-space thing.

BENJI

This is Benji's story. Benji was arguably the most unusual patient ever to come to Birchwood — more unusual than the giant Burmese pythons and more unusual than the deadly poisonous fish. This kind of ranking is very subjective, of course, but in my opinion Benji comes out on top. Benji was an African lion. He was a cub, mind you, but an African lion nonetheless.

Benji came to Birchwood well before my time, so it is not technically "my story," but it's the clinic's story and it's my clinic, so I'm going to claim it.

Dr. Al Clark, the founder of clinic, doesn't remember exactly when this happened, but the mid-1960s is likely. One morning he got a call from the Hudson's Bay Company downtown. It seems that Sunbeam, the makers of small kitchen appliances, thought that having a live lion cub in their display would make for a nifty promotion. It was the mid '60s, so people did stuff like that. And they used words like "nifty." This three-month-old cub was in a small cage beside the stand mixers and blenders. His name was Benji and he was extremely cute. Whether this helped sales or not is unknown, but it certainly attracted attention. The Bay was on the phone because Benji had become ill. Could

Dr. Clark help them out? It was basically just a big house cat, wasn't it? Same diseases and disorders?

Al immediately did two things. The first thing was that he told them to bring Benji right down. The second thing was that he found the phone number for the top Sunbeam executive in Toronto and gave him heck for subjecting a lion cub to that kind of stress and absurdly inadequate housing. Once Benji arrived at the hospital, Al declared that he would have to stay and would not be sent back to sell toasters and electric can openers. Benji was basically depressed and poorly cared for, and had picked up a secondary opportunistic infection. Chastened, there was no argument from Sunbeam or the Bay.

The nurses then set about pampering Benji back to robust health. Initially, they went down to the Dairy Queen at Ronald and Portage every day and brought back hamburgers for him. Then it occurred to someone to phone the zoo and ask for advice. With his diet improved and with all the medicine and care, Benji was soon on his way to a full recovery. Once he was well enough to leave the hospital, Al would sometimes take him home, and the neighbourhood kids would play with him in the yard. Can you imagine? Your neighbour is a vet and brings home a lion cub and lets you play with it? Different times . . .

After a couple of months Benji had grown from cocker spaniel size to small Labrador size and was becoming "a little nippy." Clearly, a long-term plan was needed. This had been on Al's mind for a while and he had made inquiries. The best solution seemed to be the Okanagan Game Farm, a sprawling exotic wild animal park near Penticton, British Columbia, where there were other lions and there was lots of space for Benji. It was tearful day for everyone when he was loaded into the back of a staff member's car and they headed west down Portage Avenue.

Several years later another staff member was on vacation in the Okanagan and decided on a whim to try to visit Benji. She walked up to the fence and peered out across the fields and clumps of trees. There were no animals in view. In the heat of the day the lions were probably in the shade somewhere. So, she called out, "Benji! Benji!" and wouldn't you know it, but a beautiful fully grown male lion came bounding up out of the distance and put his paws up on the fence. It was Benji.

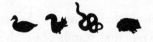

HUEY

The Assiniboine Park Zoo veterinary service has its own ultrasound machine now, but there was a time, perhaps five to ten years ago, when I would regularly field calls from one of the vets there that would go along the lines of:

"Hey, Philipp, can you ultrasound a *<insert name of strange zoo species>*?"

"Um, never done that before . . . But sure, why not?"

Of these, the one that stands out is the wolverine. The quick among you will immediately make the connection between the title of this essay and the species in question. Yes, the wolverine was named Huey because of a movie starring Hugh Jackman as a superhero whose outstanding feature was that he had somehow acquired wolverine characteristics. Forgive my ignorance regarding films based on comic books, but when I looked up the movie poster, I was unable to see any resemblance between Mr. Jackman and Huey from the zoo. Nevertheless, that's how he got his name.

Speaking of names, though, the wolverine's Latin name is *Gulo gulo*, which translates as "glutton glutton." Saying glutton once was apparently not enough. Looking at the list of his potential prey, it's easy to see how he acquired this double glutton reputation. Wolverines have been known to eat porcupines, squirrels, chipmunks, beavers, marmots, moles, gophers, rabbits, hares, voles, mice, rats, shrews, lemmings, caribou, white-tailed deer, mule deer, sheep, goats, cattle, bison, moose, elk, martens, mink, foxes, lynx, weasels, all manner of birds, and coyote and wolf pups. For dessert they have roots, seeds, insect larvae and berries. *Gulo gulo* indeed. And he was coming to my clinic.

On the appointed day the back-door bell rang, and a couple veterinary technologists sprinted to open it. Everyone was very excited that Huey was coming to visit us. I'm not sure what they had imagined, though, as they seemed a little disappointed to see that Huey was carried in soundly asleep. Something strong enough to take down a moose was not going to be managed with just a muzzle and a light sedative. Something strong enough to take down a moose was going to need to be rendered fully immobile and unconscious. The zoo vet had blow-darted him. Even in this comatose state he was still highly impressive. I don't recall his exact weight, but it was probably around 50 pounds, and stretched out flat he took up the whole length and width of the exam table. While the zoo vet and tech busied themselves with hooking up monitoring equipment and gas anaesthetic for maintenance of his slumber, I looked the guy over carefully. The first thing that struck me was his coat. It was a mahogany reddish-brown running from somewhat lighter, as if bleached, on his sides and head, to a much deeper, almost black, tone on his legs and back. I know it's a cliché, but the coat could only be described as "lustrous." Plunging my fingers into his fur was a strange thrill, as it was thicker, plusher and softer than anything I had felt before, yet at the same time I knew that being able to do this while keeping my face attached to my head was a rare privilege.

And then there were the famous claws. One of the staff explained to me that this was the signature feature of the movie wolverine character. Mr. Jackman's were apparently made of steel, whereas Huey's were regular keratin, like yours and mine, but much bigger, harder and sharper than any I have seen this side of a grizzly bear. Very impressive. The teeth were also as impressive as one would expect given his noted gluttony. This, however, brings me to the first of his problems. Huey had dental issues and was going to get four root canals. This may sound bizarre and even a bit silly, but keep in mind how important teeth are to a wolverine. Also, the dental specialist (yes, there are veterinary dental specialists) who was brought in for the procedure was donating her time, so it was a reasonable thing for the zoo to be able to afford. Huey needed to be in top form because Huey was going to the Zoo Sauvage ("Wild Zoo") of Saint-Félicien in Quebec to meet his new girlfriend.

Captive breeding is one the core missions of any good zoo. Sadly, there are few wildlife species today that are not vulnerable in some way, so anything that can be done to increase their numbers is helpful. Wolverines, however, are rare in captivity, with only about 80 in zoos around the world, and they are notoriously difficult to persuade to breed. There was a story in the news about four years ago concerning a Norwegian male wolverine named Kaspar, who was being flown to meet Kayla, his prospective mate. Upon arrival in Newark Airport in New Jersey, Kaspar proceeded to completely trash his cage with those famous claws and teeth, almost managing to escape. Huey, however, wasn't even going to get the chance to freak out airport personnel on his way to his tryst if he didn't get his health issues sorted out first. There were those bad teeth and then there was the mass in his abdomen. That's where I came in.

When matchmaking negotiations began with the Quebec zoo, the first step was to blow-dart Huey and examine him thoroughly to make sure he was in reasonable breeding condition. He was 11 years old, after all, and a confirmed bachelor with no previous breeding record. During this examination, the zoo vet identified those dental issues and then came across something more worrisome — he could palpate a spherical object in Huey's abdomen, where there should be no spherical object. It was roughly the size of a mandarin orange. It made sense for me to look at this with ultrasound before the veterinary dentist began what was expected to be a four- or five-hour procedure, because the sad truth was that if this mass looked like a cancer, there wasn't much point in fixing his teeth.

Fur blocks ultrasound, so I always have to shave. Given how gorgeous Huey's coat was, I kept the shaved window to a minimum. The clippers really struggled, but soon there it was, his dark pink belly skin. I applied the ultrasound gel and everyone around me stopped what they were doing to watch the monitor. The room fell silent. It took me a moment to get oriented to his anatomy and then there it was, a ball-like object that did not seem connected to any major organ. It was smooth and even in consistency and there was no blood supply into the centre. It did not look like a cancer. It was probably a benign and incidental cyst. Huey could have his teeth fixed and Huey could go on his blind date.

I did not hear how things went for him in Quebec. I tried to find information online about wolverines at the Zoo Sauvage of Saint-Félicien and the only story that popped up was about one escaping from it. I like to imagine that it was Huey, bored with married life, deciding to try his shiny new teeth out on a moose somewhere deep in the wilds of Quebec.

HOW TO MAKE A SHEEP SIT

"Ask her to sit!" a classmate to my left shouted out, laughing.

"No, don't ask! Tell her! It's a sheep, you dork!" another called from behind me.

"She said sheep sit!" a third laughed. "Try saying that three times quickly!"

The professor gave them each an indulgent smile and then stepped up to the sheep in question, a young Suffolk ewe.

"None of you know then?" she asked.

We all shook our heads.

The professor, a stout middle-aged woman in neatly pressed green overalls and shiny black rubber boots, gave the sheep a pat on the head and said, "Alright then, watch closely."

She positioned herself beside the sheep's left shoulder, facing the animal, who appeared to be entirely unconcerned, chewing her cud, thinking her sheep thoughts. The professor then leaned over the sheep and with her right arm reached under the animal's chest, almost encircling it. Then, in one startlingly swift movement, she grabbed the sheep's left front leg — the one closest to the professor — from underneath and pulled it to the right and slightly forward. This caused the animal to topple onto its bum, cradled in place by her toppler.

The sheep looked more resigned than concerned and continued to chew her cud and, presumably, think her sheep thoughts. We burst into applause. None of us had imagined it would be so simple or, honestly, that the professor, who normally seemed plodding and even a bit clumsy, was capable of such a deft manoeuvre.

She then went on to explain what we could do with a sitting sheep, which was not "play patty-cake" as one of my classmates loudly suggested, but rather to be able to perform a complete physical examination, especially of the udder, genitalia and feet. Sheep were her favourite patients in large measure for this reason. There was no making a cow, horse, pig or goat sit placidly while you probed their nether regions. Don't even try.

Then it was our turn. We were let loose in the barn to go find a subject and make it sit. I found mine in a far corner. I had always been fond of sheep, albeit in an abstract sort of way. I was, after all, a city boy who had managed to get into vet school without any large animal experience whatsoever. Everything farm related was fully new to me. At that point I was just pleased to have gotten through the first few weeks of the large animal medicine course without getting kicked in the head by a horse or compressed into the wall of a stall by a bull, both being real possibilities for the inexperienced and naïve. And boy, was I inexperienced and naïve. Consequently, I greeted the sheep lab with relief.

I said hello to my sheep and crouched down to give it a good ear scratch and make it clear that I was not a threat. At a distance sheep are lovely creatures, all fluffy and benign, but up close they have these weird rectangular pupils that make them look more alien and demented than I had expected. It was like seeing little antennae sprouting from someone's head. But I was undeterred; this was still a sheep after all, and creepy eyes notwithstanding, we were going to make friends and then she was going to sit for me. Praise from the professor would follow. Not such an urban fool after all, that Schott.

I scratched the sheep's ears some more and patted her. I decided to call her Nancy. This was fun! I looked around me to see if everyone else was having fun too. Most people's sheep were already sitting. The effect was comical, as the sheep looked like they were getting ready to watch a movie or perhaps have their nails painted. I smiled but realized that I had better get down to business. I gave Nancy one last scratch, got into position, reached around her and tugged at her left front leg from underneath.

Nothing.

Nancy didn't sit. She didn't so much as budge or even bleat.

I tried again, changing my angle, and whispering encouragement to her.

Still nothing.

I tried two or three times again before I became aware of a presence behind me. It was the professor. I was the last student to get their sheep to sit.

"Philipp, you're being too gentle. You really have to yank on that leg. It doesn't hurt them."

"Yank" on Nancy's leg? How did she know it didn't hurt?

But obedient student that I was, I did it. I yanked hard and Nancy sat. Just like all the other sheep, she looked entirely unperturbed. *Another autumn. Another batch of green students. Whatever. The food's good here.* Those were likely the nature of those sheep thoughts. And for those of you who guffaw at the idea of sheep having thoughts, let me encourage you to look up the recent research on the ability of sheep to recognize human faces. They are apparently as good at this as the great apes. In one study, sheep were trained to recognize Jake Gyllenhaal, Emma Watson and Barack Obama. Conclude from that selection what you will.

So there. Now you know how to make a sheep sit and you have new respect for their intellect. But before you go, you really should try to say "she said sheep sit" three times in a row.

LOVE, FROM A DISTANCE

I love all my patients. I do not necessarily love all my clients, but I do love all my patients. Some admittedly more than others, but all of them in some way. It may be a naïve perspective, but I feel that even the psycho Siamese and demented dachshunds are innocent deep inside their hearts. They're just scared. Or having a bad day. Or don't know of any other way to show their disapproval of my close inspection of their private parts. And while I love all my patients, I don't love seeing all my patients. Some are best loved in the abstract, from a reasonable distance. This may be because seeing them can lead to injury, as with the aforementioned psycho or demented ones, but it may also be because seeing them can lead to frustration. This is the case with hedgehogs.

Hedgehogs are in some ways adorable, but in many ways frustrating. At least for the veterinarian tasked with performing a physical examination. Take the case of Prickles. (Incidentally, it is a well-known fact that 90% of hedgehogs are named Prickles, Spike or Needles. The other 10% are named Sonic. There may be some rounding errors in these statistics.)

Prickles was an African pygmy hedgehog — the common pet species — and he belonged to a lavishly pierced and tattooed young couple who had just moved in together. Somewhere deep in the bowels of the internet they had found advice that a hedgehog makes the ideal starter pet. This is untrue. But more on that later.

"So, what brings the little guy in today?" I asked.

"He's been wheezing lately," the young man said.

"And he's less active," the young woman added.

"How's the eating, drinking, pooping and peeing?"

"That all seems OK, but the wheezing is really bad!" The young man had Prickles wrapped in a towel in his lap. He held him up towards me. "You can probably hear it from there, even through the towel."

Indeed. Hedgehogs are usually relatively loud breathers, making a range of snuffling sounds, but this was different. Not only was Prickles audibly wheezing, but his breathing sounded laboured too.

"You're right, that is loud! Let's have a look." I motioned for the owner to place Prickles on the table. He unfolded the towel, revealing a sphere completely covered in spikes, every last square centimetre, like the ball in a game of catch for masochists. Prickles had, like the great majority of my hedgehog patients, assessed the threat, found it to be significant and had decided to roll himself into a tight defensive ball. I could examine the tips of his spines and I could hear the unhealthy breathing, but that was it. You would think that this would make for a short appointment, but in fact it makes for a very long appointment because the preferred technique is simply to wait. In theory, eventually the hedgehog will decide that his keepers have perhaps not taken him somewhere to be attacked after all, and consequently he will gradually begin to relax. As he relaxes, he will consider unrolling. Once he has unrolled, the trick is to wait even longer because if you plunge into the full examination too quickly, he will immediately roll up again. So, you wait a little more, suppressing your temptation to look at your watch, trying mightily to tune out the sound of the wheels slowly coming off your schedule's wagon.

Sigh.

As you wait, the hedgehog will hopefully begin to explore the table, shuffling slowly, twitching his little nose as he sniffs, attempting to identify danger molecules or whatever. And if you are very lucky and you have judged your moment perfectly, you may begin to gently, with painstaking caution, examine the little beast.

So, it was with Prickles. The three of us watched and waited. We chatted about Prickles's health, we chatted about the weather and we chatted about their tattoos, but every time Prickles unrolled and began to wander around the table he would roll up in a flash again when I would so much as generate the thought that I might like to examine him now. What to do? A full examination increasingly seemed impossible without sedation, but sedation was not an option because there were some conditions that caused wheezing that would make sedation dangerous. At a minimum I wanted to listen to his lungs and see his face, especially his nostrils, up close.

The former we managed to do by placing the stethoscope in the owner's palm with Prickles on top. Eventually he unrolled there, and the owner was able to lightly press the bell of the stethoscope against the hedgehog's chest while I listened without looking at Prickles so that he wouldn't get the wrong idea. The latter was accomplished by placing a sheet of Plexiglass on the exam table (it was the lid of an anaesthetic induction chamber). After Prickles unrolled on this the owner slowly lifted it up so I could peer at him from underneath. I was able to get much closer to his face this way than by coming directly at him. Prickles was presumably too confused by the sensation of standing on solid air to notice my attention.

This examination was far from optimal, but enough that I could hazard an educated guess that Prickles had pneumonia. Treatment was with a strawberry-flavoured antibiotic liquid that the owners felt confident they would be able to give. Apparently it worked and I did not see Prickles again. When I next saw the couple a few years later they had a kitten. They had given Prickles to a friend who was much more of a night owl and who was a little less fastidious. Recall that I said I would explain why hedgehogs are not ideal starter pets? Hedgehogs are nocturnal and they love to run on their exercise wheels, making a startling amount of noise through the night. Also, for some incomprehensible reason, hedgehogs like to do their bathroom business while running on the wheel, so when you wake up (assuming you slept), there is often a nasty mess to clean up. Some people apparently don't mind, but many do. Keep in mind that hedgehogs are just as cute in photos, so loving them from a distance may be the better move.

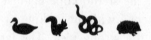

THE FERRET GUY

"I hear you're the ferret guy." This surprising statement was made by a short young woman with green hair, a nose ring and scribbles in blue ballpoint pen all over her hands and arms. It was a surprising statement because it was the first time I'd been called that, to my face anyway, and I had probably seen only half a dozen ferrets since I started at Birchwood Animal Hospital.

"I don't know about that!" I chuckled.

"Well, that's what Rhonda says," she replied, smiling.

"Rhonda?"

"From the MFA."

Ah. Now I knew. The Manitoba Ferret Association lady. She had come in a couple months prior and I had diagnosed adrenal gland disease in her ferret. I had mentioned to her that I had studied ferret diseases in vet school, in a special exotic pets rotation I had signed up for in fourth year. I suppose this made me a "ferret guy" in her mind, or, apparently, *the* "ferret guy." This reminded me of when my wife, Lorraine, who is also a vet, offhandedly mentioned to the owner of a Shar Pei (you know, those super wrinkly dogs) that she had attended a lecture on Shar Pei diseases at a conference. This client subsequently proclaimed Lorraine to be a "Shar Pei specialist." At the risk of offending the scattered few lovers of that breed out there, I can state that this is not the type of dog you particularly want to attract to your practice. In comparison, being known as the "ferret guy" wasn't so bad.

The ferret in question, a lightning-fast cylinder of fur named Hector, had just darted behind the vaccine fridge. Ferrets operate in a different dimension of physics and geometry, and can fit into impossibly small spaces. Ferret owners soon learn not to sit anywhere without first ensuring that the little beast is not hiding under the cushion.

"Hector, get out of there! Come meet your new doctor!"

While the woman wrangled the reluctant Hector out from behind the fridge, I asked, "So, what brings the happy dude here today?"

"He acts like he's stoned sometimes. All of a sudden, he'll just stop and kind of start swaying and staring at nothing. It's creepy!"

Bingo. I knew what this was. Maybe I was the ferret guy after all.

"And how is he the rest of the time, between episodes?" I asked.

"Yeah, he's great otherwise. Tears around with Humphrey, Harold and Henrietta. Does the weasel war dance! Gets into everything!"

I could picture what she meant. Having a ferret is like having a permanent kitten. Their talent for chaos is unparalleled. Most people enjoy kittens because they are cute, but most people also quickly get to the point where they look forward to the kitten growing up and becoming a mellow adult cat. Ferrets are for people who never want their kittens to grow up. These tend to be young singles and childless couples. You never see busy families with ferrets. And you never see frail seniors with ferrets.

"How often does he have these episodes?"

"It's several times a day now."

Hector squirmed out of her hands and dashed off behind the fridge again.

"When did he last eat?"

"He had breakfast this morning around seven."

"So, that's seven hours ago, which counts as fasted for a ferret. Good. You see, I think Hector might be having low blood sugar episodes. Normally his body should be able to maintain a minimum blood sugar level, even when fasted, at least for a while, but with this condition it drops quickly. So, if I take a blood sugar sample now, I'll get a pretty good idea."

I went on to explain what an insulinoma was while she dragged Hector out from behind the fridge again. It's a small tumour in the pancreas and causes what is essentially the opposite of diabetes. Diabetics don't have enough insulin, so their sugar stays high, whereas insulinoma patients have too much insulin, which is secreted by the tumour, so their sugar goes too low. In other species this is very rare, just as the form of adrenal gland disease in ferrets is very rare in other species. In fact, these conditions are also very rare in ferrets outside North America. The leading theory is the "founder effect" is to blame. That's where a small number of ancestors pass their genetic faults to many descendants and, in fact, all pet ferrets here are descended from a handful of breeding pairs. The other theory relates to the difference in ferret diets between here and other parts of the world.

Hector was back on the exam table but looked ready to bolt again. Normally they can be persuaded to stay still by feeding them something like FerreTone, which is a brownish liquid nutritional supplement that most ferrets are intensely addicted to, but I wanted to get the blood sugar reading from him first.

"I'm going to take him to the lab so they can get the blood sample and then I'll properly examine him afterwards when we can feed him FerreTone."

And indeed, his blood sugar was too low. Otherwise

he was fine on physical examination. Hector had an insulinoma. These can be removed surgically, but as he was older, she elected to use medication to block the insulin instead, which can work well for quite a long time. Hector got his FerreTone — lots of it — and his blood sugar surged up again. He was happy, the owner was satisfied that she knew what was wrong, and I was happy that I could at least partially justify my new nickname.

I went on to give some talks at MFA meetings. The following year I turned 40 and the staff decorated the clinic with 40 pictures of ferrets. The ferret guy indeed. But those couple of years ended up being peak ferret for me. I shifted my focus to ultrasound and ferret owners discovered other veterinarians who didn't recoil at the thought of treating their pets (there are surprisingly strong biases against ferrets, unjustified it must be said, among elements of the profession). I haven't been called the "ferret guy" in a decade now. I still see some ferret patients and I enjoy it when I do, but I know that the torch has been passed and out there somewhere someone else is being called the "ferret guy" or "ferret girl. I'm OK with that.

ANOTHER THING I AM TERRIBLE AT

Another? Yes, there is a list. See the chapter entitled "A Thing I Am Terrible At" in my first book, *The Accidental Veterinarian*, for the first example. It involves collecting dog semen. Enough said. If I write a third book, there'll be a chapter entitled "One More Thing I Am Terrible At" and so on. I suppose I could put more than one of these examples in each book, but as some of the readers of these books are also my clients, I am reluctant to alarm them too much. A little alarm is OK, but let's not go overboard.

Now, I don't want to be falsely modest. There is obviously plenty I am good at, too, but sometimes the positive and the negative represent two sides of a coin. Take my memory, for example. I have a good memory for esoteric trivia. A very good one, actually. Thirty years after last having had to answer the question, "How many nephrons are there in a rat's kidney?" I still know the answer: 30,000. I can also list the first 20 Roman emperors in order (Augustus, Tiberius, Caligula . . .) and I can name the capital of Burkina Faso (Ougadougou), and, for that matter, of every other country in the world. But I have observed that people like me who have a head for this sort of thing can also tend towards bouts of absent-mindedness. I'm sure you've observed this too. This is the other side of that particular coin.

To keep my clients' alarm at this revelation within manageable limits, I will hasten to add that the intensity of my job generates a level of attention and focus that usually blocks this defect from being activated at work. It's usually only when I'm relaxed and off duty that the absent-mindedness can assert itself.

But that was all preamble. This is actually a story about baby squirrels and about how I should not be put in charge of releasing them.

One unsung aspect of veterinary practice is the handling of orphaned, or allegedly orphaned, baby wild animals. It's a rare week where we don't get a call about what to do with a young animal that appears to be on its own. And often people just show up with their "rescues." Frequently they are brought in shoeboxes perforated with air holes. I suppose such boxes could occasionally contain a pet hamster or gerbil, but those usually come in cages. No, the shoebox is the near universal signal that tiny wildlife is inside.

Before we go on, I need to issue a stern proclamation: "Don't do it." Kind of the opposite of Nike. If you find baby wild animals, it is almost never a good idea to assume they are orphaned. Unless you see a dead mother nearby, they are probably not truly orphaned. And even if they are orphaned, the chance of survival for most wild babies brought into captivity is very low.

However, in the case I'm about to describe the mother was known to have died and the four orphaned squirrels were old enough that the period of foster care before weaning was expected to be brief. It probably goes without saying that the older the orphan, the better the odds of success. Moreover, the prospective foster mom was an employee at the clinic and had an above-average knowledge of animal care. Besides, euthanizing a box of tiny baby squirrels was nobody's idea of a good time. We'd give them a chance.

Squirrels are tough and they are bold. Many other wildlife species go into stress overload when handled by humans and can essentially die of fright, but some squirrels just don't seem to care: "Human, shmuman, just gimme the food." And so it was with this little gang of four. They allowed themselves to be bottle-fed as if they were trying to bulk up for some sort of Junior Mr. or Ms. Squirrel competition. They bit, they scratched, they pooped, they pissed, they climbed, they ran around and they generally behaved like tiny, hairy barbarians on meth. The Genghis Khans of the baby animal world. But they had sparkly anime eyes and twitchy little noses and gorgeous bushy tails, so everyone was charmed. At first.

We estimated their age when they were found at about six weeks. You can begin weaning baby squirrels onto solid food at eight weeks, finishing the process in a further two to four weeks. We picked two weeks. And even then, it did not feel fast enough. It was clear that they needed to be released at the earliest possible date before they actually conquered the foster's home, expelled the humans and unfurled their barbarian squirrel flag (acorn and crossbones?) in the front window. But where to release them? Despite the fact that the love-hate relationship that had developed was beginning to tip towards the hate, there was still ample love and nobody wanted to see the little bastards get run over right away or eaten by crows or attacked by dogs or otherwise meet a rapid demise.

"Philipp, you have a big yard by the river with lots of trees where you could keep an eye on them . . ."

"I do have a big yard by the river with lots of trees where I could keep an eye on them . . ." Although how exactly I was going to do the latter was unclear to me. However, it seemed as good an idea as any.

And so it came to pass that one evening at the end of my shift I was handed a cage containing four rambunctious young squirrels, careening around like self-propelled ping-pong balls. My kids were delighted. My cats were intrigued. We didn't have a dog in those days. I looked out on our yard. It is essentially a forest. We already had a healthy population of squirrels and I didn't know how territorial they were, although I suspected the answer was "very" given the number of squirrels I saw chasing other squirrels.

Hmm. What to do.

Then I hit upon a brilliant idea. We had a screen-sided gazebo down near the river! This would be the perfect place to release them. I would put food in, and the crew could hang out in there for a few days, chilling while the other neighbourhood squirrels got used to their presence. Less shocking and sudden for all concerned. Clever, eh?

This is a good point to pause and remind you about the

title of this story: "Another Thing I Am Terrible At." It turns out I am terrible at releasing baby squirrels because I can be absent-minded. And what fact was absent from my mind?

This fact: screens do not stop squirrels.

The next morning, I brought Lorraine and the kids out to see the little charmers. They were gone, and there was a jagged tear in the side of gazebo. At first, I had the irrational thought that some alpha squirrel had broken in to get at the interlopers, but Lorraine pointed out that it was far more likely that our squirrels had taken one look at the bare interior of the gazebo, compared it with the lush forest outside and said to themselves, "Screw this!"

Fair point. At least they were back in the wild, albeit at the cost of a gazebo screen.

For years after I would look at the squirrels rocketing around our yard and wonder, "Which one of you is a Genghis?" The baddest one, obviously.

PET MOUSE / WILD MOUSE

In 2011 Hal Herzog published the bestselling book *Some We Love, Some We Hate, Some We Eat.* Herzog is an anthrozoologist, meaning that he studies the relationships between animals and people. In that book he specifically tackled the weirdness of how wildly different our treatment of closely related animal species can be. Sometimes this weirdness even applies within a species. When Lorraine was a little girl, she was horrified to see a hand-lettered sign on the side of Henderson Highway, just north of Winnipeg, that proclaimed: "Rabbits: For Pets or Meat." This conundrum was on my mind when we failed our practice inspection a few months ago.

Every few years the veterinary association sends out an inspector, who goes through an exhaustive checklist covering everything conceivable to do with our equipment, drugs, record keeping and facility. It's not unusual to fail on one or two picky technicalities, so I don't get too stressed about it. We are always given a grace period to make the necessary corrections and life goes on. This time we failed because we had a mouse. A wild mouse. The inspector poked around in the cupboards and deep within one found a scattering of mouse droppings. The staff confessed that for several weeks they had noticed pet food bags with the corners gnawed open. It was then that I was told that the mouse had actually been brought in by a client who had found him in their house, stunned by their cat. Before anyone could even look at him, he escaped and darted off, smelling the pet food and realizing that he had arrived in mouse heaven. The staff had taken to calling him Mr. X.

A rather emotional debate followed. Poison was out of the question for obvious reasons, but even deadly traps that could not possibly harm any of our patients were ruled out by many of the staff because none guaranteed an instant painless kill. Can a veterinarian deliberately inflict suffering on a sentient creature, even when it is not a pet? Even when it is ruining bags of food? Even when it endangers the re-certification of the practice? The answer was no. A veterinarian cannot, in good conscience, do such a thing. Not when there was a reasonable alternative. So, live traps were set out.

On the same day that this drama was playing out I saw Hickory, Dickory and Doc, three pet mice. Well, I only actually saw Dickory, as Hickory and Doc were hiding under the wood shavings in their cage and were in any case not the reason for the visit. They were just along for the ride. Dickory, however, was a source of worry. The mice lived with a young man who I think had mental health issues and lived on some sort of income support in the inner city. He was often accompanied by a social worker. Whatever challenges he might have had in his life, they were not evident in the care of his mice. He was meticulous, yet reasonable, and he was very knowledgeable. In fact, after the first time he came in I felt compelled to read up a bit more on the medical care of mice, because I was not going to feel comfortable giving him vague answers. It is not a species that receives much veterinary attention, so I had little previous experience with them (outside of the undergraduate research lab, but that's another story entirely).

"Is he hand-tame?" I asked, as I looked warily at the tiny piebald rodent. Mice are notoriously wanton biters.

Dickory was staring back at me with bright wee black eyes, but her facial expression and body language were inscrutable.

"Oh yes. Doc's a biter but Dickory's a lover."

"What about Hickory?"

"Depends on the day."

At least the non-bitey one had gotten sick. I scooped Dickory up and placed her on the small kitchen scale we use for the micro pets. Twenty grams. Six thousand, two hundred and fifty Dickories could fit in one Albert, my largest patient. You will meet Albert in the next story.

"Oh, I see the problem," I said as I gently turned Dickory over, revealing a lump on her belly.

"Mammary cancer?" the young man asked.

I carefully felt the lump. It was hard and knobby and associated with a nipple. "I think so. You're probably right. I'm sorry."

"Shit," he said quietly. "Sorry for swearing. I have such terrible luck with these guys."

"Maybe, but they have great luck with you. Not very many people care as much about their mice as you do. Also, mice are unfortunately really prone to cancer, so your luck may be more average than terrible."

"Is there anything we can do?"

"Well, in theory surgery, but I'm not going to recommend it. As you know, she's really old for a mouse. at two years of age . . ."

"Twenty-eight months," the young man interrupted.

"Right! Wow. And this doesn't seem uncomfortable for her, so it's better just to let her enjoy her life for now until it becomes a problem."

"OK. I needed to know for sure what it was and that there was nothing I should be doing for her."

"No, just love her."

As I said this, I was acutely aware of the irony of recommending love for a mouse when at that very moment traps were being ordered for one of the mouse's distant cousins. In fact, it was in a cabinet in this very room that Mr. X had been doing the pooping that caused us to fail the inspection. I wondered whether perhaps he was watching this strange drama of a captive sick cousin being stroked, and allowing itself to be stroked, by the enemy. And if he was watching, I wondered whether he felt pity or envy for Hickory, Dickory and Doc's living arrangement. These are of course entirely foolish thoughts for me to have, but I cannot claim to be immune to them.

Dickory died peacefully in her sleep about a month later. It was probably not even due to the tumour, but rather just to old age. Meanwhile the hunt for Mr. X went on. The live traps were always empty, but we still found poop in the cupboards. One of the staff pointed out that the tasty bait we had set in the traps was probably not working because he still had access to the pet food, so we went through the laborious process of putting it all out of reach, but still no dice (mice?). Mr. X was one wily customer. I was convinced that it was in fact a Ms. X who had many little baby Xs, but the staff were sure that it was a single mouse with no babies. And they were right because one day the mouse vanished. No more poop was seen. No more bags were nibbled on. Mr. X clearly knew that he was pushing his luck and decided to move on. After all, there was an empty building right next door that used to house a Chinese restaurant. More freedom. Less stress. True wild mouse paradise.

MY LARGEST PATIENT

I'm not a horse vet, so my largest patient is not a Clydesdale, and I'm not a cow vet, so it's not a Charolais bull, nor am I a zoo vet, so it's not an elephant either. I'm a pet vet. Normally this means that my largest patient would be a Great Dane or some sort of obese mastiff, and that was the case until I met Albert. Albert was a 200+ pound (125+ kilogram), 20+ foot (6.6+ metre) Burmese python. And these are estimates. There is no way to weigh a python and while we could have used a tape measure, he never lay straight or still, so we didn't bother trying to confirm how long he was. What I do know is that four people struggled to carry him into the clinic, cradled in the crooks of their arms, like eight wobbly shelf brackets, and I know that he was quite a bit longer than my 16-foot-long room.

Now, to be absolutely honest, I am calling Albert "my patient" when in fact he was an ultrasound referral from another clinic, so I only saw him the one time. Albert had been sent to me for ultrasound because he had stopped eating. His favourite food was whole chickens, feathers and all, and he hadn't had one in several months. This might sound drastic, but they can go a very long time between meals, especially when they are hibernating. The owner was concerned, however, because this was not Albert's normal time to hibernate. The temperature had been kept warm, the humidity high and his habitat generally conducive to being active and eating. The referring veterinarian had done x-rays — many, many x-rays — to cover most of the length of his body. If you're picturing 20 x-rays taped together side-by-side running along one wall and then around the corner onto the next, I have disappointing news for you — they were digital, so there was just a whole lot of scrolling. On one of these x-rays he thought he spied a mass or object of some sort near Albert's heart. This is where ultrasound is useful. Whereas x-rays show shadows, ultrasound shows what those shadows are made up of. I had never ultrasounded a snake before, let alone one this humungous, but I figured it couldn't be that hard. Everything was laid out in a tube after all. Barrel-shaped animals, like obese mastiffs, are difficult because image quality degrades the further the sound beam has to penetrate into the body. I was excited. And the staff were beyond excited.

"He's here! He's here!" Amber, the receptionist, looked ready to pop with an upwelling of pure delight. "I told him to come to the side door so he's as close as possible to the ultrasound room!"

A throng of us gathered at the side door. I opened the door to see a man about my age with unruly grey hair and an Iron Maiden t-shirt get out of a rusted-out maroon-coloured four-door Chrysler.

"Where's the snake?" several staff asked at the same time. We walked down to the car and I introduced myself to the snake's owner. He was soft spoken and polite and insisted I call him Rod. He thanked me repeatedly for agreeing to look at Albert. In the meantime, the staff peered in the back windows of the car.

"He's in there! Oh my God, he's huge!"

And indeed, he was. Albert was in there, curled up on the back seat, partly under an afghan, and he was huge. A scrum of volunteers ensued, jostling to be one of the four designated snake carriers. Rod stayed at Albert's head and I led the way to the ultrasound room. Albert was set on the floor and immediately began to slither about, examining this new environment. I had to shoo several staff members out of the room so that we'd have enough space to work. Then I set about starting the ultrasound examination. Or, more accurately, trying to start the ultrasound examination. There was a problem. I should have foreseen this, but in my eagerness to have a giant Burmese python as a patient I hadn't really given it any thought. The problem was that I did not know where Albert's heart was.

In mammals and birds and even other reptiles such as lizards, there are external landmarks that guide my probe placement. I generally know, within a centimetre or two, exactly where to find the heart, based on the position of the limbs, the ribs and the breastbone. Snakes don't have limbs (duh) and you cannot feel the ribs or breastbone under all that taut, rippling muscle. The taut, rippling muscle caused another problem as well, but more on that in a minute. The literature and anatomy diagrams indicated that the heart should be about a third of the way along the snake. This was still a lot of territory to cover. Fortunately we had booked enough time, so there was no hurry. I sat on the floor beside Albert while Rod cradled his head end and I began scanning from as far forward as it seemed possible the heart could be. This is when the taut rippling muscle problem asserted itself. Albert began to move and coil.

"Sorry, Doc, if he wants to go, he's going to go!" Rod chuckled.

He was absolutely right. There is no way you can stop a snake this size from doing what it wants to do, and at that moment, Albert wanted to coil a little, so Albert coiled a little.

"Don't worry, he's peaceful." More chuckling.

I wasn't really worried. I mean, other than the occasional unfortunate small child, how many people have actually been killed, or even badly injured, by Burmese pythons? According to Google, there were only seven fatalities between 1978 and 2009. That's way less than those caused by lightning strikes or choking on hot dogs. Also, although Albert was extremely powerful, he was also quite slow. If I sat there long enough to allow myself to be squeezed to death, then there was probably something else wrong with me. But back to the "extremely powerful" muscles again. The muscle power under those scales was nothing short of jaw-dropping. When he first began to push against my hand, I think my mouth did fall open a little. It was like being pushed by a hydraulic lift. I no more considered pushing back than I would consider pushing back against a transit bus rolling forward.

"OK, I guess we'll just go with it then!" I said, as I shuffled myself along beside Albert, trying to maintain the position of my probe. There were no clear internal landmarks, either, so when I lost position it was difficult to remember exactly where I had been. I resorted to calling in a staff member to put a hand down as soon as the probe slipped away (imagine ultrasound gel plus slippery scales) to mark my spot. This was laborious, but gradually we made progress. Albert kept moving and we kept readjusting, but eventually, using the Doppler to identify blood flow, I found the heart. And then I found the problem. Just ahead of the heart was the mass my colleague had seen on x-ray. He and Rod had hoped it was just a cyst that could maybe be drained, or possibly even just an artefact (something that appears to be there on x-ray, but isn't), but I could see that it was real and that it was solid tissue with a good blood supply. It was positioned so that it blocked most of the esophagus. That's one thing about having a tube-shaped body — anything extra in there can more easily squash adjacent structures. It wasn't clear whether it was a tumour or possibly what's called a granuloma, which would have been a reaction to, say, a chicken bone piercing his esophagus, but either way it would mean surgery.

Rod was very sad. He loved this python no differently than I love my dog and my cats. Albert was too old for surgery and it would have been technically very challenging anyway. It was a much quieter and more subdued crew who picked Albert up, cradled him again and carried him in a kind of slow-motion conga line back to his Chrysler. I ran into my colleague about a year later and he confirmed that Albert had eventually died. Rod had other snakes, including a spectacular gold-coloured one that I also saw for ultrasound, but none as large as Albert or as dear to Rod.

EPILOGUE

FOR THE LOVE OF ANIMALS

I am a bit of a restless soul. I am constantly tinkering with and adjusting aspects of my life and my surroundings. Rarely anything major, mind you. Mostly just little tweaks. When I was a child my parents called me Zappel Philipp, meaning Fidgety Philipp in German, after a character in a 19th-century children's tale where Zappel Philipp is so fidgety that he accidentally yanks the tablecloth off the table and thereby ruins Sunday dinner. (I never did that.) The physical fidget is long gone, but the mental fidget is still there. Starting an essay titled "For the Love of Animals" with an excursion into an old German story featuring no animals whatsoever is an example of this mental fidget. But sit tight, we'll get there.

This mental fidget seeps into various aspects of my work. I'm always wondering, is there a different way, a better way? All veterinarians are professionally obliged to continually improve based on new knowledge when it comes to medical protocols, but in the management arena it's much easier to become complacent. The staff are probably exhausted with my constant refrain of "let's try this, let's try that," knowing that only a small percentage of the changes will actually stick. But when they do, I'm happy and proud. For example, and relevant to this discussion, in my 30 years at Birchwood we've had four logos, and I think this one will stick. It's not so much the predictable dog and cat silhouettes, rather it's the motto underneath. It came to me in a flash early one morning about ten years ago when I was out walking. "Birchwood Animal Hospital. For the love of animals since 1959." I'm immensely proud of that motto. No more fidgeting about that.

Putting aside the "since 1959" part, isn't "for the love of animals" what it's all about? Aren't you reading this book because of that (unless you're one of my handful of petless friends)? Didn't I write this book because of that? Didn't I enter this profession because of that? And reeling back the chain of events to the beginning, didn't I beg for a gerbil in 1977 because of that? Yes, becoming a veterinarian was an accident, but it was an accident made possible because of the love of animals. You generally can't get hit by a car unless you're in the street in the first place.

I've written before of how love is not a finite emotional space where loving animals must come at the expense of loving people. In fact, I often find it's the opposite. It's a positive feedback loop which increases your capacity for love. In my fidgety mind I've occasionally wondered why that should be. Is it that more open-hearted people are more likely to connect with animals in the first place? In other words, do I have cause and effect backwards? I suppose that may sometimes be a valid explanation. But I have another one too. I have come to see that the love of animals requires a pure form of empathy. Empathy for people is necessarily and inextricably bound into a larger unspoken, often even subconscious, social contract. If you are good to other people, other people will hopefully be good to you. Perhaps not the specific people you are helping at the moment, but generally you are contributing to a larger society upon whose wellbeing you ultimately depend. It is much easier and more realistic to put yourself in the shoes of the person you are empathizing with than to put yourself in animal's . . . er . . . paws. That requires a far greater leap of imagination and you know that it is impossible for you to ever actually be in that animal's position. This is what I mean by pure empathy. If you can cultivate this sort of pure empathy, then it is easier to cultivate the ordinary sort of empathy required for our fellow humans.

But ultimately, even if I am wrong about this and even if it doesn't lead to world peace and universal harmony, the love of animals is enough on its own. For each of us must live the best life we can, one day at a time, and are each of those days not made better by the pure, unqualified happiness in a wag or a purr? Love is also its own reward.

Afterword

There are probably a few you of who picked this book up on the basis of the title alone. And now you've come to the very end and you still don't know how to examine a wolverine. The answer was touched on in Huey's story, but it might not have been obvious. Perhaps you feel let down, or even cheated. I apologize for that.

Here, then, is how you examine a wolverine: when he has been rendered profoundly unconscious. It's the only way. Nobody, and I mean nobody, examines an awake wolverine. There are no wolverine whisperers. And muzzles and welder's gloves are not enough. I'm sorry if this comes as disappointing news. It's either tranquilizer-filled blow darts, or it's what we in the trade euphemistically refer to as the "distant exam," i.e., with binoculars. Incidentally, this doesn't just apply to wolverines. In fact, I once knew a Chihuahua who . . . Never mind, that's a story for another time.

ACKNOWLEDGEMENTS

In *The Accidental Veterinarian* I focused my acknowledgements on various mentors and inspirations, and left the key people to a short paragraph at the end. This time I will acknowledge them front and centre. These key people are my clients, past and present. If they hadn't trusted me with the care of their pets, there would be no stories to tell. It's that simple. Thank you.

In addition, this time I want to acknowledge another group of equally key people — my readers. If they hadn't picked up my first book and enjoyed it, this second book would not be in your hands right now. Thank you to them as well. This means that if you are that rare, brave soul who has read my books and who has also been my client, consider yourself doubly thanked. To have one marvellous career is more than many people can hope to enjoy, and you readers have generously gifted me a second bonus one.

There's still space left on this page, so I'd be remiss if I didn't use some of it to acknowledge the astonishing work of the people at ECW Press. Their good humoured patience with writers appears to have no bounds. My gratitude to them also has no bounds.

And finally, my wife, Lorraine, who was nudged out of the dedication by the pets. (There may be a metaphor there, but don't read too much into it.) Thank you. Thank you for so many things, but relevant to this book, thank you for drawing me into small animal practice in Winnipeg. It may have been a kind of accident, but it has been, and continues to be, a happy one.

This book is also available as a Global Certified Accessible™ (GCA) ebook. ECW Press's ebooks are screen reader friendly and are built to meet the needs of those who are unable to read standard print due to blindness, low vision, dyslexia, or a physical disability.

Purchase the print edition and receive the eBook free!
Just send an email to ebook@ecwpress.com and include:

- the book title
- the name of the store where you purchased it
- your receipt number
- your preference of file type: PDF or ePub

A real person will respond to your email with your eBook attached. And thanks for supporting an independently owned Canadian publisher with your purchase!

Printed on Rolland Enviro.
This paper contains 100% post-consumer fiber,
is manufactured using renewable energy - Biogas
and processed chlorine free.